THE RYDER OF THE NIGHT

FLYERS OF THE FIRST KINGDOM
BOOK 1

EDEN EAVES

ABOUT THE RYDER OF THE NIGHT

I am half of a whole.

A dragon without a ryder.

My kind are on the brink of extinction, I should be out there fighting, leading the flyers of the First Kingdom. But without my ryder I'm grounded.

She was the key to my magic and my future. But as soon as I found her she was stolen away, hidden somehow from even our bond's pull.

I'd searched the Twelve Kingdoms for over a decade and lost all hope. Until my brother discovered her—living in a cult in the middle of nowhere, growing the very poison that's killing my kind.

Raised with no knowledge of magic or creatures like me, she thinks I'm a monster from her nightmares come to life.

Admittedly, kidnapping her probably wasn't my best move, but I had to get her out of there.

Now I need to convince her the life she knew was a lie, but time is slipping away. If she doesn't accept who she is and learn to harness her power, it will consume her—leaving me ryderless again.

She wants to go back to that lie of a life I rescued her from. Too bad we didn't leave anything to go back to. But the more she refuses the truth, the closer I get to losing her again. So I make her an offer she can't refuse.

Only, I don't know how I'll keep my end of the bargain, because I can't let her go now I've found her. She is more than just my ryder.

But that's a secret for another day. We have training to do.

Lesson one: Ryde or die.

TRIGGER WARNING

Eden Eaves

AUTHOR

LOVE IS MAGIC

For all of us who dream of flying.

THE NORTH SEA

THE TWELFTH KINGDOM

THE FAR NORTH

THE SECOND KINGDOM

THE SEA KINGDOM

○ THE OUTPOST

THE WILD MOUNTAINS

THE TENTH KINGDOM

THE STORM KINGDOM

THE NIN[...] KINGD[...]

THE RAINFOR[...] KINGDO[...]

THE SIXTH KINGDOM

THE MOUNTAIN KINGDOM

THE MIDDLE SEA

○ THE CAPITAL

THE FIRST KINGDOM

THE DARK KINGDOM

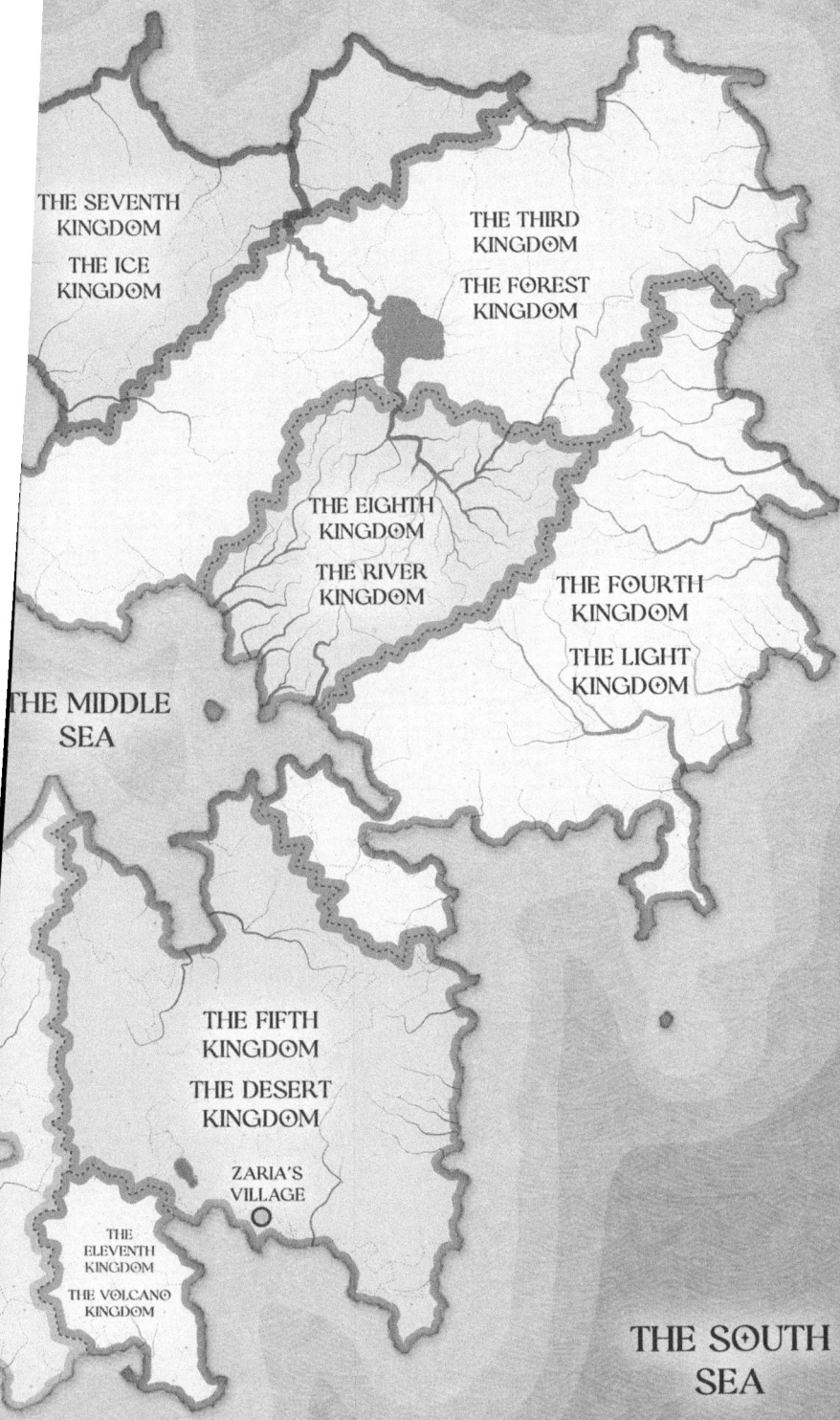

THE SEVENTH
KINGDOM
THE ICE
KINGDOM

THE THIRD
KINGDOM
THE FOREST
KINGDOM

THE EIGHTH
KINGDOM
THE RIVER
KINGDOM

THE FOURTH
KINGDOM
THE LIGHT
KINGDOM

THE MIDDLE
SEA

THE FIFTH
KINGDOM
THE DESERT
KINGDOM

ZARIA'S
VILLAGE

THE
ELEVENTH
KINGDOM
THE VOLCANO
KINGDOM

THE SOUTH
SEA

FOREWORD

If you've read the novella The Lost Ryder please go to Chapter Seven.

ONE
ZARIA

"You know I'm going to get in trouble for this," Luka teased as he held up the practice sword.

"Only if they find out," I countered, lifting a similar sword he'd gotten from the practice hall. They'd never missed anything else he had taken in the years since I'd made him show me what he had learned.

"You said they were beginning to notice your absences." A frown pulled at his handsome features as he parried my attack with ease.

"Only because Aeryn told on me." My sister loved to brown-nose. She would always be everything I could not be, and I'd given up trying to live up to my parents' expectations. "She doesn't know what I'm doing."

"How will you prevent her from following us?" Luka attacked.

"I've done it so far. Have you so little faith in me?" I deflected, stepping under the blade to cut a quick attack at his thigh. "Besides, I won't make that mistake again. My chores are done. There is nothing for her to tell on me for."

He barely dodged the blow, coming around quickly to swing at my head. His breathing picked up speed, and his brow glistened with a light sheen of sweat in the late afternoon light.

"I don't want you to get in trouble." A slight hitch came with his words when he recovered, and we reset our positions. "And I don't want you wearing yourself out."

"You know this is the only hour of the day I have energy enough to spare." I exhaled heavily and dropped the point of my weapon.

"We could try at dawn. She'd still be asleep, less risk," he offered.

"I can't. It's worst at night, and I'm too weak even for breakfast some mornings."

Luka's eyes softened with the sympathy he knew I hated. I hated all the looks. The judgement from the field workers because I was too fragile to work alongside them, when a mere moment spent in the fields would bring on an attack. The withering looks from my family. No doubt the shame of having a child who could not contribute to our community's needs like the rest, only burdening them instead, was difficult to bear. But the sympathy I so often saw in Luka's eyes was the worst of all.

"Don't look at me that way, Luka." I growled, turning away, tired of the same old conversation. "I need to do this."

Luka took my hand and tried to turn me back to him. "Why, Zaria? Help me understand. Don't mistake my meaning, I love our time together, but why use what little strength you have learning a skill they will never let you use?"

I whirled on him. "What would you have me do? Lie down and die? I can't help with the crop because it makes me sick. I can't hunt or gather. All I can do is use the few hours of the day that I'm not bedridden to do chores where I can. I'm a burden, Luka. And if raiders come? Those who can fight will defend the crops first, themselves second. I need this. I need to know I can protect myself, even if they would never let me fight. Who will fight for me? Should I pray to the Goddess to be married off to the first fae who offers my father the right price?" I scoffed.

"You're the only girl I've ever met who'd rather work in the fields than have a husband to provide for her."

I wrinkled my nose, but I couldn't articulate why nothing about my existence and planned future sounded appealing. "The only reason I haven't been married off yet is my reputation for being difficult."

Amusement colored his expression. "Maybe you haven't met the right man."

I laughed, rotating my shoulder to ease an ache. I don't know how I would have survived the last few years without my best friend. He was the only one I could talk to, the only one who didn't see me as a burden. "No one desires a headstrong wife. They want docile."

"Not everyone." Luka lunged, using the distraction to attack, hacking cut after cut.

I backed up, blocking blows. My heel hit a rock, and I stumbled. He tried to use it to take me to the ground, but I was too quick for him, slipping out of his grasp to spin around and bring the edge of my sword to his back. "Yield."

"I yield." He turned, dark gaze meeting mine. "Would marriage be so bad?"

"We've talked about this…" I trailed off. "What is that noise?"

He cocked his head, listening. "I hear nothing."

I strained, closing my eyes, searching for the sound, but nothing came. "Strange." I opened my eyes and found him with that look he sometimes got. Longing, hopeful, far too intense. I

3

quickly looked away, seeking an escape. "I should return to my chores before my absence is noticed."

"Zaria, will you talk to me?"

"I can't." I didn't want to hear it. I knew what he wanted to say, and I didn't want our friendship to change. I took the sword out of his hand and tucked both back into our hiding place before smoothing my hair. "How does my dress look?" I dusted stray grass from it, but there was nothing to be done about the stains.

"It's a little stained, Zaria. What if they think—"

I knew exactly what they would think if they saw us together outside of lessons and prayer. We were too old to continue friendships with the opposite sex. It was considered improper, and they would punish the transgression.

I held up a hand so he wouldn't say anything more. "Don't take this away from me. I need it. It's—" Another sound silenced me. "Did you hear that?"

He shook his head, looking at me like my parents often did after my nightmares. "I hear nothing, Zaria."

I let out a breath. "I have water to fetch."

He lingered in the clearing while I collected my bucket and basket. He wouldn't return to the village with me. We knew better.

I made my way to the well, listening all the while, but no more of the strange sounds came. I don't know what I expected. Nothing exciting ever happened here.

I was lugging the heavy bucket toward the house when screaming drew my attention away from my task, sending water sloshing down the front of my skirt as I hefted it to rest between my feet. The air shifted, and the strange noise returned. Like the beating of birds' wings, only...magnified. I turned in a circle, seeking the source of the shriek. This wasn't the cry of children at play but blood-curdling screams. They grew closer, striking fear into my bones. My heart hammered in my ears as the cries grew louder.

My blood ran cold when I laid eyes on the carnage.

I couldn't process the scene. Huge, winged creatures, like those of my nightmares, darted through the air, igniting our small village and the surrounding fields with streams of fire that poured from their ferocious mouths.

This couldn't be real. Had I fallen into a fever dream? But even my nightmares had never been this terrifying.

I stood rooted in place, fear keeping me in its clutches. Crops burst into flames all around me and the storehouse exploded, finally pulling me from my catatonic state.

"Our crops!" I gasped. We would lose everything if we didn't act, and I knew that's where everyone would be. Saving the crops. I had to go find them.

The acrid smoke laced with the familiar scent of the herbs hit me, and I hesitated—my intolerance. I was breathing them in. The air was thick with fumes. No wonder I was experiencing waking nightmares. I needed to get away from the poisonous air.

But I couldn't hide while we lost it all. I heaved with the indecision, finally giving into the fear of loss and snatching up my bucket, sure I'd find the village forming a water line to put out the fires.

Downdrafts beat overhead, the massive wings drawing my attention to the heavens and to the monstrous creatures. A shriek died on my lips. It wasn't real. It was the smoke and my terrible imagination. Fear tightened in my gut, and my hands shook. My throat burned, but no more sounds came from me. Every instinct told me to run. To hide. To get away from the visions from my nightmares.

No.

I wouldn't allow myself to cower. I ran toward the fire, but the village wasn't collecting to put out the blaze. Instead, they fled. I called after them, but few listened, too concerned with their escape.

"We will lose everything!" I screamed in frustration.

5

"Azariah." I heard my mother before I saw her, and by the use of my full name, I could tell she wasn't happy. "There you are. Come quickly!" Mother called urgently from across the yard, her voice full of fear and indignation.

"We have to save the crops," I insisted. We'd endured too many winters after bad harvests where we all starved and the weakest didn't make it, through many months surviving on roots and what Father could bring back from the barren woods.

This was so much more. Our entire livelihood burned, and I was only one girl. We needed to come together to save as much as possible. Even if I could get close to the fumes without them sending me into an attack, I could hardly do anything with one pail. I turned from the flames as mother stormed toward me.

She grabbed my arm, digging her nails into my skin. "You will never listen, will you? Insolent child. Your life is in peril, and your head is in the clouds."

"I—" I objected, but she yanked harder, dragging me away like we weren't under siege.

"We must go." Her voice carried an emotion I couldn't place. More than fear, deeper.

The tone got my feet moving, forcing me to run to keep up with her long strides. Questions died on my lips, knowing this wasn't the time to test her. My questions were never welcome, and in this mood they would only bring forth her wrath. I'd rather walk toward the flames than subject myself to her anger.

We rounded the corner in front of the gathering hall, but she dragged me past the doors.

"Where are we going?" I waved at the fae filling the small space. "We need to organize—" But my words faltered when I laid eyes on the fae who were carrying sacks and crates into one of the root cellars.

Mother didn't break her stride when Father appeared with a large bag over one shoulder to fall in beside her.

Wails of pain echoed in my ears as they pulled me down the

6

cellar stairs beneath the earth. A wall of cool air hit us, making the intensity of heat from the fires above more apparent. My eyes slowly adjusted, and I found my sisters already here huddling with my brother.

Why are we hiding and not helping?

Surely there was a better use of our time. We couldn't just let it all go. We'd dealt with raiders and bandits, starvation and drought. We could fight this.

This felt fearful and against the Goddess' teachings. It was cowardly to gather in a safe place while others fled. My stomach turned over in realization—Luka was still out there!

I tried to tell Mother so we could search for him, and that was when I recognized the barrels and sacks of dried herbs stored down here. They were already making it harder to breathe. I stumbled back, only to be caught by the back of my neck.

"We are safe here, Azariah," my mother scolded.

"But my intolerance." I ripped out of her grasp. They would all be fine, the herbs had no ill effect on them, but it wasn't safe for me. My breath caught in my throat while my lungs tightened. My throat swelled and burned, and my eyes watered. I could barely choke out words. "I can't stay down here."

I yanked out of my mother's grasp and ran out of the cellar, ignoring my parents' cries. I darted past more fae hauling our sacred herbs toward the cellar and pulled my scarf from my pocket to tie it around my face, heading toward the gathering hall. I had to find the elders. They would do something, or I could try to convince them not to give up. Luka would head to the gathering hall to help. I would find him there.

The wind shifted, blasting the full force of the fire's heat in my face, and sending thick smoke in my direction. It was too late to change my course, and smoke consumed me, cutting off my oxygen while blasting lungfuls of herbs down my throat. The handkerchief barely helped, and my eyes watered while my chest burned. I fell to my knees, doubled over with pain. The burn choked off my throat until I could hardly move. I crawled, forcing my limbs into motion, but I grew weaker by the second. Every breath brought more agony. Blinding torture.

The world spun, and my vision darkened. The chaos engulfed my senses—screams, cries, roaring, and destruction. It was almost peaceful, in a twisted sense.

My limbs gave out, refusing to carry me any farther, and I sank onto the scorched earth. I prayed for the fires to consume me. A quicker death than the herbs would bring.

Before the Goddess took me, a deep, terrifying roar rattled my bones.

TWO
NYX

_"_**A**_re you in a place you can talk?"_ My brother spoke directly into my mind, pulling me from the report I should have been reading but couldn't focus on.

"I'm in the Regent's Library." I glanced around for any wandering eyes, but the other advisers who lingered after council meetings tended toward the serious type, not gossipers. _"But I'm not busy."_ Sharing a mind connection wasn't a normal occurrence except between flyers and their ryders, or bonded mates. Occasionally, twins possessed the ability, but it was not a certainty, so we kept the ability and strength of our twin bond to ourselves.

"It's better if you're alone." There was a hitch to his mental inflection I couldn't place. It gave me pause. I knew his mind as well as I knew my own, considering we'd shared a womb.

"Give me a few minutes." I slipped out of the Regent's

library, where I spent a good deal of my time. *"How alone are we talking?"*

"I know how well you hide your expressions, brother. I wouldn't want to put you in a tight spot." There was humor in his words, which tempered my anxiety. *"But this is time sensitive."*

"I'm on my way to my chambers. Give me a moment."

"Okay." Impatience bled into his words.

"Kol, if it's that urgent, just tell me."

"We found something on the south coast. Way out in the Fifth Kingdom." Kol's mind voice seemed cagey. He spoke of a barren place few lived. The kingdom was largely arid dessert. As unforgiving as the fae who lived there.

"I'm alone, out with it," I demanded, growing impatient with his games. I closed the door to my suite of rooms.

"We found a village."

"And?" Settlements sprung up all over the place. The barons of the outer kingdoms gave away large swaths of hostile land if fae were willing to inhabit it.

He knew all this. The Twelve Kingdoms were vast, and my brother wasn't new to patrol. *"No, we were told to check out a possible band of rebels but found a village there instead."*

"Great, case closed. I'd inform the Regent myself, but I think it would give us away." Why was he wasting my time with this?

"Will you shut up and listen?"

I gave a mental wave for him to continue, crossing my arms over my chest.

"They are Sisters of the Sands."

"I don't know what that is."

"Neither did I until we got here. They live without magic. Any type of it. They deny its existence."

I scoffed. *"That is ridiculous. No one lives without magic."*

"These fae do. It seems like the elders of the Sisters broke away from our society generations ago and have raised their

progeny without magic. They considered it a dark practice and separated themselves from everything associated with it."

"What nonsense? Magic is magic. A gift from the Goddess Kalilah for those she favors. Nothing more. There is no dark and light." I laughed at the absurdity of it. It was like denying gravity. *"Show them some. Hard to deny something used in front of their face."*

"It's not that simple. Magic exists whether they deny it or not, but they almost certainly cover any evidence of it with superstition and religion. You know how these remote communities can be with their religion, brother."

I sighed. I didn't need a rundown on the madness infecting the outskirts of the Twelve Kingdoms. *"What does this have to do with me, and why is it urgent?"*

"At times, I wish you were less dense. What if they are hiding her here? Think about it. What better place? They could tell her any lie they please if they raised her away from magic entirely."

Ice ran though my veins. It clicked. How they could have kept her so well hidden all these years. If they raised their kids so they knew nothing of our kind, nothing about magic, and lived so remotely there was no contact from the outside, their lies could have brainwashed her even into adulthood. This could be it.

"Where are you?" I demanded.

"About a hundred leagues south of Cortona, off the coast." He pushed a vision into my mind of the coastline and the landmarks they'd followed to get there.

I tempered my expectations. I wouldn't allow myself to live on false hope any longer. I'd made a vow to myself.

"It will take me at least a day and a half to get there. Are you sure?" I didn't know how I'd explain my absence.

"Leave now, Nyx, and fly hard. I think they are going to order us to burn the settlement." Fear edged into my brother's voice.

"What? Why?" These fae might be unbalanced, but they were likely harmless.

"Because intel suggests they are growing Dragon's Bane."

"But you said it's a village, not a grow site."

"I don't know. We are trying to get eyes on their fields, but the terrain is difficult, and they are watching every inch."

"Surely command won't order a fire strike if they know there are females and children there?"

My brother hesitated. *"Maybe. We are waiting for the last scouts to return and will be sending word to the Regent imminently. That's why I'm letting you know now. Once we know and it goes up the chain of command, there will be no stopping what comes next. You know that."*

"They wouldn't destroy a whole village." It was unconscionable. I was confident in my assessment. They would destroy the deadly plants and possibly send the fae to prison camps in the far north, but they wouldn't senselessly harm females and children.

"I don't have a good feeling about it, Nyx."

"Could you be mistaken? Perhaps you missed your target along the coast?" They had to have the wrong place.

"We didn't miss an entire damn grow site..." Kol sighed, his annoyed tone coming through loud and clear. *"This is the place. There isn't another settlement for a hundred leagues. If they're growing Dragon's Bane, we haven't seen it yet, but it's not a small band of rebels like the intelligence suggested. It's families —there are kids here. Either it's both or neither."*

"I can't just leave. When will you call it in?"

"As soon as the scouts return, our report will be sent, good or bad. I can't prevent it."

"I have a small council meeting this evening." I rubbed my forehead, thinking through the excuses I'd have to make if I missed it, unsure if my brother's bad feeling was bleeding through

our bond or if my gut implored me to go. It was madness to try and get into a target settlement with our teams surrounding it; I would be spotted, and how would I explain that? Although, in flight and at speed, my twin and I were similar enough to be mistaken, so if I was fast... *"Are you pulling back, or will your team be going in?"*

"Not my call, but you need to come regardless."

"Are you sure?"

"I don't think you should wait."

"Fuck." I stripped off my shirt and then shoved off my trousers before throwing open the doors to my balcony. *"And you can't feel her?"*

"You know I can't. No matter how close our bond, it doesn't cross."

I flexed my jaw as I vaulted the parapet, letting my dragon form stretch out as the wind rushed by my ears. Eyes closed, my body took its true form, filling out to the far reaches of myself. Wings, claws, scales all manifested mid fall, and I transformed into a dragon. My power ignited in my veins, connecting me with the element my magic was gifted from. Fire in my lungs, and the wind against my wings, I took flight.

Freedom.

My wings stretched out to catch the air before I came close to the ground. I turned toward the north, beating my wings to gain altitude. I inhaled, the magic in the air recharging my stores. Staying in our fae form too long prevented us from maintaining our full power; I'd let myself get far too depleted.

"Keep me updated."

"I'll do my best to put them off, but if they confirm Dragon's Bane, there is little I can do."

We could cover ground much faster than horses or even other winged beasts, but we still had limitations. Flying headlong and even using every last bit of my stamina, it would still be more than a day. I'd have to fly overnight, and it would take me well into the morning, but thankfully, they couldn't get word to the capital any faster.

"Where are you?" my brother asked as dawn crested, bringing the Goddess' blessing to first light.

"Nearly there. What is it?"

"They think they found something. I'm going into the settlement with Elvar now." His tone had changed. He'd taken his fae form.

"If you get caught disobeying orders…" I didn't need to finish the warning. He knew the risk.

"Relax, brother. Orders have changed. Elvar and I are approaching the gates posing as followers of the Sisters of the Sands seeking lodgings. We will have eyes in the village in a few moments."

"Good. Look for her."

"I won't be able to feel her—"

"Dammit, I don't care if you can feel her. Look for a girl in her early twenties with blonde hair and green eyes," I hissed.

I sent him an image of her. The only one I had. A girl with blonde curls and a baby face. She wasn't more than three. An unusual age for a flyer to find their ryder, but it happened when the realm had need. When the Goddess granted the gift as young as she had for us, it was so we could begin training our magic early. It always foretold great power and future conflict for the Twelve Kingdoms. The conflict already pushed in on our boarders and threatened to explode into a full-blown war. We'd needed that time together, but it had been stolen from us before we could begin.

I'd spent two decades searching for her.

"Don't take this out on me. I'm trying to help you." Kol was

taking a great risk wandering into a village suspected to have Dragon's Bane. It could be hanging in every building for all we knew, and it would prevent him from taking his dragon form for hours. Days, even, if he came into contact with enough of it.

"*I know. I'm sorry.*" I redoubled my effort, climbing even higher, seeking the good air. I had to get there.

THREE
ZARIA

A large beast slammed into the ground before me, rattling my bones. I peered up and saw wings and scales on a creature so frightening, he had to be real. No imagination could produce such a thing.

Fear paralyzed me, turning my body into living stone as he snatched me up in his razor-sharp talons.

I expected to be torn apart, my death delivered quickly by the Goddess, saving me from the long, agonizing death the herbs had promised. I lifted my face, accepting my fate at the hands of the Goddess Kalilah in all her mercy. I would walk on her Shores of Avalon as a willing servant.

But death didn't come. Instead, we shot into the air. My stomach turned as it tried to stay on the ground, and I groaned at the sensation, my lungs too choked and my mind too lost in the hallucination to muster a scream.

I realized my eyes were closed, but when I pried them open, my body found the capacity for a scream after all. Terror bled in the sound that left my lips. My stomach lurched, and I fought to keep my last meal. The crops rushed by beneath us, the village a speck beyond them. Smoke and flames engulfed everything, and we soared up and above it all.

Air finally rushed into my lungs. Clean air, free from the suffocating smoke and the herbs which altered my mind and made me sick.

I heaved in the life-giving freshness, and my body came back. I was still choking from the smoke that had seared my lungs, but free from the danger of the herbs in the air at least. Maybe the Goddess had spared me?

No. If She had spared me, I would not be in the grips of a demon, being carried off to the Goddess knew where. To be torn apart and eaten? What else could such a monster want with a girl like me? To be its captive? I went cold at the thought of what sinister deeds such a creature could—no. I scratched the thoughts from my mind.

A deep sound emanated from my captor. It almost sounded like a chuckle, if such a thing were possible.

My mind was my enemy. Mother was right. All the dreams of such creatures I'd had must truly have been a sign of some evil within, and now my mind would be my end.

"Oh, for the love of the Goddess," a deep voice spoke with a hint of amusement.

I didn't have time to figure out the source before it dropped me. A yelp escaped my lips, but my feet found the ground before the sound materialized. I crumpled to my knees, my legs still weakened from all that had happened to me.

I lifted my fists and steeled myself for the attack, but none came. I frowned and squinted up at the beast. He breathed hard, his massive body laboring while his nostrils flared with the effort. For a moment, he just stared, then abruptly, he moved.

I cowered, my voice too raw from the smoke to make a sound. He moved past, bending low to dip his enormous head to a stream. I sidestepped to get as far away from the creature as possible and used his distraction to take in his vast body and wings.

WINGS!

It had looked like the gatekeeper of the Valley of the Dead as it swooped in and stole me away. But now? He was majestic. Mother always said Uriel would be beautiful. Like the Goddess had hand-painted him.

I didn't want to look too closely at the fascinating details only for him to turn around and swallow me whole, but now that those huge, savage wings that had lifted us into the skies were folded so neatly against his sides, they seemed almost delicate, not fearsome.

They were a deep indigo and tipped at their joints by sharp points that glimmered like jewels in the sun. Their matte, leathery texture contrasted with the rest of his body, which was covered in shimmering scales in a whole spectrum of purples, blues, and jades that seemed to shift in the light, the way the oil from a lamp does when it is spilled on the surface of water. It set me on edge. He was much too beautiful for a monster.

He took a long drink while I took another sidestep. But what could I do? Run? Fight?

What could I actually accomplish if he turned to feast on his prize or—

His chuckle vibrated the loose stones beneath my feet this time. I shook my head in refusal. Monsters didn't chuckle.

By the Goddess! Monsters didn't exist!

My imagination must have been running wild in death. It was the only explanation that made sense.

"Then, who just saved you from that fire, Sol?"

The monster turned his vast body to face me again and just stared...expectantly? His seemingly endless tail snaked lazily past as he settled on his haunches, brushing my foot as it went.

I staggered back. It must have the herbs. I was hearing and seeing and even feeling this awful creature I'd dreamed of since childhood because I'd inhaled the herbs. That was all this was. It couldn't be more.

"Awful?"

I gasped, then glanced around.

"I—I—How are you doing that?" I demanded, immediately shutting down the weak stammer that was threatening.

It had to be him speaking to me. We were alone. But how? He wasn't even speaking, he was thinking, and it was...entering my head? I hated it. It felt itchy.

"Doing what?"

"Putting words in my brain." I had to be hallucinating. Visions to trick me in my last breaths.

"It's called a bond, Sol."

"I don't care what it's called. How are you doing it? How can you put thoughts into my head?" Was he putting the visions in my head, too? Did it make me mad to speak to a creation of a fever dream? I probably shouldn't be trying to make sense of a hallucination. But I had to know more. "Are you a servant of the great betrayer?" If mother was right about my dreams, I'd hurl myself off a cliff. I couldn't bear it.

Confusion flickered in his expression and then he laughed again. *"We have a bond, so we can speak to each other's minds. It's the only way we can communicate when I'm in my dragon form. Do you truly not know any of this?"*

"How would I know any of this?" I said through my teeth, unwilling to let him see my fear and confusion, though it threatened to pour out of me. "And what in the name of the Goddess is a dragon form?"

His expression changed, becoming almost sinister with massive teeth on full display while his laugh curled his mouth and vibrated through the soil. *"Still cute and fierce to your core, I see, Sol."*

Indignation swelled in my chest. "Are you mocking me?"

"Mocking you? No. You just amuse me. I rescued you from certain death, and in thanks, you call me a monster and believe I am a servant of the great betrayer. Not to mention some of the deeply fascinating if not twisted scenarios you seem to have imagined involving you being my captive."

The humor in his tone irritated me. If a dream monster could give a lascivious look, that's exactly what he did.

I huffed in denial, attempting to mask the blush I felt warming my face. "Don't change the subject."

"Don't worry, Sol. We can come back to that intriguing subject later," he purred in my mind, causing a shiver to snake its way down my spine before I could fight it.

"A dragon is this 'monstrous servant of Uriel' you believe me to be. I shift between two forms—one is a dragon, and the other —a little less daunting for you—is the form of a fae." he said, flaring his wings a little to illustrate his point.

I startled at the movement, sidestepping another pace, but he quickly returned them to his sides.

"You don't need to fear me, Sol." His low voice whispered directly in my mind, almost as unnerving as his appearance.

I scowled, jutting my chin out. "Why do you keep calling me that? It is not my name."

"It was what I called you when we first met. You were young and would not share your name."

"I don't know what you mean. My name is Azariah Sorelli. I go by Zaria. I don't know a Sol, and I have never laid eyes on you before."

He puffed out a breath of disgust.

"What?" I demanded.

"You have been hidden away and lied to. You know me. Do you not remember?"

"You lie!"

"Can you not feel it?" The closeness in the curl of his tone sent a shiver down my spine. He didn't have to be near to make me feel as if he was.

"I don't know what I'm supposed to feel other than afraid, but I know that if I had ever met a—a—'dragon,' I think I would remember."

He growled low. *"I told you, I have another form much like yours."*

"Prove it," I challenged.

"I can't," he conceded.

"Oh, well, I'll just take a demon at his word then, shall I?" I almost laughed at the absurdity of this situation. Was I arguing with a dragon rather than running away like anyone else would?

"For now, you have no choice."

"There is always a choice. If you say you know me but not as…this"—I gestured to his body—"then change and prove it to me." I broke out in a fit of coughing, noticing for the first time that the smoke had reached the hilltop and was surrounding us on all sides.

"It's not possible with all this Dragon's Bane burning. I can't shift."

I didn't know what he was talking about, but my heart lurched at his words, and the thickening smoke suddenly reminded me that I had been standing here arguing with this… thing while my family was in danger and our village was being destroyed.

"My family!" I turned to look down at the burning village, but the smoke was too thick to see. I had to get back there. The terrain was rough on the slope, but I had no choice. I made to start the descent, but in a flash of wings and scales, the dragon was barring my path. *"You can't go back there. It's too danger-*

ous, and if we don't leave now, before the bane weakens me, I won't be able to fly us out of here." He lowered his chest to the ground. "*Do you think you can ride?*"

"I'm not going anywhere with you. I have to go back. They need help down there."

"*It's too late for them, Sol. We have to leave before it's too late for us too.*"

"You don't know that! I have to try—" Deep body-wracking coughs seized me, and I fell to my knees, unable to catch my breath.

My vision tunneled, and before I could right myself, he scooped me up with one...arm? I guessed it was an arm. Claws pressed against my ribcage, digging in as he vaulted into the air.

My stomach flipped. I was going to be sick.

"Put me down! Where are you taking me?" I screamed over the wind, only for my voice to be swallowed in the beats of his wings.

"*I can't hear you,*" he replied in my head.

"I don't know how to speak in your mind!" I yelled to the skies, knowing it was futile, but it made me feel better.

"*I can hear you if you just think it.*" There was laughter in his tone. "*That's how I know about those delightful dragon's captive fantasies of yours.*"

"*Evil demon,*" I thought at him, not sure if I was doing it right and if he could hear me.

"*Loud and clear, my Sol,*" he confirmed.

I hated this name he was using. Who was he to call me by any other name than the one the Goddess had given to my parents? "*My name is Zaria.*"

"*Sol is how I knew you. You liked it.*"

"*I don't believe you.*" I still wasn't entirely sure I believed he was real at all. Monsters didn't just appear from the sky and kidnap girls.

"Do you really not remember me at all?" he asked with a sort of hesitation that made my brain even more itchy.

"I think you are mistaken, dragon. Let me go. I need to help my family." I beat my fists on the claws around my middle in frustration.

"My name is Nyx. Tell me you don't know me." He ignored my efforts.

"I don't know you," I said with certainty.

"You do."

We fell into silence, which was worse than his mocking.

"Please," I caved, need taking priority over indignation. *"You have to let me go. I have to go back. I don't know you. You have me mistaken for someone else."*

"I cannot. I just saved you from death, Sol. And I'm not mistaken. I feel you," he pressed, driving some sort of connection between us. *"You can feel it too. I'm sure of it."*

My entire body tingled, and as if a string tied around my chest tightened, I felt it between us. A thread. But it had to be a trick of Uriel.

"I do not know you!" I screamed aloud, then descended into a coughing fit that left me seeing black spots in my vision. Hot tears pricked my eyes, and before I could stop them, they trickled down my face.

"Take me back. You can save them, too," I begged, pride be damned.

"They're gone, Sol," he said softly. *"It's too late. I only just got you out."*

I sobbed. They couldn't be gone. They were all I had.

It wasn't a great life. It was hard living, and there was not much in the way of affection, but I knew they loved me in their way. They held strong beliefs, and we lived with other like-minded fae in a remote community.

We didn't mix with the outside world. Some of the fae would occasionally travel to trade our harvest for provisions with distant towns, but the outside world was full of evils that my parents had left behind. So the sudden realization that I had been taken out of the safety of the compound into a world my parents had deemed too corrupt and rotten to continue living in was chilling. I had never left the compound before, and I was alone, in the clutches of a winged monster, being taken to the Goddess only knew where.

We flew in silence as I began to grieve.

"I'm sorry," he said after a long while.

I didn't reply. I had nothing to say.

What was he sorry for? Destroying my home? Murdering my family? Abducting me?

"It wasn't like you think," he countered.

"Get out of my head," I snapped.

Rage, the likes of which I had never known burned inside my veins as we flew on in silence.

But as I watched the land rush by, another body-wracking coughing fit overtook me. Darkness crept into the corners of my vision, and I cast a final prayer to the Goddess for salvation as my world went black.

FOUR
ZARIA

Dawn was upon us when I stirred awake. Panic immediately took hold when I opened my eyes to find the land far below and rushing by at great speed. It wasn't a dream.

I shivered from the chill morning air, and he seemed to hold me closer to his body in response.

The world below was showing more signs of life than I had ever seen before. Occasional crops and pastures had become villages, then towns, and as we flew, I grew more and more fearful of our destination. I lifted my head and looked toward the horizon and gasped as my worst fears were confirmed. A city grew in the distance. At least, that was all I could imagine it to be. Though still tiny in the distance, I could see the density of the buildings. I had heard tales of the cities and their sins, but seeing it was more daunting than I ever imagined.

"Thank the Goddess," he huffed softly into my mind.

I stiffened. The memory of what had occurred flashed through me at the sound of his voice, and the itchy feeling of his thoughts in my head was just as keen. What was he thanking the Goddess for, exactly?

"You've been unconscious for hours, Sol."

Through the night, if the morning light was any sign. My stomach soured at the knowledge that so much time had gone by since he took me. Were my parents safe? Would they be worried?

"Are you well?" he asked.

I spat a laugh. *"Well? What does the state of my health matter? A creature I still don't believe is real has kidnapped me. My home has been destroyed and my family—"* I bit back tears. I would not show him my pain. *"Where are you taking me?"* I tried to sound strong, but I was feeling afraid and alone, and I was weaker than before. I felt the effect of the herbs more than ever. I tried to shake it off. It didn't matter where he was taking me, he couldn't keep me. I wouldn't allow it.

I felt the rumble of a growl through his body. He clearly didn't agree.

"Well?" I demanded.

"I'm taking you home."

"You took me from my home," I thought defiantly, but even the voice in my head wavered and betrayed my uncertainty. Was this another trick of Uriel? Could he make me believe I knew him?

At that thought, a faint connection pulsed between our chests, like we had an invisible string tied between us. It was a feeling that felt familiar. Something I'd long felt if I really thought about it. A strand of myself reaching out beyond the world I knew, searching for something more. Only now, he was at the other end of the strand.

"No," he corrected, cutting into my thoughts. *"They took you from—"* he hesitated like he kept something back.

"What was I taken from? What aren't you saying?"

"Our kind. You know it to be true. I feel your tug on the bond." He had dropped his voice, keeping it low, almost like a lullaby. Was he trying to hypnotize me? The beat of his wings, the steady rhythm, combined with the reaction from my intolerance, lulled me back toward sleep.

I had to fight this hypnosis he had placed on me. I shook my head, trying to clear the fog. *"Take me back."* I hit my fist feebly into iron-hard scales, knowing it was futile. Even if I wasn't weak from the herbs, what could I do against such a beast?

"Do you want to die?"

"I'd rather die with my fellow fae than be taken to the Valley of the Dead to be your prisoner!" I fought back a sob. Would Luka be there? My siblings? Were they all dead? Would the cellar have given them enough cover? Would they be able to escape into the woods, or would the beasts have set them all ablaze?

"I won't let that happen. If you die, I could too."

I could feel his sadness in the words. I felt the same sadness. I gasped. *"What have you done to me?"* My parents had warned me of this. Uriel's beasts could attach themselves to your spirit and use it for power. They did it to siphon our energy and soul, stealing our soul so they could prowl the Twelve Kingdoms.

"What are you talking about?"

"You're stealing my spirit." I clutched my pendant. That had to be it. My intolerance alone wouldn't explain it. The pendant seared my hand, burning hot against his evil. I had to resist. I searched my memory for all the ways we were taught to fight against the siphon.

"Goddess bless. The brainwashing they put you through… We have been tied since we were born. I'm a dragon, and you are my ryder. The Goddess willed it. I wouldn't have picked you either, given a choice." Annoyance crept into his words. *"You will see the true world as soon as we get to the capital. If our bond can't convince you, that surely will."*

"Stop with your tricks. I won't believe anything you say." I tried to fight back against the thread that connected us, to throw him off or push him away, force his voice out of my mind, but the strain made my head ache. The more I fought, the more the herb weakened me. It was like quicksand.

I hissed, rubbing my chest where my pendant sat. My vision narrowed, and my thoughts became slower. I'd inhaled too much of the herb. I'd be sick for days, even without him stealing my spirit. The extra energy it took to fight him was killing me. Maybe that was his design.

I wouldn't let him poison my mind, though. I had to steel myself against his tricks.

The strain was too much. I shook with it.

"What are you doing?"

"Trying to get away!" I kept fighting the pull of the string, thrashing in his arms.

"Stop fighting the bond. You can't break it, and you're sick. You need to save your energy."

"It's you!" I fought the sleep that called, trying to suck in as much clean air as his grip on me would allow. *"I'm not ill. You've done this!"*

"No, your breathing is erratic." Concern showed in his voice. *"Did you inhale too much smoke? Do you need a healer?"* He beat his wings with a new vigor.

"It's the herb. I'm intolerant to it. It makes me ill." I didn't know why I was sharing my weakness with him; he was drawing confessions from me now, and I was powerless to stop him.

"Well, that is an interesting twist." He cradled me closer, sharing his warmth. *"You think I'm a servant of Uriel when your own family was actively poisoning you?"*

"How could they control my intolerance?"

"It's not an intolerance. You're a dragon ryder. Dragon's Bane will kill you as surely as it will me. You must have inhaled

too much before I got to you, and it's taking hold. I'm taking you right to the healers."

"You're lying," I gasped, but any fight became useless, and I fought to stay conscious.

"The only ones lying to you were your parents. You would have died if I left you there. They were willing to sacrifice you rather than let you be with your kind. Their lies were more important to them than your life."

"And what are their lives worth? You killed them all!" I screamed, only to have my words lost on the wind.

"I wasn't responsible for that, Sol. I can promise you that."

"Your kind was."

"I know." He didn't sound remorseful, but there was a feeling accompanying his words in my mind. Regret, maybe? Sadness? Something.

"If I could have stopped them, I would have, but I had to get you out."

"It's not good enough. They were killing them all." My body heaved with sadness. My parents. My brothers and sisters. Luka.

"They were only burning down the stores of Dragon's Bane. I don't think they were harming your villagers." He was lying; I could feel it.

"Stop lying to me." I beat against him again, not caring if I did die. How could I live when they were all dead?

"Stop straining."

"Put me down."

"Sol, do you have a death wish?" We came to an abrupt halt, and my stomach lurched.

I nearly lost it all over him. Swallowing bile, I found myself on my feet, and realized we must have landed. I wavered. *"Death would be better than being your captive! I would join my family on the Shores of Avalon."*

"You're not in your right mind." He rolled his eyes. *"You need a healer."*

"Don't bother." My knees went weak, and I reached out to save myself from falling, realizing to my annoyance that I was still speaking into his mind even though he could hear me clearly now. "You're trying to trick me. I won't give in."

In a flash, a fae stood before me.

A naked fae.

He was close, far too close, and grabbed my arm to keep me steady.

My cheeks heated, and I averted my eyes, lowering them. Which was the wrong choice. I got quite the view of bronzed skin and hard muscle and—I swallowed, closing my eyes.

He pressed in, his warm breath on my ear. "You know me. Feel it, Zaria. You are my ryder. This is where you belong." His voice... It was familiar and yet not. A voice I knew in my soul yet had never heard. It curled around me, delivering some sort of comfort.

My entire body reacted to him, growing warm from the inside out as a shiver ran down my spine.

Even if he was lying about the rest, I was beginning to sense this much was true.

I knew him.

But I didn't know what that meant.

FIVE

NYX

She passed clean out. Thankfully, she hadn't backed far
enough away, and I caught her before she could go over the
edge of the landing. I carried her through the open doorway into
the healer's wing.

"What do you have for us, Nyx?" Kiera asked, gesturing me
toward an empty bed.

I laid Zaria where I was directed and looked my old friend in
the eyes. "She's my ryder, and I think she has Dragon's Bane
poisoning."

Kiera gasped. "No. You jest."

"No jest. I found her. But there was Dragon's Bane burning
all around her. She inhaled a lot." I stepped back as Kiera
pressed a stone to Sol's chest. I didn't fully understand the sacred
symbols and crystals used for healing magic, but I knew she'd be
checking her lungs and blood.

Dragon's Bane could lead to blood poisoning if respiration didn't fail first.

"Where did you find her?" Kiera shot me a half glance.

"It's best you don't know," I said carefully, not sure how much trouble my brother would get into for all of this.

"What did you do?" She gave a flat look. We'd started our training the same year, and Kiera had never taken any of my shit. She saw through my charm from the moment she met me; it made me appreciate her more.

"Will you focus on the patient?" I said in a poor attempt to change the subject.

"I've already diagnosed her. Her blood will need to be cleansed to remove the poison, but she will be fine in a few days. You haven't found your ryder only to lose her." Kiera straightened and fixed her healer's robes, then grabbed a pair of sweatpants to toss at me.

I caught the sweats and exhaled, letting some of the tension and exhaustion out of my shoulders. "Thanks."

"I should go into the sweatpants business as often as you lot need them. I'd make a fortune." She signaled to a healer's apprentice to take over Sol's care and slipped from the sectioned-off area. I felt torn, but Sol was in the best hands, so I followed, pulling on the pants.

"If you do, can you dye them more favorable colors? Gray is entirely boring. I'd love a cobalt or azure." I leaned against her herbal prep counter while she gathered what she needed.

"As if you need anything more to bring out those eyes of yours. It's already sickening how the ladies in the court follow you and your brother around."

I flashed a grin. "It's because we are dragons, not because of our looks."

"It can be both."

"At least you're immune."

"You don't have anything I fancy, and marrying a flyer

sounds exhausting. I'll pass." She handed me a bundle of herbs and a knife before looking me over. "Do you need something? How long have you been awake?"

"A couple of days?" I closed one eye, trying to remember as I took them and prepped them the way she'd shown me years ago. This wasn't my first time lingering where I didn't belong. Hiding in the healer's wing became my sanctuary a long time ago. "You're smart to stay away from flyers. We don't make great partners—too much time in the skies. I wouldn't wish it on anyone."

"Is that why you refuse to marry?" She side-eyed me as she prepared a small potion. She pushed it into my hands, and I gladly downed it. Liquid energy wasn't the best thing to consume, but it would keep me upright to deal with the consequences of my excursion.

"Obviously." There was more to it than that. A female ryder was never a good arrangement for an unwed male flyer. Any fae I'd marry would be jealous of our close bond and the time we spent together, and I'd known all my life that was coming if I ever found her again. Now I had the extra battle of dealing with a ryder who didn't even want to be here. I shook my head and forced a smile to my lips. "I'll be too busy training my ryder for some time to come."

Kiera giggled. "Every time one of you calls them a ryder, my mind goes straight to the gutter."

"Don't say that in front of her. She may never look me in the eyes again."

Kiera's brows rose. "Is she a maiden?"

"I didn't ask. I thought it might be impolite considering it's the first time I've seen her since she was three years old. And things have been...complicated."

Kiera kept laughing and shook her head before taking what I'd roughly chopped and giving me another bundle to work on.

"I'm happy for you, Nyx. I know you've suffered a long time with her missing."

"Will she be okay?" I asked. If she died... I couldn't let myself follow that train of thought.

"She will. You got her here fast enough, and it's not as bad as it could have been."

I breathed easier, but it was only the first battle. "I'm not sure things are going to be any easier now that she's found."

She met my gaze. "That bad?"

"I think so. Maybe it would have been better to leave her."

"She'd burn herself out. I'm surprised she hasn't yet." Her brows creased, and she paused her work. "Even if she hates you, her place is here. She has to be trained. She won't be the first reluctant or ignorant ryder a flyer has dragged in from the far reaches of the Twelve Kingdoms. She will find her place."

"It's not ignorance. It's..." But I couldn't give away more. Not before I knew what I was dealing with and how much it would give away my bond with my brother. "It's more. She really doesn't want to be here."

Kiera was silent for a long time. "She'll come around. She has no other choice." She was right, but I wasn't sure we'd ever get that across to my ryder.

Kiera treated Zaria and left us. I returned to the landing, sure it was best if I went to scope out how much trouble I was in.

"Did you plan on telling me you found your ryder, or are you so obsessed with her already that you forgot your bond with me?" My brother's voice came in the flesh this time and not in my mind.

I looked up, finding him perched above where I stood. "How long have you been there, creeper?"

"Long enough to know you're more depressed than before you found her." He hopped down, landing in a crouch in his fae form.

"She's ruined. What if she never takes to flying? I'm no

longer the dragon missing his ryder; I'm the dragon with the religious nut job who won't ever be willing to fly with him." Why would the Goddess do this to me?

"Others have overcome worse. Ryders come from all over the Twelve Kingdoms, from different backgrounds. We've had just as bad before." He put a hand on my bicep. "The teachers are used to this. Let them have some time with her. She will let go of those silly notions as soon as she gets a glimpse of the real world."

"Kiera said the same thing, but honestly, Kol, name one as brainwashed. They deny magic exists. She thought I was a nightmare come to life. How do we even start her training with that kind of ignorance built in?"

"I told you, she'll see magic for herself and believe. Pretty easy to prove."

"She thinks we are spirit suckers sent by Uriel himself straight from the Valley of the Dead. It won't be as easy as you think."

He laughed, but when I shot him an angry look, he cut it off. "Surely it's not that bad?"

I closed my eyes and sent the memory through our bond.

My brother grimaced. "She has some work to do, but she will come around."

"After you all killed everyone she knows in front of her?"

"Point taken. That might have made it worse. But we didn't kill them all. A bunch of them escaped, and I accidentally forgot to mention it to the commander." He put his hands up. "Bad memory. What can I say?"

"That's not an excuse for everything, you realize?" I scrubbed a hand over my face. "We're both going to be charged with insubordination."

"They will not get rid of two dragons. Especially now that you have a ryder. Plus, the law states a flyer can go wherever and whenever their ryder calls. As soon as you feel them, you go.

Everyone knows this. Just say you were called. How else would you know she was there? My being there is merely a funny coincidence." He grinned, showing off teeth. "What can they say? No one in the capital knew what we found when you left. They don't know about our connection. We can chalk it up to twin mystery!" He waved his fingers around.

I scoffed, but he was on to something. "I suppose I am protected. We don't have to notify anyone when called by a ryder. It's a primal call." I paced the length of the balcony. "This might work."

"It will. Don't say more than you must. You don't know, so don't speculate. Let them do it for you. It will give you both an added layer of protection." He was right.

SIX
ZARIA

U nfamiliar sounds woke me from nightmares worse than I
had ever experienced. I startled when I remembered the
horrors my dreams had visited on me. I had to check on my
family. See for myself that it was all a dream. But as I opened
my eyes, I knew I was not in my home.

I rose while my eyes slowly adjusted to the dim light and the
room. This was not my cramped chamber with the low ceiling
and the crumbling stone floor. This was crisp, well-maintained
stonework, and hanging curtains sectioning off my bed from the
rest of the room. Instead of candles, there were little balls
producing light. I squinted at them, trying to make out what in
the Twelve Kingdoms they could be.

One of the curtains was pulled back to reveal open doors
onto a balcony overlooking... I had no words. So many
dwellings, such vast buildings that I could not imagine how

many families must occupy them. The scale alone was alarming, but the fae. There were fae on the ground, on balconies. At a single glance, I could see more fae than I had ever seen in my life.

Strangers, all of them, with the Goddess only knew what for morals. I had heard about the places the fae in my village had left behind, and if this place was anything alike, I was deep within a den of sin. My chest heaved with the need to escape, and I looked around, trying to form a plan.

They had dressed me in a thin sleeping gown. Heat rose in my face as I considered how they dressed me this way without my knowing. The length of the gown was highly inappropriate, and I shot back within the room when I realized I could be seen in this state from many vantage points. The very thought scandalized me. I snatched the curtains and drew them across the door to shield myself from view and set about looking for my own clothes.

Still light-headed from all that had happened, I steadied myself on the bedpost and drew in a slow breath to calm my racing heart. The action set off a rattling cough, which forced me to a seat on the edge of the bed.

My chest and throat felt painfully raw, and I was weak from the coughing, confirming that my dream of the fire was real. I had truly seen my world destroyed, and with it all the ones I loved. Guilt flickered within me at how false that statement was. Had I truly loved them? Could you truly love fae who'd shown you nothing of the like in return.

In my heart I knew I was born of love, created by the Goddess to be the product of my parents' love for each other, and in turn I was shaped by their love. But life at the compound was tough, the land was unforgiving, and necessities were in painfully short supply, so love was not a high priority. Survival was all that mattered.

They valued only those who could provide, and I was not

among them. I could not be near the herbs we grew for trade, and even living in their proximity weakened me. I was a liability. Someone to feed and clothe who could offer nothing but swept floors and clean pots in return.

I knew my worth, and it was not the same as my worth to them. So I gave them the love due to them as my family, but it was not the full extent of the love I knew was within. A part of me always held the knowledge that I was not fully sincere in my offerings. And now they were gone and the guilt of having only loved with half my heart was crushing.

I wept with the weight if it all, letting the guilt, my sorrow, and my fear consume me for just one moment. It was all I could afford. I had to be strong now. I had to survive this new reality on my own.

I wiped my eyes and breathed away the emotion. I used the breathing technique I was taught by our healer when I was young. It helped when I had an attack brought on by the herbs. It calmed my body and my mind. When I felt stronger and clearer of mind, I stood.

That was when he spoke.

"Are you done?"

I gasped and turned to find him sitting in an armchair, looking for all the world like he ruled a kingdom of his own. He was fae in every way, but I knew in my heart it was him. The dragon who took me, the one with the jade eyes and the pull on my soul.

As I had been succumbing to the attack, I'd seen him with my own eyes change from the beast he was, into this male who now sat assessing. But even if that was just a hallucination of the herbs, I'd still know it was him. I could feel it. Much to my disgust and his obvious amusement, he was right. There was an almost tangible thread of connection between us.

"Well, that was easy. I was prepared for battle with you, but at least you aren't being deliberately difficult. You admit you feel our connection. It's a start." He set his crossed leg to the floor and rose.

He was so tall, so…my mouth went dry as he approached. All the bronzed skin I'd glimpsed when he'd first changed was still on display. His pants the only clothing he had bothered to put on and they hung low on his sculpted hips. I dragged my eyes away from the defined cut of muscle that disappeared beneath the fabric of his pants, over a light trail of dark hair, hard muscles, a broad chest, a square jaw, and right to the glowing jade of his piercing eyes.

I baulked. I was only wearing this scrap of fabric, and he was shirtless and barefoot. I retreated to the other side of the bed, snatching up a blanket and holding it to my chest.

"What are you doing here—dressed like that?" It was the wrong question to ask, and I knew it as soon as his teeth appeared in his self-satisfied grin.

"What's wrong with how I'm dressed, Sol?" He looked down at himself casually and then returned his intense gaze to mine, offering nothing else.

The Goddess have mercy. He was magnificent. The fae I had known were lean from hardship even if they were toned from hard work. A body like his had never seen such struggles, I thought as my gaze began to drift lower again.

"Sol?"

"Hmm?" I snapped my eyes to his, remembering he'd asked a question. The curl of his lips told me I wasn't hiding my thoughts. Even if he was not able to hear them, I was certain they were written all over my face. Goddess spare me. What was the question? Oh, yes, his state of dress.

"It's highly improper," I snipped, deciding offense was better than defense. "You can't be here unchaperoned and in a state of undress." I pressed my lips together, chastising myself for again pointing out his clothing choice, or lack thereof. I did not want him thinking I had even noticed. He was nothing but my captor.

He chuckled. Again. It was becoming a highly annoying habit of his.

"There you go again with those fascinating dragon's captive ideas of yours. Tell me, are they a new thing, or have you always fantasized about being kept by a mighty beast?"

I growled with indignation. "How dare you suggest—"

"Suggest? I'm not suggesting a thing. I'm only voicing your thoughts." He took a step toward the bed, and I backed up.

"Do not come any closer. What will they think?"

"In the world you come from? I imagine they'd be scandalized." He rounded the bed and closed in. "Here, though?" He stepped into my space, the warmth from his body and his scent surrounding me. "I don't imagine anyone here would care."

"Sinners," I hissed. The word a conditioned response, quite in contrast to the reaction of my body.

"You should see the lust in your eyes, Sol. It's you having the impure thoughts. So is the sin not actually yours? My thoughts are totally pure." He raked his gaze down the thin material I wore, and I suddenly felt as bare as he was. His accusing words curled around my body, awakening feelings within me I didn't know I possessed while making me hate him at the same time. I didn't want him to affect me in this manner.

"I am not a sinner!"

"Then, why would this bother you?" Nyx brushed his fingers down the curve of my neck, raising goosebumps where our skin made contact. He shouldn't be able to affect me this way. It was more evidence he wished to lead me away from the Goddess.

I flinched away from his touch. "It doesn't."

"Liar," he all but purred.

"What do you want with me?"

"Now, there's a question."

I watched him expectantly, but he looked away, seeming to war with himself. I wanted to know his thoughts, but it seemed like he could choose which he shared with me, whereas I had no such choice.

When he looked back into my eyes, he seemed resolved. "I want you to stay. The life you were living in that place was a lie. Your place is here."

"My place is not in this den of sin," I snarled. But even as the words left my mouth, I knew they were empty. They were the words of my mother, and I could feel the falseness of them while they still hung in the air. I knew nothing of this place.

The male stood before me was not evil like they led me to believe all city dwellers were. That much I knew on instinct alone. I felt it. He might be a sinner. He certainly was a kidnapper, a liar, a monster…but I knew in my soul he was not evil.

"See, you know the truth."

"I don't want to be here." It wasn't about him, or maybe it was. "This isn't where I belong."

"You can't go back. You will die."

"I don't care." I seethed. It was the truth.

He grasped my chin with his thumb and forefinger, forcing my gaze to meet his. His eyes changed to those of the beast, and the anger rolled off him in tangible waves.

"Well, I. Care. Sol."

For a moment, we both just stared. His statement seemed to catch him as off guard as it had me.

"Why?" I whispered.

He drew in a deep breath and then his mask of indifference seemed to slip back into place. "Because you are my ryder. I know you don't understand what that means yet, but you will. I have been in limbo my whole life, knowing you were out there alive, yet somehow hidden away. Unable to claim my full power or my rightful place because you were missing. And now you are here. So I need you to open your mind and find out about the real world, accept your place is here, and learn who you are and what you can do, so that I can finally move forward with my life."

His words were cold, resentful, and I didn't understand the change, but I did understand one thing: this was all about him.

"This might shock you, dragon, but I don't care. I want to go home, and if you won't take me, I will find my own way."

He snorted a highly derisive sound.

"You think you can just make your own way back? Your compound, Sol, was days hard ride from here if you prefer to ride beasts with no wings, and weeks if you hope to travel on foot. I flew nonstop for a full day and night to get to you, and let me tell you, there is a reason your compound was so isolated. It is beyond some of the most inhospitable lands in the Twelve Kingdoms. I wish you luck finding willing conveyances for a journey like that, with no contacts and no coin. "

I sucked in a breath. I was trapped here, and if he wouldn't help me, I might never get back.

He seemed to thaw slightly. "They're gone. There is nothing to go back to. I'm truly sorry for that."

"They can't be!"

"They are. I'm sorry. I don't know why it happened, but I will find out."

His words cut deep. He could be right, but I had to see for myself. I had to know. And if they were gone, I would see them into the Goddess' arms with dignity. The only way that was going to happen was with his help.

Then his words fully registered. "It wasn't you?" I asked. I had to know.

"I was only there to rescue you," he said solemnly.

I let out a relieved breath. It shouldn't matter in the grand scheme of things, but he needed something from me, something I couldn't even begin to understand. But clearly it meant enough to him to snatch me from my home and bring me to this place. Enough to justify his actions as right in his mind. So if he wanted my cooperation in that, then I'd needed to hear that he wasn't there to burn the village. And if he was making demands, then I had my own.

"I want to go back—" He started to protest, but I held up my hand, silencing him. "I need to see for myself. If what you say is true, I want to give them the proper burial rites. They will not find their way to the Shores of Avalon unless I lay them to rest in the way the Goddess decreed."

He said nothing.

I didn't know if that meant he was considering my words or the opposite. His face gave nothing away, so I continued. "I will do as you ask. I will find out about this place, and I will help you 'take your rightful place', whatever that means, if you will agree to take me back so I can find out the fate of my family."

He considered me for a long moment, then nodded. "I can work with that," he said casually, as if we hadn't both just been bargaining for our lives. But something told me he was making light.

"So, do we have an agreement?" I urged. I needed him to say the words if I was going to trust him to deliver.

"We have an agreement, Sol."

He finally withdrew his hand from my space and lowered it, slipping it into the pocket of the soft, loose trousers which sat so low on his—Goddess, save me. I had followed it with my gaze and now I was staring.

If the low chuckle I felt to my core was anything to judge by as he turned and walked out of the room, he had very much noticed.

SEVEN
ZARIA

My knees went weak, and I slumped to a seat on the bed as soon as he left the room. Being in his presence did something to me. What in the Goddess' name had I agreed to? I didn't want to help him—I wanted to get away from him. He took me from my life and left it burning in his wake, and here I was agreeing to help with *his* needs, so he would return me to what's left of it. Perhaps he used the power of the dark spirit to make his offer sound reasonable?

I had to stay strong. I wouldn't help him. I might have agreed for the moment, but it was only to buy myself some time. At least that's what I told myself.

I rubbed my head, realizing it was swimming. I didn't know how long I had slept since the attack but getting up quickly and then running through all those emotions was catching up. I felt off balance having had that confrontation with him. *Nyx.* The

She helped me arrange the blankets until I was settled. "I'm Kiera. I'm a healer here in the capital. You were asleep for a few hours—you had Nyx worried." She chuckled.

Worried? It had seemed more like I had inconvenienced him by not waking sooner and making him wait.

"But we cleansed the Dragon's Bane from your system, and you should suffer no ill effects now that you have rested. Are you hungry?"

My instinct told me I should leave and not accept anything more from these fae, whether it benefitted me or them—I had to get my bearings quickly and find out if there was a way to get myself home since I couldn't exactly trust my deal with my kidnapper—but my stomach disagreed and responded on my behalf.

Kiera smiled again. "That's a good sign. I brought you some stew and bread," she said, lifting the tray and placing it on my lap. "It's nothing special, but the cook is used to feeding these hungry brutes, so it's hearty and will give you strength."

It smelled wonderful, but I knew it wouldn't give me strength. The evenings were always harder with my condition. Although I felt well, considering the situation. Perhaps after sleeping through the day, I was well rested where I was usually exhausted by the evening meal.

"Thank you," I managed, realizing I was virtually mute. I had to try to assert myself. Own my weaknesses and show my strengths where I could, otherwise these fae would see me as an easy target. And if I had an attack, as I was prone to do at night, I would need a healer without my mother to tend to me.

"I have a condition," I admitted. "I suffer from weakness, and I have breathing attacks, especially at night. They come with fevers and sometimes uncontrollable shaking."

Kiera's eyebrows drew together. "Hmm. Have you had this for long?"

"All my life," I told her, eyeing the stew. My stomach grumbled again in longing at the sight.

"Eat," Kiera insisted, nudging the tray. "You need it. You can tell me all about yourself while you do. So, this condition... Does it have a name?"

"Not that I know of. The healer just called it a condition." I took a spoonful of the stew and groaned; it was divine. More flavorful that anything I was used to from our limited stores. There were chunks of meat, many vegetables, and the flavor was so rich. If we had meat at the compound at all, they stretched it among so many, you were lucky to get one or two pieces. This stew was bursting with it.

"And they didn't know the cause?"

I shook my head, finishing my mouthful. "No. They just helped me manage the worst of the attacks. There was a tea that sometimes helped with the breathing and the fever, but if the shaking came on, all they could do was tend me until it passed."

"Were there no other healers nearby who could identify it?"

"Our community is very remote. We never mix with outsiders at all." I paused my spoon, realizing this healer obviously knew little about where I was from. I wondered if she even knew the dragon had taken me against my will and that my community was... "It *was* remote, I mean. It has been destroyed now."

Kiera offered a sympathetic frown, telling me she knew something of what had happened. She reached for my arm, squeezing reassuringly, and I could have cried from the gesture alone. I did not know this fae, but for her to offer me, a stranger, comfort not as my healer, but as an equal who sympathized with my plight... It was much needed.

"I know you have been through a lot, Zaria, and you have much to overcome. My job is to get you well so I can help you face it strong. Okay?"

I nodded, going back to my stew before emotions took hold.

"So, you had a healer in your community who did not know what ailed you but couldn't consult other healers to gain insight?" she prompted, urging me to continue.

"Yes. She was old and had lived with the Sisters for many years. She did her best, but her abilities were limited. As were our supplies. So, she was not always able to do more than offer comfort."

"Well, if she had not been in contact with other healers for many years, she would not know how our methods have improved. We know much now that we did not know a generation ago. I wonder if I can identify your condition and help you." She worded it as though it was merely amusing, but her tone told me she was confident she could.

"If the Goddess wills it," I said, immediately feeling strange saying such a thing in this new world I was so unfamiliar with. My parents had always warned of the sins of the rest of the kingdoms. Especially the capital. Did the fae here even recognize the Goddess?

Kiera smiled. "Our work is always in service and reverence to the Goddess, Zaria. Her will is our purpose. It will be my honor to use the gifts she has bestowed upon me to improve your health and strength."

This fae was kind, there was no denying it. Her warmth poured from her in every word and gesture. I didn't want to trust anyone in this place, but I knew she was someone I could place my trust in.

"Tell me about your condition. What triggers it?"

"The herbs. I can't be near them without a breathing attack coming on. But even if I stay away from them entirely, I still have the weakness."

"All the time, or does it come and go?"

"It comes and goes. If I am well rested, I have energy and can do chores that don't involve working in the fields. Then in the evening, I weaken. The work takes its toll on me, and I get exhausted. I usually can't take part in anything after the evening meal and take to my bed. If I'm lucky, I wake in the morning feeling better and have a good day. But if I have an attack in the night, sometimes it takes a day or two to return to full strength."

"I see. And the Dragon's Bane was growing in large crops?"

I scowled. Nyx had mentioned Dragon's Bane to me, but I had never heard of such a thing. "I don't know what that is. We grow an herb used in ceremonies and offerings to the Goddess. It's the sacred herb. It has no other name I'm aware of. The crops were large, though. It was our sole income."

"Did any others have this same intolerance you describe?"

"No, it was just me." I lowered my eyes, focusing on finishing my meal. The shame I felt at being the only weak member of my community was still heavy.

"It's not your fault, you know," Kiera assured me.

"Our healer was not kind like you. When we were alone, she sometimes insinuated that my sin had angered the Goddess, and this was my punishment. Though I don't know what sin I committed. I have suffered this way since I was a small child. I may have angered the Goddess as I've grown, but what sins can an innocent child commit?"

"By the Goddess! I have never heard such nonsense," she exclaimed, looking affronted. "The Goddess does not punish her children. Healers especially should know this. The Goddess nurtures and heals the earth and her fae. We healers are her hands for this task. The idea of placing blame on a patient for an ailment is beyond me. It goes against all our teachings. Perhaps isolation led her to forget these values over time."

I found my lips curling into a smile for the first time in an age at this. I liked the idea of a place where this was the thinking, even if being out of the commune was terrifying in every other way. "Thank you for saying that. It appears we come from very different worlds."

"So it would seem. I must assure you, though, some fae are

just intolerant to things in the environment. Most can be treated, though, even with the old ways, so it puzzles me that nothing could be done for you. I will take to my books tonight to see if I can find any solutions we can try."

"Please don't waste your free time on me," I begged. I liked this fae, and I didn't want her to invest her time when I didn't plan to stay. "I know there is no cure, and I have accepted that. I will try not to be a burden while I am here, and I will leave as soon as I am able."

"You are no burden. You belong here, and my work is to help those who do. And don't be fooled by the term 'work.'" She smirked. "My passion is solving the unsolvable. I enjoy nothing more than finding clever ways to treat mysterious ailments. Indulge me." Once again, she gave me that knowing and understanding smile. "While you are here, at least."

I chose not to respond in case it sounded like a promise to stay. Instead, I finished my stew, eating beyond my stomach's capacity because there was never enough food. I groaned as I placed my spoon back on the tray.

"Good?" Kiera asked, taking the tray.

"Wonderful, thank you."

She chuckled. "I seldom hear such praise for the cook's stew, but she will be delighted to hear it. I could bring you some more if—"

I held up my hand to stop her. "I couldn't eat another bite, but thank you. "

"And how do you feel? Are you tiring? Weakening?"

I searched myself for any of the usual signs of an attack coming. I felt…good. "No, I feel rested and well. Perhaps a result of sleeping the day away."

"Perhaps." She stood, straightening her robes with her free hand. "I will leave you now to get some rest."

My face must have shown my immediate panic at the thought of being left alone in this strange place again.

"Do not worry. A healer is always stationed outside these rooms at night. You are the only patient under my care tonight. There are wards set to alert me if you have an attack, as you say, and I will come immediately. And we ward the healer's wing at night so no one can enter without permission. You are completely safe."

I didn't know what wards were, but I relaxed somewhat at her reassurances.

She drew back the curtain to step out. "There is a bathing chamber here." She waved toward a door I had not yet seen. "The curtains are just for privacy if we have several patients, but as it's only you, I will leave it to you to close them if you wish."

I nodded, taking in the room again without the distraction of the dragon.

"Sleep is what you need to heal, Zaria. Do that and then you will be ready to take on the rest, okay?"

"Okay," I agreed.

"I will see you in the morning."

EIGHT
NYX

W hat in all the kingdoms was that?
I pressed myself into the shadows outside the healer's wing and drew in a deep breath. What had I been thinking? She'd had her life turned upside down. She was in shock and afraid, mostly of me. Yet every time I opened my mouth to her, nothing but belligerent alpha nonsense came out.

And then I went and touched her. By the Goddess. Why did I do that?

I don't think the Goddess herself could have stopped me, though. My Sol was beautiful. I had known she would be. When her body went limp and I caught her in my arms on the landing, I held her against my chest and felt the rightness of her there. The curves of her that fit exactly to mine. Then her scent hit me, and I knew I was done for. She seemed so small when I laid her on the bed, but Goddess, she was strong. I could feel it, her strength of will.

Her hair was still pure sunshine, and those green eyes that lived in my memories all those years were just as knowing as they had seemed back then. Except now they were filled with fear and disgust. Yes, there had been lust there, too, but that didn't matter when she looked at me like I was the one who had destroyed her world.

This would kill me.

The Goddess would never give us more than we could handle, though, right? My mother always whispered so under her breath when she was angry at my father. But they weren't ryder and dragon. They were both dragons.

And she didn't hate him. At least not when they met.

I found myself faced with the impossible task of trying to train my ryder, and quickly, when she wanted nothing to do with me or this life. I had to suspect she would reject her magic, too, because it went against all she knew. How did you make someone want what they never knew existed and accept something they were programmed to reject?

An impossible feat.

Blasphemy sat at the tip of my tongue. Why had Kalilah done this to me? I would have words for her when I met her in my afterlife.

I ground my teeth, keeping back the curse I wished to scream at the heavens. It wouldn't change my stars.

It was all made worse by the torrent of free-flowing thoughts that poured from Zaria's mind unchecked. They were messing with my head. It had to be that. I had to help her get that under control quickly for both our sakes. Although...knowing the places her mind went when she was backed into a corner was very enlightening. But, fuck. If I'd had to listen to much more of it, I couldn't have been held responsible for slamming her into a wall and devouring that pretty, vicious mouth of hers.

I smacked my forehead and raked my hand down my face.

"Going well, I take it?" Kol's voice came from deeper in the shadows.

"Fuck!" I jumped half out of my skin.

Kol's gravelly laugh came from the darkness, but my eyes shifted without a thought, revealing everything the darkness shielded from most eyes. "You might be *the* Dragon of the Night, but you are not the only dragon of the Asra line in the palace. Beware the shadows, brother. You know better than anyone. That's where you'll find me."

I could usually feel him approaching in my mind. I couldn't let myself be so unguarded again. I rolled my eyes and walked over to where he was reclined against the plinth of our father's statue. It was an eyesore, appropriately situated in the shadows of the palace walls to honor his service and his sacrifice to the kingdoms. I hardly noticed it anymore, so of course, Kol hung out there.

"You need to see someone about your skulking tendencies," I grumbled, taking a seat beside him.

"I was merely waiting for you to finish..." He waved his hand in the air, leaving the possibilities unspoken.

I scowled, not taking his bait. He had no clue what had just happened, and it was going to stay that way.

"Did you fuck it up already?"

I shot him a look.

"Oh, calm down. Your glowy-eyed, Dragon of the Night bit doesn't work on me."

I scoffed. "You used to cower when Father did it."

"Pft! It wasn't me who pissed himself that time he—"

"Yes, yes." I waved him off. "The general was a scary bastard. But you could show me the courtesy of being equally afraid of me once in a while, you know."

"You were born six minutes before me, not six decades. We

shared a womb, so your firstborn shit doesn't work with me, either."

"I beat you out, though, didn't I, little brother?" I nudged him.

"That great big head of yours was blocking the exit!" He nudged me back.

I laughed and shook my head. I always thought I needed to be alone with my thoughts, but Kol was always there to remind me that what I really needed was this.

"But seriously, though…did you fuck it up already?"

I sighed, smoke streaming from my nostrils in my frustration.

"Goddess, have mercy," he muttered.

"She's…" I searched for the right word. I could have given him a list of the things she was: argumentative, stubborn, opinionated, ignorant, terrified, alone…beautiful. Mother, have mercy, I was an arse. What she must have been feeling, and I just… but she… I settled on the only word I could: "Frustrating."

Kol smirked, and I frowned. Damn him, there was no way he could hear my thoughts. I had them on tight lockdown.

"I can't hear you, Nyx, but never forget I can feel you. Especially when your emotions are so intense. I get it, though. She's come from a bad situation, and her learning curve is going to be steep. You're just desperate to get airborne with your ryder. But you have to be patient. Educate her, help her adjust, and above all, give her time."

"You don't get it at all," I snapped, getting to my feet and pacing. "She will never want to be my ryder, Kol. She thinks I'm responsible for what just happened to her and her family. Even if she believes what I tell her and I give her time to let it sink in, how will she ever get past that?"

"It will not be easy, especially if you go in there all fire-breathing dragon, trying to force her to see things your way."

I paused my pacing, guilt crawling up my spine. I hated the feeling.

"You're such an idiot sometimes, Nyx. You went in there all fire-breathing dragon already, didn't you? Fuck!"

"In my defense, she has seen me as my literal fire-breathing dragon already, so I cannot see how my attitude is going to intimidate her further."

Kol jumped up and stalked toward me. "She is alone, probably scared to death, and you"—he jabbed his finger in my chest —"with your 'I'm the alpha dragon, so it's my way or the highway' bullshit is the last thing she needs." He looked at where his finger met my bare skin. "And while we are on the subject of not scaring the new girl shitless, where the fuck are your clothes?"

I smacked his finger away. "I flew in. Since when does my state of dress concern you?"

"Please, you have nothing I haven't seen a thousand times. Your ryder, on the other hand, comes from the most extreme of those batshit religious groups and was living on the damned edge of existence. I doubt she's ever seen so much as an exposed bicep, and you're parading around in all your glory acting like you don't realize what you do to the fae of this court in just your gray sweatpants and nothing else."

I chewed on my lip.

"Fuck my life, you're impossible. You knew exactly what you were doing going in there like that, didn't you?"

I opened my mouth to respond, but he cut me off.

"Don't even bother denying it. You like her. I can smell it on you. By the Goddess, Nyx. Really? Do you think having a thing for your ryder is going to help the situation?"

"You're one to talk," I threw back. He was nailing me to the wall, and I wasn't just going to take it, even if he spoke the truth.

"My ryder was not just yanked out of his life of lies and thrust into this whole new world where an arsehole dragon thinks he can call all the shots and use his glowy eyes and muscles to get what he wants, was he?" He huffed, annoyed with himself for

59

taking my bait. "Your ryder is going to need a friend, not a turn around your bedroom, Nyx."

I bit back my annoyance at how right he was. I sighed, tipping my face up to the sky and letting a plume of smoke drift up and away as the fight went out of me and the tension bled from my body. "Zaria. Her name is Zaria," I said after a moment, admitting without words that she was more than just my ryder and we should call her such.

"Beautiful name," he replied, the tension gone from his voice now, too.

A beautiful name for a beautiful fae. I was so screwed.

Kol's soft laugh pulled me back to him. I was broadcasting too much, apparently. I'd never needed to keep absolutely every feeling and emotion from him before. But then I'd never actually had anything I wanted to hide from him this badly. Thoughts were easy to close off, but everything? I was going to have to work on that.

"You need sleep, Nyx. Go to bed." He assessed me and rolled his eyes. "Or ignore me and go fly back up to your little perch on the roof across from the healer's wing and watch her balcony all night like the possessive alpha dragon you are. Whatever. Just be nice to her when you see her next. She has been through enough. She needs a friend."

He didn't wait for a response, just walked away.

My wings shot from my back as soon as he rounded the building, and I took off. I didn't shift fully, just wings. I didn't want to lose the sweats and have to sit on the roof all night naked. The nights in the capital were balmy enough to allow it, but sitting with my dick out while watching my new ryder's window all night was not a good look.

NINE

ZARIA

I awoke to the morning light filtering through the opening I had left in the curtains that surrounded the bed. I had originally closed them, then felt vulnerable not being able to see the rest of the space, so I settled on having them open a little after I used the bathing chamber and then settled back in bed.

I was restless and wondered if I would sleep at all, having slept for hours during the day. But with a full stomach for the first time in living memory, sleep quickly took over and held me all night.

It was strange. I'd had no nightmares for the first time I could remember. No attack, no dream-laden and fitful sleep. Just deep, sound rest, and in the morning, I felt different.

Alive.

I went to the bathing chamber and found that moving was

easy, not like it could sometimes be after a bad attack had kept me in bed for a day. My head was clear, and I had energy.

A healer came to check on me and brought a breakfast tray with her. They told me Kiera had been called away first thing to tend to an injury and would return soon to check on me herself.

Once again, the food was plentiful and delicious. Probably a special concession to the patients of the healers to boost their strength and aid their healing. I doubted everyone in the capital ate this well.

"Are you feeling any better?"

I startled at Nyx's voice, but then his face came into view between the curtains, and I frowned. The voice was the same, but the face was ever so slightly different. Less harsh. Perhaps sleep had softened him from the brute he'd been yesterday.

"Nyx?" I said, keeping the quiver out of my tone. I didn't think I was mentally up to dealing with him yet.

"Close. I'm Kol." The identical image of Nyx slipped through the curtain, and I would have called him a liar, but he held himself entirely differently than Nyx did. He carried an ease to his body language while Nyx held tension. "I'm his brother. And you must be the infamous Zaria."

"Are all males here identical copies of you two?" I asked, surprising myself with the hint of attitude.

He cocked his head and lifted a brow before laughing. "Yes, every single one of us. A bunch of copies."

I laughed despite myself. Clearly, this male didn't set me on edge quite the way his brother did. They may have looked similar, but their auras were worlds apart. "Twins?"

"How did you guess?" He smirked, venturing farther into the room and picking up a candle off the end table. He brought it to his nose to sniff.

I watched him, fascinated. I had never seen identical twins before, only heard of them. It was incredible. I was watching the fae I'd had an extremely intense and frustrating interaction with yesterday, yet it wasn't him. "You are not like him at all."

He was all around softer, or maybe gentler. His voice wasn't so harsh, and his movements were less brash. The tiny details added up to make a completely different fae.

"We have the same face." He returned the candle to its place and turned to me.

"Similar, but not the same," I countered.

"You're the first fae in my whole life to say as much."

"At first glance, yes, you do, but they aren't really seeing you if they think you two are the same."

His smile spread across his face. He had a simple underlying joy to him Nyx didn't possess. "I like you already," he said warmly. "My brother better not fuck this up."

"What do you mean?"

"You know, Nyx... Tall, dark, and douchey? I think you two have met." He gave me a type of grin I couldn't help but laugh at, although I did not know what the term meant.

"I'm familiar."

"He's a lot to deal with. Believe me, I know. I had the pleasure of growing up with him." Kol winked.

"Has he always been like that?"

Kol nodded vigorously. "Even as a baby. Always serious. My mother used to joke about it. My father said it would make for a good general one day. But he does soften once you get to know him."

"I'm not sure I believe you."

"I'm not sure I believe me, either." He laughed, warm and rueful. "So, what has you confused?"

"What do you mean by: he better not, um, mess this up?" I cleared my throat and felt my cheeks heat when he smiled at my change of wording.

"So proper, little sunshine." He grinned, as if we were old friends.

I blushed even more. I was not opposed to such language, though the fae who worked our land and traveled to trade the herbs used it frequently. I sometimes use it myself in select company when the situation required. I was just so conditioned by our ways and the expectations of the females in our community. And perhaps, most of all, my mother's expectations of me. Was it fair that they held us to different standards? I never felt it was. It was okay for the males to push the boundaries of propriety, but they always expected the females to comply. And for reasons I could never understand, my mother always seemed especially focused on my behavior and ways.

"Don't worry. We will chase those habits out of you quickly, I promise. You'll be giving us a hard time before we know it."

I wasn't so sure. I felt like the use of language was only half the problem. He seemed to exude confidence and was uninhibited in ways I could not comprehend. I was raised to be the exact opposite. Never speak up, never cross lines. These ways were so utterly foreign to me—I'd never catch up. Besides, I wasn't staying in this place once I could leave on my own.

"I think you're great is all," Kol cut into my thoughts. "I don't want him to mess things up and push you away." He winked again at that.

So, the brothers hadn't talked. Kol didn't know I wanted to leave or about the arrangement Nyx had pushed me into, unless this was a well-executed plan to get me to lower my guard. I'd have to stay diligent, as this was a war from every side, and all the players knew each other but me.

"Mess what up? Your brother acted as though he rescued me, but it was more of a kidnapping than a rescue. It's hard to misinterpret that."

Kol bit his lip. Whether he was stifling a smile or some other emotion, I couldn't tell.

"I can see how it seems that way to you, but he saved you,

Zaria. I swear it to the Goddess. He brought you here to save both of you. You are his ryder—you need each other."

"I don't know what that means." I sighed.

"By the Goddess, please tell me he told you why he brought you here?"

"He told me I'm his ryder and that he needs me here to claim his full power and his rightful place, but none of that means anything to me." Frustration seeped into my words as I recalled his selfish requests.

Kol looked at me, agape. He didn't seem like the type of male who was often struck speechless, but the silence stretched on between us.

He slowly shook his head and then pinched the bridge of his nose. "Goddess, forgive me. I'm going to strangle him."

I almost laughed, he looked so serious.

"Zaria," he said earnestly, taking my hand. I fought the urge to snatch it away. Such familiarity was not permitted in my community, and it was a conditioned response. I was not used to such tactile ways, but Kol just seemed to ease the need to reject it, and I relaxed. "On behalf of my idiot brother, I apologize. Please do not base your opinion of the rest of us on him, I beg you. We are not all so…"

"Douchey," I supplied, still not knowing what the word meant.

He burst out laughing. "I was going to say selfish, but sure, douchey works."

I stifled a laugh.

"He really told you he brought you here because he wants you to help him get what he needs?"

I nodded. "Yes."

"And you're still here?"

"I don't exactly have anywhere else to go. I don't even know where I am," I admitted quietly. "Aside from in the healer's wing, I mean. I know that much. But what it's a wing of and where in the Twelve Kingdoms that is exactly, I do not know." My face heated, and I suddenly felt stupid. The whole scene yesterday was so disorienting, it hadn't even occurred to ask.

"Oh, my sweet little sunshine." He grabbed me in a hug, and I stiffened. Kol's easy nature aside, I was unused to such casual physical contact from anyone. Affection was not something freely given in my home. "Sorry, I should have asked first," he said, not making any move to let me go. In fact, he seemed to squeeze me tighter. "Some fae don't like to be hugged, but you looked like you could use one, and I'm a hugger."

I giggled. I didn't want to, but I liked Kol. I didn't want to like anyone in this place. I wanted to get away as soon as I could find a way. But first Kiera and now Kol... Maybe he was right that I should not base my opinions of a whole kingdom on the actions of one. And despite never having or thinking I needed comfort in this way, it was... nice.

As fast as he had grabbed hold of me, he let me go. "You must be entirely confused, little sunshine. What can I tell you to ease your mind?"

I shrugged. Every new piece of information just brought more questions. I needed facts, but I had to be able to process them one at a time. If I showed him how vulnerable the not-knowing was making me, he could take advantage of me in so many ways. I didn't know where I was, didn't understand why they wanted me here, what they expected of me, if my family still lived, or if I would ever see them again. They were all weaknesses I wasn't willing to reveal by asking every question on my mind. I would have to try and hold back where possible.

"Okay, let me tell you what I know," he declared, apparently unconcerned that I had not answered. "We should sit," he suggested, gesturing to the small sitting area.

I took a seat, and he dropped into the chair Nyx had claimed yesterday. Nyx had made it seem like a throne because he had somehow infused it with more power and presence by just name felt heavy and fundamental in my chest when I thought it. Like that thread between us he insisted was true was reminding me he was vital even though he'd left.

My feelings about him and what he'd done aside, my body—or my soul, I suppose—seemed to feel his importance at just the thought of his name. I didn't like it. How could I begin to process all that had happened when even my soul felt drawn to the fae who caused it all?

Another wave of sadness hit. I couldn't imagine what terrible fate had come to my family. I had to shut down those thoughts to prevent another emotional outburst. I was not in a safe place, and I would not indulge that show of weakness until I was.

I quickly wicked away a single escaped tear with my finger before they all tried to fall and used my breathing exercise again to calm myself.

"Hey now," a soft voice said from the curtain.

I looked up to find a robed fae entering, carrying a tray of steaming food.

"I heard you were awake," she said, closing the curtain behind her and placing the tray on the side table.

I could do little but blink in response as she approached and quietly busied herself checking the heat of my skin and the rate of my heart in the way the healers did with their fingers on my wrist.

"How are you feeling?" she asked once she was satisfied.

"Um, okay," I replied weakly. There were no words for how I was feeling, and I couldn't pour it out to this fae even if I could find them. I did not know who I could trust in this place.

She offered an understanding smile. "I know you've been through a lot. Zaria, isn't it?"

I nodded as she gestured for me to get back into bed. I had planned to find some clothes and leave, but she had this gentle but forceful manner that had me obeying and slipping back under the covers. A healer's nature, I supposed.

existing in it. With Kol, it was simply a chair. Not that Kol had no presence—quite the opposite. But Kol wasn't intimidating. It was inviting, warm, and a little chaotic.

"Okay, firstly, you are with the healers because you suffered Dragon's Bane poisoning. You were unconscious for a while, but the healers treated you, and now you are on the mend."

"Oh, that much I know," I interrupted. "I saw Kiera last night, and she told me I'm recovering well. "

"Ah, good. Kiera is the best. You are in good hands." He glanced out of the balcony doors. "As for where you are, what this grand healing facility is a wing of…Well, little sunshine, you are in the beating heart of the First Kingdom. At the palace of King Viktas and his aerial legion, the famed Flyers of the First Kingdom."

"I understand you said some words, but if those words have meaning to you, they don't to me."

He stopped and stared. "What didn't make sense? You surely know about the kingdoms, don't you? The King? What did you not understand?"

"I did know we have a King, but not his name. I know there are twelve kingdoms, our village was in the Fifth. That's about all I know. "

Kol gave a low whistle. "I guess I'll start with the basics, then. King Viktas rules the Twelve Kingdoms. They are each governed by barons who represent the King. This is the First Kingdom, also known as the Dark Kingdom, and this city, Amaya, is the capital of all the kingdoms."

"Why is it known as the Dark Kingdom?" I asked.

"Good question. The nights here are longer than the other kingdoms. Our night skies are the most beautiful you'll ever see. You were in the Fifth, which is known as the Desert Kingdom."

"Is the whole kingdom desert?" I asked, feeling like I knew nothing.

"It's mostly desert, yes," Kol confirmed.

I didn't see the point of telling him it was to keep us all safe. The Sisters of the Sands chose to live outside of the rule and law of the rest of society. They were protecting us from the great evils of Uriel. They knew this place to be wicked.

"I know the life you lived is all that you know, but the world outside of your compound is entirely different from what I suspect you were told. And the fae who kept you there... They were hiding you from this world for a reason."

"I only know they felt it wasn't safe for them to bring up their children around such..." I didn't want to use the word 'sin' in the face of someone who seemed, on the surface at least, to be kind.

Kol chuckled. "It's okay, sunshine. Not much is known about the Sisters of the Sands, but I'm aware of the kind of religion they followed and the opinions they likely held of the rest of us. They choose isolation for their own reasons, I'm sure. But the lengths they have gone to in order to conceal you, knowing what you are... They had to be working tirelessly to achieve that. They had to have a really strong reason to go to that much trouble."

"What I am?"

"Your magic," he said, like I should have known what that word meant.

"What is magic?"

"Shit." Kol scrubbed his face. "This is hard. How can I describe magic to someone who has never heard of the concept?"

Was he asking me? I had no clue.

"Okay!" He jumped up, startling me, and went to the table where the healers kept an array of items for their practices. Some were familiar to me from our healer in the village. He picked up a candle and came back, putting it on the low table in front of me. "How do you light this candle?"

I frowned. "What kind of question is that?"

"It's not a trick. Just tell me how you would light it."

"Well…at home, we always have a fire for cooking or warming. I would light it from that or with a lamp. "

"Okay, but imagine there is no fire burning. How would you light it?"

I searched the healer's table for fire lighting tools. "Do you have a flint? We would need something to create a spark and some kindling."

"Right, see, they have taught you how to survive without magic, because they kept magic completely out of your world. But we are made of magic. Magic is in our veins. If we don't learn how to wield it, it can consume us, but it's not all bad…" Kol merely glanced at the candle, and it lit!

I pulled back so sharply, I may have stumbled if I wasn't sitting. "H—how?"

Kol reached out to stop me from escaping him and blew out the candle. "It's okay. Relax. I was just showing you how things are in a world of magic."

"Fae here can just set fire to things with a thought?"

My mind went back to the destruction at my village. Huge monsters pouring fire from their mouths. I got up and paced.

"Is that how my village was destroyed? At a mere thought?" I couldn't fathom it.

"Zaria, please come sit. There is so much more to it than that."

I did sit, but only because I wanted more answers. "Explain it to me, please. What is magic?" I asked as rationally as I could.

"I suppose you would call it power. We all have power inside us we can draw on and direct. The kind of power and its strength depends on the individual, but it can do many things. Some as simple as lighting a candle, for example."

I scoffed. "Simple?"

"To us, they are simple things. We all have different powers and ways we use them. There used to be great power in the kingdoms, but over the centuries the power has lessened. Some say it is because our connection to the Goddess grows weaker. Who really knows? But most fae are at least born with the powers of their bloodline and some powers native to the kingdom they originate from.

"So, powers come from the kingdoms?"

"Like I said, before we were united into the Twelve Kingdoms, territories were divided by their very nature. The fae of old lived with those like them so powers were linked to the lands they lived on. We all evolve into our magic differently. Some can connect to the Goddess through her ley lines to draw on other powers, too. Some have more access to this than others; ability varies, as does natural strength. That is something which is prized. Anyone who can harness greater magic is revered. That's why you are so important."

"Because of what I am?" I clarified, trying to understand.

"Yes."

"And what is that, exactly?"

"Those who can take flying forms, such a dragons, are innately able to come into great power as we mature. But only if we come into contact with our other half. We call them ryders, for obvious reasons. The Goddess blesses us with this symbiotic connection to another, and when we make that connection, both flyer and ryder come into more power than is normal. Both individuals will already be powerful as the gift is only bestowed on those with much magic already. And the change doesn't happen until the two connect and bond. But once they do, their powers meld, and the power between them amplifies. They charge one another, and the result can be incredible."

I shuddered and the hair at the back of my neck rose. My entire body rejected it. I knew what he was inferring. I knew he was trying to say I was his brother's other half, but I couldn't be. It went against everything I knew. Against the Goddess and my parents. They'd never forgive me if I walked this path of evil.

"I have no power," I assured him. Quite the opposite, truly, although I wasn't giving him a list of my many weaknesses.

"This was my original point. You *must* have great power. The Goddess would not have created the bond between you and Nyx unless you were equally matched. And Zaria, Nyx is powerful."

"But I can't—"

He stopped me. "There is so much for you to learn before you can understand any of this, but somehow, some way, your parents cut you off from what you really are. They raised you without magic, but they know it exists in everyone and everything. To not use it is harder than to let it be free. I'm uncertain what their motives were, but to hide you so effectively from Nyx, and to suppress your power so effectively took work. A lot of work. I don't know how they did it, but now that you are together, sunshine, that power of yours is going to come out, and you need to trust us to help you tame it, or it's going to... Well, let's just say it's going to be a lot to handle."

I felt sick. I didn't believe even half of what he said could be true, and whatever he was not saying was even more terrifying. How could such things be real and be completely kept from us? If this power existed in everyone and everything, then my parents and the elders were hiding it? It made me question everything I thought I knew.

"If what you say is true, how could it be hidden from all of us born there? If we all have this power, wouldn't we know?" I was thinking of my siblings, of Luka, and how they never showed any signs of being anything other than ordinary.

"It's likely they didn't have power like you. It's not common anymore, and those that live on the fringes of our world might have so little power that it would be easy to cover up by simply not educating them in how to use it. They would never know what they could do. You, though... They were suppressing it somehow. Otherwise, Nyx would have been able to find you years ago."

I just couldn't see how it was all possible or how to reconcile it with my beliefs.

"I know it's a lot. But I'm here, which is a good thing, because it looks like my brother is doing his best to bury his head in the sand." He chuckled, leaned forward, and reached out his hand to offer me comfort. Despite my warring emotions, I accepted it. I needed it. He gave my hand a light squeeze.

I sucked my lower lip between my teeth. "Are you a…" Was it rude to ask if someone was also a demon in disguise? What a strange world I found myself in, trying to figure out etiquette for literal beasts.

"What?" Kol asked.

"A dragon," I said, the word tasting unfamiliar. "Like…your brother?"

"We are identical twins. It would be kind of strange if I wasn't also a dragon—some would say the more magnificent of the two, but I will leave you to be the judge of that when you see me take my true form."

I instantly felt proprietary toward Nyx at those words, then realized how absurd that was. Yes, I had thought his dragon form quite magnificent in the moments I was able to set aside my crippling fear. But I should hardly care which was the more magnificent beast between the brothers. I had no loyalty to either.

Even as I thought it, that invisible thread I had always felt reached out to the outside world and latched onto something. And now, I knew it connected me to him. To Nyx. As if that proprietary thought had tugged it to touch base with him.

My dragon. The most magnificent.

By the Goddess! What was I thinking?

And it was with that thought I remembered Nyx's ability to know my thoughts. I prayed to the Goddess that only worked when he was close by. I did not want him thinking I felt any claim on him.

I put my face in my hands.

"Oh, sunshine. I know it's got to be so hard to have your entire world ripped apart like this. I'm sorry," Kol said softly, misinterpreting my reason for hiding my face. But I was happy he didn't know my thoughts like his brother, and I was not about to correct him.

He gently pried my hands away, taking them in his. "I'm not trying to make it harder on you or convince you of anything. This has all got to be a huge shock."

"Why do you call me that?" I asked, realizing I had already accepted another pet name that had no logical reason.

He beamed. "Because it's you. You're a ray of sunshine. Your golden hair shines as bright as your soul...and you're little." He patted me on the head.

I brushed his hand away in mock annoyance. "Compared to you and your brother, maybe, but that doesn't make me little. That makes me normal."

"Fair point. Dragons are pretty big, and our fae forms reflect that."

A thought struck me. "Will I...change into something?"

Kol smirked. "Like what?"

I rolled my eyes; he knew what I was asking.

He laughed in response. "No, you will not change. You won't grow wings or anything else. That is why ryders ride, because they cannot fly with us."

That made sense...if anything could in this bizarre world.

"Do you want me to go on?" he asked, searching my face.

"Please."

"It's a special bond we have with our ryder. When our magic is first awakened, we become aware of something out there we are drawn to. It's hard to describe."

"Like a part of you is reaching out for something?"

"Yes! You felt it?"

I regretted the admission, but it was too late to take back. "Maybe. I don't know. I always felt like there was more out there calling to me. I just thought it was because we were isolated, and I yearned to know what was on the outside of our compound. But leaving wasn't an option, so I shut it down."

"Interesting." He studied me, and I didn't like it.

"Go on," I urged, trying to get the attention off me.

"It happens differently for every pair, as the Goddess wills it. But somewhere between our innate magic first awakening around the age of two and maturing into adulthood, when our origin powers awaken, we get the call. The magic we share begins to awaken between us, and the pull gets stronger and stronger until getting to the other person is a need. It's impossible to resist the call." His eyes brightened as he spoke.

"That didn't happen for me, though," I insisted.

"No, I believe it did. You were so young. New to your magic. You don't remember?"

I shook my head. "Nyx mentioned something about it, too, and I thought he was lying."

"He wasn't," Kol said carefully. "Nyx was called to you. He was only young himself, around eight years but already powerful. We think that's why it happened so young for you both; the strength of your combined power triggered it early. It's not unheard of, but the Goddess only calls on one so young if their power is important. It foretells a need. Your powers combined must be crucial to the future of the kingdoms."

"I don't remember. Is there a chance he's wrong? Maybe it wasn't me."

"You know it was you, Zaria. You must be able to feel it inside that you know him on a level that doesn't exist with anyone else. Besides, it's not something you get wrong. The connection is undeniable."

I sighed. "He said that, too...that I knew him. I didn't believe him, and since I was being carried off by a winged beast, I didn't want to believe a word he said."

"Understandable. Being kidnapped by a dragon doesn't sound so great." He chuckled.

"That's what I'm saying. Who would respond well to such a thing?" I threw up my hands. "Even another dragon agrees with me."

He laughed, and I joined him. "He was trying to save you from the fire and the Dragon's Bane, though."

I grumbled, not wanting to give Nyx any credit, even if a little was due. Very little. It was the dragons who started the fires in the first place. I couldn't forget that. My face must have betrayed my train of thought because Kol looked contrite.

"I'm truly sorry for what happened to your village. It's a complex situation that you'll come to understand better, but suffice it to say that the herbs your village grew are the reason dragons are dying off. The crops had to be destroyed."

"And the fae?" I snapped.

"That was…unfortunate." He shifted uncomfortably. "Dragon's Bane on that scale could completely wipe out what's left of our kind. It's dangerous enough to those tasked with destroying it from the skies. To go in while it's all burning like that… only a dragon like Nyx could survive it. He only just got you out."

"Maybe he should have let me die with my village," I mused.

"You'd rather be dead than be here?"

I couldn't answer that. The person I was before the fire would have begged the Goddess to take me along with my family to the Shores of Avalon. But everything I thought I knew could now be a falsehood. Where did that leave me?

Would I rather be dead or find out the truths that had been kept from me my whole life, and maybe discover there is more to life than what I'd been given?

"You don't have to answer that. I'm sorry. Everything is too fresh for you right now. You need time to process. But you are safe, and when you're ready, you'll see that you belong here."

"Fae keep saying that."

76

He smiled softly. "Because it's true. It's destiny, the Goddess' plan. Don't fight it. Just know I'm here for you. I know I'm a stranger right now, but you are my twin brother's ryder. That makes you family in my book."

I didn't know how he had the ability to lighten even the darkest of moments. "Thank you."

"I mean, don't get me wrong, his ryder or not, if it turned out you were an arsehole, you'd be on your own. He would deserve it, but I wouldn't be getting myself involved with that kind of mess. I like a nice, easy life."

"So, that's why you were worried Nyx would mess things up? Because I'm supposed to be a ryder, and he is supposed to be my, erm…dragon?" I cringed internally at the absurdity of saying such a thing out loud. "You're worried we won't be able to get along?"

"It happens, and it's a nightmare for everyone who has to work with them or just be around them."

I cringed because if I really was stuck here and, Goddess forbid, destined in some way to be a part of this world, then I could only foresee that kind of relationship for Nyx and me.

"Do you have a ryder?" It suddenly occurred to me to ask.

"I do." He smiled, giving more away than he knew.

"You must really care for her. It shows on your face."

"Him, and I do care for him deeply. He's one of my closest friends."

"A male?" I didn't know why it surprised me.

"Not all ryders are female, not all flyers are male, and they don't have to be opposite sex pairs. It is simply as the Goddess wishes."

"Why do you call them flyers and not dragons?" I asked. I had so many questions.

"Because they aren't all dragons."

"Oh. Right." He had said that. My mind ran away with the possibilities. "Then, what are the other flyers?"

"We have gargoyles and pegasus... There are all kinds of flyers."

I couldn't begin to imagine what manner of creatures they were. "Why so many kinds?"

He lifted his shoulders. "I don't know. Ask the Goddess."

"Do they all have that fire thing? Or is that only the dragons?"

"We all have powers, but what kind of power is unique to each of us. It's a complicated thing." He pushed to his feet to walk to the balcony doors. I could already tell he was the type who couldn't sit still for long.

"Do you know what mine will be?" The words were tough to form, as asking the question was acceptance of so much that seemed impossible. But each answer just led to the next question.

"Impossible to know." He turned to face me, his eyes bright. "Do you want to get out of here?"

TEN

ZARIA

"I don't know if I can." I eyed my surroundings, unsure I could just leave, and if I could, where would I go? I didn't know what was out there. All I could imagine were the horrors my parents had described. But with all I was learning, those lessons were now tinged with suspicion in my mind. Would I question everything I thought I knew?

I didn't know how to process any of this, and I didn't think I would anytime soon. It was too much, and I was overloaded by my own thoughts. Maybe a change of scenery would help me get out of my head for a while.

"I can show you around and give you a feel for the place. It's so much better to show you than to try and explain it," he suggested in an encouraging tone. I could tell he was itching to go. I was right; he could not be contained for long. It would drive him mad.

"Yes. I'd like that. Do you think it will be okay?"

"I'll take the blame if it's not." He offered me his hand, wiggling his fingers with a tiny, mischief-filled smile.

"Why do I get the feeling you're up to no good?"

"Because I am, but only in the best ways. I promise."

I laughed again. It felt easy with Kol.

I was about to tell him I couldn't go out dressed like I was when Kiera appeared through the open door.

"I see you have found trouble already, Zaria," she exclaimed, breezing in with a bundle of clothes in her arms.

Kol straightened, withdrawing his hand. "I did nothing, and I admit to nothing."

Kiera rolled her eyes, offering me a secret smile as she turned away from him to hand me the bundle.

"I was told you'd finished treating Zaria and I could spring her free to show her her rooms and give her the tour," Kol offered in his defense.

"We have," she threw at him before returning her attention to me. "You're good as new, so you can go with this one as long as you don't over do things and promise to come and see me in a few days so we can discuss your condition. I have some theories, and would like to do some tests."

"I will. Thank you."

"Those are just a few things to get you started," she said, referring to the clothes. "Yours were ruined, I'm afraid. I don't think the Dragon's Bane smoke would have ever come out of them. I had them burned so they didn't harm anyone."

"Thank you." I took them gratefully, trying not to show emotion. My clothes being gone felt like another part of me had been taken away. Even though I hated them, it was just another tie to my life, cut.

"I'll change now. I don't think I can go out like this." I'd found a light dress and undergarments left out for me this morning, which

I assumed were only intended for wear in the healer's wing, though. I wouldn't feel properly dressed going outside in it. I was used to the heavy, itchy robes we made at home, which covered every inch of skin lest we be tempted into sin. I hated them, but I would have liked their comfort right now. I felt too vulnerable and on show.

"You look fine," Kol interjected.

"I can't wear this out."

He lifted a brow but didn't comment.

"I'm serious. This is barely a robe."

"It looks fine to me," he said cautiously. Kiera shot him a glare. "But if you aren't comfortable, you should change," he added, backtracking, and holding his hands up to protect himself from Kiera's dagger eyes.

I unfolded the first thing in the pile and blinked. "Pants?" I exclaimed before I could catch myself.

"Yes," Kiera said, confusion showing in her voice.

"Am I allowed to wear them?" I pressed when neither she nor Kol said more.

Kol laughed. "I take it you weren't allowed to in your village?"

I shook my head, eyeing the garment.

"Females can wear anything they want here," he informed me.

"But…" I looked at Kiera. "She's in robes." Her robes were long and more closely resembled what I was used to. I had just assumed it was the standard here, too.

Kiera joined Kol in laughter. "I have to wear these only while I work. It makes healers easily identifiable so we can be found for help when we are needed, but in my leisure time, I can wear what I want."

"Oh." I ran my fingers over the soft material. When I was small, I used to beg my parents to let me wear pants like the boys because the skirts were always so heavy and restricted my movements, making it nearly impossible to keep up with the boys when we played.

"I'll step out so you can change," Kol said, then headed for the door.

Kiera followed, stopping before the doorway. "Take things easy, Zaria. At least until we have a better handle on your condition. I have had your rooms warded the same way I did here last night. If you suffer an attack at night, I will be alerted."

"Thank you." It didn't seem enough for the kindness and comfort she had offered, but I only had my gratitude to give.

"It's my pleasure."

She left so I could change. I put on the strange clothes and found they fit fairly well. When I stepped out of the room and into the hallway, Kol clapped.

"Excellent. How do they feel?" he asked.

"Fine." I glanced at myself, feeling self-conscious. "Strange."

"Enjoy your day. I'll come check on you later if I'm able, Zaria." Kiera squeezed my arm before disappearing into another room.

"You'll get used to the pants. You can't ride a dragon in a skirt. At least not easily." Kol gestured for me to follow, and I did.

"Where are we going?"

"Do you want to see your rooms first or go in to the city?"

"Rooms?" I asked.

"Yes, every student gets their own. We'll go there later. Let's get some fresh air first."

"Student?" I frowned, halting my steps. This was going to be a long day if he couldn't speak a word I didn't have to question.

He placed an arm around my shoulders and smiled reassuringly. "It's okay to ask all your questions, little sunshine."

I didn't know how he did it, but I was at ease again.

There was a pause, and I realized he was waiting for me to ask a new question. "Student?" I repeated.

"Ah, yes." He urged me to walk with him again. "Well, under normal circumstances, a ryder would come into their powers and have the relevant education as they grew up. Then when the call came to their flyer, they and their flyer would relocate here to the palace to become students of the legion. Trainees, really, who will eventually join the ranks of the Flyers of the First Kingdom."

I must have looked at him blankly because he made the face I was coming to know as a friendly form of exasperation.

"I'm sorry," I offered. "It feels like I know nothing, and I can't tell you how confusing that is."

"I'm here, and I will help you learn. You can always ask me anything," Kol promised sincerely.

I nodded, biting back emotion I didn't want to allow in right now.

"Anyway," Kol continued. "Your journey on that learning path took a diversion, but you are here now, and you have much to learn, so, yes, student. Welcome to the legion, trainee."

I swallowed. "You want me to learn how to ride a..." My mouth went dry. Because it wasn't any dragon they wanted me to ride. It was *him*. I couldn't do it.

"Don't look so worried. There's more to it than flying lessons. Think of it more like a crash course into the world outside your village for now. Flying comes later." He looked away, muttering words to himself that sounded very much like, *"As long as we can keep my damned brother on the ground."*

My stomach churned, and breakfast threatened to reappear.

"How long does this education take?" I asked, trying to ascertain how long I would be expected to stay here.

"It depends." Kol shrugged. "We all get the call at different times. Some are still young and will stay and learn until they fully mature. Others come later and only need to pass the standards for flying and magic wielding set by the legion to join."

"Are you a student?" I knew the question was absurd as soon as it passed my lips. Of course he wasn't. He was too...authoritative to still be training. "Sorry, that was a silly question. Neither you nor your brother can still be students."

Kol laughed. "And why would you think that, sunshine?"

I studied him. He was the exact image of Nyx, and Nyx could not be considered anything more than the finished product of whatever he had studied to be. "I, uh...I mean that you're both too...commanding, too self-assured..."

I realized too late that there was no way to explain my meaning without stroking the ego of a male...beast, who I was quickly realizing did not need such positive reinforcement to have a high view of himself. And *his* ego seemed small compared to his brother's. I closed my mouth before I could betray my thoughts any further.

Kol grinned, and I wanted to die from embarrassment.

"I think the word you are looking for is arrogant," he suggested.

I opened my mouth to assure him I didn't mean that but knew it was futile, so I closed it again. He seemed to take everything in good humor, and I refused to dig myself a hole.

He laughed heartily and shook his head. "You are quite right, sunshine. I graduated into the legion a few years ago, but the enlisted flyers and ryders work closely with the trainees at all times."

I didn't miss that he was only speaking about himself, but I was loathed to seem interested his brother. Curiosity won over, though, and I asked, "And Nyx?"

Kol's expression changed. Was it regret or guilt, maybe? "Nyx is a special case."

I realized with sudden clarity why that would be. "He couldn't attend without his ryder."

Without me.

Kol sighed. "Ordinarily, no. A flyer without a ryder would not qualify to even come to the capital to train. But we are something of a legacy around here. Our father was the last general of the legion."

I swallowed. "Was?"

Kol nodded. "He was killed in action two years ago, and Nyx…" He paused, looking away.

"I'm sorry for your loss," I offered.

Kol shrugged. "Thank you. But he was a general to his core. It was written in his marrow to lead the fight and die for the kingdom. It was always going to happen. We are from a long line of high-ranking flyers. General Asra was The Dragon of the Night, head of both the legion and our family line. He was right hand to the King, and leader of the Dragon Council. He was the head dragon of all the kingdoms basically, and Nyx should have immediately filled his shoes as his first born, but…"

My eyes widened as the weight of what Nyx had meant when he said 'take my rightful place' finally settled on me. "But he couldn't without me."

Kol shook his head. "The King appointed a regent to govern in the interim, but Nyx must take his rightful place as soon as possible."

"You're his twin. Couldn't you?" I was grasping at straws, knowing if he could have, he surely would.

"The Regent is a place holder offered by the King, because we all know the next General Asra should be Nyx, not me. If I take the place of the first born, that will be it. It's more than a rank. It's the hereditary role of alpha dragon of all the kingdoms. Being an alpha physically changes you. I couldn't fill in for him and then pass it back. The alpha is the alpha until he dies. He would have to challenge me and kill me to claim his birthright back, and neither of us would ever…"

I nodded, understanding the primal nature of what he was

explaining, while also grasping that I was the missing key to Nyx's whole future.

"So, will he have to challenge the Regent?" I asked, wondering how that would be different to Kol filling in.

"No, the Regent is a dragon not of our line, so he can't sit at the head of the family. As general and interim head of the Dragon Council, he holds the responsibility, but he can't become alpha without a challenge. And since there are no bloodlines left capable of challenging Asra dragons, without the Asra blood in his veins, he would simply die trying."

It was all fascinating, and I found my interest troubling, because I would not be staying, and I did not need or want to know more about the politics I'd unwittingly become part of.

Kol led the way silently for a while as we both digested the weight of that information. We walked through winding passages and up flights of stairs, then out onto a massive courtyard.

I froze, the sight hitting me. The palace sat above a massive city—one I saw in the distance from the air. It stretched farther than the eye could see. If I hadn't been looking at it myself, I wouldn't have ever been able to imagine so many houses in one space. The sheer number of fae must have been overwhelming. How could they all live so close together? It must have taken them a day to walk across the expanse of the city.

"Sometimes I forget what a sight it is," Kol whispered.

"How are there so many fae here?"

He shrugged. "I don't know. Very different from what you're used to, I imagine."

I nodded in awe. "Did you grow up here?"

"I did. The general was stationed here, so we were born here, but most dragons live within the capital now."

"Why?"

"We are rare and becoming more so every day. There aren't many of us left, so living alongside the legion and the majority

"Which kingdom are you from?" I asked cautiously, not sure if the question was offensive.

"The First. My father was the General of the King's armies, and his father before him, and his father before him. Right back to when the kingdoms were united. Before the Twelve Kingdoms were formed, the lands were divided by the terrain, the climate, how the fae lived, and named accordingly. Those names predate the numbers and have stuck around. Our identities lie in those places."

"Why did they unite?" I asked when he didn't elaborate.

"We were at war. The Hundred Years war, between what is now the First Kingdom and the Fourth. Dark and light. The war only ended because the realm was attacked by the Vivi Mortui, an undead army. It was come together or perish. At the time, the King of the First Kingdom held the most power, so they united under the First Kingdom. It was a brutal war against the Vivi Mortui, but the fae were victorious. But the losses were immense across the entire realm, and the kingdoms had to stay united to survive. It was a hard time, but it brought the fae together." Kol's voice carried pride. "The legions of flyers who fought in the war became the King's legion and have been stationed in the First Kingdom ever since."

"So, there are beasts—dragons in all the kingdoms?"

"Flyers. We aren't all dragons, and there can be, but we all come to the First Kingdom to train with our flyers. It's the best way to make sure we all learn together with the best teachers. Which is why you're here."

I frowned, understanding, but still aching for my home. For Luka and my parents. "I don't want to be here, though. I belong with my family."

"I know." He got up and sat on the arm of my chair. "But I can promise you this is where you're meant to be. I don't know why they took you away, but it wasn't fair to you or to my brother."

of our kind protects us before we come into the use of our powers and can defend ourselves." His words were solemn.

"Why are you becoming so rare?" 'Dying off' was the phrase that came to mind, but I would avoid those words at all costs.

"Dragon's Bane," he said simply but bitterly.

"I'm sorry." I still didn't know exactly what role my community played in that, but it was clear it was something not good, and I didn't know how to feel.

"It's not your fault. I'm glad you're here now. Things can finally be how they should be."

I frowned, a pang of guilt hitting me in the chest. I didn't want to stay here or help Nyx... at least I didn't *want* to want to. But things were complicated and becoming more so by the minute. How could I reject Nyx when it would affect his twin, too? Twins were a gift from the Goddess. A soul living in two bodies. They were sacred to her. They shared connections others would never understand. While Nyx felt closed off and cold, Kol seemed to wear his mood on his sleeve. I could feel his worry and stress over his brother.

I rubbed a hand over his arm. "I can tell you worry over him."

"Someone has to." He forced a smile back to his lips.

"He's that bad?"

"Worse than you can even imagine!" His eyes danced with amusement. "But he's a good guy deep down."

I scoffed. "He must have buried it deep."

"He hides it well." He put his hand over mine. "Come on. We have places to be."

ELEVEN

NYX

It was almost too early when I went to the Regent General's Office, but I knew Octavian would already be there.

"I'm ready to take my place," I rushed out as soon as I entered. I could have kicked myself for not finding a less desperate-sounding way to phrase it, but here I was. I needed to get things moving as quickly as possible.

Octavian lifted a brow as he looked up from the parchment he was reading. "I heard you found your ryder. Congratulations."

"Yes, and I want to get her up to standards as soon as possible." We both knew what it meant.

"You mistake my congratulations for agreement to your request. You can't expect me to throw you into the field with an untrained ryder and simply hand over the most significant roles in the kingdom to you in such circumstances."

"I am of age, and my birthright—"

Octavian cut me off. "I am well aware of your birthright. If you think anyone has forgotten, you are mistaken. It's what has afforded you the privilege you have been extended during the years your ryder was missing."

I sucked in the snarl threatening to leave my lips. As if you could call a desk job on the sidelines of a legion I should have been leading a privilege. I settled my mind so my tone wouldn't match my rage. "I understand what has been done for me, but the time has come for me to take my command. Our war with the Vestar grows worse by the day. She can learn in the field. We can't afford to lose more lives, and putting her through the full training is a waste of time." Time we didn't fucking have.

"Those are the rules, Nyx, and while I understand you are impatient considering the circumstances, this process can't be rushed. I can't risk losing you like we did your father. An untrained ryder in the field will only put the entire wing in danger. I've heard she isn't even showing signs of magic yet." Octavian gave me a sympathetic look, which only enraged me further.

"Who told you that?" She'd barely been here two fucking days.

"Do you think for a second, as Regent General, that I don't keep tabs on when any dragon brings a ryder into this city, least of all you?" Octavian wasn't a bad guy, nor did I think he was against me, but he didn't get to where he was without political maneuvering. I'd been stupid to not be aware of how it might affect my position before now.

"Who told you?"

"I am responsible for all dragons in this city, and even if you don't know it, the healers do. They filed the appropriate reports… Something I would also have expected from you." He said it in a matter-of-fact way, but it stung. I did not enjoy disappointing a fae who had held the respect of my father, something few fae could claim. It was akin to disappointing father directly, and nothing was worse than that.

"Everything happened rather quickly, and I—" I cut myself off before I started making excuses. "I apologize. I should have reported it to you directly. It has just been a shock."

"Yes, I heard her rescue was somewhat dramatic." His brow creased in a way that could easily be mistaken for concern, but I knew him too well. Suspicion was laced in his frown, too.

"It was. Thank the Goddess I got the call in time," I said with as much casual confidence as I could muster. I did not want him looking too closely at this.

"Indeed. Which is all the more reason to let her settle in and recuperate before you begin her training. She has a long way to go before she will be ready for the legion. The war will be there when she's ready."

"But how many lives will we lose in that time? She will come into her magic quickly by her proximity to me. We can take our place, and she can train in the field. She's not an adolescent."

"No, Nyx. But she is an adult fae who has been forcibly removed from her home by her family's murderers and taken to a world she could never have imagined. At least if she was a youngling leaving a normal home for the first time, she would be somewhat prepared."

I cringed at his frank assessment. "I meant that she has maturity on her side. She will learn quickly."

"I understand your feelings on the subject, but I think your judgement is clouded. Why would you want to put your ryder at risk that way? Do you want her to die?" Octavian tilted his head like he was trying to figure out my intentions, but I couldn't tell him the deal I'd made with her.

"I can protect her," I returned, letting my tone slip into a growl.

His brows rose. "Nyx, your father was my closest friend,

may he rest with the Goddess, and I knew better than anyone how he could be dragon-headed when he thought he knew best. But this line of thinking is irresponsible even for an heir of his. If his death has taught us anything, it's that all dragons are valuable."

"Please leave him out of this." I crossed my arms over my chest.

"I can't, in good conscience, approve of you taking your untrained, unproven, and, if reports are correct, uncooperative ryder straight into the field. We don't even know what her abilities will be."

"She's not going to kill herself or me, so what does it matter what her powers are? They will come when they come, and I think training with a bunch of green ryders will only hold her back. Field work is more valuable to her than sitting around a classroom. We both know good ryders are made in the field. We have lost so much time already, Octavian."

The thought of the excruciatingly slow process of educating her from absolute scratch was killing me. Where would we even begin? I was more and more convinced that throwing her in at the deep end was the only way to break her in.

He thought over what I said before replying. Octavian was good at his job because he listened to those under him. I couldn't say that about all the commanders within the First Army.

"I understand where you are coming from, Nyx, and I know you want to fast track her through so you can finally take your place. But I must put her welfare and that of the other flyers first or I would not be doing my duty. She must go through training as any other ryder would. Until she has a grasp on her magic, she is a danger to herself if no one else."

"I can keep her safe. You know my magic is strong enough even without hers. I'm one of the strongest dragons in generations. Keeping me here is a detriment to the legion. We are losing flyers left and right, and we don't have enough to be losing any at all." It was true, but it wasn't my most pressing concern. I needed to get out there and lead the flyers so I could prevent the loss of any more flyers. But I needed her in order to do that, and if I couldn't even keep her here long enough to train, then I was fucked. She would leave if we didn't get moving soon enough.

Octavian frowned. "I'm sure you're concerned for your brother and want to be out there with him," he said with sympathy, confusing my fear of losing Zaria with my fear of losing Kol. Whatever helped me convince him to let me lead, I'd roll with it. "But I can assure you I am keeping our flyers safe. We are all cognizant of the losses—all flyers feel them—but I can't risk more lives by putting her out in the field before she is ready."

"The fleet would be safer with me in command, and you know it," I snapped, losing patience.

"I'm not only speaking to the safety of flyers. I am worried about the safety of our entire kingdom. She could cause some sort of natural disaster by coming into all that power at once with no knowledge of how to control it. She could kill other flyers who aren't naturally protected against her power like you are. The instructors are used to powers going rogue and are trained for it. If her power is as vast as yours, she could wipe out the fleet you wish to protect, not to mention the civilian casualties we could see." Octavian's words were final. He pushed to his feet, and I was sure I was going to get scolded, but he softened as he moved around his desk to put a hand on my shoulder. "Focus on helping her. That's all you can do. Let me worry about keeping the fleets safe."

I nodded because there was no use fighting it. There was nothing else I could say to convince him right now, so instead, I said what he wanted to hear. "Yes, General. Thank you for your time."

"Anytime, Nyx." He turned back to his desk, effectively dismissing me.

I left, launching into the air as soon as I cleared the hallway, with my powers flickering around my knuckles, which quickly changed into talons in a display of my frustration.

I had to calm down before I destroyed something.

TWELVE

NYX

W hen I returned to the healer's wing after a flight to burn
off my frustration, Zaria was gone.

"Where is she?" I demanded.

Kiera seemed surprised I didn't know, but not in the least
intimidated by my commanding tone. She was immune and
didn't suffer arseholes gladly.

"With your brother. He didn't tell you?"

I ground my teeth and tilted my face to the sky, not sure if I
should be cursing my brother or thanking him. It was hard to
know with Kol. He had his own ideas of what was best, and
there was no convincing him otherwise.

"I'm going to guess by your reaction he didn't." She brushed
her hands over her apron, smoothing it. "I'm sure she's in good
hands."

"But why?" I paced the small room, sure it would annoy

Kiera but unable to stop myself. I had to find a place to put all the pent-up emotions I'd been carrying for so long. "Couldn't he have let me handle it?"

"Were you going to?" Kiera side-eyed me while she grabbed an old recipe book and flipped to one of the marked pages. There were stains on the well-worn paper, but she dragged a finger down the page, muttering to herself. "Maybe he is trying to help. Someone needs to show her around. Would you rather it be someone else? Someone who has a less favorable opinion of you?" She gave a hint of a smile when she said it.

"No one has an unfavorable opinion of me."

This time, her look wasn't so subtle. "I think there are those who wouldn't wish to see you take your place among the command, or are comfortable with the status quo. I think Kol looks out for you, even if his ways are unconventional."

"Which might be true, but the more opportunity Zaria is given to avoid her reality, the closer we come to disaster." I didn't want to burden her with all my fears, but some of them leaked out.

"What were you going to do? Pick her up from here and deliver her straight into lessons? Goddess, Nyx. She needs to settle in. You won't speed things up by forcing her before she's ready. Maybe Kol could see that and took her before you could crash in and cause more harm than good. Hmm?"

I growled. I wouldn't have delivered her straight to a lesson. I'd have shown her her rooms first. Ugh, she was right.

"She will come around," Kiera assured me.

"Do you really believe so?" I knew Kiera had to have over-heard some of what we'd said to each other by the nature of how the healer's ward was set up, but she hadn't seen the conviction in Zaria's eyes or felt the strength of her will like I had. Zaria was the same child she'd been when I found her all those years ago, and that child was fierce and stubborn. No one would make her do what she didn't want to do. I'd admired those parts of her, but now they scared me. Her parents had hidden her away and turned her against this world, and all of this felt so fucking hopeless.

Kiera abandoned her potion and placed her hands over mine. "I truly believe so, Nyx. You have to let her see you. And I mean the real you, before you argue. Not the unbending alpha you become whenever you think about having to fill the general's shoes."

I rolled my eyes. "You realize I only get that way because it's an impossible amount of pressure, right? I don't enjoy it."

Kiera smirked, returning to her potion. "Really?" she deadpanned. "Because you're so good at it."

"Give me a break, Kiera. Try having a destiny hanging over you that you can't reach without your other half while a ticking clock counts down to when the goodwill of the King runs out and you lose it all forever. Then talk to me about how unbending I can be when I think about it all."

Her eyes softened in sympathy, but she still didn't cut me any slack. "That may be, but if you pull that attitude with her again, she will run as far and as fast from you as she can, and then where will you be?"

I groaned. She always knew how to hit me where it hurt most. "Fine. You win. Be nice, I got it. Now, tell me where they went so I can go and be my delightful real self so she will want to stay."

Kiera shook her head in mirth. "Goddess have mercy on that poor sweet girl."

"Sweet?" I scoffed. "You didn't hear all the very not so sweet things in her head. Trust me, she is tougher than she looks."

"She needs to be; she's got to keep you in check for the rest of her days."

I swallowed. I always knew our bond would be forever, but hearing those words reminded me that together, our forever could be a very long time. It'd been centuries since the majority of flyers and their ryders had lived anything close to their potential life spans. The Hundred Years War was centuries ago, but in reality, one conflict had bled into another since then, and peace had been a distant dream. Meaning most flyers' lives were cut short in service to the kingdoms. It was the nature of war.

In peacetime, bonded ryders and flyers could live for many hundreds of years, rather than the normal fae lifespan of around a century. Now I had found her, the thought of our potential future together just raised the stakes.

"Where did you go?" Kiera nudged.

I blinked. "Sorry. Just thinking."

"Well, do yourself a favor and put some of that thought into how you can win Zaria over. She's alone and must be terrified. If it wasn't for your brother, she would have had no one to lean on."

I nodded. "I'll try. Where did they go?"

"I think he was going to show her to her new rooms and get her set up with some clothing and whatever else she needs. She has nothing, remember?"

"Shit," I grumbled. "I should be buying her things." She was my responsibility, but even setting that aside, I wanted to provide for her. I'd longed for this chance all my life, yet my brother was stepping up because he thought I wouldn't.

"Indeed. Maybe it should have been you settling her in and providing what she needs to feel welcome and safe. Thank the Goddess for Kol, I guess."

"I guess," I grumbled before heading for the door.

"Oh, and Nyx? Kol told me to tell you he's putting all of it on your credit account. He looked like he was feeling generous, so I hope you're good for it."

The small satisfaction that he was at least letting me pay for what Sol needed helped ease my guilt for thinking about myself first his morning and going to Octavian rather than Zaria.

I left the healer's wing in a hurry after that. I could have asked Kol through our bond where they were, but I didn't want him to give me shit for not being the one to do that stuff. So, I went out looking for them where I thought they would be. I finally caught sight of them in the market square, heading for the tailor's quarter, and I followed at a distance. For a fucking hour!

They seemed to be having a great time, and there I was, skulking in the shadows, silently fuming. I felt her laughter in all the wrong places when they stepped out of yet another store. My brother was doing his best all-around great guy act to keep her smiling, and it got to me. How could he be that way with her so easily when all I felt was frustration?

She was pointing at something in the window of a shop, and Kol tilted his head, suggesting she go in silently, as if they had been friends for so long they could communicate through body language alone. He stayed outside, obviously tired of all the shopping.

"What the fuck was that?" I asked, jumping into his mind now he was finally alone.

"Hmm?" Kol asked, playing ignorant.

"You know what you're doing."

"I can't imagine what you mean. Obviously, this arsehole bit you're doing isn't working well for you, and I'm just compensating. But if you really wanted me to play a specific part, you would needed to have told me before I talked to her." He turned in a slow circle, trying to spot my vantage point.

"I've been behind you two for a fucking hour. Great monitoring skills."

"I'm not her bodyguard."

"Then, why are you out with her?" What was his damn angle?

"I'm helping your ryder settle in after her traumatic experience. Would you prefer for her to hate this place more by being totally isolated from her peers?" He finally found my hiding place perched on the edge of one of the palace walls. *"You creepy*

bastard. *Don't you have anything better to do than sit and watch us? Some paperwork to get to or maybe training to arrange now that you have a ryder?"*

It was a low blow, but I wasn't taking his bait. *"You seem to be doing what's necessary, getting her set up with everything she needs. I'm shocked you haven't arranged her training schedule, too."*

"And?" Kol asked, smiling at Zaria as she exited the shop. He let me listen when I half expected him to close me out as punishment.

"They have some nice things," Zaria replied. "But really, you got me more than enough already."

"We should order you a couple sets of uniforms now that you have enough regular clothes. You also need ink and notebooks. We'll have to come back once you find out what your focal stones are and get those, too."

"What're focal stones?" Zaria asked.

"They are crystals and stones which match with your power's origin and type. They can aid in storing, focusing, and replenishing your magic. The instructors will help you narrow it down once your magic comes out." Kol's voice carried a smug tone just for me that made me want to strangle him.

"What is your end game in all of this?" I asked him in his mind, hopping off the wall to let myself free fall most of the way to the ground before my wings snapped out and caught me, softening the landing.

"Do I need one?" Kol asked flippantly. *"I wasn't aware I needed motivation to make friends with someone who will be around for the rest of our lives."*

I scoffed. He knew what I was dealing with. *"You know she isn't going to stay. They've brainwashed her beyond belief."*

"She won't if you keep acting this way."

"I'm not acting any way. I'm being practical with my expectations. I need my magic, and then she can do what she wants."

Kol turned again to search for me, but he didn't find me on the wall. *"If that's what you think, then you're more stupid than I believed."* He laughed through the bond without showing any outward sign of it to Zaria. *"Honestly. you can try telling yourself that if it helps you, but you know damn well it doesn't work that way. You have to work with her so she wants to stay."*

"Can anyone get over that much brainwashing? She doesn't know this world, and she won't ever be comfortable here. Any hope of her being happy was taken from me, so I need to be rational and plan for the worst."

Kol internally frowned, which was a strange contrast when I could see him smiling and listening to Zaria chat. "This way to the uniform store," he said to her before replying to me with, *"Why wouldn't you give her a chance to settle in before you write her off, considering what she is to you?"*

"Lots of flyers don't get along with their ryders."

"You know that's not what I mean." Kol's voice carried disapproval.

"Then, what do you mean, exactly?"

"Don't act like you can't feel it," he scolded. *"She needs us, and she needs to learn this is her home. You're not helping."*

I huffed. *"She won't give me a chance."*

"Maybe if you were nice, she might."

"So, let me crash your little shopping trip."

"Only if you're going to be pleasant," he warned.

I just scoffed and appeared beside them. "Hello there."

Zaria jumped and let out a little sound I shouldn't have liked as much as I did.

Kol shot me a flat look. "Can we help you?"

"I wanted to see how Zaria was getting settled in and take her to the lead mage to get her put into classes, but she wasn't in her room." I glanced between them, but Zaria wouldn't look at me.

"She needed clothes and things before she thinks about any of that. I'm showing her the best shops."

I didn't like that he wasn't giving me an in. We always had each other's backs, but Kol was playing this one differently.

"I'm sure Kol can introduce me to whoever I need to meet once we are finished," Zaria said when I didn't reply.

"See? I can introduce her, so if you'll excuse us." Kol held the door open to another tailor.

She slipped through, muttering a thank you.

I flattened myself to the wall outside to listen in, loathing how desperate it made me look.

"You didn't have to do that. He's your brother, and I'm just a stranger to you," Zaria whispered, but with dragon hearing, I could easily hear her.

"Just because he's my brother doesn't mean I won't look out for you," Kol answered, his voice softer now. "You deserve space and loyalty, too. You don't have to believe me yet, but you can trust me."

I shoved off the wall and took to the skies before I did something I would regret. I wanted to fly far away and leave my troubles behind, but I couldn't waste more hours flying around to let off steam, so I headed for the only place I could sit and think in the palace.

The general's quarters, unlike the rest of the legion stationed in the capital, which was housed within its own section of the palace grounds, were up in the royal residence. The upper palace which looked over the entire capital was lavish and ridiculous, and no place for the military leader of the legions. But leader of the dragons was not just a military rank. Dragons had no monarchy, but The Dragon of the Night, head of the Dragon Council, was a hereditary right and a governing position, and as such, the role came with a place in the royal household, lands, and titles.

Such things meant little to dragons, but the accord between the dragons and the ruling family had kept the kingdoms safe from outside foe for centuries since the kingdoms united. The trappings of the royal position were merely a symbol which enforced the partnership in the minds of the fae.

Kol and I were raised here, right beside the King's own children. Educated as princes, and afforded every luxury of the station, we wanted for nothing…except our father's love. The general was his role. With only one exception I could recall in my whole life, nothing came before his duty. Because of that, I'd loathed this place by the time I left for the legion barracks in the lower ward of the palace. That was what I considered my home, and the idea of moving back up here and living this life where I would become my father turned my stomach. That was not the life I wanted. My place was in the barracks, and even once I claimed my birthright, I'd want to live among the flyers I commanded. The trappings of the office my father seemed to love held no allure for me. I just wanted to lead honorably.

I would never come up here again if I had the choice…but my mother's garden was a place of solace. I never set foot in the apartments; they just sat empty in wait. But I often found myself gazing out over my mother's roses whenever I needed comfort.

It had been well maintained by gardeners since her death in my childhood. The queen was her closest friend and kept it in her memory. Only members of the royal household could access it, but they seldom did, so it was my safe place.

With my elbows rested on my knees, I sat on the bench Kol and I had had made in her honor, thinking about the mess my life had become in such a short space of time. After years of being ryderless, and all the problems that had brought me, I was in a worse position than ever.

"Nyx, my boy. What a pleasure."

I managed not to stiffen when the King's hand patted my shoulder. How deep in my thoughts had I been to miss his approach?

I lifted my head and made to stand. "Your Majesty."

"Please, sit. We are at home here. No formalities amongst family."

They were pretty words, but King Viktas was as ruthless as my father at times. I never knew which side of him was the truth and which was for show. It was another reason I chose to be with the legion. Royal head games were exhausting.

"What brings you to Lady Asar's garden? Have you finally decided to move in?"

I shook my head. We'd had this discussion on a rolling loop since my father's death. Without my ryder, I could not take my place, so I saw little point in moving into a home I dreaded even visiting. And even with my ryder now found, I would earn my role leading the legion by flying with them first. No flyer would respect a general who had never seen battle, and no dragon would accept a leader who had lived in a palace of fae all his life, never seeing firsthand how dragon kind was being wiped out.

The titles were mine, as they had been all the Asars before me, but my forefathers still climbed the ranks, and so would I. I would take the rank and titles and delay the trappings as long as possible.

"Not yet. The time has not come." It was the same reply I had given a hundred times.

The King sat beside me, taking a relaxed pose, which made me see how rigid I was.

"I thought with your ryder now safely by your side, you might have come to your senses."

So, he knew. It was a fool's wish that the news had not yet reached him, but I had hoped I would have had a little more time to bond with her before we came under his scrutiny.

"She is still adjusting. We have some work to do."

"So I heard, but no better mentor exists in the realm. You have been preparing for this moment your whole life. She is in good hands."

I hung my head. "We need to come to terms with some things between us first. She is holding some false ideas of our kingdom, and our initial meeting was...traumatic for her." I didn't know why I was sharing this information.

The King patted my knee. His demeanor was fatherly today. I always found this side of him suspicious when I knew he could be so cold at times, but I would never show him as much.

"You'll get her to where she needs to be, my boy. I have every faith in you." He rose, never one to indulge in pleasantries for too long. "Bring her by, Nyx. Your brother, too. The queen misses you both, and I'd very much like to meet her."

THIRTEEN
ZARIA

After we visited every store Kol could think of, I went to the rooms that were apparently mine to put away all the new things he had bought for me. I told him I would find a way to pay him back for everything, but he insisted they were his welcome gift. That just made me feel worse about intending to leave.

I needed some basic clothes, and I was extremely grateful, but he also got me books and things for training, and uniforms for flying. Things I didn't want or ask for, but he insisted I would need.

There was a knock, and I froze.

"Zaria?" Nyx's voice carried through the door, and my stomach churned.

I didn't want to see him, but at the same time, I glanced

around my unfamiliar new space and felt relieved I had some company. Reluctantly, I went to answer.

Nyx was leaning on the doorframe.

I took him in, shirt stretched tightly across his broad chest, muscles bulging in his folded arms. I lifted my gaze and found him smirking. His intense jade eyes seemed to glow with amusement.

With just his look alone, I knew. I was broadcasting again, and he was enjoying it. My blood boiled, but before I could speak, Nyx held up his hands.

"Let me help you with that," he said with a warmth I hadn't heard from him before. He pushed off the frame and squeezed past me into my rooms without an invitation.

I stood agape and watched him take in the sparse space. I didn't like the way it felt to be so exposed. I had nothing. I was used to having very little, but we all had very little back home. This felt different. From what I saw today, the fae of this place had plenty, but I truly had nothing except what Kol had given me, and none of that felt like mine. I was alone in this, and anger rose in me again.

"What is it you think you can help me with?" I demanded.

He turned to face me. "With keeping your thoughts under control, Sol." He skimmed a finger over the stack of notebooks on the small desk.

That took me by surprise. I wouldn't think he would want to help with that when he seemed to enjoy it so much.

"You really doubt I would help?" he asked, and a look of hurt flickered across his face.

My lips parted to reply, but I honestly didn't know how to. Yes, I did doubt it. How could I not? But then that connection between us seemed to want to correct my assumption.

"Sol, after I searched for you relentlessly for most of my life, and never gave up on finding you, why would I abandon you now that I've found you?"

He looked so serious, and it softened him, but I had to protect myself. "But you did."

"I deserve that, I suppose." He shook his head. "I had an early meeting. I wanted to help you get settled in, but when I went to the healer's wing, I found that Kol had beaten me to the job. I would have taken you to get the things you needed, but I'm glad you had some time with him."

I smiled, recalling the day. Despite my circumstances, Kol had made it a day I could remember fondly. "He was very kind."

"He's like that," Nyx agreed. "Did he get you flying leathers?"

I nodded, shame heating my cheeks when I thought of the bill for all the things he insisted I needed.

Nyx huffed a laugh, and I stiffened. I was doing it again.

"Think of it like a river."

I frowned.

"Your thoughts, Sol. Think of them like flowing water. Right now, they are a raging river flowing unchecked. You need to build a dam so you can keep them contained, then learn how to open the dam enough to let a small stream flow out when you want it to."

"And how do I do that?" I asked skeptically.

"Visualize it," he said simply. He gestured me closer to him as he perched on the desk, and I stepped toward him, drawn into his space by that thread. "Close your eyes," he all but whispered.

I complied, questioning my sanity for trusting him even as I did as he said.

"It's good that you question whether you should trust me."

My eyes snapped open.

He reached out and took my hand in his. "You can trust me, of course, and you know that from our bond, but it's good that you question and don't do it blindly."

I tried to snatch my hand back, but he held tighter. "Why should I trust you? You just showed me you are still stealing my thoughts, and that's the least of my reasons to never trust you."

"I'm not stealing them, and I'm about to show you how to stop them from being thrown in my direction. Now, close your eyes and picture the river."

I closed my eyes again and visualized the river near the compound.

He laughed. "That's not a river, Sol. It's barely a trickle."

I jerked in his grasp. "How do you know what I'm picturing? You can see what I see?" Goddess, have mercy, this was just getting worse.

"Not quite. I can't look through your eyes, but you can send me images and memories in the same way as you send your thoughts."

"That's...disturbing."

"It can be very useful."

"If you say so."

He sighed. "Imagine a big river for me so I can help you build a dam."

"I only know one river," I murmured, embarrassed once more of my closed-off existence.

Nyx smiled. I couldn't see him, but I could feel it in my mind. What an odd sensation. "I will have to take you to the River Kingdom one day."

The kindness in his tone shocked me, like showing me a place he loved would be a pleasure for him.

"*Okay,*" he said into my mind, the feeling still unfamiliar. But unlike when we were flying, it was made all the stranger because I was staring at him, and his mouth didn't move. "*I'm going to show you a river to help you visualize. It's just a memory from my mind to yours.*"

I braced, not sure how it would feel, but I nodded, anyway.

Suddenly, I saw a vast river with raging waters. It filled my mind as if I were looking at the sight myself. I gasped. It was unbelievable.

"You see it?"

I nodded, unsure whether or not I should open my eyes. I blinked my eyes open, and the image was gone.

"Okay, now I want you to imagine building a dam that will stop the water from flowing away."

"H—how? I stammered aloud.

"Bring in logs, pull down trees. It's your river; stop it however you can. Build a wall to stop the flow. Imagine with each log you add that the thoughts have a harder time flowing away until you have them all contained."

I tried what he suggested, but I felt silly.

"It's not silly, Sol."

I grumbled that he was answering my thoughts again.

"Stop me, then. I'm going to keep answering them as long as you let me hear them. "

I rolled my eyes, but I tried it. I imagined stacking up huge logs across the water. It slowed the flow until they walled it in completely, creating a calm pool.

"Good," Nyx said softly.

I opened my eyes to find him grinning.

"Did it work?" I asked, surprised.

"It was a good first effort."

My shoulders fell. "So, you can still hear them?"

"I can feel a barrier. That's a big achievement for your first time. You'll be able to strengthen it with practice and allow it to open and close at will once you have it perfected."

I allowed a small smile. It was something. And I would practice. The less he knew of what was in my head, the better. It was the best motivation to work hard at that skill.

Suddenly conscious that my hand was still in his, I pulled it away, and it was as if I burst a bubble. I stepped back, creating some distance, and covered the movement by busying myself with the things I still had to put away.

Nyx rose, clearly intending to leave. He peered over my shoulder into the bag of supplies, and I instantly felt judged. I closed the bag to prevent him nosing into my things.

"I see you got all the necessities."

I did not want to get into the many objections I made, nor Kol's insistence. That was not his business. "Your brother was very generous," I told him simply.

Nyx laughed and headed for the door.

I spun to face him. "What is so funny?" I demanded.

"If you think I would allow my brother to provide for my ryder when she is in need, Sol, you are very much mistaken."

I opened and closed my mouth. What did he mean by that?

"Strengthen the dam," he ordered, and unbidden, I obeyed. He nodded. "Better. And what I meant was…you're welcome. If there is anything else you need, anywhere in the capital, simply put it on the Asar account."

I glared. Did he mean that he had paid for these things?

He was still laughing as he let himself out of my room, while I growled in frustration and hurled one of my new boots at the closing door.

FOURTEEN
ZARIA

I was lonely.

It was a cold, hard fact I could no longer ignore.

I guess if I thought about it, I had always been isolated in many ways from the family and community around me. But there, I knew my place. Here, I was alone, and sitting in this set of rooms that was now supposed to be mine, I felt it.

I wished I had gotten something to read. Kol had bought me writing supplies but nothing to read. Apparently, I would be given texts to learn, but I didn't have those yet. I had organized my new things in my space. I had bathed and dressed. Now I felt lonely. I hadn't thought I'd have the energy to be awake long enough to feel homesick if I was honest. After an attack from the herbs, I should have been long abed.

Evening was approaching, and I didn't even know where to go to get food. I wondered if I would be able to find my way back to the healer's wing to visit Kiera since she was the only other person I knew in the palace. But when I thought of leaving this room and encountering strangers in the halls, I balked and stayed put.

I should have asked Kol where I could go after I settled in, but it wasn't his fault. He couldn't be expected to think of everything. He had his own life to live. If it was anyone's responsibility, it was Nyx's, but clearly, he wasn't concerning himself with my welfare, so I was on my own.

I sighed. It would not be the first evening of my life I went without a meal.

Chatter in the corridor filtered under my door, and I tensed. Just the thought of how many strangers I was sharing space with unnerved me. I had checked the lock was turned before I bathed, which was the only reason I could relax in the amazing, pre-warmed water they had here.

The innovation astounded me when I first saw it in the healer's wing, but to find it available in my chamber too was a shock. I had to learn how it was done. It poured into the tub already warmed from pipes that ran along the walls. I didn't know where it came from, but I was exceptionally happy to soak in clean, warm water, which I had not had to heft from the well and heat over the fire. It felt almost too indulgent.

The voices grew louder as they passed by my door, then a knock sounded.

Before I had the chance to wonder who it was, Kol called out, "Little sunshine! Come out to play!"

I smiled involuntarily and rushed to the door, so glad of the company I was craving. I flung the door open and stopped dead. Kol wasn't alone. Three strangers crowded the corridor with him. With smiles on their faces and the same energy that Kol exuded, they seemed friendly enough, but I still withered. I could feel it creeping under my skin and I couldn't stop it. When I shrank back and put my vulnerability on full display, I wanted to kick myself.

Kol's face fell as he took in my unfortunate reaction. "Oh, hey, sorry. I should have warned you I'd brought friends."

I quickly pulled myself together and shook my head vigorously. "No, it's fine. Sorry. I was just surprised." I summoned the courage to look at the others and plastered on a smile. "Hi."

"Where are my manners?" huffed Kol. "Zaria, this is Maxen, Casimir, and Elvar, my ryder," he said, pointing to each of his friends.

Maxen, a male as large as Kol and Nyx, extended his hand in greeting, and I took it tentatively, unused to greeting anyone new. The very few traders that ever came to the compound were kept away from us, but I had seen this greeting exchanged from a distance. It was just the first time I had tried it myself. It felt right, though—a way to connect with a new person and measure each other at the same time. This male was physically strong, and while I was sure he had to have formed the opposite opinion having measured me, he had a warm smile and a light touch. "Pleased to meet you."

"We came to take you out," Kol informed me.

"Oh," I replied.

Brilliant. Just brilliant, Zaria, I scolded myself.

"We are headed into the square to our favorite tavern," he explained. "Their roasted beef is the stuff of legend."

"And their ale isn't bad, either," joked Casimir, nudging his friend.

I had been desperate for company minutes ago, but could I really do this? It sounded like more than I could handle. Kol had pointed out several 'taverns' while we were out, and I was intrigued, but they were bustling with fae inside and out, and I wasn't sure I was ready for such an immersive experience.

"Come on, Zaria," Kol urged. Then he said the one thing that could make me agree: "We're going to get Kiera next. She will be so happy to see you."

"Okay," I agreed before I could stop myself.

They whooped in unison, and I looked down at myself, wondering if I was wearing the appropriate clothing.

"You look perfect. Come." Kol reached for my hand to drag me out of my room.

"Wait. I need my key," I insisted, turning to collect it from the desk. I might not have had much to secure, but I had to keep my sanctuary safe.

Once my door was locked, I was on my way to the healer's wing to collect Kiera with Kol and his friends, and I made sure to note the way so I could visit any time I wanted.

***

"And then you came out of nowhere and nearly knocked me out of the damned sky!" Rowan accused Kol.

Kol shrugged. "I'm stealthy. What can I say?"

Laughter erupted around the table I was sitting at among a dozen ryders and flyers after a delicious dinner. Some of them had consumed several of the large mugs of ale. It was clear flyers, at least the larger ones, had a high tolerance to the effects of alcohol. Though I was not averse to ale, I did not have such a high tolerance and did not want to feel at a disadvantage in such lively company. So, I tried a fruit juice Kiera had suggested, and she was right; it was remarkable and unlike anything I had ever tasted before. Sweet and refreshing.

"You need to wear a bell at night is all I'm saying," Rowan said.

"And where is the fun in that?" Kol argued. "I'm a night dragon. I'm made to sneak up on you. It's my special skill."

"How about you, Zaria?" Rowan turned the conversation to me. "Got any special skills?"

I shrank under the sudden attention. "Umm."

"Zaria's powers have not fully revealed themselves yet," Kol jumped in. I didn't correct him and say that I had no power whatsoever. It was clear he was limiting what I had to share with these new friends, so I'd follow his lead.

"Yeah, but what about non-magical skills?" Casimir threw out.

"Leave her be," Kol defended, and I was touched. But actually I did have some skills they would probably see as useful. It was just difficult to know what they would think of a female having such training. Though, from what I had heard this evening, it was obvious there were very different societal standards in this place. Just a glance around the table showed that half the flyers and ryders were female, and they, by all accounts, were battle-hardened warriors.

"I'm good with a sword," I offered tentatively.

"No shit?" Kol said.

I nodded. "I learned in secret, though."

"You had to hide learning to fight?"

"Yes. Only the males learned in my village. The females were not permitted... especially me."

Frowns gathered around the table at my words.

"I was always sick," I explained to the group. "They wouldn't have let me learn even if females were allowed."

"So, how did you?" Maxen, Kol's muscular friend, asked.

"I had a friend who taught me" A pang of sadness hit me at the thought of Luka. I felt his loss deeply, but there was so much loss to process, it just kept hitting me in pieces. I looked at the expectant faces around the table. I would not succumb to grief here. I swallowed and continued, pushing the grief down for another time.

"I wanted to know how to use a sword, and he didn't mind showing me."

Luka didn't mind doing anything for me. Nothing was ever too much. I had always known he would have taken any opportunity to spend extra time with me, and that old guilt threatened to join the grief I was already feeling. He would have made a good husband, but I was not the wife for him. Perhaps the part of me that reached beyond our walls for an unknown connection was the obstacle in my way of accepting that future? I would never know, and I would always feel guilty for it.

"Are you okay, little sunshine?" Kol asked carefully.

I looked up and saw the concern in his expression. In fact, the whole table was watching me, and I had gotten lost in the grief I had been so desperate to hide. I shrugged. "Just thinking about my friend."

Kol's expression softened, and he placed a comforting hand on my arm. "I'm so sorry, Zaria."

It didn't need to be said. He was sorry for both my loss and the part his people played in it.

"Were you close?" Kol asked.

"He was a good friend." I smiled through the impending tears, wanting to only remember the good and not dwell in the pain. "He was a good teacher, too."

Kol took the cue and steered the conversation away from my heartache. "And you're good, you say?"

I smiled, grateful. "I believe I could put up a good fight. I've never had to use the skill in a real situation, but I could take Luka down, and he was among our best swordsmen."

"Fascinating," Kol mused. "The arms master will be happy to hear that."

"Arms master?" I asked.

"That's the instructor in charge of weapons training," he clarified.

"Oh. Why would they be happy to know?"

"Because you start your training soon." Kol beamed.

I went cold.

"Don't pull that face."

I schooled my features. "How soon?"

"In a few days. You do have a magic wielding session tomorrow, but that's really more of an assessment of your powers."

"Well, that shouldn't take long, then," I muttered. Assessing nothing would take no time at all.

"Do you have some other plans tomorrow, little sunshine?" Kol teased, nudging me playfully.

I shook my head while the pit of my stomach churned at the reality of this whole new life they expected me to jump feet first into. I didn't ask for any of this... but I agreed to do it in exchange for getting back to see what was left of the compound and my village. And honestly, what else was I going to do? Sit in my rooms all day and stare at the walls?

"One of us will come and get you on the way to breakfast and show you the kitchens and mess hall, then at least you'll never go hungry. The kitchen is open pretty much constantly since patrols are in shifts, so you can go there any time," Kol said.

"Shouldn't Nyx be showing her the ropes?" Casimir asked.

My stomach turned at the mere mention of his name.

Kol groaned. "My brother has his head up his arse today. If it was up to him, our Zaria would still be twiddling her thumbs in the healer's wing."

"Well, his loss is our gain," Kiera added with a warm smile.

I liked this group. They were clearly close, and the feeling of family among them gave me hope that there was a new family for me out there, whether it was here or somewhere I had yet to go. If these fae could come together from all over the Twelve Kingdoms and make a family together, I could have that one day, too.

When the drinks were finished, we all walked back to the flyers' accommodations in the palace grounds.

"So, how have you been feeling?" Kiera asked in a hushed voice to keep the words between us.

It was the first time I had really thought about my health since leaving the healer's wing this morning, and it hit me then that I was well. More than any kind of 'well' I had ever felt. I hadn't had weakness, attacks, or any kind of symptom whatsoever since I woke here after the fire.

"I, um...I haven't ever felt so well," I told her, unsure of what that could mean. The day had been such a whirlwind, but living it without my usual weakness and ailments felt like a different life. After such an attack in my village, I'd be weak and bed ridden for days. Even being awake this late would have been beyond me. The difference resonated deeply. I didn't know how to feel about it, or if it made Kiera right about the herbs.

Kiera nodded, looking contemplative, as if she had expected the answer.

"Maybe your treatment has had a lasting effect and delayed my regular attacks from returning?" I suggested, looking for reasons.

"I don't think that's it," Kiera said carefully. She stopped walking and turned to me while the others carried on ahead of us. "Zaria, I think it's possible they were poisoning you."

I stared at her in shock.

"I tested your blood when you were first brought in, and you had concentrated levels of Dragon's Bane—our sacred herb, as you called it—in your system. That's not possible from inhaling the smoke. It had to have been ingested."

I couldn't form words. Who would do such a thing? And why?

"The smoke from the fire could certainly have brought on an breathing attack, but given how you have described your ongoing condition, I have reason to suspect you were being dosed with Dragon's Bane daily as a way to cut you off from the magic in the rest of the kingdoms."

I sucked in a breath. "But…"

"I have looked into your list of symptoms, the duration of your condition, and nothing else fits. Plus the fact you were living at a Dragon's Bane growing site. It makes sense. They probably spiked your evening meal, which explains why you were always worst at night, and how you had better periods in the middle of the day when the dose was likely wearing off from the night before. And think about it: you have had no attacks or weakness since you got here despite a bad dose of it. I believe it's because the poisoning has stopped."

Kiera placed a hand on my shoulder in comfort. "Listen, I know it's a lot to take in, and I'm here for you. If you need to talk through any of this"—she gestured around us—"I'm here. Come find me any time, night or day… or you can talk to Nyx or Kol."

I scoffed at that. Kol was someone I thought I could count on, but Nyx? Unlikely.

"What are you two doing?" one of the group shouted from yards away.

We didn't respond—I couldn't even if I had wanted to—but we took up our walk and followed them once more.

Kiera let me digest for a few moments, probably expecting a barrage of questions. But right now, I only had one.

"Why?"

I didn't really expect her to know. I just had to put the question out there.

"Well, they were living without magic—raising children to never know it existed—so they had to find a way to block yours. When it emerges, it would be too much power to cover or hide. Plus, they had to mute your call to your flyer or he would have found you years ago, no matter where you were in the kingdoms."

I recognized the stairs we took and knew they led to my corridor. I had so many questions, but I had no more time to ask them tonight as we arrived at my door. The whole group had delivered me safely back on their way to their own chambers, and I was about to be left alone with nothing but my own thoughts and hundreds of unformed questions.

Kiera obviously recognized this. "I'm sorry to just dump that on you out of the blue. Come and see me when you have time between lessons. We can talk it over properly."

I nodded, dazedly accepting the goodnight hugs of my new self-proclaimed friends.

One thing I was sure of as I let myself into my chambers: I was not sleeping tonight.

FIFTEEN
ZARIA

I laid awake most of the night, tossing around what Kiera had said. I'd had difficulty believing a lot of what I had learned since arriving here, but I had to admit, very little of what had revealed itself to me seemed impossible.

I could even believe Kiera's theory. But where did that leave me, exactly?

When there was a knock on my door, I was surprised to find Maxen, the extra muscular dragon I met last night. He was all smiles, and it set me at ease.

"I'm on my way to get chow, and I promised Kol I would take you to breakfast and then show you where to go for magic wielding afterward."

I felt my cheeks heat. "Well, thank you. It's very kind of you all to help me find my way around. I don't want to be a burden to anyone, though."

"It's no bother. I'm going that way, and you need to eat."

I was happy to leave my thoughts behind to find some breakfast and distract myself for the day. The mess hall was almost as lively as the tavern last night, and I tried not to get overwhelmed by the rowdy strangers I now lived among. I was sure I would settle in and feel at home here eventually. Then I caught myself. I wasn't planning to stay, and I didn't like how easily I was beginning to think otherwise.

True to his word, Maxen made sure I was fed and then escorted me to where I was due to be assessed for magic.

"This is where I leave you," he announced in the doorway to a large hall. He nodded to someone inside. "I'll see you later."

"Thank you," I said, already half-distracted by the next unknown to cross my path. When I peered into the room, I immediately wished I had stayed in bed.

Nyx was waiting with his arms folded across his oversized chest and surly expression in place. He was listening to an older fae who was talking rapidly, but his focus was solely on me.

The other male seemed to realize his attention was else-where, and he turned to see what the distraction was.

The new person was unlike anyone I had seen before. His wiry frame was hunched at the shoulders. There wasn't an ounce of muscle on his body—the opposite of the imposing figure beside him. In my limited experience of this world, I could confidently say he was something other than just fae. That is to say I felt sure he could turn into another type of creature. He had a serpent like quality. I really needed to find some books. I needed to know more about...well, everything.

As I drew nearer, the man's sharp, narrow-eyed stare unset-tled me, and the elongated nostrils on his blade-like nose flared. Scenting me? I felt like I was being assessed as a tasty meal, and I wanted to run.

"*Hold your ground, Sol,*" Nyx said softly into my head.

I dared a glance for a second. His eyes offered encouragement, so I returned my focus to the fae with the snake stare. *"Is it safe?"* I replied to his mind.

Nyx's amusement was clear in his tone. *"I would hope so. He is an instructor. If he made a habit of eating trainees, I think command would have done something by now."*

"Then, why is he looking at me that way?"

"He is assessing you. Just hold your ground."

I stood, waiting.

"Interesting," the instructor said at length, then at last took his fixed attention off me and looked to Nyx. "I sense no origin powers. Are you sure about her?"

My lip curled at the way he spoke about me as if I was not here.

"I am certain," Nyx said firmly. "I was called to her when she was only three years old. Power that can call a flyer at that age can't be mistaken. I could feel it then... I just can't now."

He was doing it, too. Acting like I was not here.

"And what kind of power did you sense?"

Nyx looked defeated. "I was young, Rakan. Hardly an expert in origin power types. It was strong, that's all I can tell you. Can you draw it out?"

Rakan returned his snake stare to me, and I lifted my chin. I would not cower.

"Hmm. We will see. She is spirited, though. I hope that doesn't get in the way."

I couldn't take being treated like livestock another moment. "I'm right here," I snapped.

Rakan arched a brow, making the features on his face pull sharper. "Spirited," he repeated, more to himself this time.

"I'm Zaria." I shot Nyx a glare. If he wasn't going to introduce me I'd introduce myself. He offered a nod, letting me know I was doing okay. I felt like I was facing down a wild animal and the wrong move could see me mauled. Maybe that was closer to the truth than I imagined. It was impossible to know in this place.

Rakan offered a single nod, not letting up an ounce of intensity.

"My apologies. Zaria, this is Rakan, a magic instructor. He's going to help you with your power development. He has the power of siphoning, which makes him well equipped to help us."

I tried to make sense of the words he spoke. "Why would siphoning help?"

"Because if he can draw your powers out by siphoning, he can help you understand what kind of powers you have and help you to draw on them better," Nyx said, not unkindly, but it all made me feel like more of a failure.

Rakan grunted a greeting and gestured for me to come and stand before him. I did so, even though my whole body wanted to do anything else. He eyed me, intense and stern in his assessment, his scrutiny pulling his gaze tight. I stilled, fighting the uncomfortable stare as he began to circle me. I waited, half expecting him to lift and examine my feet one at a time and then return to inspect my teeth.

When he finally completed his circle and faced me again, he frowned. "No aura," was all he said.

What did that mean?

"Let him work, Sol," Nyx said through the bond. He sounded hopeful, as if this process was the key to unlocking my so-called magic and I should just trust this bizarre process.

I didn't want to have magic. I didn't have any, so why did disappointment cling to me like damp clothes? I couldn't get away from it. The way Nyx looked at me... I could see it in his eyes. I was letting everyone down, and I hated the feeling.

Rakan waved Nyx forward and positioned him in front of me, then he placed my hands in Nyx's.

"Okay," he said, setting his palm across my forehead. "Begin."

"Wait!" I cried out loudly—louder than I intended—and pulled my hands out of Nyx's. "Begin what, exactly? You haven't said what I have to do."

Rakan muttered something about the Goddess. "You do nothing for now." He pointed to Nyx. "He will call to your power. Draw it out."

He set about repositioning us into the hold again, and I tried to calm myself, but it wasn't easy. I was way too on edge, and this wasn't helping.

"*Breathe,*" Nyx soothed through the bond, but it did nothing to calm me.

"*How can I when I have no idea what's happening? Is it too much to ask to be told what's going on? What is expected? And stay out of my head. There's too much happening to build one of your dams right now.*"

Nyx smirked but switched to speaking aloud. "I am going to try calling to your power. Rakan will work to draw out any power that answers my call. All you have to do is open yourself."

"And how, by the Goddess, do I do that?" I asked them, glaring at Nyx. "*Information! I need information,*" I scolded privately down the bond.

"*I thought I was to stay out of your head?*" His satisfied smile was going to turn me violent.

"*Just tell me what I need to know,*" I demanded.

Aloud, he told me, "It's the opposite of what I showed you yesterday. Let it flow. Don't hold it back."

"Let what flow?"

"Everything. You, your essence. Hold nothing back."

Rakan's hand touched my forehead again. "Begin."

SIXTEEN
NYX

"This isn't working." I broke off from the contact and thrust a hand into my hair, my temper spiking. We'd been at this for days with Rakan to no avail, and we were all frustrated.

It was like she wasn't even trying at all.

No matter what Rakan attempted, Zaria seemed immune. He could not draw a single ounce of power out of her, and if a serpentine flyer with the strongest siphoning powers in the kingdom couldn't draw something out of her—fear ate the inside of my chest raw. She couldn't have no powers. It wasn't possible. That's not how things worked. Our powers had to be equal to meld.

Could her parents have permanently taken her powers from her? I hadn't slept in days, going over and over it.

"Don't act like this is my fault." Zaria's chest heaved like she'd just carried water up the side of a mountain.

"What do you feel?" Rakan asked her.

"Nothing. Nothing at all," she huffed.

I ground my teeth and pressed my eyes closed. "How can you feel nothing?"

"I don't know," Zaria snapped. "Maybe there is nothing to feel!"

I turned on Rakan, ignoring her. "What do you feel when you try to draw on her powers?"

"Nothing." He crossed his arms over his chest. "Are you sure this is your ryder?" he asked again and eyed me like I was lying.

"Do you think I'd drag some unwilling girl who doesn't even like me into training if she wasn't really my ryder? To what end?"

Rakan narrowed his eyes. "I've never seen anything like it then. What kingdom did you say you found her in?"

"Desert, on the border of volcano."

"But you met her once before?" His snake-like eyes moved in ways a fae's shouldn't. It was unnerving.

"Yes. She was here in the First, just outside the capital. That's where she's from… or so I thought as a child." What else made sense?

"Do you think she could have dampening powers?" he mused. I hated the way he looked at her like he judged her. Like her lack of power was somehow her fault. It made me want to snap at him, even though I knew I was doing the same thing, blaming Zaria for things that were not in her control. I hated myself for it.

Rakan just had a way about him I wanted to protect Zaria from. Volcano flyers and ryders were odd, but I guess growing up in a place where every day could bring disaster made a fae different. He was jaded, but I could never nail down why.

He hadn't had a ryder in many years, which took him out of the flying forces. Not every flyer who lost their ryder could handle life after, but Rakan made it work. His reputation was that of a good teacher.

But that didn't mean I liked dealing with him, even if I couldn't deny he had the best chance of bringing out Zaria's powers.

I lifted my hands palms up. "I don't know her lineage. I couldn't tell you unless we learn more about her blood, and either she doesn't know or won't tell us."

"Stop talking about me like I'm not here," Zaria demanded, not for the first time.

"Stop acting like this is so inconvenient to you, and maybe we will," I barked, losing the last of my patience. She didn't deserve it, but I was frustrated and lashing out.

"If I could bring out some powers, I would!"

I wasn't sure I believed her. Either my face expressed the thought, or I was so spent I was broadcasting to her like a youngling with no control. Or, like her, a complete novice. Goddess forbid.

"Don't you think if I could do it I would just to get you off my back?"

Rakan ignored our back and forth, continuing with his own musing. "Without knowing for certain where she's from, it's hard to even know where to start, especially since I can't draw her powers out with siphoning." He crossed his arms over his chest, moving to look at the map of the Twelve Kingdoms that took up an entire wall in the training room. "She is a risk for dampening if she's from the First Kingdom."

"Can one of you please explain these things to me? What is dampening?" Zaria asked.

Rakan shook his head. "I have never..." he muttered, trailing off under his breath. If this was like the last few times he began muttering to himself, he'd just go on in disbelief at how Zaria knew absolutely nothing of this world and had no discernible power, and yet if she was supposedly the ryder to the great and powerful (his words, not mine) Dragon of the Night, she should be showing signs of it.

We ignored him.

"Remind me to get you some books on the basics." I sighed. "So, if siphoning can draw power from others and channel it or store it, those with a dampening power can suppress the power of others, leaving them powerless for a period. If you are dampening him or both of us without knowing it, maybe his power isn't working."

"Which is why we can't let you move on to other forms of training. Especially flying; it's too dangerous," Rakan added, then finished muttering for now.

Zaria frowned at us both. "Why?" She sounded genuinely disappointed to hear we couldn't fly until we knew.

I had to remind myself that it was because she was trying to get back to the life she lost, not because she wanted to be mine. My ryder, that is. Nothing else. Fuck.

Who was I kidding? She was more than that, and I knew it in my soul. I just couldn't let her find out because she would never accept it.

"A siphon has to have close or physical contact with their target to draw their power. However, dampening is far more dangerous because it can target a wide area, not just an individual," Rakan informed her. "If it turns out you can dampen, and your power level is a match for Nyx's, as it should be, you could accidentally use it in the air and knock your flyer out of the sky since you don't know how to wield it or control it. And not just Nyx. You could take out anyone else who is flying with you. You are a danger until we know what you can do." Rakan's words were harsh, like she should have known better.

"So, we are stuck here until I use a power I can't even feel?" Frustration bled into her words. I felt for her. She was, once again, being told to stay in one place, and not given any freedom or control.

"I'm afraid so. It's too dangerous, knowing nothing about your heritage, and since you can't feel your powers."

"I think I'd know if she could dampen. I would feel it," I tried for Zaria's sake. I didn't want her to think of this as her new prison. I wanted her to want to be here, and nothing that had happened so far was getting that future off to a good start.

"Maybe, maybe not." Rakan wasn't budging. "You can work on other things, but I can't, in good conscience, allow you into flight training until we know for sure."

"Fine." Every day we spent in this room put us another day behind. Every day we were behind was another day I couldn't take my place, and another day she might figure out what she really was to me and want to leave even more.

I had to find a way to draw her magic out.

"I am going to consult with some of my colleagues who specialize in dampening. Maybe they will be able to help. Same time tomorrow?"

"Thank you," I said, even though he'd achieved nothing in the last week.

"Have a good afternoon." He left before us, probably hurrying off to another student.

"Never did I think I'd meet someone more insufferable than you here," she shot.

I scoffed. "There are plenty. You just don't know very many fae."

She rolled her eyes. "I'll keep that in mind. See you tomorrow."

"Where are you going?" I asked when she turned the opposite way in the corridor. "We have combat arms now."

"It doesn't matter. I can't be trusted around others, can I?" She quickened her pace like my legs weren't longer and I couldn't keep up with her.

"It does matter. Combat arms isn't magic, and we will be on

the ground. You just can't be in the air with others. It's too dangerous."

"How do you know I won't kill someone on the ground when my magic comes out?"

"Because I will be able to manage it. As long as you don't knock me out of the air, I can handle you."

"Then, maybe I just don't want to go."

I stared at her. "You love fighting, don't you?"

She threw up her hands in frustration. "I can't do this. I don't belong here. Everyone knows—you just won't admit it."

"You do belong here," I said, blocking her way. "You have to do this."

"I can't, and I can't be trapped. I can't breathe in that room."

"And what is your solution? You heard Rakan. They won't let us train with others or in the air. We are a danger to everyone here until we know what your powers are." It wasn't what I wanted either, but I accepted it.

"Take me home. Just let me go back—*please*." Her beautiful green eyes went glassy as tears gathered, and it pained me to see.

"You know I can't do that."

"You can do it, you just won't." She put her hands on my chest and shoved, trying to push me out of the way.

I didn't move an inch, but my lip curled up in a snarl. "No, I won't. We have an agreement, and you are not upholding your end."

"I am trying." Her tears turned to anger, and her hands into fists.

"Try harder."

She screamed and beat her fists against my chest. "What would you have me do?"

"Stop repressing your powers." I wasn't sure it was actually her fault or if it was the brain washing by her parents, but she had to snap out of it, and no one could do it for her if Rakan couldn't.

"I'm not holding back! I'm trying my best." She dropped her hands, breathing hard from the exertion.

"Well, something is blocking you."

"Such as? I don't know the first thing about magic. If I did, I'd surely have used it against you by now," she said with a sneer.

I didn't believe her, but I lifted a brow, leaning closer. She took a step back, and I mirrored it until she found herself pinned against the stone wall. "What would you do to me? Kill me, Sol? Ruin this place? Get back to your family? You are the only one stopping you. You are the only one leaving yourself helpless." I fed her the words, trying to push her into a reaction.

"Get off me." She shoved again, but I only pressed in closer until we were chest to chest.

A smile curled over my lips. "Make me."

Her fingers dug into my pecs, nails threatening to break skin. "I'll scream."

"And? Who will hear you through these stone walls? And who will care?" Not the truth, but she didn't know that.

"You...you...monster!"

My head fell back, and I laughed, long and hard. When I regained my composure to look at her, her cheeks were pink with rage, but her body was warm. Flushed. She didn't hate being pressed into the wall at all.

Fuck.

Our gazes met, and emotion passed between us—flashes of things I couldn't quite pinpoint. Our bond wasn't strong enough yet. Arousal flooded through me, though. I tried to tell myself to back off, but I couldn't bring myself to. I wanted this. Craved it.

Her pupils dilated.

My lips curved up.

"You're unbelievable." Her words only sent more blood flowing beneath my belt.

"Am I? I feel you through our bond, Sol."

"Get out of my head." She shoved again, and this time, I let her push me back, but I only gave her enough room to breathe, and enough so she didn't feel my hard-on.

"No. I won't be doing that." Smugness bled into my tone.

She made a sound I expected to accompany a stomp of her foot. "May I return to my chambers now? Since you're my jailer."

I stepped aside to let her pass.

SEVENTEEN

NYX

"I feel like an arsehole."

"Are you being an arsehole?" Kiera asked, looking up from what she was reading, finding me standing in her open garden door.

She had a garden-level suite of rooms far out of the way on the other side of the palace. She'd never wanted to be near the courtiers or the training when she wasn't working in the healer's wing. With a big family of healers like hers, I found it funny she craved the quiet.

"Maybe? Yes? I don't know." I sighed.

She closed the book in her lap and sat back. "Sit and tell me what's going on."

"Must I?" I asked as I did what she told me to.

"What else did you come all the way over here for if not to talk?"

137

137

"I'd considered splitting a bottle of spirits."

She leaned to look out the door I'd walked through. "It's barely dinner time."

"Better to start early and pass out early, because we both have to work tomorrow."

"I have the overnight shift, so I couldn't even if I wanted to."

"I probably should keep working, but Zaria isn't speaking to me." I grunted.

"What did you do?"

"How do you know I did anything?"

She looked at me over the rim of her mug. "Don't make me answer that. You won't like the response."

I narrowed my eyes and held out my hand for her cup. "Because it's wrong?"

"Hardly." She gave me an inquisitive look but passed it to me. "What are you doing?"

"Making you a fresh one. Knowing you, that tea's been sitting there for hours." I moved to her small kitchen, which was a luxury for the palace. It was a tradeoff for being this out of the way. The more desirable rooms were smaller but closer to the courtiers.

Kiera didn't get up. "Two cubes of sugar. Thank you."

"If you think I don't know how you like your tea by now, I'm offended." I held my hand over the small stove. Only a little warmth lingered from when she'd heated water earlier, so I picked up the kettle and used my own fire to heat it. No need to waste the firewood or the time it would take to heat. I dumped her mug and grabbed myself a fresh one.

"You never know how much males actually listen."

I made a rude gesture before adding the sugar to both our mugs and bringing them back to her little sitting area. I sat back with mine and sipped the warm liquid.

"Are you going to fill me in? Or are we to sit in silence and pretend this is nothing more than you coming to see your oldest friend."

"I don't want to sound like a bastard." I pushed my fingers into my hair, half wanting to pull it out.

"What is it? Zaria's magic, you two not getting along, or everyone expecting you both to be brilliant from the moment you found each other?"

"All of the above, with an emphasis on the last."

"One of the reasons I'm so happy I come from a long line of healers. We all get the healing gift. Some better than others, but there's no pressure to be anything more than what the family has been doing for centuries."

"I am expected to fulfill the obligations that come with my family name, only I couldn't until now. So, every minute we aren't living up to expectations, we are a disappointment, and it's turning me into a monster, Kiera." I scrubbed a hand over my face.

"You're frustrated," she reasoned.

"I am, but I'm taking it all out on her, and it's not her fault, I know that. But can I stop myself from being a dick to her? No. I don't know what's wrong with me."

"Alpha male conditioning is what is wrong with you," she said flatly.

I looked up at her and narrowed my eyes. "Excuse me?"

"Oh, come now, you know that's exactly how the General dealt with frustration, and you hated it. But the conditioning got in deep anyway, so here you are."

I blinked at her.

"Don't look so affronted. It's not your fault you were raised by an emotionally unavailable, grumpy bastard." She sipped her tea, and I relaxed slightly, until she spoke again. "But it is your fault you're allowing yourself to act like one."

I grumbled into my tea as I took a sip so that I didn't lash out. Fuck, she was right, and I hated myself.

"You're both under a great deal of pressure, but that's no excuse for this kind of behavior, Nyx. You're not helping her. You're compounding the pressure."

I nodded, feeling chastised and guilty.

"Perhaps she doesn't do well under pressure," Kiera continued. "And why should she have to? She's been thrust into this life she knows nothing about, and they are trying to train her faster than any ryder ever. It can't be good for her. Magic is a finesse. She can't just be expected to produce it out of nowhere, especially if she's been repressed her whole life." Kiera shook her head. "The pressure will make it harder for her to bring it out."

"Tell everyone else that. In their minds, she's been chosen as a ryder and, therefore, should be blowing magic out of her arse."

"If she was blowing magic out of her arse, I'd be impressed." Kiera grinned, and I laughed. "But in all seriousness, is she showing any signs of it awakening at all? The Dragon's Bane should be fully out of her system by now, so it's not that holding her back."

"None at all. Not even a spark. I'm worried they stole it from her permanently somehow." I hadn't spoken that fear out loud to anyone before. It felt good to get it off my chest.

"I don't believe that's possible, but before you brought Zaria here, I wouldn't have believed it possible to hide a ryder and suppress their magic, either, so maybe I'm wrong. But I do believe magic is intrinsically tied to a soul and cannot be taken away. Would she even be a ryder anymore if her magic was forcibly removed?"

I lifted my hands palms up. "We've never dealt with anything like this, so how can anyone know? But I am beginning to feel like if she doesn't show signs soon, they will try to replace me."

Kiera gasped. "Can they?"

"I think the King could do anything he wanted." I'd thought about it a lot. There was nothing stopping him.

"Surely, Octavian can't continue to be the general. He's not an Asra."

"There's always my brother."

She made a face. "Kol doesn't want it."

"Can he refuse?" I exhaled heavily.

"Can they force him?" She had a point.

"It's a mess, and every day they add more pressure, and Zaria hates me more." Every turn felt like a dead end. Like the universe was blocking me.

"Can you tell them to back off ?"

"I've tried, but I am just a flyer, not a teacher. They think they know better than me, but I can feel her pulling away." I set my half-finished mug aside and slumped lower in my seat. "I can't find a balance."

"You've got to find her some room to breathe."

"But how?" I asked rubbing my temples. "We aren't allowed to fly, which takes away the best part of training. I've waited my whole life to get to fly with my ryder, and now she hates me."

She came over to sit next to me. "You have to let her see you. This you."

"When? While we are training and she's frustrated, when my brother is dominating her attention, or when I'm getting asked when she'll be ready in every council meeting?" I winced and softened my tone. "I'm sorry. I'm not trying to take it out on you."

She rubbed my shoulder. "I know you're not, and Kol is hard to ignore. It's just his personality."

"Believe me, I know, and usually I like the pressure taken off of me, but with Zaria, it's all made harder by everything." I wanted her to have friends and build the support she needed. I just also wanted her not to hate me.

"I can't imagine. There has got to be a way to take the pressure off her."

"Is there anything I can do to help draw her magic out? Or figure out why it's repressed?"

"Hmm..." Her mouth twisted in a frown. "Have you gone through the texts to see if there has ever been a ryder with this issue before?"

"All the ones in the library."

She thought about it for a moment. "Maybe you should try the healer's library."

"Can you let me in there? I'd ask permission but..."

"You don't want bureaucratic hang-ups, and healers hate letting anyone have access to medical texts because they just misdiagnose themselves?"

"Or so healers tell us." I gave her a grin.

She rolled her eyes. "I'm torn on that one. Fae should be able to research their own ailments, but not everyone is carrying a rare curse that makes their brain bleed. Sometimes it's just a headache."

I held up my hands in defense. "I'd love it if Zaria's condition was that easy. Will you let me in?"

"Come tonight."

EIGHTEEN
ZARIA

After the disaster of yesterday's magic session, I refused to leave my rooms for the combat arms lesson. I couldn't handle another run-in with Nyx. I'd intended to hide out in my rooms all night, skipping dinner so I would not see him at all. But Kol had better ideas, and we ended up at his favorite tavern again. It was a late night, but I enjoyed the fruit drink again and left the ale to the dragons.

In the morning, I braved the mess hall for breakfast on my own for the first time. After that, my intention had been to find Kiera for some pleasant company or just keep to my room. However, a note was handed to me in the mess hall, inviting me to meet with the arms master.

I could very easily tell Nyx I refused to go, but a direct summons from some unknown weapons expert was not something I was going to refuse. I was hard-headed, not foolish. However, the arms master was not at all what I had expected.

"Good morning. You must be Zaria." A petite female crossed the space to greet me. She couldn't have weighed more than seven stone soaking wet, and she was at least half a head shorter than me. "I'm Hazel, the arms master."

My face must have shown my surprise, but she was all business and seemed in a hurry to get started as she pointed to a side room in the hall. "You can find some gear that fits in there, then come over, and we can see where your skills are."

I shouldn't have, but I stared, and I couldn't form words.

"You do speak, don't you?" she asked, but not unkindly.

"Forgive me…" My brows pulled together as I tried to remember what she'd said.

"Spit it out. I've heard it all before." Her words would have seemed sharp if not for the knowing smile that broke across her face.

"I didn't expect a female to be the arms master," I admitted.

"Most don't, but we don't discriminate in the Storm Kingdom. We are a tough breed of fae, prepared for anything. The general, may he rest with the Goddess, loved to recruit us as teachers for the more unusual skills as well, like tracking, hiding, and dead reckoning, and all the best of us are female." She winked. "But you shouldn't be so surprised. I hear you have some skill with a sword yourself."

Just how had she heard that? My cheeks heated. "I had to learn in secret because I'm female, so you'll have to be the judge of my skill."

"What backward arse place thinks females shouldn't know how to defend themselves?" She huffed, but when I cringed, she apologized. "I mean no insult to your blood. There are more reasons than combat for females to know how to defend themselves. I think everyone should know their way around a knife or a sword, but my culture differs from most."

"I lived in an isolated community in the Fifth Kingdom before I came here. Females were subject to many more rules that males, but I agree, we should all know how to defend ourselves. That was my motivation, mistress." She was a teacher, so I deferred to her as an elder, even though she seemed not many years above my age.

"No need to call me that. Hazel will do fine."

"Hazel." Calling someone in authority by their given name felt strange, but I didn't want to end up on her bad side.

She smiled, and I relaxed a little. She was nothing like Rakan, thank the Goddess.

"Are you a flyer?" I asked, knowing I'd got the term right, but still feeling weird about asking.

"I am. I'm a dragon like your flyer. Most of us from the Storm Kingdom are." She nodded at the supply closet. "Go get some gear so I can see your skills." She was a busy type, obviously. Happy to converse but not while idle.

I nodded, always feeling like I knew less than everyone around me. I didn't even know the simple facts like which kingdom Storm was. Our elders only called the kingdoms by their numbers—another indication that my education was full of holes, which left me looking like an idiot at every turn. I needed to ask Kol if he could get me some books, so I could at least learn the basics.

When I returned with the proper padding, Hazel offered me a wooden sword identical to the one I used at home. Even the weight felt familiar in my hands. I pressed my eyes closed for half a second as sadness hit me square in the gut. Luka. Sorrow twisted in my chest. I didn't know if he was dead or alive—I didn't know if any of my family was. Nyx had rescued me from danger in the moment, and I understood that. But I still didn't understand why I couldn't go back now the danger had passed, nor could I really grasp why we'd been persecuted.

A light touch jarred me from the grief. "Are you okay?" Hazel asked.

I nodded, sucking in a slow breath so as to not embarrass myself further.

"Do you want to come back tomorrow? There will be students here in an hour, but I wanted to assess your level, so I know which class to put you in. I have a free hour tomorrow, too, though, if that would suit you better." Her empathy hurt my heart more.

"No, I only need a moment." Perhaps I should have taken her up on her offer, but I needed to be doing something. Whatever it took to gain the skills I needed to allow me to return to my home. I couldn't justify putting it off. Not with the accord I had with Nyx.

I centered myself, a skill I'd learned as a child when faced with any aspect of my life I felt was unfair or that I couldn't change. "I'm ready."

"Are you sure?"

I nodded.

She lifted her sword. "This is a practice sword; it's a hand and a half. We use them for sparring."

"I'm very familiar with them," I assured her, moving to lift mine, but I wavered. "Don't you need padding?"

"If you can hit me, I deserve the bruise." She gave me the type of smile I was starting to associate with dragons. It was roguish and sly but playful. Closer to Kol's than Nyx's. It disarmed me, but I knew better. Anyone who believed they didn't need padding when sparring was either a master of the craft or a moron, and I knew enough about Hazel already to know she wasn't the latter.

Luka and I had never used padding while sparring. It was too difficult to slip out of the practice hall, and we learned to live without it. It helped that we knew each other's styles so well.

I sank into a familiar posture, right hand on the hilt, with my left lightly resting on the pommel. I made the decision to move, but she came at me first with a mid-downward cut before I'd even registered her movement. I barely got my blade up in time to block the blow. I deflected and spun around to be ready for her next attack. She wore a smile as she came at me again, this time in a whirlwind combination of blows. I was slow, but I managed to defend myself.

I was sweating by the time I fell back, but I wouldn't give her a second to form another attack. I launched myself at her. She parried my cuts with ease, only using one hand on the heavy wooden weapon. Her strength impressed me. Even the most skilled fae in my village weren't near her level.

We went back and forth, and she landed a couple of blows on my padding. They'd sting later, but she'd pulled them. I'd been hit full force by Luka and knew hers would be more than anything he could deliver.

"Stand down," Hazel said at length. "Well done. I didn't expect your form and footwork to be as practiced as it is. I'm impressed. How did you become so accomplished if they didn't allow females to train in your village?"

I glowed under her praise. "I trained secretly. It wasn't easy, but I wanted to learn."

"You did good by yourself."

"It wasn't entirely me. My friend helped." It wasn't fair to take all the credit. I wouldn't insult Luka's ghost that way. "I practiced as much as I could."

"I am impressed, and it's very hard to impress a fae from the Storm Kingdom."

My cheeks heated from more than the exercise.

"Let's work through some drills so I can see more before I put you in one of the group classes. Anything you've missed, I will put aside time to tutor you privately to get you as well rounded as the class will be. Does that work?"

She was asking me?

I nodded. "Yes."

She walked me through some simple drills and then we had a quick sparring match again. This time, she went harder on me.

By the time we stopped, my lungs burned, and I sucked in breaths. I wasn't used to this much physical exertion, but my body wasn't letting me down for the first time in my life, and I had to think, once again, about the possibility of why that was.

A clap sounded from the doorway, startling me out of my train of thought. We both turned to find Nyx leaning against the frame of the double doors. He kept clapping. "Bravo. What you lack in magic, you exceed in weapons."

"Thank you." I didn't want to like his praise, but I warmed from it, too, and I was sure I turned a brighter shade of pink. I hoped my flush from the physical exertion hid it.

He shoved off the wall, venturing farther into the practice room. "Does this put her in the advanced class?"

"It does. Will you be joining us to train with your ryder? It would be a pleasure to have the future general back in my class again." She turned to me. "Nyx is the most accomplished swordsman I've ever trained, you know."

My gaze flashed to hers. She wasn't kidding. Her expression was that of admiration. A flush stained her cheeks, which took me by surprise. Even she was not immune to Nyx's appeal, it seemed.

"I can't be. I know how many excellent warriors you've developed, Hazel."

Her smile widened. "But none so amusing as you and Kol."

"Kind of you to include me with his praise." Was he being humble? Who was this standing in front of me? Surely not the same fae who'd carried me off. "I would like to come help if I wouldn't be intruding."

"It would be an honor to have you, and I have a few students you could knock down a peg or two for me. I fear a female beating their arse will never be enough."

He smiled, showing off his teeth. "You know it's my favorite pleasure, putting little shits in their place."

She laughed and pulled him into a hug.

Maybe I didn't like her so much. I swallowed the possessive growl building in my throat. Why in the Goddess' name was I feeling jealousy? I shuddered at the thought. No. I wasn't jealous, not in that way. Perhaps I was jealous of their easy friendship when every encounter with him was such a challenge for me. But I was annoyed, too. Why couldn't I have one space I enjoyed? Did he have to taint them all?

I let out a breath and returned my weapon to the rack. "When does the advanced class start?"

"Every afternoon at half past three." She glanced between Nyx and me, maybe sensing the tension in the room. "I expect you there today."

"I will be here."

"So will I," Nyx added, grinning.

Insufferable male.

"I look forward to it. And Zaria?" Hazel said.

"Yes?"

"Change into your training uniform. They allow you more freedom to move, and I don't want you damaging your own clothes."

I glanced down at the clothes Kol had helped me acquire. They were modest, much like what I would have worn at home. There had been so many other choices, but it was comforting, and I was unfamiliar with the styles of this kingdom and these uninhibited fae. But this was my life for the time being. Maybe I could embrace some new ways. I'd always envied my brothers and how they could run in their pants.

"We ordered some uniforms, but I don't have it yet."

"That will be dress uniforms you ordered. They have that specially made in the River Kingdom. Have you not been fitted for your training gear yet?"

I shook my head.

She lightly hit Nyx in the chest. "You're slacking. Take her to the kit stores immediately. I expect you both back here in time for the advanced class."

"Calm yourself. That's why I'm here." He feigned hurt from her blow, and I bristled.

Nyx's eyes flicked to mine with a look of smug satisfaction, and I immediately realized I had completely forgotten the whole dam in the river thing he showed me. I was broadcasting again, and it hadn't even occurred to me.

"*Jealous, Sol?*" His voice slipped into my mind unbidden.

My upper lip lifted in a silent snarl. "*Jealous that she gets to stay here while I have to go with you, maybe.*"

He sent laughter into my mind but kept his features unaffected.

"Well, off you go, then. You know how slow they are down there. If you don't go now, they will still be measuring her when the class starts this afternoon."

Great. Now I had to spend the next few hours with him?

I reluctantly stripped off the pads whilst keeping half an eye on Nyx and Hazel conversing like comfortable friends. I cut my thoughts off before they gave him any satisfaction about the way I was feeling.

Build the dam, Zaria. Stop the flow.

Once I was ready, Hazel bid us farewell, and we headed out together.

"Are you hungry?" Nyx asked when we were halfway down the corridor.

"Hazel told us to go directly to the kit place," I challenged.

"Relax, It won't take us long, so we have time to eat first. They will have everything we need on hand." He scanned over me, but his gaze lingered longer than it needed to.

"Oh?" How would he know such a thing?

"They can tailor things for you if they need to, but they will have a set that's close enough to hand you today, and the tailoring isn't really necessary, anyway."

"Why not?"

His eyes raked over me again, and I felt heat roll over my frame.

"Why are you looking at me like that?" I said under my breath so no one else would hear as we rounded a corner into a busier corridor.

"*Am I not allowed to look?*" he spoke in my mind.

"Get out of my head," I hissed.

"*You know dragons have great hearing, so lowering your voice doesn't prevent any of them from eavesdropping.*"

"*Of course, they do.*" I reluctantly switched to speaking in our minds. "*Why were you looking at me like...*" I couldn't say how I thought he was looking at me.

His lips curled into a devilish smile... like he'd won. "*Am I not allowed to admire?*"

"*Admire?*"

"*Yes, Sol. I was admiring you.*"

My steps faltered, and I stopped walking. I couldn't even touch that statement.

"*How can you be so sure I won't have to get things tailored?*"

"*Because you are underweight right now from going without enough nutrition for so long. A couple of weeks eating three square meals a day, and you'll fill out perfectly.*"

His eyes flashed at the thought, and I was happy it wasn't only me who was letting feelings slip. I just didn't know what to do with his.

The way he purred the word "*perfectly*" into my mind felt heated.

I adjusted the way my clothes sat on my thin frame and fidgeted uncomfortably.

There were fae passing us by in this hallway, and it suddenly became apparent to me that, to everyone else, it looked like we were just standing staring at each other.

Nyx must have realized the same because he spoke aloud again, "It won't take us long. We have time to eat first."

I was about to shoot him down when my stomach rumbled.

"You can't deny me now. However will you keep your energy up to fight me if you starve yourself?"

I gave him a death stare before turning to storm off the other way.

He had to jog to catch me by the time he realized what I'd done. "The kitchen is the other way, Sol."

"Maybe I'm no longer hungry." Again, my stomach betrayed me.

"Where are you going?"

"To Kol's chambers to ask him if he'll take me to get my training uniforms."

"*Have it your way.*" He rolled his eyes, then, without warning, ducked out of a side door and launched himself into the air.

Did they just have those exits all over the palace? At least I was rid of him. Now I just had to remember where Kol had pointed out his rooms when we walked by on the way to the tavern.

It took me a while to find my way, which I would never admit to Nyx, but I was feeling very pleased with myself as I finally crossed the courtyard that led to Kol's rooms.

I lifted my hand to knock on Kol's door, and my self-satisfaction slid off my face as Nyx pulled it open with a sandwich in hand.

"What took you so long? I brought you lunch, but I was hungry, so I started without you. I hope you don't mind." The smugness as he bit into his sandwich was infuriating.

"I'm not hungry." I shoved past Nyx to see if Kol was even here.

Kol gave a sheepish shrug when I found him lounging in a robe, only half tied. "Good morning."

"It's past noon." I took a seat beside him as to not be forced to sit with Nyx.

"And? It's my day off, and I was rudely awoken by whatever ever this is." Kol picked up his cup of tea. "You'd better have brought me lunch, too, brother."

"Do you think I would forget you?"

"You seem to have lost all of your manners when it comes to Zaria, so I'm sure you're capable of all sorts." Kol gave Nyx a flat look.

Nyx rolled his eyes and handed his brother a brown, paper-wrapped package. "I had a feeling you'd be late out of bed."

"As I said, it's my day off, and we were out late." Kol scoffed, and his attitude amused me, but I wouldn't let on in front of Nyx. He opened the package and softened. "You're forgiven. Where did you find fresh wild boar at this time of year?"

Nyx handed me a wrapped package too before taking the opposite couch. "You can thank me, but it was the chef. He's working magic. I snatched up half of what was left because I love you."

"You *do* love me," Kol moaned explicitly after taking a bite. He gave me a sideways glance. "I'm shocked you're as cheery as you are since you were out late, too."

I grinned. "I didn't drink the ale like you," I reminded him.

"Excuse me?" Nyx's eyes fixed on mine.

I didn't meet his gaze, keeping mine on the sandwich.

Kol didn't speak, either, too busy eating.

"Is someone going to explain?" Nyx said through gritted teeth.

"I didn't realize we have to explain ourselves to you," Kol said between bites.

Nyx turned his attention to me, and I took a bite and shrugged so I didn't have to reply.

"Whatever." Nyx shoved to his feet and stormed out.

Kol broke out in a laugh. "Grumpy bastard. What are you two fighting about this morning, anyway?"

"He was supposed to take me to get training uniforms from the stores, but he decided to try and charm me into lunch, and I wouldn't agree. So, I came here to see if you would take me, but he beat me here to prove a point." I picked at the bread.

"I can take you, but I think you now have a bigger issue." Kol grimaced. "Sorry. I didn't think he'd blow fire over you coming out with us."

"He has no right to. I'm new here. What does he think, he can just put me in my rooms when he's done with me, and I'll stay there like an obedient child? I have to be here, but I'm not a prisoner, am I? So, what's wrong with trying to enjoy it?"

Kol pulled a face. "I don't know. He's always been a bit of a grumpy bastard, but this is taking it to a whole other level."

"Well, it must be me because every interaction we have seems to end like this. And now I've got to spend the afternoon weapons training with him."

"It's not you. He's just...Nyx. Come on, I'll take you to get uniforms and then come with you to weapons so you don't have to take the full brunt of his temper for my indiscretion." Kol strolled to his wardrobe, letting his robe fall off his shoulders on the way.

I blinked, staring. His shoulders were massive like his brothers. Huge muscles rippled with the action, cutting all the way down to his butt, which was now out because he'd dropped his under garments. I turned away with a tiny gasp.

He laughed. "You're going to have to get used to it, sunshine. Flyers don't have a thing about nudity like some fae. When we shift, we either strip or wreck a set of clothes bursting out of them. Then when we shift back..." He shrugged. "Clothes just aren't a priority when you spend half your life in animal form."

"I'm not sure I'll ever get used to it." I put my hands over my cheeks to try and absorb some of the heat. "It's weird when it's you."

"You've seen my brother naked."

"Yes, and..." And what? I didn't know why it was weirder with Kol than with Nyx. They were both stunning, but my body didn't have the same reaction to Kol.

"And?" Kol prompted.

"You're identical. It reminds me of him," I blurted. I couldn't believe I'd admitted it aloud.

He returned to my line of vision dressed in sparring clothes, with one eyebrow raised. "Is that a bad thing?"

"It is when I go scarlet thinking about it."

Kol narrowed his eyes, processing the information. "Do you like him?"

I swallowed.

He smirked. "Sunshine, do you like my brother?"

"Yes. Or at least something inside me does, but it's rather against my will." I wanted it clear that the feeling wasn't voluntary.

His lips curled into a sly smile. "That's an interesting twist."

"Why?" I demanded.

"A lot of ryders end up sleeping with their flyer at some point or another. We spend a lot of time together, and training can be intense and rather intimate. That closeness can bring on feelings, or it can be mistaken for them in some cases. Or, honestly, sometimes it's just convenient to have a fuck buddy when we are out on tours for months. So, everyone blowing off a little steam rolling in the fields isn't uncommon, but you can't be at that point yet. Usually, it takes months."

"What are you saying?"

"That maybe you just actually like him?" He laughed again,

shaking his head with a shrug. "I'm not sure what it really means. It's interesting, that's all."

I made a face, my lip curled in disgust. "Goddess, save me."

Kol softened, sitting on the coffee table in front of me and taking my hands in his. "He's not a bad guy, Zaria. Believe me— we spend a lot of time in each other's heads. If anyone would know, I would."

"Doesn't make him any less insufferable."

"True, and I can't help with that. He came out of our mother's womb that way." He squeezed my hands. "Come on. We need to get your uniform before your lesson."

NINETEEN

NYX

M aybe I'm a glutton for punishment, but I tried to pry in
my brother's mind while they were getting her uniform.
I was blocked though. I guessed he didn't feel bad for not
inviting me to go out with them last night. If he did, he wouldn't
be shutting me out. He should feel guilty. How could he take
Zaria out when he knows damn well I can't get through five
minutes with her without us clashing? I mean…that's obviously
why he didn't invite me, too, but damn it, he shouldn't have
invited her, either. She's *my* ryder. Mine. If she goes out with
anyone, it should be me. Or I should get a fucking invite, at least.

I had paced a fucking rut in my floor last night, feeling bad
that she was stuck in her rooms alone, annoyed that because she
was so stubborn, she probably didn't eat so she wouldn't have to
risk seeing me. I almost took her food or had some sent, but I
knew it wouldn't be welcome. So instead, I just stewed in my

room, guilt ridden that all I seemed to do was make a bad situation worse for her. All the while she was out with my brother, probably holding court with half the legion at the Flaming Pegasus.

So, yeah, Kol should feel guilty for not inviting me, even if I would have ruined the mood. Or at least fucking warned me he was inviting her so I didn't look like such a clueless bastard. I was not talking to him. I would put up with him because Zaria was leaning on him, but he and I were not friends right now.

Kol was his own person, and while we were incredibly close, we lived very different lifestyles. He had friends from his unit that I couldn't be as close to—not when I was grounded here while they were out fighting and bonding. He liked to party in the city with them in his time off while I felt like I wasn't part of that scene. Even when I finally joined them in the field one day, hopefully soon, I would be leading them, and I had to be above reproach, so I'd never truly be a part of what they had.

Now I finally had my ryder—the one person who should have been by *my* side for the rest of my life. *My* partner, *my* one. But she didn't want to be that, and then I came to find that she'd managed to fall in with the very group I had to stay on the fringes of, no doubt fitting in perfectly and making them all love her, too. Things were hard enough before, but with practically a whole legion ready to welcome her with open arms, it felt like I was under even more pressure.

Goddess, what if Zaria took a liking to one of them? I was going to lose her in every way.

I had to cool down and find some way to work with her both in and out of training so that I stopped driving her away. If I could achieve that, maybe she would feel more at home and her magic would unlock. Most bonded pairs melded their magics soon after bonding, but she didn't even have magic yet, and if we didn't meld, she would stay in the dark about the extent of our bond. I sure wasn't going to be the one to tell her. It was far better she discover it for herself.

I arrived at the advanced class well before Kol and Zaria with my own gear.

"Did she ditch you?" Hazel joked.

"How did you guess?" I deadpanned.

We'd known each other since she was brought here as a little dark-eyed twelve-year-old who could already school all of the trainers, except the then weapons master, who was also a dragon from Storm. In all the years since, she'd never had the call to her ryder. Duds were rare, but they happened. They were the flyers whose ryders may have died in infancy or simply never came to be. It was hard on them because they would never know definitively who their ryder was, just that they must be gone.

Hazel wasn't past an age where it was a foregone conclusion. She could still be called. Her ryder might yet emerge. She had not given up hope. But I knew the pain of the hope and the wait. My circumstances were the same but also altogether different. I met my ryder, and even when she was gone, I knew she had not gone to the Goddess because our thread was not cut. I just couldn't locate her.

Once that thread of connection links, after a pair meet for the first time, we know if it's cut. That alone is what has kept me from going insane over the years. So, I admired Hazel for keeping herself level and becoming so invaluable. All I was able to do was sulk around the palace, doing a job I hated because it was the antithesis of who I was. But not Hazel. When the old weapons master retired, she'd stepped into his shoes. She didn't need to meld her magic with a ryder to be useful at her job like I did. It almost made me jealous, but she deserved her post.

"She is going to keep you on your toes, that one," she quipped.

"Believe me, I know."

"She's not a fan?" Hazel raised a brow.

"You always were nosy."

"What have I got to do until I find my ryder except live vicariously through those of you who have?" She sat on the floor and waved me over to help her stretch.

I knelt behind her to push on her back. "I hope yours wasn't raised like mine and at least knows that magic exists when you do find them."

She craned her head back to look at me, her expression twisted into shock and then quizzical. "You're kidding?"

"I'm not." I let up on the stretch and sat across from her, both our legs open in a V to help each other by grabbing hands.

"She didn't know magic existed? That's..." She took my hand and let me pull her forward. "I gathered from meeting her this morning that her upbringing was unusual, but no magic?"

"None," I confirmed.

"Imagine spending your entire life not knowing magic exists. I can't. We'd die in Storm. Our lives depend on our wards and warnings from the lightning." The fae from her kingdom were the only fae I'd ever come across that weren't afraid of lightning. They loved it, lived in it, and harvested it like other kingdoms harvested crops.

"I don't want to live in a world like that." I released her arms, and we rearranged our feet so she could pull me forward.

"So, how did they explain her power if magic didn't exist to them?"

"She doesn't have any," I murmured, figuring if I didn't speak the words clearly, they would not be true.

"What?" she choked.

"It was blocked somehow, along with her bond to me, as far as we can work out. Kiera is confident it will emerge now we are together, but nothing so far."

"Unbelievable. Where do you think her magic is? It has to be as strong as yours. How would they be able to block that kind of power?"

oned with when she found her ryder. "Occasionally, I get fond of a fae or two. Very occasionally."

Every eye in the room was on her. Even Zaria was drawn to Hazel.

"Glad to be on the right side of your selective admiration." Kol stepped toward the middle of the room, and the trainees parted like the sea, allowing him to walk to the front of the space.

As a decorated flyer, Kol had the instant respect of the trainees—damn, of most of the kingdom. I, too, commanded respect, but it wasn't earned; I'd inherited it from a fae who'd been nothing like me. He was feared, cold, and driven. An asset to the King and the Twelve Kingdoms, but not worth shit as a husband or father.

It was not a legacy I wanted. I knew I'd never live up to what my father was, but I had to forge my own success to maybe live up to what they all expected of me. I yearned to part crowds the way Kol did. Because fae saw the deeds I had done to defend and serve the kingdom. If I could get my ryder in the skies, it might finally start happening for me. Until then, I had to settle for fae scattering in the halls to clear a path for me should it be a case of like father, like son.

"Consider yourself lucky, Asra," Hazel quipped to Kol, pulling me back from my thoughts. She waved Zaria forward. "Join us."

Zaria crossed the room without ceremony. I could tell she was uncomfortable under the stares of the class, but she did it for Hazel. I knew it was irrational, but I was jealous of Hazel and the ease with which she clicked with Zaria. She was going to drive me to resent all the fae I cared about by simply being herself and making them love her.

Hazel directed the class through stretches and then had them pair off to begin warm-up footwork.

"Not him," Hazel said to Zaria when she stepped over to pair up with Kol, who had stayed purely to boost his ego with all the adoration.

"Who would you like me to work with?" Zaria asked, side-stepping away from me.

I shot Hazel a look, and she pressed her lips into a line, which told me enough.

"I'll work with you while these two manage the class," Hazel replied without missing a beat.

"So, you have us here to do your job?" I hid my disappointment with the tease while sifting through the practice swords to see if my favorite was still in use.

Hazel rolled her eyes and turned to Zaria. "See what I have to put up with?"

Zaria glanced between us. "I think you set yourself up for that one...but I do think he could use something to occupy his time so he's not nosing into other fae's business." The cut stung.

I lifted my upper lip and let my teeth show but quelled the dragon. "I like my hobbies as they are. Stalking, kidnapping, and hoarding—those things that are most important to us dragons."

She shifted, avoiding my gaze, clearly flustered.

"Can you not give all of us a bad name?" Kol groaned.

"I'd deny it but, sorry, Kol, Nyx is right. If I found the right male, I'd carry him off and keep him to myself, too." Not a flicker of apology from Hazel.

Zaria covered her mouth, and at first, I thought it was in horror, but then I heard her laugh. "I'd watch."

All three of us turned toward her, stunned. She even seemed shocked she'd said it.

"Excuse me?" Kol asked slowly, sounding certain he must have misunderstood.

Zaria's shock quickly turned into a grin. "What? Look at her! She's beautiful. Any male she deems the right male... well, they'd be worth watching." She shrugged.

Kol tipped his chin. "She has a point."

"You'd better believe I have good taste." Hazel smirked at me, and I wanted to know what was on her mind. "Now, all of you, stop distracting me. I need to see how her footwork is."

"Then, you can't blame me for taking you, Sol," I said into Zaria's mind, so Hazel wouldn't get pissy.

"I can do whatever I please," Zaria said out loud before taking her position in front of Hazel.

Kol snickered, elbowing me. "She is a handful."

"Thanks, by the way," I said, still sore about earlier.

"She is a person, Nyx, with feelings and needs. She needs to know she has support, and she wasn't getting it from you."

I had no rebuttal. That just made me feel like shit since I knew he was right.

"She needs a life. Let her have one."

"I'm not against her having a life." I was against her being unwilling to do what we needed to do. Even if it would kill me, she could do whatever she pleased after our magic melded. I had to accept that before we got too close.

"You are overbearing, and while I know plenty of fae seem to like that about you for some reason, it's only in the bedroom they like it. It's a little exhausting when it's all the time."

My brother was never one to spare my feelings, but these truths hit hard. He said nothing more, leaving me to stew over what he said.

I moved to correct a trainee's footwork while he corrected the angle of a cut with another. Then we moved into drills, and all the while, I kept one eye on Hazel and Zaria. With a few fixes, she'd slotted easily into the class without much work on her part.

"Great work, everyone!" Hazel called out. "We are going to spar for the last hour of class. Grab the padding and helmets." She wiped her brow with her forearm. As the students broke off to claim gear, Hazel handed Zaria a helmet. "With some practice, you will break those habits. I'm sure Nyx can help you there so you catch up faster."

Zaria openly recoiled. "I'll ask Kol."

Hazel raised a brow, meeting my eyes over Zaria's shoulder. "Kol won't be here long. His flight will be back out soon, and I'd offer to give you extra lessons, but I have classes to teach. Nyx has more time than me, and you couldn't ask for a better partner to learn from."

"Does he not have duties?" Zaria hissed, obviously hoping I wouldn't hear.

"He does, but those are mostly suspended while he's back in training with you. His duty is to his ryder until you are ready for the field."

"Oh..."

"Once this footwork is second nature and you stop over-thinking it, you will be a formidable opponent."

"Thank you," Zaria said softly.

"I want you to spar first with Nyx."

Zaria's attention snapped up, and her body coiled with radiating tension. "Shouldn't I pair off with another student?"

"Since you can read his mind if you allow yourself, he's a better first opponent than those ahead of you in this class. Plus, he has a vested interest in not hurting his ryder. I don't trust the rest of these morons to be careful with you. Sometimes their egos get in the way of their better sense. So, until you catch up, you will be sparring with him, both with swords and in hand to hand."

I heated at the thought of grappling with her and had to catch myself before it had a chance to develop.

"Shall we, Sol?"

TWENTY
ZARIA

Hazel's reasoning made sense, but it didn't make me any less annoyed.

"Don't look like someone punched your sprite," Nyx snapped through our bond.

"My what?"

"Never mind."

Kol laughed and tried to cover it with a cough.

"Can he hear us, too?" I glanced between the two of them.

Nyx made a face that told me Kol could.

"For the love of the Goddess!" I was reeling. Kol had been my safe place in all this, and to think he was hiding that he also knew all my thoughts and fears while I trusted him… I was going to be sick.

"Take a breath." Nyx caught my arm as I tried spin away from them and leave. *"It's not like you're thinking, Sol."*

"Oh, really? How is it, then?" I bit out aloud. I knew I had only known him for a couple of days, but the idea of Kol being secretly inside my mind too left me feeling so betrayed.

Nyx wouldn't release my arm when I tried to pull away from him, though, and I eyed his hand on me. If he was not careful, our sparring would be a real battle. I was sure I could do some damage with a practice sword if I tried.

He smirked and slowly let me go, but he closed in on my personal space as if to catch me again if I tried to run.

"In short, I can hear you, and you can hear me. And I have the same bond with him. You can't hear each other. It's only me in there, Sol." He tapped my temple so lightly, it sent a shiver down my spine. *"He hasn't betrayed you, and yes, I hear those thoughts. You aren't practiced enough yet to prevent emotional outbursts flowing through, but you're doing great. Just know you can trust Kol. Always. He is the best of us."*

I felt immediate relief and glanced at Kol to find him watching us with concern and yet warmth in his eyes. I guessed he could hear Nyx's kind words about him. I looked back to Nyx, my mind a whirling storm, making it hard to focus on what was most important in the moment. I believed him. Kol was good—I felt it—but I was so angry with Nyx about everything that I couldn't help pushing back.

"Don't preach to me about trust. You don't know the meaning of the word."

His eyes flashed bright jade, and he stepped even closer. *"You want to know what I know of trust, Sol? I know that I'm trusting you with something of life-or-death importance right now. In a room full of fae, I just handed you my most guarded secret. My brother's most guarded secret. Something we have kept our whole lives to protect each other. Twins are rare, but those with the bond we have are nothing more than legend. If it got out..."* He sighed, cutting a glance Kol's way. *"I will explain more but not here."*

I was speechless. I didn't need to wonder if what he was saying was true; it was tangible between us. He was trusting me with something that could potentially harm his brother and himself right in front of two dozen fae I could easily tell.

"Just know that Kol is on your side and wouldn't betray you. It's not who he is."

I nodded, watching them both exchange looks. Now I realized they were conversing, but it was so subtle, you'd never know.

"So, no one knows you can speak to each other this way?"

"No."

"And he won't ever be able to do it with me?" I needed to know if I was going to be forever blocking two fae out of my thoughts.

"No, Sol, he won't."

"Not even once we meld?"

"It's our power that merges, not bonds."

"So, when our magic melds, we'll share power?"

"Yes and no. We can meld our abilities and combine them, but it's not always that straightforward. It depends on how well our meld goes, and how deep our connection is."

He was holding something back again. Did Nyx doubt my ability to meld? Or did he doubt the ability to share magic with me for some reason? My parents had always kept secrets from me, and I hated it. He would only hinder us by keeping secrets from me now.

"Will we be able to use one another's powers?" I asked for more clarification.

"It's not an exact science, Sol. We will have to see how it goes, but sharing power like that is the purpose of melding. Two powers melded are infinitely stronger than the individual powers alone. And we can share power reserves too, so if one of us is running out, we can draw from the other."

"You can run out of power?" I asked, surprised.

"I don't know. I can't figure it out. Our bond is still intact, but magic-wise, I feel nothing from her, and I know I felt something when we were young. She definitely had her first sparks of magic then—I felt them. Now, they're gone."

Hazel asked the question I was too afraid to: "Could they have done something to her to make her lose her magic entirely?"

"How? There is no way in the known world to remove someone's magic except what a siphon can do temporarily. Don't you think if there was a way to extract magic and destroy it, we'd know, because we'd all be living in fear of it?"

"True. It would be the ultimate weapon."

"Exactly."

"But I'm confident it's there; she just can't access it."

"I hope the Goddess grants you the answers soon, my friend."

We switched to doing our own stretching and were just finishing up when the other students began to join us. Zaria slipped into the back, with Kol by her side. He lifted a shoulder in an unapologetic shrug and stayed in the back where they wouldn't be noticed.

But their anonymity didn't last long. "Don't try to sneak in here, Kol Asra!" Hazel called when she spotted them. "How long have you been back?"

"Not for long. Only a few days." Kol wasn't allowed to say much about their missions, and Hazel would know that.

"You never come by and see your favorite arms master. You know how much I've missed having you two in class." There was a hint of teasing to Hazel's voice.

Kol grinned. "Are you admitting to possessing feelings, Miss Storm?"

Her eyes were like lightning, and the air in the room charged. It seemed to connect all of us. She would be a force to be reck-

"Powers are like any other part of us. Our energy needs to be restored through rest and sustenance. If you keep burning through power, it uses up energy, and yes, eventually, the well will run dry and need to be refilled. We all have ways to recharge that are unique to our powers." He offered me a soft smile. *"There is much to learn."*

I couldn't disagree. I was feeling overwhelmed by just these few revelations. But my questions never stopped forming. *"So, if my powers run out, you can give me some of yours?"*

"Yes. Most bonded pairs can pull from each other's reserves."

"Isn't that dangerous?"

"It can be, but it comes back to trust again. We will trust each other with our lives when flying and with our magic. But I think that part is the least of our worries." He had a point. My head was spinning. There was far too much I didn't know.

"Let's get this over with." I lifted my sword, suddenly keen to stop the barrage of new and concerning information I would need to find time to digest.

"So eager?" He smirked, taking my change of focus and rolling with it. He fastened his chin strap and stepped back, lifting his own weapon while dropping into the posture.

"To get it over with? Yes. I need to prove myself, so I don't have to train with you anymore." I feigned a left attack and spun right, catching him off guard.

He caught the blow with the flat of his weapon, deflecting it at the last second. *"I'm sensing a theme."*

I wouldn't catch him by surprise again. He moved directly into an attack, driving me back, and I fended off his blows with ease, giving it back with full voracity. I wasn't worried about conserving my energy; I had more now than I'd ever had in my life. And even if Nyx trained regularly, my life had been carrying water a dozen times a day, even when it took me three times as long as anyone else because I could only carry half as much, cleaning, cleaning, and more cleaning, all before having to spend hours in the kitchen every day. I was no stranger to endurance, even as weak as I was.

"You are good." He did nothing to mask his surprise.

"Did you doubt Hazel?" I blocked a blow right before it hit my face mask, pushing with all the strength I possessed while he used his height to force the practice blade closer to my face.

He laughed, falling back. *"Learning to converse while sparring is imperative."*

I scowled, hacking forward. I knew my footwork wasn't the best, but my anger got the better of me. He deflected them with ease, and my back hit the floor, knocking the wind out of me, and I couldn't figure out how I'd gotten there. He stood over me with the tip of his sword to my throat.

"I yield." I shoved the blade away from me and kicked up to return to my feet.

Nyx didn't comment, but his expression said he was impressed.

"I can converse. I did it all the time with—" I cut myself off and eyed Nyx.

His reaction was transparent. I could see it was a punch to his gut. He had his river firmly dammed, of course, but his face held all the questions: *'Who did she just stop herself from naming? Someone who meant something to her? A male?'*

I knew it was cruel, but I was happy he was concerned about those things, and I wasn't going to offer him any context or reassurance. Instead, I continued like I had never made the slip.

"But I didn't have endless hours to play with swords growing up. I only had whatever time I could snatch between chores when no one was wondering where I was."

Nyx softened. *"You must have really loved it to go to that effort to steal time for it."*

"I always have," I admitted, softening myself.

We went a few more rounds with me lasting longer each time.

"Why do dragons learn this kind of combat?" I asked when we took a break to get water.

"Because we do run out of magic, and while we can shift into our dragon form with low reserves, we can't always breathe our magic weapon since it's a function of our reserve as much as anything else." He downed a cup of water and then poured one over his head. It soaked into his white shirt, making it cling to his pecs.

I turned away, not wanting him to think I was staring. *"Couldn't you just eat someone if you can't use your magic?"*

"I guess I could, but I wouldn't want to." He burst out laughing. *"But no one would taste as good as you look, so I'd be disappointed."*

I sputtered, knowing how flushed I must be. *"Why wouldn't you want to?"* I asked, just ignoring the other statement.

"Because I'm fae, even when I'm in my dragon form. I wouldn't want to begin a trend of eating other fae."

I looked at him and knew it was a mistake. He glistened in the light filtering through the high windows, glowing from the exercise.

His mouth twisted into a smug grin. *"See something you like, Sol?"*

"Not a thing." I returned my focus to my cool water. *"I guess I wouldn't want you to eat other fae, either."*

"Break's over. Strip off the pads. Now that everyone is good and warm, let's do some hand-to-hand work," Hazel called.

My gaze snapped back to Nyx's. *"Please tell me I can spar with someone else?"*

"Not a chance unless you're better at hand to hand than you are with a sword, and somehow, I doubt it."

"Goddess, save me." The last thing I needed was to have his body pressed against mine.

172

His lips curled, spreading the grin across his smug face. "*I'll take that as a no.*"

"Do you have any training in hand to hand?" Hazel asked me when we returned to the mats.

"Not much. Only what went into disarming and some grappling. I didn't know it was part of the advanced class. Maybe I should spend time in the beginners until I'm proficient." I would do anything to avoid this.

"No, the sword play is more important, and you'll be bored in a lower level. Nyx will work with you outside of class to catch you up with hand to hand and knife work." Hazel gestured for Nyx to take over.

"Show me what you know of grappling so I can get an idea where to start," Nyx said, far too smugly. If only I had secret skills so I could put him on his back. I'd have to work hard to get there to not give him the enjoyment. Maybe Kol would help me, too.

I went over the drills I knew with my weapon, and then he had me put them together without a sword. Every movement brought us closer—his warm breath against my ear, his damp chest pressed into mine, hands pulling uniforms. Thankfully, my flush from the exercise hid the color in my cheeks.

I tried another move Luka had shown me, but Nyx was too quick.

He flipped me over and rolled on top of me, pinning me to the mat under him, nose to nose. "Nice try, Sol."

My mind instantly blanked of all the counter moves for a pin, filled instead with the way a fae his size could toss me around. Warmth stirred in my chest.

"*Naughty.*" He didn't move to get up.

I clamped down on the flow of my thoughts. I realized I was improving that skill. "*You can't possibly know what I'm thinking.*" I closed my eyes and tried to hook a leg around his hips to flip us.

He grinned down at me, thwarting the move with his weight alone. *"I don't need to know what you're thinking. I can sense other things."*

"Like what?" I tried to get a knee between us.

He pressed lower, not giving me an inch. *"I can scent it on you."*

"What?" Horror struck me cold.

His eyes gleamed. *"I'm sure you can put it together."*

"You're kidding?"

"Dragon senses are more sophisticated than your fae senses. We can see, hear, and smell things better."

Goddess, no! Did that mean that if I was—I could hardly think it—aroused, every dragon nearby would know it? I moved again like I was going to try and flip him, and when he tried to block me, I shoved a knee between us.

Nyx's reflexes were quicker, opening my knees and shifting to press his hips to mine. It was only for a half a second, but I felt everything...and we were in a hall full of fae.

We shot apart like magnets connected the wrong way, both on our feet, not making eye contact. Kol stifled a laugh, turning around to disguise it, while Hazel met my eyes, giving me a long, questioning look.

"I need some water," Nyx announced, like it wouldn't draw even more attention to us.

"I think that's enough for today. All of you go do a couple of laps around the outdoor track and then stretch out before you go." Hazel looked like she was going to say something else, but I slipped out the door with the other students before she could, not ready to face anyone.

TWENTY-ONE
ZARIA

I went back to my rooms after the laps, sweaty and in need of my bathing chamber, but as I turned into my corridor, I found Nyx sitting outside my door. He didn't follow to do the laps, so I figured we were done for the day.

When he saw me, he climbed to his feet, looking serious.

"Can we talk?" he asked as I approached.

"I need to clean up," I told him, hoping to brush him off.

"I can wait." He moved like he was going to return to the floor and wait out here.

The thought of everyone seeing him there was embarrassing somehow, so, reluctantly, I stopped him with a hand on his arm. "You can wait inside." My tone was begrudging.

I let us both in and went straight to my wardrobe for some fresh clothes. I ignored my comfort robes, like those I was raised in, instead picking some pants and a tunic like the other female trainees seemed to favor. Was I trying to impress Nyx? Goddess, I hoped not.

Nyx sat on the chair at my desk, looking worried.

"I won't be long," I told him before heading for the bathing chamber.

I washed quickly, unsettled by the knowledge that he was just on the other side of the door. Dressing in the unfamiliar clothes, I ran through all the things about today that could have him looking so worried.

When I returned, he was staring at his hands, deep in thought, and his head snapped up.

We just held each other's gazes for a beat before I broke the stare, turning to dispose of my dirty clothes in the laundry basket.

"I need to know that you won't reveal our secret," he said out of nowhere.

I spun to face him. " I thought you already pointed out that we have that trust in our connection. You know I won't betray you to anyone."

"I'm not worried about me, Sol. I need to know you'll extend that to my brother."

I didn't hesitate. "Of course. He is part of you."

Nyx's shoulders slumped with relief. This really was life and death.

"Can you tell me why it's such a secret?"

"Sit. You must be exhausted," he said, surprising me with his concern for my wellbeing.

I took a seat on the bed while he re-took his chair at the desk. I couldn't help thinking the distance was deliberate. He parted from me as quickly as I had from him in the sparring hall.

He gathered his thoughts before he spoke again, and I watched him.

"Twin dragons of old were born bonded, able to share thoughts, feelings, powers—every part of themselves. Through history, especially during wars, they were exploited—separated and used for espionage since they could share information over distance through their mind bond. It was a great advantage for any kingdom to have, and it constantly put twins in perilous situations. So many were lost across enemy lines, leaving their twin alone. The pain of losing your twin, Sol... I can't put into words what that must be like. I never want to find out."

"I can't imagine."

"Twin bonds haven't been known since the Hundred Years War. Perhaps the Goddess stopped gifting them to prevent any more twins from dying—who knows? But my father discovered ours when we were just boys, and he knew what it would mean for us if anyone ever found out. He knew he would have to be the one giving the orders that could see one or both of us put at risk. So, to protect us, he told us we could never reveal it to anyone. He made us make a vow." He looked into my eyes, and I knew how serious it was for him to tell me this. "I've never broken that vow and never told a soul...until you."

I gasped. "Will something happen now you've broken it?"

A small smile crept over his serious expression. "No, Sol. We are bonded, too. Our trust is built-in and can't be broken. You are the only person I ever could or would tell. I'm sure Kol told his ryder, too."

"So, if you know our trust can't be broken, why do you have to ask me to keep the secret?"

He stood abruptly, walking across the room. "Because I know I can't break it...but I don't know what you'll do. You could break it. It would expose us and put our lives at risk. It would bring up a lot of questions as to why we kept it to ourselves. But you might ultimately choose that rather than keep my secret." He faced me again, emotion in his eyes. "But I'm begging you not to do that, for Kol. Someday, I will be the general, and I will have to order him out there to be put in danger —more than he already is. And if he dies, Sol, under an order from me because I told our secret and it became known, then I will die too. I won't be able to live with that. I just won't."

I pushed to my feet and crossed over to him in three steps. I didn't think about my pride, holding back, or any of the nonsense that plagued my every thought since he took me from my village. I just acted from a place inside me that knew one thing for sure: this bond we had was more important than anything in all the kingdoms.

I took his face in my hands and looked deep into his watery eyes, stroking my thumb across his cheek to feel his skin against mine. It was a new sensation. I never felt anything when touching another person, but with him I felt everything: need, want, hope.

And it was all reflected back in his eyes.

"Your brother's safety is as important to me as yours. Your secret will never leave my lips, I swear it."

A beat passed…and then he moved.

Nyx closed the distance between our lips before pressing his to mine. My mouth parted for him automatically, and his tongue swept over mine, deepening the kiss. He hoisted me into his arms and wrapped my legs around his waist. When the wall met my back, he pressed against me fully, and this time, we did not jump apart. He moaned at the contact as he kissed me deeper.

He ground our hips together, the feeling of him hard against my core forcing a yearning sound from me as well. It shocked me, and I tore my lips from his, dragging in air. We were both panting, but he didn't release his hold, and I didn't try to escape him. We just stared.

What had we done?

TWENTY-TWO
NYX

After leaving Zaria's rooms, I walked around the palace aimlessly, feeling purposeless—something I had not felt since my father died.

I could not believe I had just crossed that line. I wanted her more than I could admit, even to myself. But this was bigger than my wants and needs.

Every minute I didn't have a functional ryder, I was allowing more flyers to fall to the Vestar. Their deaths sat on my shoulders. I felt every loss to my soul and knew I'd be weighed and measured for the failures in the afterlife. Even if it wasn't by the Goddess, it would be by my father, which meant I had to get Zaria up to speed with her training to take command. But I also knew it wasn't right to force it. No one learned well that way. I knew I was the issue, but I couldn't figure out how to stop being the damn problem and become the solution.

"Why are you pacing the halls like a kicked puppy?" My brother slipped into my head.

"Why are you awake?" I closed my eyes to enter his mind, finding him flying over the outer walls of the city on guard duty.

"As you can see…"

"I'll join you." I ditched my clothes on the nearest landing platform and took to the skies, flying north to the edge of the city.

Kol didn't change directions, knowing I'd catch up soon enough. We circled each other, riding the thermal lift to take us higher. We came out on top of the clouds. The moon was nearly full, making the tops of the clouds illuminate with the bright reflection. They shone on my brother's oil-slicked scales, emphasizing the purples and turquoises mixed into his coloring.

"You didn't answer me about the pacing. What happened?"

"Do you really want to hear about it?"

"Why wouldn't I?"

"Because she's your new best friend."

"You're my brother. You will always be half of my soul." Kol's mind voice carried more hurt than spoken words ever would.

"It feels like there is distance between us," I replied at length, not sure I could even describe how it felt. We'd always been close. I didn't want anything to drive a wedge into that.

"I thought you were giving me space so Zaria had a friend."

"I don't know what I'm doing moment to moment. I know she can't stand me, and I know that's my fault, but I can't seem to stop myself pushing her when I know it's the wrong move." I heard Kiera's words playing in repeat. *"Kiera says I'm acting like father."*

"Ouch!" Kol laughed. *"But she's right—you are,"* he added, not even trying to refute it or save my feelings."

Hearing him agree hurt, but I had known he would, and I

deserved it. *"I want to stop being an asshole, but how do I let up when fae are dying? I don't know what to do or to say to her. We seem to either be at each other's throats or all over each other."*

Kol's gaze burned into the side of my face.

"What?" I asked.

"Get on the fucking ground and explain yourself."

I dove, only spreading my wings when I was just above the ground to shift and land in a crouch.

Kol was on my tail, the beat of his massive wings blowing the waist-high grass around us before he landed an arms-length from me.

"Explain yourself," he demanded as soon as he straightened.

"Did we have to be on the ground to do this?" I asked, setting my hands on my bare hips.

"Yes, because I want to look into your eyes when you tell me something happened between you two and I'm just hearing about it."

"So you can punch me, more like." I huffed.

"Trust me, if you are screwing with that poor girl, I wouldn't bother punching your face when I could knock you out of the sky."

I smiled ruefully. "Damn, you sound like her brother, not mine. Relax. It's not all that."

But it was. I could still feel her body pressed into mine, and how right it felt. More right than any fae I'd ever touched, only confirming what I'd known since the first time I saw her.

"We kissed. She—" I exhaled heavily. "I love her."

Goddess, it was out there now, but telling him felt necessary. I couldn't take it back, and I didn't want to.

"I love her more than I thought possible, honestly. But I'm making her hate me."

"And doing a real good job of it, too. Like you're the expert arsehole." He rubbed a hand over his chest, looking to the heavens. Rays of moonlight cut through small gaps in the cloud cover, casting down all around us. The Night Kingdom was the most beautiful place in all the Twelve Kingdoms. I hated that we couldn't enjoy it more, living the way flyers did with the wars always over our heads.

"I know, I know. I wish it were as easy for me as it is for you. I'm losing her. She wouldn't even go to combat training today. She was supposed to meet Hazel and be assessed, but we had a fight, and she stormed off. She's frustrated with me, the situation, Rakan."

"Can you blame her? You're being an arse. Rakan's not exactly easy to deal with, either." Kol spoke like he had a bad taste in his mouth. "He's always put me off. I think he and Octavian are too close. I've never liked it."

I nodded, running over my interactions with Rakan in my head. "Do you think? I can't decide if Octavian is on my side anymore. I used to believe he wanted the best for me, but now it feels like he doesn't want to give me my place."

"Power corrupts, absolutely."

"Do you really think there can't be any good in someone in his position? I don't want to fall prey to that legacy when I take over my command." Why did politics have to seep into every aspect of our lives?

"I don't know. I don't like the way he handled the burning of Zaria's village. I tried to talk to our commander about it, but he said the order came from Octavian, and there was nothing he could have done. I just don't think it's right to destroy an entire community because of some wrongdoing there." Kol shook his head.

"It's been bothering me, too. I've wanted to bring it up to Octavian, but I've been too busy with Zaria."

He nodded. "You should. I don't want to be a part of a system that thinks that's okay. It shouldn't even be on the fucking table."

I stepped forward to put my hand on his shoulder. "It never would be if I were in command."

He nodded, letting his head hang heavy. I'd missed how much it was affecting him. "I know, which makes this worse. Zaria didn't deserve to be orphaned."

"You said some got away... could they be her family?"

He didn't lift his head, his grief bleeding from him. The war took from us all. "I don't know. The commander reported there weren't any survivors, which makes me think they found them, and I missed it. I thought they'd at least capture them and bring them in for questioning, but they didn't even do that. Why?"

"I don't know... but I am going to find out."

We were quiet for a long time before Kol spoke again. "You have to be on her side above all else. Even above mine. You need each other, and until you figure that out inside yourself, she's going to feel there is distance and conflict between you. You have to trust her like you're asking her to trust you." Kol met my eyes, his still that of his dragon. Bright and intense jade, just like mine. "You can't expect her to leap when you won't."

"You're right."

"I'm always right." Kol laughed.

"Thank you for being there for her."

He put his arm over mine and his hand on my shoulder, sealing us in the embrace. "You're welcome. But don't forget I'm here for you, too."

I squeezed him briefly before I let him go.

"Now, I'm going to go finish my duty so I can go fuck my ryder before he starts his day." Kol grinned, all teeth and mischief.

"Wait, he's not with you." I realized for the first time.

He gave me a 'no shit' look. "We're only back here for provisions and some training. So, he's on days with that ryder stuff, and they put the flyers on night watch duty since there's really nothing to do."

"Well, go get your morning delight, then."

"And you enjoy those blue balls until you learn to not be an arsehole." He took off before he could see my rude gesture.

TWENTY-THREE
NYX

I t was too easy to forget, at least for a few days, that there was a war waging out there—the very reason for the urgency to get Zaria trained. That was until they pulled me out of one of our training sessions to meet in the war room. It was already filled when I slipped in. The section leaders were all gathered around the large table in the center, which held a model of the Twelve Kingdoms, while the Regent gave an update.

"...northwestern front with no warning, which concerns me. We need to send troops to see if the outposts in the Second Kingdom are overrun."

"How could the outposts be overrun without some warning? We have systems in place for this," I asked as I stepped into a space at the opposite end of the map. "What about the fire signals?"

"I don't know." Concern pulled his harsh features. "They

either failed, or the outpost didn't have enough time to ignite theirs."

"None of the pyres were ignited?" I asked since I'd missed the first part of the brief and was lacking some context. We had a system of pyres to ignore across the border of the Twelve Kingdoms to alert for emergencies. They stretched all the way across every kingdom and were checked and manned around the clock. It was the responsibility of each of the barons to keep the pyres in their kingdom in working order.

"None of them. When the Third Flight went to relieve the Fifth Flight at the outpost, it was empty."

"Empty?" My voice was strained. The Fifth Flight was a unit with eight flyers and their ryders. Even if they'd been ambushed, they should have been able to hold off the attack long enough to ignite the pyres to warn the rest of the kingdom.

"Wait, you said the northwest? Not the southwest?" That information threw me. We didn't have any enemies in the northwest. There wasn't much inhabited land, and the North Sea created a harsh environment to live in. I chose my words carefully, knowing the gravity of what I had to ask, but I knew Octavian, and he was withholding something vital. "You don't think it was the Vestar, do you?"

Octavian fixed me with a stern look, confirming my hunch. Maybe he would have withheld longer, but I wasn't about hiding information or even theories. Our units out in the field deserved better. I might not be general yet, but I would still make sure that our kind were not hobbled by misinformation out on the front line.

He shook his head slowly. "I think it's the Vivi Mortui."

A gasp rippled through the room. Even I hadn't seen that coming.

I said what the entire room was thinking: "We haven't seen an attack from the Vivi Mortui since the Twelve Kingdoms were united."

"I know, but what else could it be? If it were the Vestar, surely there would be evidence of an attack. Even their death magic couldn't vanish an entire outpost overnight."

"When was the last time we heard from the outpost?" I placed both hands on the map, surveying the area, but I had it memorized. I didn't need to look. I knew we had nearly a hundred lives there.

"Four days ago. The Third Flight arrived two days ago."

"And we're just hearing of it?" I said through gritted teeth.

"They had to conduct a full area search before reporting. You know the protocol, Private Asar, or do you need a refresher course while you are back in the trainee program?"

I had struck a nerve, and Octavian was not someone to cross, no matter who he was to my family. I wasn't surprised he would take the opportunity to remind me, along with the entire command, that I held no rank, nor was I even through training on paper.

But I didn't take his bait and ignored the derision. I stepped around the group to get a better look at the villages around the outpost. "Did they fall back?"

"They did—to the village here." The Regent used his magic to point to a village two hours inland from the outpost.

"It's got to be safer there for now." Or at least I hoped. If we were dealing with the Vivi Mortui, it was completely unknown. They were the reason the Twelve Kingdoms originally united. To defeat the undead enemy, we had to come together. The last time we fought them, we had an abundance of dragons and lost far too many driving the Vivi Mortui back into the sea. If they were back during a time when we were bleeding dragon lives, what hope did we have against them?

"I'm sure the commander of the Third Flight had similar thoughts."

"What of the missing outpost residents?"

"No trace," the Regent replied curtly and stepped back to sit in his chair. "I'm open to ideas on how we move forward before I bring this to the King."

Soft chatter broke out in the room among the advisers.

I closed my eyes, trying to rationalize. The North Sea bordered most of the Second Kingdom and was a bitterly cold place this time of year. It didn't get much better in the height of summer. No realms beyond the freezing waters had reason enough to risk the crossing for an attack. If the Vestar braved the North Sea to surprise us from that side of the realm, I couldn't imagine why. Even so, the undead army? I couldn't fathom that, either.

"*Kol?*" I spoke to my brother through the bond.

"*Yes?*" he answered quickly but seemed distracted.

"*Can you go find Zaria to make sure she's safe?*"

"*Sure. What's going on?*" he asked, and I heard him make excuses to the fae he was with.

I filled him in on the basics. It was only a matter of time before it spread around the palace.

"*What do you think of all this?*" Kol asked in my mind.

"*I don't know. I have a hard time imagining the Vestar ships making the voyage.*" They had one of the best navies in all the realms, but no one built boats to withstand the North Sea for long. It froze often, and the shifting ice plateaus broke up even the best wood and craftsmanship.

"*Did you know any of the flyers at the outpost? Who was assigned there?*" Kol wasn't privy to the movement and assignment reports I was, being on the council.

I nodded before I realized I had eyes on me. "*Two of them were in our training year.*"

"*Goddess. Who?*"

"*Torrence and Atara.*"

"*How many flyers?*" Kol asked solemnly.

"*Eight, at least. But I haven't seen the—*"

"*EIGHT!*" The pain in his voice hit me in the chest.

"I know. It's a colossal blow."

"In a time when we get fewer dragons every year..." Kol sent me a mental image of Zaria sitting in the mess hall. *"She's safe."*

"Thank you. I know it's irrational..." But I had a gut feeling we were facing something we couldn't explain, and everything in me said to protect Zaria. I couldn't put my finger on why.

"Nyx," the Regent said, beckoning me forward.

"Yes, sir?" I approached his seat, clasping my hands behind my back.

"I know you can't really afford to be away from your ryder and training right now, but I need an impact report and a threat assessment in the next hour for the King. He will want to reinstate the outpost, so we need to know what kind of enemy we are facing."

"I understand. I'll get to it right away."

Fuck. Hours of work and answers for questions we didn't even know how to ask now had to be ready to hand over to the King in one hour. How could I propose a solution with an unknown enemy? An impossible task, and I knew it wasn't to screw me. The Regent trusted me, and I would have his input, but if we put another unit there, would it end in more lives lost? Could we even hold the ground? We could not protect that front if we lost the outpost. The kingdom's security required a strictly maintained series of defenses and warning systems. Leaving it empty could lead to an enemy force getting a foothold in the Second Kingdom and unspeakable loss of life without us even knowing. And if the Vivi Mortui were behind the attacks... I couldn't even bring myself to imagine.

I rubbed my forehead as I took my usual desk in the Regent's library. Half an hour later, I hadn't come up with any sort of real solution for how we could combat an enemy we couldn't identify. If it was the Vivi Mortui, we had the entire history of the war to consult. Detailed battle plans which had been used to successfully to defeat them the first time. But I poured over old texts about the war, and they had never wiped out anything without leaving a trail. They killed indiscriminately, then consumed our dead to absorb our magic, but they weren't quick in their ritual task.

We also didn't know when the outpost went down. It could have been any time in those two days, but still, two days was not enough time for the Vivi Mortui to consume a hundred dead and leave no sign. And with a full flight of flyers present, there should have been a battle, so there would be signs of that at least, right?

If there were enough undead, I guessed anything would be possible. Could they have spent the few centuries amassing a force capable of such destruction?

I scratched out the last line I'd written and tossed the parchment aside.

I knew what I had to write, but I also knew what it would do. We'd have to move two more flights to the Second Kingdom, leaving the First and Sixth vulnerable to the Vestar. We didn't have enough flyers to fight on two fronts, and we'd have to send as many dragons as possible to the Second Kingdom if it was the Vivi Mortui, because the dead didn't stay dead unless they were made ash. Dragon fire was one of the only ways to penetrate the magic and get enough heat to burn them.

Fifteen minutes later, I met the Regent in his office.

"Tell me you have something."

"I do, but neither you nor the King is going to like it."

"Brief me before we take it to the King."

I filled him in on my recommendation and found that he'd come to much the same conclusion.

"I hoped you would see something I missed." He nodded, processing the information before shoving to his feet. "We have to brief the King."

"We?"

"Yes. Your ryder is here now, so you will take over your duties eventually. Better to be in it from the start than to be handed a war in the middle."

Maybe he wasn't trying to block my taking over the command after all.

"Can I ask you something?" I said as we waited for our audience with the King.

"Go ahead." Octavian nodded.

"Why was the entire village destroyed in the Fifth Kingdom?"

"Why are you bringing this up?" he asked, like it was insignificant.

"It was an entire community. There were females and children there." He didn't say anything, so I went on. Maybe I hadn't made my point clear enough. "It felt excessive. We could have burned the Dragon's Bane and taken the males into custody so they could be tried for their crimes."

"We have to stomp out all extremism. The whole village helped to cultivate and grow the Dragon's Bane. Those extreme religious views are dangerous, and if they aren't stopped they will keep growing their crops and spreading their poisoned ideals. They will kill all the flyers if we let them. We can't leave half of it to come back. We have to get it by the roots."

"I disagree." The loss felt so monumental and wrong, but arguing with him in this moment felt like starting a fight that would blow up in my face. I had to be careful with our dealings until I had the command. With outposts falling and lives lost, he could make the argument I wasn't up to leading if I wasn't going to protect our people.

I would make changes when I took over, and he couldn't stop me.

TWENTY-FOUR
NYX

"W here are you?" I reached out to my brother's mind as I stormed toward the main library.

He sounded exhausted when he replied, "*I just finished a pointless formation exercise with the new flight trainees. I don't know why they get us involved when they are that green. It's just to parade the famous flyers around for inspiration, I assume, but it's a colossal waste of my time.*"

"*Can you meet me in the main library?*"

"*Now? I stink.*"

"*What's new? Just meet me. I need you to do something for me.*"

"*I'll have you know I always smell fantastic, thank you.*"

"*It's not something you can mask with your cologne, brother, trust me.*"

"Good luck with your library mission," he mocked as I felt him pull away.

I rolled my eyes. *"Wait! Please. I could really do with your help."*

He grumbled, but I could feel that it was with love. *"Fine. Is there anything else you need, General, or will my presence be enough for now?"*

"Yes. Can you stop by and see of Kiera can join us, too?" I *hadn't found anything in the healer's library, but I was sure she could help me sift through stuff in the main library.*

"Unbelievable," I heard him mutter before he blocked our connection.

I arrived at the library and got straight to pulling texts. By the time Kol and Kiera arrived, I was at a table with a couple of books open and three neat stacks beside me.

"Here we are. What couldn't wait for me to bathe?" Kol asked as he peeled off his jacket and took a seat opposite me.

Kiera pinched her nose, pulling a chair slightly away from him and sitting. "Goddess, spare me. You do smell."

"I warned him. Apparently, this couldn't wait."

Kiera turned her attention to me. "What's going on?"

"I'm going out of my mind," I told her. "Zaria still has no powers. Rakan still won't clear us to fly until they show themselves in case she can dampen and takes me out in an uncontrolled burst."

Kiera frowned. "Is that likely?"

"It's possible, but I doubt it. She's from this kingdom, we think, but if she was born near the border of the Fourth and Fifth Kingdom, there's a chance. The issue is she is showing no power whatsoever, and he doesn't trust her around the future leader of dragon kind." I rolled my eyes at that. "Until she proves she's not a risk."

Kol leaned forward. "But even if her main power is dampening, you'd be able to manage it if she had an outburst. You have some dampening in your blood, and you have intuition, not to mention the control of gravity you have from your night bloodline. Surely, he realizes that? After all, you are the 'strongest dragon in generations'." He used air quotes to mock his own words.

"I don't know what his problem is, but we are grounded until she has her powers and can wield them properly, and I don't have endless time for that to happen."

"Zaria will be as powerful as you are—let's not forget that. If she comes into her power suddenly, don't forget her age, either. It's going to be her full power all at once. Not the first powers of a child," Kiera countered. "I know you can manage most things, Nyx, but could you really manage that in the air if it took you by surprise? I'm not saying Rakan isn't being over cautious, but there is a risk."

"That's the thing. I don't think she could take me by surprise. Our bond is getting stronger every day, and I think if she was about to come in to that much power, I'd sense it. I could land us safely; I'm sure of it."

"So, what's your plan?" Kiera asked. I knew she was really asking what role she would be playing in it.

I glanced around to check we were not being observed, then swiveled the ancient book to face her. I tapped the page, and Kiera's brows lifted.

"Can you make this for me?" I whispered.

Kol leaned over to look and whistled.

Kiera nodded and pushed the book back toward me, closing as she did so the potion was no longer visible to any nosy passersby. She had her own copies of just about every potion's text in existence in her personal collection, so I knew she wouldn't need to check out this volume and potentially get caught. Not that a recipe was available anywhere. That kind of magic was outlawed during the unification of the kingdoms, but

Kiera had access to things that should not exist. She could make it happen.

"It will take me a few days to get what I need," she told me quietly.

"Thank you," I said, sincerely.

"And what am I doing in this mission?" Kol asked, knowing there was more.

I checked our surroundings again. I wished I could tell him through our bond, but we had never told a soul until Zaria. That included even our closest friends. After a group of trainees passed our table, I lowered my voice to a whisper. "I need you to get me a dampening night stone."

Kol sat back in his chair, never taking his eyes off mine. "You understand that's completely illegal, right?" he said low and slow.

I shook my head, exasperated. "And you'll never convince me there's a point in that law when fae are born with that power but they are allowed to exist."

"Yes, but few are powerful enough to cause significant harm, and the only reason for acquiring a stone like that is for nefarious purposes. You could render the entire city helpless for a week with one stone if wielded by a strong enough fae." He looked at me pointedly, suggesting I had that level of power.

"It's just insurance—I hope not to have to use it—and I plan to take her to the Shadow Valley, well away from other fae. If I'm forced to use it, no one will be harmed."

"So, that's the plan? Take her away so you can rush her training in secret? You know they will notice if their highest profile trainees just disappear."

"You let me worry about that. I need to get her flying. I can't waste any more time. I'm left with no choice."

"What do you mean?" my brother asked, a frown pulling at his dark brows. "You have time. Octavian is working out well, and no one is expecting you to suddenly have a proficient ryder after what you have both gone through. She needs time and care. Don't fuck this up."

"I'm not fucking it up." I didn't like the stance he had taken against me. We'd always been a united pair, almost the same person with as much time as we spent in each other's heads. Now, for the first time in our lives, it felt like he was shifting his allegiance. "I know what I'm doing."

"Is that so?"

I huffed.

"You two are like younglings, the way you bicker," Kiera scolded. Her expression was fond, though. "I need to check on a patient. I'll leave you to it and get to work on that *energy tonic* for your ryder."

I thanked her, and she wafted her hand over her nose. "And you—take a bath," she told Kol.

He pulled out his shirt and took a sniff, grimacing.

"I don't like the way you have Zaria's back over mine," I grumbled after Kiera left.

He scowled. "You don't really believe that, do you?"

"It's starting to feel that way."

Kol rested his forearms on the table, leaning forward. "I would do anything for you, you know that." He jabbed his finger into the tabletop. "Including care for your ryder when you are clearly incapable of doing so because you have your head up your arse."

"I do not," I objected.

"Really? Because you sure aren't giving the impression you have any clue how to make peace, which you know is the only way to start making any progress as a bonded pair. I mean, sure you can just carry on pissing each other off, but you'll never meld fully like that. And that's not your destiny, is it, brother?"

I shrugged, determined not to give away that I knew it wasn't. I rocked back on my chair, trying to seem unaffected.

Kol laughed. He could see straight into my damned soul, I

would swear.

"You have a real chance to have a meld so perfect, your powers will become one if you do this right. A bond like yours runs deeper than flyer and ryder. You might fool everyone else, but not me. I saw what's between you in only a moment."

"Is that right?" I tried not to look found out.

"Believe it," he pressed. "Maybe instead of putting all your energy into standing your ground and trying to work around the rules to get her flying, you should be figuring out how to make her feel valued and supported. You realize she is forever, right?

"Goddess! Are you sure? I thought I could exchange her at the ryder store if I didn't like her."

"I sometimes wonder how we are related." He sighed. "All I'm saying is, if you stopped being your stubborn self, maybe you could find a way to meld more than just your powers." He quirked a brow.

I dropped my chair back onto four legs, my hands balling into fists at my sides. "What do you suggest... I sleep with my ryder? I seem to remember you telling me when she first arrived that I should keep my charms to myself. That's what I'm doing."

Kol scoffed and rubbed his tongue against his cheek. "That was when she first arrived. This is now. I can feel the bond between you, so please don't play me for a fool like you would everyone else in the kingdom. At this point, I think it would serve you better to be charming rather than hostile. And you both could benefit from getting it out of your system. Orgasms put everyone in a better mood."

I made a crude gesture at him. "It's a shame I'm not like you. I'm the surly twin, remember?"

"You made that choice. You can blame me for a lot of things, big brother, but not your personality." The worst part about Kol was his ability to let everything roll off his back while wearing a smile, then so easily return the insult ten-fold.

"It's not my fault my ryder was taken from me."

"No, but it is your fault you turned in to a grumpy bastard when she wasn't instantly delighted to finally reunite with you, so lighten up."

"I will lighten up as soon as I find what's blocking her magic and deal with it."

"How about you just try to stop driving her away for a start?"

"She will leave as soon as she has a choice—mark my words. That is why I have no time to waste getting her trained and melding our magic. She's only here now because I promised she could leave once she helps me. This needs to happen before I lose her again, and for good this time."

Kol's frown came back. "Then what? You'll be bonded, melded in every way, and she thinks she can walk away from that?"

"She doesn't understand what any of it means. She only sees a way to leave."

"And where will that leave you? Ryderless again, and no better off than you were before."

"No. I'll have our melded powers. I'll be able to assume control of the Dragon Council, and I won't need a ryder to be a general. Many have held the position long after they have lost their ryders. They just don't lead from the front; they lead from here. I'll figure it out."

He shook his head. "This isn't the way."

"I am out of choices." And running out of time. My gut told me that if she went back and found the bodies of her family, she would follow them to the Valley of the Dead rather than carry on, and I couldn't risk losing her like that before we melded. Too much rested on me gaining what was mine by birth.

Kol shook his head, clearly listening to my thoughts.

"Get out of my head."

"You catch more ryders with honey than with whatever this broody shit is."

"And to think I came to you for help with fixing things," I muttered under my breath.

"That was your first mistake." Kol broke out laughing.

I let him laugh it out, secretly wishing I had it in me to be like him.

He collected himself finally. "Look, I don't think, deep down, she really hates you. She could blame me for what happened to her family, but she doesn't."

I stared at him. "Did she tell you that? What did she say?"

"I can't tell you."

"Are you kidding me?"

"I'm not betraying her trust."

"You're my brother."

"Which doesn't mean I'll be a bad friend, especially when it looks like I'm the only one she thinks she's got. You should know me better than that."

I was speechless. Kol stood and picked up his jacket.

"I'm going to go bathe and then look into sourcing some contraband for this stubborn idiot I know. I'll see you in the weapons hall for a trainee session tomorrow. Hazel wants us back.

Apparently, we went down well with her trainees." He flipped his jacket over his shoulder and sauntered away.

Bastard.

I watched him until he turned the corner and then dropped my forehead to the table, banging it five times. When I lifted my head, I noticed a couple of ryder trainees eyeing me curiously. When they met my eyes, they lowered their heads and quickly turned in the opposite direction.

I dragged myself out of my seat and gathered the books into my arms. I had already checked them out, so I carried them out of the library and headed for Zaria's room. She would not be there now, which was for the best, but I would leave them outside for her to find later.

TWENTY-FIVE

ZARIA

A fter another futile week of sessions with Rakan, I had a headache setting in from the mental strain of trying to find a place in my body and mind that magic somehow existed, unbeknown to me. It was like I was blind to a part of myself everyone else seemed to think I had. A phantom limb or third eye. It was starting to feel like I was trapped in my own personal Valley of the Dead. I was surrounded by strangers who were all trying to convince me this thing was real, and it wasn't.

What made it worse was this was what I'd always wanted—a life of my own outside my tiny world, freedom to learn things, like how to defend myself, and to dress how I liked. I'd dreamed of all these things while stuck in our little village, so why did I hate it so much?

Because it was all out of my control. They were things happening to me rather than things happening for me like I'd wished. And maybe this was all punishment for always chasing for more than I had. Maybe I should have just been satisfied.

"Your thoughts are loud."

"You could not listen," I snapped.

He took a seat in one of the armchairs in a cozy nook inside the main library. I'd asked him to show me it after I found all the books he'd left by my door yesterday, so I could come whenever I wanted to. I was in awe of the space but wasn't fully appreciating it because, as usual, I was verbally sparring with my so-called partner.

"You could block me."

"Or you could mind your own business and let me enjoy this magnificent library."

"It's a little hard to do that when you're screaming at me, mind to mind." Amusement filtered through his expression.

I closed my eyes and reformed the dam like he'd shown me. It was easier to do when it was my sole focus. I felt like I was being pulled apart at times, constantly being told to block my mind one moment but open myself up the next.

"Better," he said aloud, like he was the personal judge of my struggles.

"Can you just *not* for like a day. One single day. I need a break." The more I tried to use that part of myself, the more my head seemed to hurt.

"I don't know why you're mad at me for wanting to help you." Nyx rested his elbows on his knees and put his head in his hands.

"Because you're not helping me; you're judging me."

"I'm not." He didn't raise his head.

I rolled my eyes and sank lower into my seat. "Do you think it's fun to have someone listening to your thoughts all day and all night?"

"I've had it my whole life. I don't know any other way," he said in my mind in case there were any listeners.

"It's different when it's someone who has your back."

His head came up, and his wings flickered into view. "If you don't think I have your back, I don't know what we have. I don't know how to get it across to you—I'm on your side. I need you, Sol. We are an extension of each other. One doesn't work without the other. Aside from my brother, there is no one in the Twelve Kingdoms I'd protect more. Even if you hate me, even if you don't want anything to do with magic, our lives are tied. Our fates are tied. I will always have your back no matter how you feel about me. There is no other way for me to exist."

I didn't know what to say to him. It wasn't often Nyx left me speechless. My chest ached. I knew I was straddling the line between my two worlds, and I'd have to choose or they'd both destroy me. Why was I so resistant to this place when it was all the freedom I'd ever craved?

"I just need a break. My head hurts after every one of those sessions. I feel like I'm getting nowhere. Do you know how awful it is to feel like a failure day in, day out?"

Nyx let out a bitter laugh. "I know better than you think. Day after day, I get asked by the Regent and the King about our progress and feel my failures in their silence. It's my fault your magic isn't coming out."

"Then, what do we do?" I asked, half to myself, half under my breath, needing a miracle from the Goddess.

"Maybe we should start over."

"What do you mean?"

He got to his feet and offered me his hand. "We need a change of scenery."

"What? We have arms training in less than an hour. We don't have time to go anywhere."

"We're playing hooky today. I'll have Kol make an excuse to Hazel. Come on."

I took his hand. It felt strange to accept it without resistance, and his face told me he was thinking the same.

He pulled me out of my chair and led me from the library, down the hall, and to the dragon landing. There was one on every floor, all through the palace. They looked like large outdoor terraces without rails, but I quickly learned they weren't a space to lounge in the sun as they were frequently used by all nature of flyers in the palace.

"What are we doing?"

Nyx opened a cupboard beside the landing door, and I noticed a well-stocked supply of those soft pants he seemed to love wearing around—to taunt me, I assumed. This must be where the flyers could dress after they shifted—a term I'd learned from my new books—and it looked as though there were a good number of shirts available, too. Who knew? Nyx sure seemed to miss those when he was dressing after a flight.

The wind whipped through the landing door and tossed my hair as a stark reminder of the heights the palace reached.

"Trust me." Nyx's wings formed while the rest of him began to flicker. He plucked a heavy-looking leather jacket from the cupboard and handed it to me. I took it, puzzled. "It gets cold up there. Put it on," he instructed.

I balked. "But we aren't allowed to fly."

He took a cloth satchel from a hook and stripped off his clothes, with no care of who might see. I looked away, pulling on the jacket, and ignoring the amused sound he made.

"I can keep a secret if you can." He handed me the bag, now filled with his clothes. "I want to show you something. Trust me. Please."

I was doing a good job of not looking at him naked, and I prayed to the Goddess that was not what he meant to show me.

TWENTY-SIX

NYX

I n truth, I never really expected her to say yes, so when she put the jacket on, I had to hide my shock. She was really trusting me. It gave me hope for the first time since I landed in the healer's wing with her.

She took a deep breath, steeling herself, and seemed to come to terms with the fact I was naked. She would get over it because she was going to see naked flyers a lot once she was allowed in flight training. Even though I hoped she never looked at them the way she tried so hard not to look at me.

"Where are we going?" She had a nervous expression but a sparkle in her eye that said she wanted the adventure.

My lips pulled back from my teeth as I grinned, letting more of my dragon show. "Anywhere but here."

She shook her head, but she was fighting a smile. She was truly lovely.

"You know you want to," I urged. We were both smiling, and it felt right. This was how it should be between us. I just didn't know how to keep it this way.

"*Sure you do,*" my brother's voice came into my head, crashing straight through the moment I was having with Zaria. "*Just don't be, you know...you.*"

"Stop listening in!" I couldn't do this with an audience. Was I really so rattled by this sudden shift between us that I was broadcasting to my brother without knowing?

"*What do you tell her all the time? Stop screaming in my head,*" Kol replied with a laugh.

Fuck him. I mentally kicked the door shut in his face and locked it tight.

"We have to hurry before anyone sees us, Sol," I pressed, seeing her mood change in her eyes.

"Fine. But this doesn't mean I trust you with everything."

"Of course not." I wouldn't give her any more time to argue. Letting my spirit take the shape of my dragon, my bulk filled the entire launch pad around her. I stayed low on my belly, so she'd be able to get onto my back. "*Climb up.*"

"Just climb up? Like it's that easy to navigate scales and spikes?"

I laughed.

"How will I hold on? Don't I need a saddle?" She looked like a child standing next to a tree for the first time, not sure how to. It was endearing, and so funny.

"*No one is watching, Sol. Grab a hold near my front leg and do it. You can climb, can't you?*"

"I've seen it done."

"*You weren't allowed to climb trees? You were robbed of a childhood.*"

"I was always too sick. I usually just watched the others do it. Anyway, what would you know about it? You can just poof into a dragon and fly."

"Because it's fun?"

"Well, I had to find other ways to have fun."

"Then, you're welcome for showing you what real fun is."

She rolled her eyes. "I wasn't thanking you."

"I know, but you should."

She half lifted her leg and wrinkled her nose. It was cute, but I kept the thought to myself, not wanting to discourage her. "This is a trick, isn't it?"

"How would it be a trick?"

"I don't know, but it feels like a trick. Do fae really just climb onto dragon's backs? Who invented this? Who even thought it was a good idea to mount a monster?"

This time, I couldn't hold back my laugh. *"We are fae just like you."*

"So you claim, and then you do this." She waved her hand at my scales. "And then you say 'trust me,' and that's supposed to be enough to charm a maiden onto on your back?"

"How am I doing?" I brought my face near hers.

She swatted in my direction. "After kidnapping me, I might add."

"Maybe focus on climbing before you fall off the landing and break your pretty face."

Her cheeks pinked. She liked me calling her pretty. "Shut it and let me focus."

I mentally sealed my lips, waiting for her to try and get a leg up.

She lifted the strap of the bag over her head and settled it across her body, and after an awkward minute, she made it up to my back.

"Now what?" she asked, getting comfortable on the flat plane between my shoulder blades.

"Hold on to the spikes."

"That's it? There are no more safety precautions than 'hold on, good luck'?" Fear crept into her words.

"Theoretically, magic helps us. A bit like magnets. But since ours isn't melded yet, and really, you have none to speak of, maybe pray to the Goddess?"

"You want me to pray to stay on? That's your advice?"

I could feel her losing her nerve, so I launched into the air before she could jump off.

Fingers dug at my scales, finding grips on my spikes. "What are you doing?" she shrieked.

"Flying, last time I checked."

"I'm going to f—" The wind cut her off mid-scream

I rumbled a laugh. *"Sol, I can hear you much better if you say it in here?"*

"I said I'm going to fall!" she repeated in an equally loud scream right into my mind. I cringed, but it was too funny.

"Don't laugh! I'm going to fall off, and then you'll have to explain why I'm splattered on the palace wall when they said not to fly. Goddess, save me!" She grabbed at different places, trying to find the most secure way to hold on.

"Try to relax, Sol," I said, beating my wings to get above the palace quickly. It was a steep climb that I knew would terrify her, but I wanted to get clear of the grounds as fast as possible. We really should have walked out and launched from a place outside the palace, but I was in the moment. Now I just wanted to leave without anyone spotting Zaria on my back.

"Relax? Are you out of your mind?" She held on for her life, grappling against gravity as we climbed.

I wouldn't break her focus by telling her she was doing an amazing job holding on. This was no beginner flight, and she was doing great. It was like magic kept her in her seat, but I didn't feel it between us no matter how hard I tried to reach out to it.

When I hit the altitude I wanted, I leveled out. For a moment, she went less rigid. Then I banked away from the palace.

She screamed, and I laughed.

"You're safe, Sol. It's my job to keep you on until we get better. I told you that you have to trust me."

She brought her fist down on my back. *"Bastard!"*

"So angry today. You really should work on that."

"Goddess," Zaria gasped, voice trembling.

"Too high?" A lot of ryders had to overcome a fear of heights when they began.

"No. It's beautiful up here."

"Do you not remember from when we flew in?"

"I was hardly in the right mind to appreciate it then. This is incredible."

I smiled, closing my eyes to cherish the moment. This was better than I had even hoped. *"The First Kingdom is breathtaking. Actually, all of the Twelve Kingdoms are."* I banked away from the city, turning toward the mountains.

"I want to see it all. No wonder you love to fly." She leaned over, throwing us off balance.

I had to quickly bank the opposite direction so she didn't tumble off my back. *"Woah, there! You need to keep your center of gravity over me so you don't fall off."*

"I thought you said it was your job to keep me on," she said in a teasing tone.

"With your help. Goddess, help me." I stretched my wings out to soar, riding the thermals. *"I can't keep a girl with a death wish on my back if she doesn't will it."*

Zaria laughed musically, much more amused by the idea of falling than a new ryder should be. *"What would you do if I fell?"*

"Nose dive and catch your arse."

"Could you really catch me?"

"Yes." I would not admit that I'd never expected her to hold on so well. I thought she would inevitably fall, and then I would simply catch her and carry her like I had when I brought her here. She would curse me all the way to the Shadow Valley, but

she would never be in any real danger. But she was continuing to surprise me.

"How do you know?"

"Practice. We're born with our wings. I've been flying since I could walk. A falling fae is easy to catch. Just ask my brother."

"You've dropped Kol?" She sounded horrified.

"Sol, think about what kind of trouble a wild adolescent boy can get up to when unsupervised, then add wings and a play-mate. I've dropped and caught many a thing. We came up with all sorts of games when left to our own devices."

"By the Goddess!"

"It also made us two of the best flyers in the Twelve King-doms. Probably part of the Goddess' divine plan, and why dragons are sometimes blessed to be twins."

"I can only imagine."

"Be thankful. It was also good practice for catching foolish ryders who unseat themselves to get a better view."

She made a little harrumph sound.

We flew in silence for a while. She wasn't using words, but her awe was palpable. I took us to the ridge of the mountain range that sat beyond the city, and once we crested it, I fell into a dive into the valley.

Zaria startled, but her body didn't seize like it had when we launched. She just held on tighter. I could feel her trust growing in me, and she let out a shriek that was a whoop of excitement rather than fear.

This was just what we needed. I could feel the bond between us strengthening.

I leveled out and soared low over the tranquil lake on the valley floor, the water stirring as we rushed above its surface. The valley was stunning at this time of day, the sun casting half of it in shadow and half in intense afternoon light. It was like two worlds, dark and light, existing side by side like oil and water. A stark contrast, the strength of the light not diluting the darkness but rather sharpening it.

"Beautiful," she sighed softly in my mind. I felt her wonder. For the first time, I was starting to feel…maybe not happiness, but definitely sparks of it. It was positive energy where my soul met hers. Hope filled me, but I pushed it down. There was so much resting on this plan, and I had to get her to agree first.

I wouldn't break her joy yet. She was ryding like a natural, even without magic assisting her. We had time for some fun before I had to ask her to trust me on a whole new level.

TWENTY-SEVEN

ZARIA

F lying felt like breathing for the first time. It felt like freedom and tasted like a life just out of reach. But maybe, just maybe, if I stood on my tiptoes and grasped, I'd get a hold of it.

Nyx flew in a wide circle over the lake. We soared in the sun, his wing tip slicing through the water when he flew us low and switched back so that we raced headlong into the darkness. This was pure joy. There was no other word for it. It was the rightest thing I had felt in my life, and I couldn't control the way it lit me up inside and spilled out into occasional sounds of exhilaration and a huge smile.

Guilt threatened in passing moments, but the feeling of rightness fought it away. There was time for grieving, but this was right, and I wouldn't keep holding myself back.

"What are you thinking up there, Sol?"

"You mean you aren't hearing it all loud and clear?"

"No, not your thoughts, just your emotions. I can feel how much you like this. I just wanted to know what's going through your head." He paused. *"You're surprised. I feel that now."*

"I'm not trying to block you. I was too caught up in flying to make sure I was stopping the river in my mind."

He was quiet.

"What is it?"

"I don't know. Maybe this is bringing your magic on."

"Flying?" He had settled into an easy rhythm, taking us higher around the valley.

"That's part of it. Being together and strengthening our bond is the important thing."

"We've seen each other every day," I argued, not seeing his point.

"We haven't exactly been bonding, though, have we?"

Guilt slammed into me.

"Don't do that."

"Do what?"

"I just told you I could feel your emotions, and you just let guilt overtake everything you were feeling. It's not your fault, it's mine. I should have handled things differently. You needed me, and I've been an arsehole."

I couldn't believe his words. Was this real or another trick to have me do his bidding? Even as I thought it, though, I knew it was real. *"It wasn't all you. I've been just as bad. It's a lot to accept that everything I knew is gone, and I want to grieve that loss. I am. But the more I learn, the more I believe you when you say it was all a lie. It's hard to know if I should be devastated or angry."*

"Which is why I should have been more supportive. I'm truly sorry."

I sighed. *"Look, it was both of us. We're both dealing with a whole mess of things we can't control, and we took that out on each other. But don't start being all sweet. It's freaking me out."*

I felt the rumble of his laughter through his scales. *"Noted, Sol."*

We flew in silence for a while, and I tried to find a place I could exist between grief and hope.

What did I want?

I didn't want to return to my old world. My eyes had been opened, and I couldn't go back to a life without magic, even if I had none of my own. I liked this place and the fae. Here, females could do what they wanted, could be anything they wanted. I'd seen it. I couldn't give that idea up now. It would be like going back to a cage for the rest of my life after experiencing outside of it.

It was being alone here that was the hardest thing to cope with. My past life was just gone. Any love I had, any support I needed, gone. And in this whole new world, it didn't feel like there was a place for me. They were a family. They had each other's love and support. They didn't need to make room for me. But they had, I reminded myself. It was there. I just wasn't letting myself feel it.

Choosing this life meant leaving my other behind. Was I brave enough?

It came down to trusting the fae I had around me now. Trusting them to catch me if I fell. It gave me an idea.

"Nyx?"

"Yes?"

"Have you ever lied to me?"

"Never."

"So, I really met you when I was young?"

"Yes, Sol, and I've carried that memory of you all these years."

"And you are sure I'm the one? Your ryder?"

"*Certain,*" he said resolutely, making a turn to fly us over the lake. "*You just have to trust me.*"

I did. I knew it in my heart. I just needed to prove it to myself and to him.

Before I could change my mind, I took hold of the spikes around his neck and raised myself to a crouch on his back.

"*Sol! What are you doing?*"

"*Trusting you,*" I breathed.

And then I leapt.

A roar drowned out the rushing wind as I fell.

His scream of "*Sol!*" in my mind was gut-wrenching, and fear rushed through our bond.

I'd jumped over the water. If he couldn't catch me, I hoped I would survive the fall, but there was no guarantee, and it was going to hurt.

I twisted and turned, not knowing which way was up, my limbs wheeling. Then I caught sight of the water rushing toward me. It was suddenly so close I knew I'd made a mistake.

I braced for the water, closing my eyes, and holding my breath.

A crushing grip closed around my torso, snatching me from the air, and my descent abruptly stopped. A taloned claw held me, inches from slamming into the water. I jerked with the change of direction, and groaned at the pain it caused. It had not been the gentle dive and catch I'd imagined. But he had me.

I opened my eyes, and the shore was upon us. It was too late to land.

We were going to crash.

Everything went dark, and we rolled. I could hear the sounds of impact on shale, and we rolled and bumped. It all happened so quickly.

Then... silence.

TWENTY-EIGHT

NYX

I blinked and found myself looking at the sky. The rocky beach beneath my back was a reminder of the horror that had just happened.

Sol!

I unwrapped my wings from around my body and revealed her, looking dazed but whole in my tight grip.

I eased my claws open, and she sat up, her eyes shooting to mine.

Relieved she was okay, I let my head fall back to the ground and let out a sigh that carried with it a stream of smoke.

"Are you okay?" she gasped, sounding terrified, and somewhere inside, it pleased me to know she was worried after what she just put me through.

When I didn't answer right away, she scrambled up to clasp

my huge face in her tiny hands. "Nyx, talk to me. Are you okay?"

Was I okay? Was she kidding me?

I blinked, then rolled. The movement was so fast, she was under me before she knew what happened. I towered over her, nostrils smoking in rage. She scurried back, and I advanced until we were nose to nose.

"*Are you out of your mind?*" I bellowed into her head before I pushed away, stalking across the shore, then turned and advanced on her again. "*What were you thinking? You could have DIED!*"

She shrank back, and I cooled down immediately, remembering too late that I wasn't just raging. I was a monster to her. I gave a whole body shake and shifted to my fae form, standing before her, breathing hard, trying to contain my fear and anger.

I could have lost her, and the feeling would sit with me for the rest of my days.

We stared for a long moment, our emotions raw and clear, passing between us.

"I'm sorry," she whispered.

My shoulders fell. I'd got the point she was trying to make. It was a trust fall. I wish she hadn't done something so reckless to prove it, but the truth was clear: she'd given herself over to this bond between us and shown me she was all in.

I fell to my knees in front of her and put my head in my hands. The image of her falling just out of my reach was still fresh in my mind. My nightmares would include that vision for years to come. There was a moment when I thought I wasn't going to get to her, and I felt the loss about to slam into me as hard as the water would have.

I lifted my head and met her eyes.

"You just took a hundred years off my life, Sol. Don't ever do anything as reckless as that again." My words were calm, but my meaning was deadly.

She had tears in her eyes. "I had to know."

"Had to know what? If I'd just sit by soar above and let you splatter yourself on the ground?" I shook my head in disbelief.

"No. I had to know if trusting you was enough."

"And was it?"

She nodded again, with a tear rolling down her cheek.

I sagged in relief, sitting back on my heels before eyeing her up and down. "You're okay?"

"A bit sore, but I deserve it." Her gaze roamed over me, looking for injuries, and she recoiled at her error. I was naked.

She looked away from my body, grabbing the bag from across hers. She held it out, keeping her eyes on the ground in a silent plea for me to put some clothes on.

I pushed to my feet and crossed the space between us. "You're going to have to get used to the sight of me naked if we are going to fly." I took the bag and pulled out my pants so I could slide them on.

"Are you injured?" she asked, still not looking.

I examined my arms. There were a few light scrapes, and my back felt like it had a few, too. My dragon hide could withstand a lot and protected me well, but a few jagged rocks scraped through as we rolled.

But I shielded her. That was all that mattered.

"Just a few scrapes. I'll be fine." I stood over her, offering my hand.

She checked I was clothed before she took it and then let me help her up. When she was on her feet, I wrapped my arms around her. The act felt strange since we hadn't reached a point where it seemed natural, but I had to hold her in my arms to really let it sink in.

She was okay.

I pressed a kiss to the top of her head and breathed in her scent.

"I wouldn't have survived if I hadn't gotten to you," I

admitted softly. She tensed, but I held tighter, not letting her pull out of my hold. "No, don't go. Let me hold you."

She relented, and I felt her arms slip around my waist.

I took a deep, shuddering breath and then let it out slowly, then finally letting go of the tension I was holding.

We stood for a long time wrapped in each other, and I didn't want to let go. For so many years, I had been missing a huge part of myself, my soul, my power, my identity. And even finding her didn't seem to resolve any of that turmoil. But now, with her in my arms, it felt like those things might finally be within my reach.

I had her, and she was here willingly. It was almost everything I'd ever needed. We just had to meld, and I would be complete.

For that to happen, she would have to trust me enough to put her life in my hands...and that's exactly what she had just proved she could do.

TWENTY-NINE

NYX

I eased my hold on her, and she tilted her face up to look at me.

I gazed down at her and shook my head, a laugh bubbling up inside me unchecked.

She frowned. "What?"

"You're crazy, you know that, right? Who jumps off a dragon hundreds of feet in the air?"

She shrugged. "Until today, I thought I would have to be crazy to even get on a dragon, never mind jump off one."

"You're a natural, you know."

"It felt natural. Like I just knew what to do."

I grinned. "You like ryding me."

She coughed, but instead of blushing and refuting it like I thought she would, she took it in good humor and smiled. "If you say so."

I laughed. "Oh, I do. We just need to get you fitted with a tether of some kind before I'll take you up again. My heart will never recover from that death dive."

Her face fell in guilt, and I tightened my arms around her, holding her together in case she spiraled again.

"It's fine—we're okay. I'm just not going to be letting you forget it for a while."

"Great." She huffed, pulling away from me. I reluctantly let her go, and she eyed me. She bent to pick up the bag still half full, and handed it to me again. "Put the rest of your clothes on."

I took it and glanced down at myself. My pants were still half open, revealing more of the planes of muscles and scattering of dark hair than I had thought were on display.

"Sol," I chuckled, shaking my head. Nudity meant nothing to me, and she would become desensitized in time. But to a maiden who'd been raised with strict rules of propriety, I could see why I was dressed indecently. In the name of compromise, I fastened the last buttons and pulled on my shirt.

I needed her to hear me out and hopefully agree to a risky plan so I could give her this.

"Why do you call me Sol?" she asked, pulling me from my thoughts. I smiled fondly at the memory her question brought.

"It means sun, and when I first met you, that's what you reminded me of," I told her honestly.

"I wish I could remember."

"Our first meeting?"

"Yes." She leaned back in my arms, looking up at me earnestly. "I don't doubt you anymore, I swear. But if I could remember, it might feel… I don't know, more real to me, I suppose."

"You were so young, Sol. Even if you hadn't been taken away, even if we had known each other for all the years since, you may not have remembered the meeting. I could show you…"

I didn't know why I hadn't thought of doing it before.

Zaria nodded eagerly, and I showed her the image I had held for so long in my memory.

Her face lit up, and she had tears in her eyes as she beheld the scene. Then she sucked in a breath, and I held mine while her eyes fell closed as the scene came to life in our minds, and my memory seemed to awaken hers.

It was fuzzy, partly from the passing of time, but mostly I guessed due to her age. We didn't hold on to many memories from so young. I assumed it was only mine pulling hers from her mind that uncovered it at all. I reached out to touch her, clasping the back of her neck to bring our foreheads together. I wanted to do anything I could to strengthen the connection between us. My eyes closed so the shared memory could be my sole focus.

"Ground yourself in the memory," I encouraged her, anything to hold on to it. "Feel the soil beneath your feet, and the sun on your skin. The breeze ruffling through the loose waves of your hair."

I could feel it. The sun was warm, casting a golden glow on her hair, which was the most vivid part of my memory. It was as if she was light itself. I could never forget it. I was night. I was raised to be darkness embodied. To thrive in the dark. I was her opposite, designed by the Goddess to be the other half of one another. Where her light met my dark, it did not dilute; it only sharpened. We were made to enhance each other.

When I felt the call, I didn't know what it was at first. I just knew I had to go. I was physically pulled by a need inside myself to leave the palace and sprint through the streets. I ran to where the busy streets turned to quieter roads and pastures. I ran across fields, hopping a stream, and spotting a house in a glen. When I came upon the low-walled garden, I saw a small girl playing and twirling in the falling cherry blossom.

"It smelled like cherry blossoms," I whispered. I had forgotten the scent until we woke the shared memory, and I inhaled, the fragrance so real. "They were rampant that year. The entire sky looked pink. They kept landing in your hair."

She breathed a teary laugh, but I kept my eyes closed, not wanting it to break just yet.

But then the memory changed slightly. My image had always only been of what I saw, but suddenly, I saw her view of me. It rocked me. I looked younger than I had felt. There I stood, bathed in her light, my hair so dark it was almost purple in the rays of the sun. Eight years old and ready to take on the world, but I was just a boy, not yet aware that what was about to take place would change my life forever.

She saw me and stopped spinning. She was so small—two, maybe three years old—but the power I felt from her was overwhelming as it connected with mine. I wanted to vault the wall and go to her, but I didn't want to scare her. She was too young to understand that I needed to be near her. I was barely there myself. I knew about the call, but I had expected to be a male when it came, so it was only in the moment our magic connected, recognizing their other halves, that I realized.

I was afraid for her because I knew that once they were connected, ryders were supposed to go to the palace to train. She was too young for that. I would wait for her to grow bigger so we could train together.

"What's your name?" I'd asked, but Zaria was shy. I was a stranger, after all. She backed away. I wanted to tell her it was okay, that she didn't have to be afraid. She could tell me her name when she was ready. I would come back every day until she knew me, and then she could share her name.

Then she took another step and crossed into a ray of sun that was cutting through the cherry blossom branches. Her hair lit up, and I would never forget how it felt like my whole world became light in that moment.

"I'll call you Sol," I whispered. "You are the sun."

Then a female rushed out of the house, sweeping my Sol behind her skirts.

Zaria gasped at the scene. "My mother," she breathed.

I stroked my thumb on her neck to remind her I was with her, even as my heart broke all over again, reliving the memory.

"Who are you?" her mother demanded.

Keen to put her mother's mind to rest, I proudly introduced myself with all the arrogance of a privileged young fae. "I am Nyx Asra, my lady." I bowed. "First son of General Asra, The Dragon of the Night, and commander of the King's legions."

She gasped, gathering my ryder into her arms. "Get away from this place!" she cried.

"I was called here, my lady. Your daughter is to be my ryder."

"She will be no such thing," she snapped, running back to the house.

"My lady, I mean no harm!" I called to her retreating back. My Sol peered over her shoulder to look at me as she was carried away.

Her mother ran into the house and shut the door with a bang, leaving me stunned. That fae could not hide Sol from me. I had been called. It was the law; no one could stand in the way when a flyer was called to their ryder. I turned on my heel and ran.

The memory vanished, and I was left leaning into Zaria while she processed what she had seen.

"Some of those memories were yours," I told her. "Do you remember?"

She shook her head. "I know that came from my mind, but it was like I was watching it for the first time. I don't remember that house or my mother being that young. She was so angry with you. Why?"

"I don't know. I never found out. I ran all the way home. I didn't stop until I was at my father's study door. I knocked, but it was his aide who opened the door and told me that my father was in a meeting, and I had to wait. Nothing was more important than my call to you. Maybe I should have insisted rather than waiting. But you didn't just barge in on the general, so it was hours before I finally got called in and told him what had happened."

The memory was hard to relive. I had many regrets in life, but that was my first, waiting when I could have demanded to see him. Maybe things would have been different if— I cut myself off. I couldn't go down that dark road again.

The one bright moment in the aftermath was my father's unwavering support. I may have waited hours for his attention, but once I had it, he did not let me down.

"He wasn't a particularly caring fae," I told Zaria with a wistful smile. "But a flyer's call to their ryder was not something that could be denied. So, without question, he followed me back to the glen to explain this to your mother. No one would have taken you away from her. We just needed to know each other, to bond as we grew. My father would have offered to move you and your family to the palace to take care of you."

"But she said no?" Zaria asked.

"No. You were gone. The house was empty, and I never saw you again."

THIRTY

ZARIA

I felt his loss. It was tangible between us. It was my loss, too, but I was finally feeling the weight of his suffering for all those years.

"I'm so sorry," I whispered. It felt like not enough, but what else could I say?

My mind was reeling. Why was my mother so angry when she saw Nyx? From what I had read, discovering you were a ryder was supposed to be an honor—a privilege granted by the Goddess. What reason could my family have had to run away to prevent it from happening?

What pushed my mother to fabricate a world without magic? Or pushed her to find one at the very least. The pieces of my fractured reality began to fit together.

"A ryder gets their magic when they meet their flyer…" I mused.

"You should have," Nyx confirmed. "I could feel the power inside you, but we weren't together long enough for me to know if your magic awoke."

"It must have. We met, and that's the trigger, right? So, they had to have suppressed it."

"I've tried to tell you that, Sol." His words were kind, not exasperated.

"I know, but I've seen things for myself now. It's just sinking in, that's all." I felt like the ground beneath me rolled like I was stuck in an earth shake, but it was inside, not outside.

"But how have they done it? We know it's not the poison. I'm well now that I'm free of that. It has to be something else. And how is it still blocked when they are gone? Could they have stripped me of my powers for good?" Questions came faster than I could voice them, and it all hit me harder than it had before. I could see it clearly now. It all pointed to the village, my community, my parents. "They did this to us on purpose."

He nodded solemnly.

"I'm so sorry." I'd been so terrible to him when my parents were the ones who deserved my anger. They took me away from all of this, lied to me, tried to make me less, and for what? That part hurt the worst. I could not fathom a good excuse.

"It's not your fault. Please don't say sorry. You suffered too, more than me."

"Why did they do it?" I all but begged him, though I knew he did not have the answer.

"I wish I knew, Sol. Maybe we will never know. All we can do now is find a way to access your power and make up for lost time."

My shoulders slumped. "Oh, good. The impossible task is all we have left to do."

"Don't give up now. We are so close."

"We aren't close. This feels impossible. What if they ruined my magic somehow? Is that possible?" I searched his face for reassurance.

He took my hands. "It can't be gone. I don't believe that. We just have to find it…and I have a plan."

My brow furrowed. "You do?"

He pointed over to the trunk of a fallen tree. "Let's sit. I'll tell you about it."

We walked over, and as I sat, he dug in his pants pocket and pulled out a leather pouch. He sat beside me, tipping two items into his palm.

He studied them—a small vial, and a dark stone—then drew in a breath and spoke. "There is a way we can find out what is blocking your magic."

"Okay…" I replied with trepidation, sensing hesitation from him. "Why have we waited so long to try it?"

He sighed, closing his eyes. "It's highly illegal, and so, so dangerous."

I recoiled. "Dangerous, how?" If it was such a risk, maybe we shouldn't even consider it.

He lifted the small vial from his hand and held it to the light. There was a liquid swirling inside that was a viscous, shimmering green. It was a small amount, but something as dangerous as he hinted at might only need a drop. "This is an apotheosis potion. It allows you to walk into another's soul."

He waited for me to digest that information, but he must have known it meant nothing to me. "That…sounds…" I couldn't finish that sentence. It sounded impossible, but I had to keep reminding myself I now lived in a world where the impossible was commonplace. "You want me to, what? Drink it?"

He shook his head. "No, I will drink it while we are open to one another, mind to mind, and connected by touch. Then I can cross into your soul."

"Don't we do that already? Open mind to mind when we speak?"

"It's deeper. This is more than even my brother and I are. Like sharing a mind." His words were solemn, cold even. I didn't like it.

"And that's dangerous?"

"It requires you to have absolute trust in me. They call it soul walking, but it's really access to your mind and magic center. Those two things combined are what is considered to be your soul. Once in that place inside you, I could destroy your magic, and create madness in your mind. I can't kill you, but the damage I could do would make you wish you were dead." He blew out a long breath.

"Why would anyone do such a thing?"

"In the old world, before the kingdoms were united, there was dark magic. Now we understand there is no real good and evil in magic. All magic comes from the Goddess. It's the intent of the magic wielder that changes its character. When the kingdoms were formed, these practices were outlawed to bring order. It's thought the practice was developed for healing magical bonds, but it's so invasive and open to abuse, it was made illegal, and all records of how to brew the potion and successfully carry out the process were destroyed in the unification. Along with many other archaic methods which were used for ill intent."

It was a lot to take in, and I had so many questions, but I mostly wondered how he had the potion. "How did you get it?"

"Not all records were successfully destroyed across the kingdoms, Sol. There are those who have painstakingly collected fragments of information over time to properly catalogue the history of magical practices. They believe in the importance of preserving history but recognize that certain information must be kept in safe hands. I have a source whose family have been the safe keepers of magical history for centuries."

"Kiera?" I knew it as certainly as I knew I could trust him absolutely.

"How did you know?" He looked taken aback.

"She told me she has a passion for healing magic and said that many answers can be found in history. It was just a hunch."

"No one must know." He looked panicked. "If it becomes known she has access to such information—"

"I would never tell a soul. Kiera is my friend," I assured him.

Nyx relaxed slightly and returned his attention to the potion. I watched him battling over what was right.

"Will it hurt?" I asked. It was the first question in a long line of questions I had, but they all came down to trust.

"According to what I've read, not unless I try to do harm." He turned to face me. "And you have to understand, Sol, that I could never do you harm. And even if I could bring myself to, as your bonded flyer, I would be hurting myself by hurting you. You can trust me with your life."

I looked into his eyes, not wavering in my conviction. "Did my death dive not prove to you that I know that now?"

Nyx pinched the bridge of his nose.

"We should do it now." I'd decided, and I didn't want to wait.

"You should think about this," he protested.

"I have thought about it. Tell me how it works. We need to figure out what's wrong with my magic."

He stood and paced. "If anything goes wrong—"

"We have to try."

He came back and knelt before me, taking my hand before he placed the dark stone into it.

"What's this?" I asked, turning the stone in my palm.

"If we are breaking old magic laws, we may as well break harmful artifact laws, too. This is a night stone."

I studied it. It was smooth and rounded like a pebble, and the color of night so dark it seemed to absorb light. Tiny flecks of silver, like stars, shone from within the inkiness.

"Remember, we talked about dampening with Rakan? This

stone is able to store dampening magic that has been siphoned. But night stone is found only in the First Kingdom. It has dampening power of its own, so when it's used by a siphon to store the dampening magic of a fae, it can be deadly. It's illegal, forbidden magic. It could easily get into the wrong hands and cause untold harm."

"What do I do with it?"

"I want you to hold it while we soul walk. If I do anything that is harming you, if I change in any way... if anything at all goes wrong, you rub it between your hands. The heat alone will activate it. When it warms to the touch, you press it to my skin to connect with my magic. You don't have access to yours, so you have to use mine. When it connects to the power, it will surge, dampening all magic around it, and cutting off my magic and the soul connection. You'll be safe then."

"And you?"

"I'll be okay. My magic may take some time to return, but it will."

"How long?"

"I don't know. It's powerful and unpredictable, but I will be okay. It's the only thing you can do to stop me once I'm inside."

"Will it hurt you?"

He forced a smile to his lips. "Nothing I can't get over. You have to promise me you will use it. I have to know you can stop this if it goes wrong."

I nod, closing my hand around the stone.

"I'll be able to see what you are doing?"

"You'll be with me."

"Then, we should do it."

"Are you sure?"

"Yes. We have to do it now. I have to know what they took away from me. I need all the parts of myself back to feel whole."

I hadn't yet even realized the extent of the betrayal I felt over my parents cutting that part of me off from myself.

"I want you to think about it. You only just started trusting me today."

"It's more than trust, Nyx. It's needing myself back. I can't go another day if there is a chance this will give me it back. I don't have to think about it. I do trust you, and I need to know."

"It's still dangerous and—"

I cut him off. "If you trust me, you trust me to know I've made up my mind. I want this. I understand it's dangerous. We have to trust each other."

"You are the most important person in the world to me, Sol. I do trust you. I wouldn't have brought it up if I didn't."

"Do this for me, then. Give back what my parents took."

Emotion rolled through Nyx's expression, but it settled on resolved, and he opened the vial. He took my hand and linked our fingers, while I held tightly to the stone in my other hand.

"Take a deep breath and keep your eyes on mine," he instructed. "Then I want you to open yourself up fully the way we've been practicing."

I did as he said, feeling him there.

"Ready?"

"Yes."

He tipped the vial between his lips and swallowed.

Within a moment, our mind connection deepened.

I lost sight of our surroundings and found myself standing with him in a space with no end. Light glowed from the center of the space and drew our focus. Our interlinked hands kept us tethered while we walked toward the source.

As we got closer to the light, I could see golden tendrils of it, like little vines and sparks, reaching out. When I looked at Nyx, I found the same tendrils coming from him, reaching for me. They didn't make contact, though, as if they couldn't pass an invisible barrier. It felt like a whole other world existed between us.

He gasped. "Do you feel those?"

"Yes, is that—"

"Go on," he urged.

"Is that our magic?"

"It's the pathways our magic will follow when we meld. They are predestined by the Goddess. Only ryders and their flyers are connected this way. They should reach for each other, and once they connect, we meld. The more tendrils that connect, the better the meld will be. A perfect meld would connect all facets of our magic."

I ran my touch over one, feeling the pull in my chest.

He recoiled physically. "Careful now."

"Did it hurt?"

"It's just raw." He was studying the tendrils coming from the light. We moved around it, looking from every angle. "That's your power, Sol. It's so strong and bright."

"Can you see what's wrong?"

He shook his head. "I don't understand. I should be able to feel it." He studied the tendrils, picking strands apart, following the flow and how they moved. They behaved like his, but they didn't connect.

He finally took his eyes off the light of my magic, turned to face me, and stopped dead.

His eyes narrowed, and his mouth fell open.

"What is it?"

"Your pendant," he whispered.

I looked down and gasped. Black wisps seeped from my pendant. Like smoke, it spread from me, and wherever it met a tendril of his power, its darkness extinguished the light. None got past.

"What is that thing?" he demanded.

"It's a symbol of dedication to the Goddess," I told him, automatically defensive. "We are given them when we take our first offering to the temple, and we never take them off. It's a vial of sand blessed by the priests of the Temple of Avalon to symbolize the shores we are welcomed to when we finally go to the Goddess. We all wear them…"

As soon as the words left my lips, I saw how that was the answer to this whole mystery. If they took me, hid me, kept me prisoner in a remote place, and poisoned me to prevent my magic from reaching out for Nyx, of course they ensured I always wore something to prevent our magic from connecting. We all did! It made me wonder how many others in my village had some kind of power. I knew I was the only one being poisoned, but these pendants were around every neck in the compound.

Our eyes met and confirmed this without words. Nyx let go of my hand, breaking the soul connection, and in an instant, I was back on the fallen tree with Nyx kneeling before me.

"This whole time, I've been wearing the thing blocking me?"

"I think so." He reached for it, and as soon as he touched it, he hissed, recoiling.

"What's wrong?"

"It burned. It doesn't hurt you?"

"It gets warm sometimes, but it doesn't hurt." I gasped. "No, wait! When you brought me here from my village, it hurt. It burned me. I thought it was protecting me against you…"

"Maybe it was. Well, protecting you from connecting with my magic, at least. Ultimately stopping us from melding."

I touched it and found it warm, but not too hot to touch.

I scrambled for the clasp, trying to get it off, but there wasn't one there. I tried to remember how they put it on me. It was part of the ceremony. I was young, so I didn't remember all the details. All the children made their first offering to the Goddess at our small temple. We placed the offering at the altar and knelt, they placed the pendant around our necks as we recited the prayer, and then… I gasped again. They used a tool to attach it. I remembered that it got hot for a moment. But I was so proud to be allowed to wear it, I hardly remembered the detail. Had they fused it to me?

I grabbed the pendant and tried to work it over my head. It was too tight to remove that way, though, so I yanked at it, and as I struggled, it suddenly burned my palm, as if it now saw me as a threat, too. I didn't release it, pushing through the pain, trying to snap it, but the chain held. Eventually, the searing forced me to release it with a hiss.

"I can't get it off."

Nyx took my hand, inspecting my palm. "Whatever it's doing, it's resistant to being removed."

"Like it knows?"

"Maybe. But it doesn't want our magic together—that's it's purpose."

"How can we get it off? It won't break; it's too strong."

He thought for a moment, then seemed to come to a conclusion. "Remember that you trust me."

"I don't like the sound of that."

"Cover your eyes," he demanded.

I frowned but lifted my hands to cover my eyes, unable to stop myself peering between my fingers to see what he was doing.

He pulled the chain as far as it would extend from my throat, ignoring the pain it was obviously inflicting on him.

"What are you doing?"

"Just... don't move." He leaned forward and blew a thin stream of dark flames from his lips onto the chain.

THIRTY-ONE

NYX

Z aria stiffened but didn't move. I could feel the weight of
her gaze and knew she was watching through her fingers,
but I didn't look away from my task. A hair's width in the wrong
direction, and I'd burn her. She should be immune to my fire as
my ryder, but until we melded, and because of how blocked her
magic was, I didn't know if she would be.

The chain held, and I growled, drawing deeper into my
magic, and channeling it into the flames. My fire burned black
like the night, rippling with the power of absolute nothingness—
the void, as some in the First Kingdom called it. Darkness swallowed and suffocated. It stole vision and senses. It carried secrets
and shadows.

Dark fire was a rare weapon to possess, and I used it spar-
ingly. If anything would break the chain, it would be dragon fire.
Nothing in our world could stand against it forever.

The chain softened, so I redoubled my effort.

Zaria trembled. I could feel her pain where the searing hot metal was touching her neck. It couldn't be helped, but she held strong. She was amazing.

"Hang in there, Sol," I said through our deep connection, the effort like speaking to myself after the potion.

"I'm okay. Don't stop."

"Not until it's off, I promise you."

The metal dripped, splashing on the ground between our feet. Zaria winced but kept herself still. Another drop fell, this time splashing onto my pants and burning a hole there. I put it out of my mind. We'd both end up with burns, but it was a small price to pay to get it off her.

She whimpered, and her pain radiated in my mind. I could feel she was fighting off tears.

"I'm sorry."

"Don't be sorry. I can stand it. Focus."

Strain pulled at my magic as I poured all my power into the fire.

Suddenly, the chain gave way, and I instantly cut off my fire as I stumbled back.

"It's gone!" Zaria clutched at her throat, breathing hard. "You've done it."

"Are you hurt?" I looked her over.

"I'm okay," she breathed. I could tell she wasn't completely, but superficial wounds would heal.

I half stumbled to a seat, pulling off my shirt to wrap it around the necklace. I didn't trust it, and I wasn't going to let it touch her or my skin again. I would have destroyed it if not for the forethought to have Kiera look at it and tell us what in the Twelve Kingdoms it was.

I wrapped Zaria's burned hand in strips torn from my pants, so she could hold on. I didn't try to dress where the chain had seared her flesh as it heated. I hoped the cool wind would soothe it some as I flew us home as fast as I could.

We didn't speak. We were both too consumed with our own thoughts about this thing we now carried in the bag she held beside her.

We arrived back over the palace, and I dove straight for the healer's landing. The wards would alert them of our arrival, and I hoped with everything I had that it was Kiera who attended us.

Zaria dismounted like she'd been ryding her whole life, and I shifted back to my fae form. I was just about to take the bag from Zaria so it couldn't harm her when Kiera swept through the doors and tossed me a pair of sweatpants.

"What have you two been up to?" she asked, puzzled to see us here when everyone knew we weren't flying yet. Before I could hit her with the news, another healer came out onto the landing and drew up short at seeing us there.

I threw Kiera a glance. I knew she could read a 'go with it until we are alone' look.

Nodding toward Sol, I told Kiera, "Zaria burned her hand. It was faster to scoop her up and fly her up here than walk her here in pain."

"I tried to catch a lamp that got knocked over. I'm so silly." Zaria laughed, seamlessly filling in a suitable lie to appease the other healer.

"I've got this, Sirena," Kiera informed the other fae, coming forward and inspecting Zaria's bound hand. "You go back to monitoring our other patients. I'll be along in a while to check their progress."

Sirena, who looked young and nervous, was obviously new and shadowing Kiera. "Yes Healer Noreth." She dipped her head in deference and disappeared back into the healer's wing.

I stepped into the pants and straightened, making sure the younger fae was out of earshot. "We have another problem, too," I said in a hushed tone. "But burns first. Her hands and neck."

"Come," Kiera instructed and turned on her heel. We followed her past the small wards where recovering patients stayed, past the rooms where they performed healing magic, and through to Kiera's personal rooms where she did her research. "Have a seat." She waved toward her sitting area and went to her cabinets for supplies.

I took the bag from Zaria and set it on the workbench Kiera used to prepare ingredients, then took a seat beside Zaria, helping her out of the flight jacket so she didn't scrape her burned neck.

Kiera returned and began assessing the burn on Zaria's neck.

"Are you going to tell me how this really happened?" she asked as she got to work, cleaning and applying a magical ointment I knew would have it healed before morning.

"Dark fire," I admitted.

Kiera turned a fierce scowl on me.

"I wasn't careless." I held up my hands in defense. "I swear. It was necessary."

"When I saw you, I worried something had gone wrong with that energy tonic I gave you..." Her look was meaningful. She wouldn't speak of the potion out loud. "Tell me it wasn't that."

"No," I assured her. "The tonic was exactly what we needed, thank you."

Her brows rose. "You took it already?"

"I did."

She had slipped the vial my way when she delivered reports to me that morning. Maybe she thought I would wait before going through with my plan.

"Did it help?"

I nodded. "We have answers, but we also have more questions." I lowered my voice, but we were safe in her space. As long as the potion was never spoken of aloud, we were okay. "Zaira's necklace was the problem. I had to use dark fire to melt it off her, hence the burns."

I slipped my hand into Zaria's uninjured one as the guilt for having to hurt her to free her of that thing ate at me once again. Kiera's eyes widened.

Zaria winced as Kiera swiped ointment over the worst looking welt. "Show her," she urged.

I suspected that Zaria just didn't want me hovering over her while she was being treated. I had to admit it was a huge turn-around from hardly being able to be in the same room together, but a lot had happened in a short amount of time.

I was not unhappy with the change.

I let Zaria go and went to the bench, carefully removing the bundled shirt. I placed it down to opened the fabric, spreading it out to reveal the pendant.

Kiera glanced over but returned her attention to Zaria, unwrapping her hand and treating it first. "Is that all of it?" she asked as she finished applying the ointment.

"Nyx has burns, too."

"I'm fine," I grumbled.

"Nyx thinks such things as flesh wounds are beneath him," Kiera chided, coming over to the bench and handing me the pot of ointment with a pointed glare.

I rolled my eyes and took it, going to the wash basin and rinsing my hands before dipping my fingers in the pot and quickly rubbing the cream between my palms.

"There." I returned to where Zaria and Kiera were inspecting the pendant.

Kiera shook her head at my petulance.

"It burned Nyx when he touched it. It's only ever been warm for me, but when we were trying to break the chain to get it off, it burned us both like it was fighting us off."

"Hmm." Kiera tentatively touched it at first and then with more purpose. She picked it up and looked closely, then held it up to the light. "What's inside?"

"Sand," Zaria replied.

"From where?"

"I don't know. It represents the sand on the Shores of Avalon. I always assumed it was regular sand. It's only symbolic."

"You think the sand is the problem?" I asked.

"Could be. It could be spelled, or it might contain something else. There's only one way to find out." She tried twisting the top, but I suspected that would be too easy after the fight to break the chain.

I was right.

Then she paused, inspecting the engraving on the top of the vial. She set it down and wordlessly went to a bookshelf, pulling on a large, old volume and bringing it back to us. She heaved it open, flipping through pages until she found the section she needed. Her ability to catalogue information in her mind and know where to access everything she needed in a moment always impressed me. Proving her skill, she flipped a couple more pages and ran her finger down a list of symbols. She stopped, tapped a symbol, read the line beside it, and muttered to herself.

Zaria looked at me, and I shrugged.

"Let her work, Sol. She's the best at this."

Abruptly, Kiera took the pendant and placed it in the large stone bowl she used to make many of her treatments. She took some parchment and a pen and scribbled an intricate symbol. Then she dropped the parchment onto the pendant, added some purple leaves, and set light to it using her magic.

The leaves and parchment burned hot and fast, glowing bright white before going out just as quickly. She reached in, picked the vial out of the ashes, and twisted the top. This time, it opened.

"Amazing," I said in awe.

"It was magically sealed. There's a sacred symbol etched into the metal. I'm surprised to see this kind of magic used in the remote Fifth Kingdom. Shall we see what's inside?"

I nodded but instinctively guided Zaria behind me and stepped back, so we were both at a safer distance.

Kiera tipped the vial and tapped the contents out onto the bench. Sand flowed initially, then a sliver of something more solid and as white as the sand itself fell out.

"What is it?" Zaria asked.

Kiera used some tweezers to pick it up and held it to the light, examining it from all angles. "It's Draco Fulgurite."

"What is that?" I was glad Zaria was asking. I felt like I knew the name, but after the events of today, I wasn't making the connections fast enough.

"When lightning hits sand, it melts the grains, forming these glass structures shaped like the lightning itself. That's Fulgurite." She took a small jar from a shelf and dropped the shard into it, and it made a tinkling sound, glass on glass, when it fell in. She put a lid on the jar and screwed it closed. The jars used for her line of work were specially made and spelled to contain magic indefinitely. "When the lightning is created by a storm dragon, the glass is infused with its power. That is Draco Fulgurite. And as you know, a storm dragon's lightning causes a disturbance to other magic. It short circuits the powers of natural energy fields, severing connections, preventing new ones forming."

"Has it broken my magic forever?"

My chest seized at the anguish in Zaria's voice, and we both turned to look at her. She was clutching the place where the pendant had always sat, going to it for comfort—a habit that would take time to break. She had tears in her eyes, and the fear that she would never have magic was pouring from her.

Kiera hurried to her while I remained frozen to the spot.

"No, Zaria, it hasn't broken your magic. Not at all. I'm sure now the pendant is not blocking it, it will awaken in no time."

I should have told her. I could have prevented her feeling this fear, and if I told her what I'd done, here and now, Kiera would know, too. But I couldn't leave her in fear of never having magic, not after everything she survived to get to this point.

"Sol, your magic is already free. I contained it with mine so we could fly back safely."

Her glassy eyes lit with hope, and while I held her optimistic gaze, I could feel Kiera's drilling into me. She knew.

I stayed focused on Zaria. That conversation could wait, preferably for a very long time.

"When you're rested, we can go to the wielding hall, and I'll let go," I said.

She shook her head, rejecting the resting idea. "Let's go now"

THIRTY-TWO

ZARIA

I thanked Kiera for her help, including the help we would never speak of again. Then we set off for the wielding halls.

I was nervous, but it was exhilarating. A feeling I realized I'd never actually experienced firsthand until Nyx crashed into my life. Now it seemed like every day was more exhilarating than the last.

I rubbed my hand as we walked through the corridors. The burn was already healing; it was incredible. In a life without magic, such an injury would affect a person's work for days if not weeks. Kiera told me it would be fully healed by tomorrow and shouldn't scar. Why would anyone choose to live without that?

But it was more than choosing to live without magic. They'd chosen for me. They'd not only taken it from me, but they'd poisoned me. Daily. They intentionally made me sick and weak and...

I shook it off. The more I learned, the more I resented thinking about my family. I wasn't quite ready to address my feelings about them and their choices, but I wished I could ask them why. Maybe I wouldn't understand what drove them even if I had an explanation, but I'd never know. Maybe I just needed closure to move on. But that was for another time.

"Slow down, Sol," Nyx chided, and I realized I was outpacing him.

"Sorry." I slowed some.

He smiled when I eyed him sheepishly.

I couldn't get used to this version of him. Now the walls were down, and we were more confident of each other's intentions, I realized there was a lot to like about this dragon of mine.

Dragon. Of. Mine.

I felt that on a whole new level, and it was startling.

No one had been that to me before: *mine.* I'd had siblings, but we weren't close. I was the family's burden. They didn't see me as an equal, so I was always on the outside. I had a friend in Luka, and I valued that friendship at the time. But I always knew he wanted more, and I didn't feel the same, so it was more like companionship limited by my boundaries. Nothing like what I had already built with Kol, which felt unconditional and limitless. I would be endlessly grateful he was there for me when I needed that more than anything else, and I would always be there for him.

But nothing else came close to Nyx. I could feel the possibilities developing before us. It was early days, but the foundations were being set. A partnership, an unbreakable bond, an equal. Things I never imagined I would find in this life.

I glanced at him again, and he looked away, but I saw the smile he tried to hide and knew he'd felt my projected emotions. I realized then that I was blocking him from my thoughts and found it took little effort. It surprised me. When did that get so easy? Maybe it was the freeing of my power? From Nyx's smile, though, I knew I needed to learn the same level of proficiency in shaping my emotions. But I was too apprehensive about what was to come to care that he knew I was growing fond of him.

We arrived at the wielding hall and found the main room in use. I was crestfallen after almost running here, but Nyx led me to a smaller room and closed the door once we were inside.

We stood facing each other in the center of the space, and I waited.

Nyx seemed to be hesitant.

"What is it?"

Nyx shrugged. "This is new for me. Usually, when we come into our power, it's gradual. It develops as we grow. You are past that stage in your life and have all your power, but you've never even felt it before. It's daunting to be the one about to open it up inside you all at once."

"You don't think I can take it?"

"No, I'm worried you'll blow up half the palace trying to light a candle, Sol."

My eyes went wide. "Is it that strong?"

"It's a lot."

Apprehension gripped me, and I knew I needed him to get on with it before I lost my nerve. "Just do it. Worrying won't change anything. Just let me feel it and then tell me what to do."

"Okay." He surprised me by taking my hand again, and I was surprised more by the fact it felt so natural now.

I had no idea what to expect, so I startled slightly as something—power, obviously—that was built inside. A deep well of it. And as he slowly released his hold on it, it poured into me, filling the well.

It didn't give me any hint at what it could be capable of like I thought it might. I could just feel how much of it there was, and it was far more than I expected. Nyx walked around the palace looking like magic was just a part of him—a part he had no trouble mastering. If we were equally matched, like he said, he was hiding his reserves expertly. This was overwhelming.

"You okay?" he asked softly.

I nodded.

"Breathe, then," he urged, humor in his tone.

I let out a breath I hadn't realized I was holding.

"Shall I keep going?"

"There's more?" Even to my ears, I sounded panicked.

Nyx smiled. "Only a little. You almost have it."

I felt him let go, and the remaining magic flowed in. When it stopped, I could feel my reserve was full. I hadn't expected to be so aware of how much power I would have on hand, and I sensed that I would always be aware of how much was in the reserve at any time.

"Okay?"

"Yes."

"I know you feel full to the brim right now, but you'll adjust. It's a feeling that becomes background very quickly. Give it a day or two, and you'll stop thinking about it. It's like eating. When the reserve is full, you don't think about it. When it's low, it's like a hunger to replenish it."

"How do you replenish it?"

He tilted his head in thought. "Rest is the main thing. Sleep, eat, heal. If those things are taken care of, magic restores itself naturally within a short time. There are things you can do specific to your magic and to your origin, too. Dragons can use metals to replenish; we draw power from different ones. Some more than others. You'll find that metals which are more valuable are so because they provide more power to us. Other things such as crystals can boost magic; usually those native to where your line originates give the most power. There are potions, but those are more of a short-term, artificial boost. Like a shot of energy. Good in an emergency.

And in old magic, the sacred symbols were used to connect our magic centers to the Goddess. Though, these days, those connections are weakened, and we don't rely on them anymore."

"Why are they weakened?"

He laughed. "Do you want a history lesson or a magic lesson?"

I breathed out a laugh. "Magic, please." That was the priority. "But will you tell me some time about the rest?"

"Sure." And hope grew between us for a moment about a future 'sometime' that now felt reachable. We returned to the task. "Okay, let's try something basic."

Nyx went to the shelf on the far wall and brought back some empty cans. He set them on the floor at various points around the room. I watched, quietly adjusting to the new sensations.

"I want you to draw some power from your reserve and direct it out of your hands. We are going to try and knock the cans over. I'll show you."

He described how to draw on it and form it into an energy I could use to move objects, then he demonstrated the action by waving a hand toward a can. It promptly fell over and rolled away.

Then it was my turn. I drew on my magic like he said, and I formed it into energy, which was harder to do than it sounded. I had no idea if I had done it right. Then I waved my hand, and nothing happened. I waved it again, and nothing. Frustrated, I shook my hand out, and energy burst behind me with a bang. I hunched in on myself instinctively, then slowly turned.

A burned patch of floor several feet away was smoking, but the walls were still standing.

"Okay, that was fire." He sounded amused. Relaxed, even. Was he mad?

I looked down at my hands as if they would go off again at any moment.

"Let's keep these where we can see them for now," he teased, reaching for both my hands.

I tried to snatch them away. "Don't! If I do that again, you'll get hurt."

"I can take care of myself, Sol," he assured me. "Let's try again. This time, try and bring forward less power if you can. Less is more."

I tried again, and this time, I was able to force the energy out myself. But when it impacted with the floor, a small fire bloomed and then vanished.

"Fire again." I huffed, frustrated.

"It's good," he encouraged. "Power is power. You are wielding it. Your magic is out. You have it. This is what we've been working toward. It's the first step. Think of your power as neutral. When you draw on it, you tell it what to be in that moment, then you can direct it."

"You make it sound so easy."

"It's not hard, it's just unfamiliar. It's another thing you will hardly give a thought to once you have it. But for now, just try telling it what you want it to do in your mind."

After several more tries, burn marks smoldered in several places, and all the cans remained standing. "Why am I stuck on fire?" I huffed. "Maybe we should be trying to light things on fire, not knock things over."

"What do you want to light, a barn? Because you need to dial it way back before we try a candle," he teased.

I studied my hands. The fire didn't stream from them like I might have imagined. The power was just that. Intangible and invisible until it hit, and then it ignited. Like that first day when Kol lit the candle. I never saw the fire come from him, the candle just lit. I see now that he sent a tiny amount of his power to the wick and told it what to do. The control I now realized that must have taken seemed unachievable, but Nyx's words helped me make sense of the how.

I was still using too much to have any kind of control. Even if I wanted to light a fire, it was going to be out of control outside of this safe room. I needed to work so much smaller, then maybe I could find the control over how the magic was used, too.

I took a deep breath and tried to visualize the amount of power I wanted. I was stuck with fire, so I tried to focus on a single flame's worth rather than a fireball. The power I drew felt smaller, but I wanted even less, so I tried pushing some back. It worked and felt manageable, so I took a chance and told it to push the can over. If it was fire, it was fire, but at least I knew it was a more controlled amount.

I let it burst from my hand and watched in horror as Nyx was blown off his feet. He landed on his back and skidded across the floor, knocking over a can as he slowed to a stop.

I rushed over, falling to my knees beside him.

"Are you okay?" I checked him over, but he didn't respond. "Nyx?"

He coughed and groaned, and I leaned over him, trying to see any injuries.

He tried to speak, but the words were unclear. I leaned in close. "What did you say?"

"We need to work on your aim," he said into my ear and then began to laugh.

I rocked back, relief surging, but I still shoved him.

"Hey!" he objected, still sprawled on the floor.

"You're fine," I grumbled.

"I'm not on fire. That's something, at least."

I narrowed my eyes at him. "I knocked over a can. That's more than something."

"*You* knocked over the can?" he challenged.

I shrugged, leaning over him with a smirk. "You didn't say I couldn't use you to knock it over. You should really be more specific."

The words had barely left my lips when my world flipped, and I found myself on my back with Nyx looming over me.

I drew in a sharp breath at the hungry look in his eyes.

"I'm going to kiss you now. Is that specific enough for you, Sol?"

THIRTY-THREE

NYX

I took her lips with mine, and she didn't hesitate in kissing me back with a shocking hunger. My need for her was building, and I knew I couldn't ignore it indefinitely, but I'd been trying to give her time to deal with all the changes in her life without adding more complications.

We were bound for life. There would be time.

After our first kiss in her room, she'd looked regretful, and I'd decided then that I'd let her come to it on her own. Things returned to how they had been before, and I knew it was what she'd needed. But things had changed between us again now, and I couldn't fight this.

I didn't want to.

Her hands slipped into my hair, deepening the kiss, and pulling me flush against her. I groaned in surprise at the contact of my hardening length against her heat, and she whimpered, rubbing herself against me. For a maiden raised by zealots, she was unafraid to take what she wanted, and I was not complaining. But even as I thrust against her, eliciting a moan, I worried that she was too vulnerable and inexperienced to risk our bond by rushing things.

She clearly had no such concern. Her hips rolled in a rhythm matching mine. Our kisses were only broken to afford panting breaths, and we drove each other closer and closer to the peak with each grind.

And then I heard it. Footsteps coming this way.

"Fuck," I growled, lifting off her and rolling to a seat beside her before she could comprehend what had happened.

"Nyx?" she said in a daze, raising herself up so she was sitting beside me.

Before she could even ask what happened, there was a knock, and then the door opened. "A little healer bird just flew by and told me that someone found their power!" My brother came strolling in without a care, hardly noticing the scene until he was fully inside. "Oh, shit. Sorry." He stopped abruptly and started to backtrack.

Zaria was flushed, panting, and her kiss-swollen lips and messy hair were dead giveaways. But I was no better. We were so obvious, it was painful.

Kol's grin said everything, but I subtly shook my head. I could take his shit, but Zaria didn't need to be feeling embarrassed by this. It was all new for her, and I would not have shame be a part of how she was feeling.

He said nothing, thank the Goddess, but he did give me a knowing look that was none too subtle.

"Are you two talking about me right now?" Zaria hissed.

"No, little sunshine. He has me blocked. Probably so I don't puke from all the sweet nothings he was whispering in your ear."

"We hadn't got to the sweet nothings," she countered,

surprising me again. She was not embarrassed or ashamed. If anything, she seemed annoyed we'd had to stop.

"My fault, sorry. I'll leave you to…whatever this was. Just came to let you know that it's drinks on me at the Flaming Pegasus tonight. No arguments! We're celebrating this."

Zaria lit up at the idea and looked over. I usually said no, but her face held hope, and I didn't want to be the one to disappoint her.

"Sure," I confirmed. "We'll meet you there."

Zaria let out a little happy noise, and Kol grinned before he turned and left us alone.

She turned, too, unsure. I didn't want her to question what we'd done, so I got to my feet, pulling her up with me. "I think we've done enough for your first day. I'll walk you back so you can get ready."

She nodded, and we silently collected the cans, returning them to the shelf.

We walked back to her rooms while she chatted about how the power felt and what she wanted to work on, all while I nursed my blue balls. They needed to lower their expectations. I was not pushing her and risking our entire future.

At her door, I kissed her forehead to let her know I had no regrets without starting more.

"I'll come get you in an hour," I told her, then left her to bathe and change while I went back to my quarters to take care of my situation.

"*You two need to fuck,*" Kol said into my mind out of nowhere. He was sat across the collection of tables we'd shifted together to accommodate the whole group, and he was watching me watching Zaria chat to Kiera.

I cut him a glare and went back to watching. *"Originally, you said she needed a friend, not a turn around my bedroom. Then you said I should charm her. Now you're saying..."*

"Now I'm saying just fuck her. I'm her friend. You need to be something else. And you need to do it soon because I can smell it on both of you. The smell of need is going to attract horny flyers like honey, and trust me, brother, you don't want that."

I grit my teeth at the very idea. *"I'm giving her space. She's been through enough."*

"Space to what? Take a turn around Maxen's bedroom instead while she waits for you to get your head out of your arse?"

I growled, noticing that Maxen had joined them and was speaking closely into Zaria's ear to be heard above the noisy tavern. *"Maxen is too besotted with Katara, but nice try."*

"Made you growl, though, didn't it?" He raised his drink to his lips to cover his smirk.

"Just leave it. I have my ryder—that's enough for now."

"Since when do you settle for enough?"

"Since she's a maiden, and she's had a rough time. She's vulnerable, and I'm not going to make her feel more so for my own gain."

"It didn't look like it was only for your gain earlier. She almost looked like she'd been about to come, but you pulled away and left her hanging."

"That's because we had both been about to come when I heard you stomping down the hall. A second later, and you'd have walked in on something I couldn't have stopped if I'd wanted to."

"Thank the Goddess I wasn't a second later. I don't need that visual in my head for the rest of my days."

"I don't want you having that visual, either," I assured him.

"Then, may I suggest you dry hump your ryder in more private settings in the future?"

Zaria looked my way while Maxen was saying something to Kiera, and the heat in her eyes had me shifting in my seat. She took a sip of her drink, then turned back to her conversation.

"By the Goddess! I'm going to have to go dry hump someone in a minute if you two keep that up. You could cut the pheromones in here with a knife!"

THIRTY-FOUR

ZARIA

"I'm confused," I admitted to Rakan. Maybe it was the light haze left in my head from the celebration last night, but things still didn't make sense to me where magic was concerned.

He sighed like I was a lost cause but gave his permission to continue with a wave of his finger.

"You said we couldn't fly in case my magic came out and I held a power that could take down a dragon mid-flight, but that's not at all how my magic is. Nyx explained that magic is just power until you tell it what to do."

"Girl, you are a unique case. We didn't know what your magic would do."

I waited for more, but apparently, he was done. A fae of few words. So, I looked to Nyx, exasperated.

"Normally, you'd have your innate magic and know how to wield it before you bond with your flyer, Sol. That magic can be shaped by you depending on your skill level. Once you mature, some other powers awaken. We call them origin powers. They are tied to your bloodline, to the places your line originates, and can also be associated with your environment now. Since your magic was blocked, we weren't sure what would happen when they were released. Origin powers usually reveal themselves over time and come to us when situations require them."

Rakan grunted some kind of comment but didn't try to make himself heard clearly. Nyx glanced at him and then returned to me with an apologetic look.

"Rakan was concerned that as we had already bonded, some origin powers would have awakened, and if you were suddenly able to unlock them, they might be a risk to those around you if they were to overwhelm. Luckily, that didn't happen, so we are good."

"So, we can fly?" I asked hopefully.

"No," Rakan said flatly.

Nyx shook his head. "Not until your powers are assessed and the level of risk can be established."

I huffed.

"All ryders have to do it to be cleared for flight. You aren't being singled out."

"Okay," I sighed. That seemed to be permission enough to go ahead, and Rakan set about arranging us as he had the last few times. We faced each other and held hands so we were connected.

Rakan placed his palm on my forehead, and I tensed.

Nyx spoke before Rakan could give the command to begin I had been expecting. Perhaps he knew me well enough now to know I needed more information to be able to trust the process. "I will call to your magic, and Rakan will syphon from you so he can assess what your powers are made up of."

"Will he take it all?" The idea of being drained scared me. I was still getting used to the reserve being full of power. I didn't know how I'd feel being without it.

"No, he will only take enough to sample. Don't worry. You're safe." He squeezed my hands.

I nodded, letting him know I was ready.

The first thing I felt was a draw to Nyx—his call, I supposed. Different to the almost tangible strand of our bond that always reached for him and tethered us together. This was definitely a pull from that reserve in me. I guessed this was how we could draw on each other's magic. Yet another way I was connected to Nyx. There felt like there were many ways now, and some were getting more physical.

The magic inside me responded to him, opening instinctively so he could draw what he needed. This bond between us was like a key to my reserve that no one else would have. I felt my power flow to him steadily and could feel it leave me, but it didn't feel like a loss of power. My instinct told me that by sharing magic, we both stayed safe. If one was depleted, we were both at risk, so passing it to him didn't feel like a loss.

Suddenly, a second draw pulled from that steady flow. I immediately hated it. It felt invasive. I could feel the difference between sharing magic with my other half for the good of us both and losing it entirely as the power left us.

Nyx tightened his hold on my hands, grounding me as I bore the unpleasant sensation, and I held on to his comfort, trying to stay calm as I felt my reserve draining slowly.

Just when I was starting to panic, Rakan withdrew his hand, and the drain on my magic stopped immediately. I breathed out a deep breath I was holding and sagged into Nyx's arms.

He held me while I adjusted to the new sensation of a space inside me that was previously full. There was still power there. Plenty, actually. He had taken less than I imagined. But in the moment, the sensation had felt like a hemorrhage.

"*You okay?*" Nyx asked through our bond.

"*I'm fine. I hated that feeling, though.*" I wound my arms around him, soaking up the comfort he was offering.

"*It's not nice at first. Once you see how it refills naturally, though, you won't mind it so much.*"

I tried to straighten up, but Nyx held me to him. "*Stay here a bit longer, Sol. He will be assessing for a few minutes anyway.*"

"*I don't want him to think I'm a weak little girl. He's already made it abundantly clear he's not impressed by me.*"

Nyx laughed. "*Rakan isn't impressed by anyone; ignore him. He won't even notice I'm holding you now he's got his sample. Let him work.*"

I relaxed a little. "*This is nice,*" I admitted.

Nyx pulled back slightly, looking down at me. "*I think that's the first time you've admitted you like being near me.*"

"*Want me to take it back?*"

He returned me to his chest. "*Nope.*"

After a moment, Rakan cleared his throat, and I pulled away from Nyx, turning to face him. He had his back to us, though, staring down at his notes, pouring over the texts he had open.

Nyx slipped his hand into mine.

"Her origin powers are predominantly from the Light Kingdom. I'm getting strong amplifying, enlightenment, divination." He paused to reference something, and goosebumps rose on my skin just hearing these unbelievable things he thought me capable of. A thrill of anticipation ripped through my chest, knowing I would learn all I could about the Light Kingdom and what it meant to originate from there.

"Replenishment staples will be sunlight, fire, citrine, labradorite… There's an interesting interaction with moonstone and black onyx for help with physical stress, so you can both replenish from those if either of you have an injury, since Nyx is a dark wielder and connects to onyx." He continued tracing his finger down a list.

"Light wielders make excellent healers. Don't overlook that

despite it not being your calling. You can still learn things that may aid you. Divination is strong in light wielders, paired with some intuition I believe comes from a First Kingdom origin somewhere in her line. I would recommend amethyst as her origin stone. It's native to there and enhances intuition. I'll set up a session with Oribel to go through that with you. I also recommend some work with sacred geometry. Kiera can guide you— all that is beyond me. But the Light Kingdom uses the symbols to better effect than the rest of the kingdoms. Maybe the Goddess favors them."

I was rendered silent by all the information, so I was relieved when Nyx spoke. "Light." He shook his head, squeezing my hand. "Sol…the sun. I should have known."

"Can't say I can predict how a dark wielder and a light wielder of your strengths will meld, but it's going to be interesting." Rakan somehow managed to sound utterly disinterested despite his words.

"She has some First Kingdom blood in her line, you said?" Nyx sounded slightly concerned. I just watched the back and forth, hoping I could get all of this in writing so I could actually take it in later.

"Intuition is strong, so there's definitely some First Kingdom, but she's not a risk for dampening."

"You're sure?"

Rakan finally turned to look at Nyx over his shoulder. "Certain. No dampening." He returned to his notes. "I'll get this all recorded and submit the report, but I'm recommending that you meld before you are cleared to fly with a unit. She has a lot of power, and no experience harnessing it. The meld will give you better control, and you'll be less of a risk to our flyers."

My stomach sank.

"You can start training alone. Just stay away from flight classes until you meld."

Nyx nodded, not thrilled but not putting up any resistance.

Besides, we'd flown anyway; his permission wouldn't have stopped us. At least now we could afford to be seen if we did it again.

Rakan said nothing more and resumed making notes, effectively dismissing us.

Lovely.

THIRTY-FIVE
NYX

"It's been two weeks since her magic awoke. What's the holdup?" the King demanded.

"Your Majesty, I'm not prepared to risk an entire class of trainees with such a powerful and inexperienced ryder. They will continue to train separately until they are melded. I'm just following the advice of the experts and the way we've trained ryders for a century," Octavian said.

I cringed, feeling caught in the middle. Both fae had been like family to us, and I owed them both a debt for the concessions made when I was unable to take the place of my father, having no ryder at the time of his death.

"With respect," I addressed Octavian, "I don't feel the meld is necessary to progress. Zaria is working hard. She's listening well, and we have her power under control. I believe we pose no risk to the rest of the trainees, and if you give us the opportunity to complete flight training, we will do so quickly. She's a natural ryder. We just need to complete the program."

"With. Respect," Octavian seethed, the first show of anything other than familial warmth he had ever displayed. "We have unknown enemies attacking outposts, dragons disappearing, fewer hatchlings every year, and I *will not* risk an entire new crop of capable flyers just so you can claim status and become the General. And the truth is that you do not have her magic under control. If you two had full control, you'd be melded."

I reeled. He acted like this was some moral failing of mine. Where had this come from? Had the power of the position gotten its claws in him? I'd never seen him so possessive over it before. He'd always referred to it as my position, which he was guarding for me. The regency works because it's an unrelated dragon filling it in name only, so the hereditary roles do not pass as they would, father to son. Was it possible, after two years in the position, he was taking on alpha characteristics, regardless? I didn't know how it would be, but two years was a long time with that kind of power. Perhaps he'd forgotten that it was not really his. Would I have to challenge him?

"We've done in weeks what most students take years to do." I studied him. My father's friend. My father trusted him. The King trusted him. Was I being paranoid? "This is not about status," I refuted. My tone was little more than a growl.

Octavian disregarded me and addressed the King. "We can't be certain they can control her magic without the meld. Dragons will be at risk. You don't want that."

"What I want is for the succession to take place. I need an Asar back at the head of the Dragon Council." The King banged his desk. Octavian's lips formed a tight line, but the King continued. "The dragons are restless. They need stability, and that is Nyx."

No one had ever verbalized in front of me that there was

unrest in the council because the position had not passed to me. I was under the impression that Octavian was well-regarded.

"No one wants to see an Asar back at the head of the council more than I do," Octavian said through gritted teeth, but for the first time, I didn't buy it. "But if stability is so important to the council, the meld is even more important. Nyx will have responsibility for all dragon kind. We can't hand that over when his bond with his ryder is not yet complete. Melds have been known to fail. What then? More uncertainty while we go back to having a proxy? Or would we have to hand over to Kol?"

The way he spat the suggestion got my back up. He might not want the job, but Kol was every bit the Asar I was and would lead admirably. They didn't see that because he was too carefree, but he had it in him.

The King pinched the bridge of his nose. "Well, it's been two weeks since her powers awoke. How long is it going to take?"

"These things can't be rushed, Highness. Melds come when they come, not when we desire them. I will admit that, typically, we see them happen soon after bonding, but long bonding periods are not unheard of."

"And there's nothing they can do to encourage things along?" the King asked, grasping at any hope he could find. "Because if we can't get him out commanding the flyers soon, with all this uncertainty, we may need to consider putting Kol out on the front just to appease the council."

A knot formed in my chest. It was an unspoken agreement that until I could fly, Kol wouldn't be put out on the front. He was my only surviving family, and I knew the King had always kept him close to the First Kingdom for my benefit. But now? Was it a threat or simply motivation? I didn't know.

"We are doing everything we can," I assured him. "We are spending as much time together as we can, working in every discipline, power sharing as often as possible. We can't do more. Our connection is strong, but please remember the upheaval

Zaria has been through. Her whole world has changed. She needs time to fully adjust to all the changes."

"Well, for the love of the Goddess, think of something else you can try," he boomed. "And keep me updated daily."

"Yes, Your Majesty."

"Dismissed."

I dipped my head and left the office, breathing out a heavy sigh.

Then I looked up and found Zaria standing there, and from the stricken look on her face, I knew she had heard the conversation. She was getting good at small magic, like projection and amplification, so she could listen in easily.

I sagged. She'd wanted to go to the meeting, but I'd wanted to protect her. I should have known she would come anyway.

"Sol..." I reached for her.

She backed away, shaking her head. "It's my fault."

"How is it your fault?"

"I'm holding you back. I'm sorry." She turned and took off in a jog away from me, and I felt powerless to stop her. She needed to sort through her feelings, and I knew what would help with that.

"*Kol?*"

"*At your service,*" he replied jovially.

"*I need a favor.*"

THIRTY-SIX

ZARIA

"**W**hy the glum face, sunshine?" Kol asked, flopping down in the seat beside me by the fire in the library.

I wasn't shocked he found me. I often came here to study. It felt like the best way to accept this life was to know as much as possible about it. This nook had become my escape after grueling lessons. I now knew the fire helped me recharge, too, so that explained why I took comfort here.

"No reason. Just thinking."

"Want to talk about it?"

I dropped my head back against the chair and rolled it to look at Kol.

"He sent you, didn't he?"

Kol shrugged. "He was worried."

"Well, you can tell him I'm fine. In fact, he's probably listening, so you won't have to." I clamped my mouth shut as soon as

I registered the words that were leaving my mouth. But I couldn't take it back. Glancing around, I whispered, "I'm so sorry."

Kol looked around subtly, then leaned in. "It's fine. No one is close by."

"What if—"

"It's fine," Kol insisted.

I felt just awful. They'd never slipped, and in a fit of frustration, I could have revealed their secret.

Kol returned to the topic of our conversation, brushing my slip aside. "He didn't ask me to come so I could report back. He sent me so you had a friend."

I softened and shook my head. "Why is he looking out for me after he just had to defend us to the King again?! He's the one getting pressured from every side while I hold up his career, his whole life. And he's there, making sure I have someone to talk to. It's all wrong."

"You are his first priority. Don't ever forget that. Because in the not-too-distant future, he will have so many responsibilities, there may be days you don't feel it. But for as long as he draws breath, you will be the thing he puts above everything."

I studied Kol. There was not an ounce of deception in him. I knew his words to be the truth. And yet I knew he didn't feel that way about his ryder. They had a good meld—I knew because Kol had talked about it to help me understand how melds were different for all pairs. Theirs was fairly decent, in his words.

I'd been around many pairs since then and watched their connections. Some were barely friends, but lots were obviously intimate, like Kol was with Elvar. But it was just pleasure for them, not love. Or was I foolish for trying to apply that concept to this world?

Of course, there was love here. In most ways, the fae were the same. But among the bonded few like we were, the pairings were pre-destined by the Goddess. Some had relationships outside the bond, and that worked for them. Others turned to their bonded partner for those needs, but was it laziness or just complacency?

None of that fitted what Kol was trying to tell me about what I meant to Nyx. Of course, I knew our bond as ryder and flyer was above all, but I felt like Kol was referring to our bond as more than his or others, and I couldn't wrap my mind around that when I felt so…misaligned.

That was it. I was misaligned with this path I was supposed to be progressing along. I was trying to follow Nyx, but I wasn't there, right by his side like I needed to be. I was just a little out of sync.

"Did I lose you?" Kol asked, pulling me out of my head.

"Sorry. My mind is a mess of thoughts, and I'm just trying to make sense of things."

"That's why I'm here, to help you make sense. Do you want to take a walk? We can get some air and untangle that mess of yours."

"Sure." I dragged myself out of the chair and followed him out of the library. As we crossed the lobby, I looked across the space and met eyes with a fae I'd just seen while waiting outside the King's office. He'd eyed me with suspicion, then disappeared into another office. Now he was here, watching me. What if he'd heard what I said about Kol and Nyx?

"You coming?" Kol called.

I shook it off and caught up with him. I didn't know where we were headed, but it didn't matter. I needed to get some air and stop being paranoid.

We walked along familiar corridors until we reached fresh air, and then Kol steered us along a walkway I'd never been down.

"I think I'm stuck on a different path to Nyx, and that's the problem," I admitted after I sensed Kol was waiting for me to speak.

"How so?"

"My life was so different before. It was controlled for me. It was a prison of sorts, and I see that now. The elders kept us confined, cut off from the outside, working for their cause. Then, aside from that betrayal, we know they were also poisoning me to keep my bond to Nyx cut off. It's a lot to come to terms with."

"Of course it is," Kol soothed. "No one expects you to move on overnight. You are grieving many different losses."

"That's the thing—it's the moving on. I know how to process the deaths. We were raised to face death, and our rituals were the closure we had to move on. That's missing for me. I have no closure. It's an open wound. And it's not mourning for the fae themselves, although that sounds heartless and terrible. I have a lot more work to do on understanding and forgiving their actions before I can grieve their loss."

"So, what is it?"

I thought about how to put it into words. "When I came here, all I wanted to do was get back. Even once I started to accept there was nothing to go back to, I still needed to go, because I was raised to think that a soul could not go to the Goddess without the ceremonial rites. I see now that other kingdoms have their own traditions. We all have them. So, I think I'm not moving on because, in my heart, I know those fae, not just my family, all of them, are just out there. Dead and forgotten. And I can't live with it. I can't just forget and move on knowing that."

"You want to go back to perform the rites?"

"I think I have to. I think that is what's in the way of our meld. I can't give myself fully to this new path when I still have one foot on the other, and I can't think of another way to let it go."

"Then, make Nyx understand."

THIRTY-SEVEN

ZARIA

I tossed and turned in my bed. No position was comfortable, and the weight of my thoughts was too heavy to carry into sleep. I couldn't settle. I wanted to be what Nyx needed me to be, but I couldn't find a way to make it happen.

I didn't know how to resign myself to this life, even if it was the one I now wanted. Everyone was growing tired of waiting for our meld, and every day that passed made me want to leave. It was getting exhausting, and the more I thought about it, the more I was convinced the only way forward was to go back. To see if putting that part of my life to rest would unburden me enough to complete our bonding.

I'd tried to bring it up with Nyx, but he kept shutting it down.

I needed to bury the dead. Even though I carried an insurmountable amount of anger for my parents. My siblings didn't deserve to wander as ghosts forbidden from joining the Goddess.

Luka didn't deserve to have his bones picked clean by ravens and to be a lost soul.

I often thought of how much he'd have enjoyed life at the palace, or even just life outside of our village. He would have thrived here, but because of the choices of our parents, he was dead. I hated being the only one left alive. I didn't feel like I deserved it.

All of it felt like a block on my soul.

And I would never move forward with the weight of their deaths holding me back.

I couldn't lay in my bed any longer. I needed some air.

I forced myself out and dug through my wardrobe for something to pull over my night clothes. I cracked my door to make sure no one was in the hall and startled at the sleeping form in my doorway.

The torchlight dotted along the walls gave enough light to see it was Nyx curled on the floor facing my door.

"Nyx?" I bent and nudged him, keeping my voice low. He didn't stir. "Nyx…"

Nothing.

I toed him with my boot, and he rolled slightly, opening one eye.

"What are you doing here?" I hissed.

He chuffed and rolled to his side without answering.

"Nyx, what are you doing?" I asked more forcefully when he didn't answer.

"You've mentioned leaving every day for a week, so I was beginning to think you might sneak off in the night," he finally murmured.

Was he serious? "So, you've been sleeping in my doorway?"

"Yes, Sol. And apparently, for good reason." He glared.

"For how long?"

"A few days."

"A few days?" Goddess, no wonder he'd been looking tired.

"Uh-huh."

"I could have just stepped over you," I said with a huff.

"I have been awake since you got out of bed."

"Don't lie. I just had to kick you in the chest to wake you up."

"No, you had to kick me in the chest to get me to reply to you. I was feigning sleep to avoid this argument with you," he said through a yawn. "Can we do this in the morning? We have to be up in"—he angled his head to look out the window across the hall— "two or three hours."

"I'm not going back to bed."

"Why are you up?" He sat up like it had just occurred to him that I'd come out of my rooms for a reason.

"It's none of your business." I stepped around him, not sure why I'd decided to keep it from him. Probably because he thought he was entitled to it.

"It is my business. You can't run away." He was on his feet, blocking my path before I could take another step.

My instincts screamed at me to back up, but I held my ground. "I'm not running away. Now, move."

"No." He pressed closer, forcing me to take a step to prevent our bodies from meeting.

"Back up," I said, but my voice caught, ruining any of the indignation in my tone.

"No," he said again, but this one sounded playful. He took another step into me.

I mirrored the movement, and my back hit the stone wall beside my door. "I'm going to the library, but it's really none of your business."

"Why?"

"It's. None. Of. Your. Business." I would not tell him I planned to look at maps to see if there was any chance of getting myself back to the compound.

"It is my business. You're my—" He cut himself off, chest heaving.

"I'm your what?" It was barely a hesitation, but I caught it.

"You're my ryder. It is my job to protect you."

We were at a standoff. I didn't want to tell him why I wanted to go to the library, and he wasn't going to let it go. And his body heat did something to me. I needed to get out of there before I lost myself. Every second I stood there risked him knowing I was getting aroused. I loathed knowing that dragons could scent arousal. I could have been living in blissful ignorance.

I squeezed my eyes closed, trying to get a hold of myself. I would not give him the satisfaction of pressing my thighs together to ease the ache. He would know.

Once I got my voice under control, I lifted my chin, meeting his jade gaze. "You don't have to worry about me running away. I'm merely getting some air because I can't sleep, so move."

"I'm afraid I can't do that. You could still run away."

I schooled my features. "Look, I'm frustrated, but I wasn't serious. I know I couldn't make it across the volcanic wastelands by myself. I'm not an idiot." I may want to do a little research on it rather than lay in bed staring at the ceiling, but he didn't need to know that. And ultimately, I knew I couldn't actually go alone.

His eyes softened. "I can't risk it, Sol."

Men. Luka warned me they were all like this. I hadn't believed him. "So, you're going to sleep out here every night?"

"Unless you want to invite me to share your bed?" He delivered the line with a smile indicative of his dragon. Entirely sly and leading.

I hated that I liked it. "Never."

"Then, I guess here I'll stay." Smugness dripped from him.

"You can stay here, but I'm going," I insisted.

"Not without me, you're not."

I sighed. "I am entitled to free time."

"Sure, we all are, and I am entitled to spend my free time wherever I wish."

I narrowed my eyes. "You wouldn't."

"Wouldn't what, Sol?" His lips curved up. He was enjoying this far too much.

"Start following me?"

He half shrugged. "Who knows when we'll run into each other?"

"You are insufferable."

"I know. And I know how much you like it."

"Goddess, save me from this fate." I gave up the fight. "I'm not going to the library so that you can sit and stare at me while I read. I'm going to sit out on the landing and look at the stars. If you can't trust me not to climb down a drainpipe and run away into the night, then come with me. But don't ruin it for me, or I'll push you off."

I pushed past him as he laughed. "You realize I can fly, Sol?"

Groaning, I set off for the landing. "You don't say."

Nyx followed but kept his smart remarks to himself for a change, walking in silence just behind me.

I looked at him over my shoulder. "Is this a taste of what's to come with you as my shadow?"

"Don't threaten to leave by yourself, and I won't need to follow you."

I slipped through the door to the landing platform, letting go so it swung closed in Nyx's face. I bit my lip to keep in my smile and kept walking right to the edge.

Nyx came jogging up beside me and put his hand protectively on my arm. Ignoring it, I bent down, taking a seat, with my feet dangling over the edge.

"By the Goddess, are you trying to fall?"

Exasperated, I cut him a heavy glare. "Have *you* forgotten you can fly?"

His eyes narrowed. "There will be no more trust falls in our future, thank you."

I looked out over the city and took in the sight. I was used to the night bringing a blanket of darkness down over the world. Here, there were lights from torches dotted everywhere. The palace grounds were kept lit by the watch posts around the walls, and the streets around the palace were lit by streetlamps. The all-night taverns that catered to the legion, who kept round-the-clock hours, were subdued in the early hours but still going. Traders would soon begin setting up and preparing their wares for the day ahead. The city never slept, and I couldn't get used to it.

Laying back, I tucked my hands behind my head, gazing up at the night sky. Nyx laid down beside me and watched the stars in silence for a while.

"Explain to me why you are so set on returning?" he said after some time.

"I would have thought Kol had told you my reasons."

He raised up onto his elbow and looked down. "Kol is your friend, and I'm not going to take that away from you by using him as a spy."

A smile curled my lips.

"What?" he asked.

"He said the same thing."

He laid back down. "Well, there you are, then."

Silence stretched, once again, and I felt his expectant stare boring into me.

"I think I just need it, that's all." I didn't have the energy to go into my reasons tonight.

Before he could reply, a giant mass slammed down next to me, causing me to sit up suddenly and pitch forward.

A hand snatched out, saving me from falling.

"Don't fall to your death on my account," Kol said flatly.

"Kol! You nearly scared me to death. Never mind the fall."

"Kol?" Nyx said, concern lacing his voice. "What's wrong?"

I looked at Kol, then. Nyx was right, something was wrong. Kol looked distracted, agitated. "I have to pack. I have to—"

"Pack?" I asked.

Kol raised his eyes to Nyx, and sadness pooled in them. "We've been ordered to the Second Kingdom, brother."

"No." Nyx's hand went to his mouth. "They can't do this."

"It's done. We just got called back from patrol, and I have to get ready. We fly out at first light."

"Who changed the orders? I speak to the King and the Regent daily, and—" Nyx cut himself off as he laid eyes on his brother.

"I don't know."

"We've had meetings for weeks about how to retake the outpost and make sure another flight isn't lost. How did this happen?"

"The King came into the war room this morning asking questions. He said something about my powers being undervalued." Kol put his hands over his face. "I didn't think it would lead to this. I don't know what the fuck they think I can do. I'm not a fucking replacement for you."

"No one expects you to be." Nyx put a hand on Kol's arm.

My stomach dropped. Was this because of my slip in the library? Did they know about the twin's bond?

"It looks like they think I can be." Kol didn't turn around as he spoke.

I sat rooted in place, unable to move, not knowing if I should say I thought it was my fault.

Nyx wrapped an arm around his brother, and Kol leaned into him. I almost felt like I shouldn't be watching this private moment between them.

"I thought we were being kept here because the First Flight always guards the capital. Apparently, that's not the case anymore. I'm at an utter loss."

"I'll find out what's going on," Nyx promised. I thought he

might go now and demand answers despite the hour. But Kol continued as if he hadn't spoken.

"How can we face an enemy none of us know? How can we send our best flyers to a place where a hundred fae disappeared in two days? Aren't we just throwing lives away?" Kol's voice stuttered.

Nyx didn't reply but hugged Kol.

He had to be at a loss for words.

"I have to go. I have to get things ready—"

Nyx grabbed his face with both hands, cutting him off. "I will go to Octavian and insist we have armies and another flight staged close by before you're sent in. You have me. I won't let anything happen to you, no matter what it takes."

My breath hitched. It was too much risk. Nyx would risk their secret to make sure his brother wasn't in danger.

This was like watching a disaster unfold in front of my eyes, and there was nothing I could do.

Nyx left to get answers from the war room. He was convinced the order was given in the dead of night so that they would be gone before he knew about it. But that had failed, so he wasn't going to let them go without putting up a fight.

Kol went to his rooms to pack, and I paced mine, guilt eating me alive.

A knock at my door came as the night sky was showing the first signs of a distant dawn. I threw it open, finding Kol, with a bag at his feet.

He reached for my hand and pressed something into my palm. "If I die—"

"Don't you dare say that!" I snapped.

"Zaria, I have to live in reality."

"By the Goddess, I swear, you do not get to go into this thinking you will die. If you do that, the Goddess may fulfill your wish."

Kol closed his eyes. "Please keep this for me. Please. I won't say anymore, but if I don't come back, give it to Nyx."

I took the small, folded message with Kol's seal and turned it in my hands.

A tear rolled down my cheek. "Okay."

"Put it away. Do not tell him or anyone else I did this." He looked into my eyes, more serious than I'd ever seen him. Tears swam in his eyes, too. "Promise me."

"I promise."

He pulled me into his arms, and I pressed my face into his neck, unable to stop my sob. "What am I going to do without you here?"

"Nyx will protect you." He didn't release me.

"I'm not worried about him protecting me," I said indignantly. "You are my best friend." My first real friend, I realized as I said it. I'd had Luka, but that had been different; he'd always wanted more than I could give.

Kol pulled back enough to look into my eyes. "I am?"

I nodded through my tears. "My first. My only. So, I can't lose you."

Kol's face broke out in a smile. "I'll do my best."

"No!" I smacked his solid chest.

"No?

"Do better. You have to come home."

"I know." He kissed the top of my head.

"Promise me!"

"I promise."

THIRTY-EIGHT

NYX

"Wake up." I crouched next to Zaria's bed, but she didn't stir. I stroked a lock of her hair off her face. "Zaria."

She jumped, sitting up to scramble back in her bed until her back hit the wall while her hands came up in front of her.

"It's me," I hissed.

Zaria's gaze focused on me. "What are you doing here?"

"We need to leave."

"What?" She twisted to look out the window. "What time is it?"

"Sunrise is in three hours," I told her.

"What's wrong?" She shifted from bewilderment to concern.

"Everything and nothing," I confessed. "We can talk about it on the way."

"On the way where?" she asked, rubbing her eyes as the rush

from being jolted out of sleep subsided and her body registered it was not ready to be awake yet.

"Away from here." It was all that mattered right now.

"Are we in danger?" she whispered.

"No." It wasn't a lie, but I couldn't promise we would be safe indefinitely, either. I was increasingly feeling uneasy. I felt we were being watched too closely for it to be right. The King had never shown such interest in any bonded pair, and the pressure was becoming unbearable.

On the other hand, Octavian was complacent to a fault. For how much pressure we were getting from the King, it should have followed that Octavian would be breathing down my neck to progress, too. But he was happy to wait for the meld to happen in its own time. That worried me more than the King's obsession.

"I'll tell you everything. I just want to leave before sun-up, so we don't have to explain our plans to anyone."

Zaria nodded and quietly got out of bed.

I helped her gather her things, and while she dressed and used the bathing chamber, I packed them into the two saddle bags I'd brought with me. When she was ready, we took the back stairs and left the palace by a delivery gate.

Zaria didn't ask any questions while we walked through the quiet streets to one of the less popular inns in the city. I had a stable hand waiting there with two horses loaded for travel. After securing Zaria's bags to her horse, I paid the hand and helped Zaria into the saddle. I hadn't asked her if she had ridden a horse before, but she was a dragon ryder; she could handle it. And from the way she mounted, I could tell she was no stranger to the saddle.

I took the reins of my horse and centered myself before mounting. The animal was twitchy, and I needed to give off the calmest energy I could muster—not easy when we were sneaking out of the most heavily guarded city in all the kingdoms.

I mounted, and the horse let out a startled whinny, stamping his feet, and turning in a circle.

Zaria leaned over her mount to catch my reins and help steady the spooked creature.

It was always that way for us. They sensed the beast inside and were reluctant to submit to a monster they knew instinctively to be a predator. Eventually, once they realized they weren't lunch, they settled.

She smirked when she handed the reins back to me, pleased with herself for being better than me at something.

"Thank you." They were the first words we'd spoken since we left her room. "Let's go. I want to clear the city while it's still dark."

I turned my horse and led the way, taking quiet streets to the river, then following the river trail out to the city limits. We didn't encounter anyone, and the route I chose left the guard posts out of view.

"What is all this?" Zaria finally asked when we'd left the densely populated streets of the city behind.

"We are going back to your village, like you wanted, Sol."

"What?" Her brows pulled. "Really?"

"Really."

A small smile spread, but then she studied the packs again. "Wait. Surely you don't mean to make us ride horses to the Fourth Kingdom through the volcano wastelands."

"I do."

"We could fly and get there in a fraction of the time." It amused me that she was now so accustomed to dragon flight, she couldn't fathom a need for horses.

"I don't want anyone to know where we are going, and when they realize we are gone, they will look for a dragon. I don't know if you know this, Sol, but I'm quite easy to spot."

She scoffed, then paused. "Wait, they'll look for us? Are we going to be in trouble for leaving?

I shrugged, playing it off casually. "We aren't prisoners."

She studied me. "But we are supposed to be training, and we are under some intense scrutiny, aren't we?"

"I don't think the King will be pleased we are taking some unscheduled time away from the palace, but we aren't forbidden from leaving. I see it as a gray area."

"But you felt strongly enough about us leaving now to chance angering the King?" she asked.

I breathed in the cool, pre-dawn air, and felt free for the first time in weeks. "It was getting hard to function in the palace."

"I noticed."

"I was getting the feeling if we don't meld soon, the King will start taking drastic action to try and force it to happen."

"Drastic, how?"

"I don't know exactly, since a meld can't be forced by any method known to fae. But the King has the High Priest of the Temple of Avalon in his ear, and according to Kiera, the temple has a dark history when it comes to soul bonds."

"Dark?"

"Back before the Hundred Years War, when old magic had a dark side, the priests used dark spells to force soul bonds. They guarded their rituals and knowledge fiercely among the elder high priests. They didn't record it or share it, so it lived only in the minds of the elders. They believed that if a soul could live on with the Goddess, then one could live on in this world, too. If a high priest took ill or grew old and was dying, it's thought that through a dark ritual, they could bond the soul and the knowledge of the elder into that of one of the under priests, therefore keeping the elder living on in this world, rather than him going to the Goddess, and keeping his knowledge alive."

"What in all the kingdoms?" Zaria muttered.

"Look, it sounds like an old magic tale you'd hear over too much ale in the wrong side of the city to me, but Kiera seemed to think that the elder high priests of the temple still believe in the old ways. And they are probably crazy enough to believe that kind of magic actually existed."

Even in the dark, I could see the horror on Zaria's face.

"Sol, don't look so worried. Magic like that doesn't really exist. But with things how they are, is angering the King any worse than staying and getting nowhere with our meld while he gets radical ideas in his head about how he can help it along?"

"No. Definitely not."

"Exactly, so I think it's a good time for us to head back to your village. Besides, I can't stand doing nothing to for Kol. I feel helpless. Time away will be good."

THIRTY-NINE

ZARIA

R iding beside him gave me a lot of time in my own head. It took us hours to get outside of the capital and the surrounding towns. It went on for miles. Then we were surrounded by farmlands on a busy market road, but the earth was dry, and the horses steady. I enjoyed the scenery. I'd never left my village, and in the weeks I'd been at the palace, we kept to such a small vicinity I hadn't seen any of what was beyond, except from Nyx's back.

"How are you holding up?" he asked.

"I still can't believe we're doing this." I was relieved to finally be fulfilling the other side of the bargain I'd made with Nyx, but after so long, part of me was filled with dread. I couldn't altogether let go of the idea that my family wasn't dead until I saw the evidence, but I knew it was foolish to hope. Even so, there was still a little seed buried in my brain telling me they were out there.

"Can't believe it in a good or a bad way?"

"I don't know. I guess I'm stuck in the middle. Apprehensive, but I'm grateful, too. Thank you."

"You need it. I think we both needed to get out of there."

I glanced over at him. "It wasn't just the pressure of the meld, was it?" I knew it wasn't. I'd watched him turn slowly in on himself in the days since Kol was sent to the Second Kingdom.

They'd been separated before, and he'd told me it had been hard on them both. Kol's flight had been deployed many times since they'd finished their training, but the risk was usually much lower, and the distance far shorter. This was different.

Kol had made brief contact while they were flying long days to reach the outpost, but we had not heard from him since. Nyx suspected it was a strain for Kol to communicate over such a long distance, especially beyond the Wild Mountains, while using so much energy on flying non-stop every day. I hoped that once they camped and began the task of reclaiming the outpost, he would be able to check in more regularly to ease Nyx's mind.

"It felt like I was rotting, being stuck there and knowing what kind of danger Kol is in but not being able to do a thing about it."

"Rotting?" I questioned, wanting to understand him better.

"Rotting in place, you know? I was festering in my anxiety and frustration. I can't think of a better way to explain it." He turned his head to meet my gaze and shrugged.

I knew what he meant. Nyx was being kept completely out of the loop on the First Flight's mission. He was livid and more suspicious than before. Even though he didn't yet hold the rank of general, since his father's death, he'd been included in the chain of command. He'd never been cut out, and there was no clear reason for keeping him in the dark now, other than their weak claim that he was 'too close' to the flyers to be objective.

"I understand." I paused, not sure if I should compare my own situation to what he was facing. "I think it's a little like how I felt in my village. I was kept in the dark, fearful of things on the outside, and expected to follow their rules without question. I had no control. I know it's not the same—I wasn't fearing for a loved one, but…"

"It was still like rotting in place," he agreed.

I nodded.

"No one should have to live a life kept in the dark with no choices or control," he said with conviction. "If your parents wanted to live that way and raise their kids there, fine, but it was wrong of them to lie to you. They took the choice from you."

"It feels like they stole so much." I let the grief I'd been nurturing for a little while now form words. "We should have grown up together. They stole that from us." I didn't know if I'd ever forgive them for it.

Nyx smiled wistfully, possibly imagining what we'd have been like together from that age. "You just wish you'd had two little fae with wings to do your bidding."

I smiled in spite of the melancholy. "Yes, obviously. I cannot even begin to think of all the ways I would have abused the privilege of having you two around. The mischief you would have come up with."

"You would have been as bad as the two of us." He shook his head. "Worse, maybe."

I laughed in agreement, then sighed. "Can you imagine if we'd had all those years? Coming into our magic together, bonding and growing. We'd be melded by now…" I trailed off before bitterness had a chance to take hold.

He led his horse closer, so our thighs were side by side, and reached for my hand, taking it off the reins. "Things happened this way for a reason. I must believe there is a purpose to it."

"I know we can't change it, so there is no point regretting or being angry over the past, but I don't know how to let go of the anger I carry for what they did to me."

"The Goddess has a plan." He squeezed my hand, then released it. "Even if it is unknown to us right now."

"I know you're right." I had to trust.

FORTY

ZARIA

W e made camp late each evening, always a ways off the road. We'd agreed that we'd stay away from inns and taverns in case anyone was looking for us. The nights grew longer by the day, which meant we rode long after the sunset to make progress.

We took the saddles off the horses and fed them in the dark, working silently side by side. We felt seamless. More than we ever had in the palace.

Nyx searched the underbrush for enough dead wood for a fire, then used his magic to ignite it. Every part of me was stiff by the time I sat next to the flames. My muscles craved the heat, and I scooted closer until I was nearly sitting in them.

"Death by campfire might not be the best way to go." Nyx met my eyes over the fire.

"I'm sore. Maybe we should have flown."

"You'd be sore flying for that long too, but we couldn't risk it." He crouched next to the fire, turning the makeshift spit he'd constructed to cook the rabbit he'd caught earlier in the day. I was fascinating with this side to him. In the palace, where everything was provided, it didn't occur to me he would have the skills to survive like this. Like we had in our village where everything was so scarce.

He realized I was watching and stilled, his hands almost in the flames.

"You're going to burn yourself," I warned.

He dropped his attention back to what he was doing. "Not likely. Dragons are fireproof. Even in our fae form, we have a high tolerance to heat."

I shuddered. "Does your magic do that?"

"I guess so. I've never thought about it." He sat back, leaving the rabbit to cook.

"Your scales protect you when you're in your dragon form, but you don't have those like this."

"That you can see." He smiled, and his wings flickered.

I rolled my eyes. "That does not convince me."

"You'll have it, too. At least you should be protected from my fire once we meld."

I studied his features as they flickered in the light. "Let's not test that one until we have melded."

Once again, it all rested on the meld. Just the mention brought the heaviness down on our little camp.

"Let's get a few rounds of practice in while the food heats to work out your stiffness." He got to his feet, changing the subject.

"Are you serious?"

He had both our swords. Not practice ones—our real ones, which we'd started using in training. But he left them with our packs and came to me. "You didn't think this would be a vacation from your training, did you?"

"I did think, after riding since dawn, I would get a bit of a break." I grunted as I moved, pretty sure my legs would give out if I tried to stand.

"You misjudged my dedication to getting you ready for the field." He offered a hand.

I took it, and he pulled me to my feet, but then without warning, he put his shoulder into my chest, lifting me. I gasped, caught off guard by the move, but my training was second nature now, and I hooked my leg around his back, using the leverage to break his hold.

He laughed as I regained my footing and stumbled out of his grasp so he couldn't surprise me again. I thought I had a moment to catch my breath, but I was wrong. He dove, catching me around the middle to tackle me into a pile of leaves. I grunted as we collided, only the cushion of the leaves preventing me from losing my breath. I didn't have a second to think, because he went for my arms to pin them. I dodged, bringing my knee into his chest to prevent him from trapping me against the ground.

We scuffled, rolling around, each trying to gain the upper hand, ending up deadlocked at an impasse. He'd win if I let it go on too long, though, as he was stronger than me.

"Where in the Twelve Kingdoms did you find this energy after riding all day?" I shoved against him.

"I haven't flown in days, so I have pent up energy to burn." He pressed harder as he spoke, and I was weakening. It was only a matter of time before he had the upper hand.

Then an idea hit me. It was cruel, but it would work.

I lifted my hips into his. He blanched, his eyes widening as they met mine. I used his distraction to flip us, coming up on top of him in a pin.

"Evil, Sol."

I dragged my teeth over my lower lip, releasing his arms as I sat back on him to celebrate my victory. "You told me I need to use any advantage I can find."

He groaned, eyes closing as I sat just above his pelvis. His breath hitched. "I can see how well you learned the lesson." He didn't even try to throw me off.

"Is the game over?"

"Which one?"

My brows pulled. "Our scrimmaging?"

He opened his eyes, his gaze heady while a grin stretched over his lips. "I thought we were past that game and onto a new one." His fingers skimmed up the outsides of my thighs.

"I think you'll lose that game, too." I grabbed his wrists, stopping his hands before they reached my hips, preventing both his advance and the advantage he'd gain by getting a hold of me.

"I don't know. It feels like I'm winning from down here." His tone dropped deep, carrying a bite.

"You do not know what winning feels like," I warned, not knowing which of us I was warning.

His brows lifted. "I don't? Are you going to show me, Sol?" He broke my grasp on his wrists and grabbed my hips, but his touch wasn't harsh. He was soft, stroking his thumbs over my hip bones, following them until they dipped below my leathers.

I barely restrained a groan. Warmth flooded through me, and it took far too long to come up with a retort. "Is this a new lesson, teacher?"

"You don't seem like you need to be taught."

I leaned forward until my chest brushed against his. "Wouldn't you like to know?"

Before I realized what he was doing, he had me flipped under him again, his knees between mine, our bodies dangerously close. I existed between our joined breaths, covered in a blanket of him. A blanket of darkness.

He looked into my eyes and whispered over my lips, "I win."

"Do you?" I breathed, wrapping my legs around his hips and arching into him. He was hard. Goddess, help me.

"The rabbit is burning." He dropped his face to my neck, but only for a fraction of a second before his weight was gone.

I already missed it.

FORTY-ONE

ZARIA

I was so tired of travel rations, I could have cried when Nyx told me we needed to stop in a town to replenish our supplies.

The road grew lonelier the longer we were on it. Nyx was quiet, and I didn't know if it was his concern for Kol, or a new strain between us since our tussle by the fire. I hadn't realized how much I'd come to depend on Kol and Kiera's company. Especially now with no one to question about Nyx's weird behavior.

"This is a good-sized town. They have a tavern. I think we are far enough away now, so we should get a warm meal while we are here. What do you think?"

"I think yes!"

Nyx pointed at a building down the main street. "And they

have a butcher. We've hit the jackpot. We can get more salted meat to bring with us."

"Anything for some variety." We rode at a slow pace, taking in the town. It bustled around us, fae going in and out of shops. We drew attention, but I guessed that was because Nyx was larger than most fae—and one of the most attractive males I'd ever seen. He would draw eyes anywhere. It wasn't like when we went out in the capital and fae stared because of how he and Kol resembled their father. Or because they all knew he was the flyer who would be the next general. This was curiosity, not staring.

We went into the butcher and then a bakery for fresh bread, followed by the general store for more dried foods. Our packs were bursting by the time we finished, and my stomach growled. I turned to head to the tavern when a colorful display caught my attention.

I took a few steps away from where our horses were tied to look in the window of a shop. All kinds of colorful little pieces were displayed. They shone like jewels. Farther in, I watched as a female rolled out what looked like colored glass.

"What are you looking at?" Nyx said, coming up behind me, close enough that his breath was warm against my ear.

"This colored glasswork. Are they making windows?" I guessed that must be the case, but I couldn't figure out what the little pieces were for. Maybe jewelry? I glanced back at him.

He stared, then started laughing.

"What?"

"Are you making a joke?"

"A joke? About what?" I asked, gesturing at the window. I really hoped I wasn't hallucinating.

"It's candy." He said it like I should know what he was talking about.

"Candy?"

"Are you trying to tell me you don't know what candy is?" he asked, disbelief creasing his face.

"I don't know what candy is," I confirmed.

"It's made with sugar. It's a treat. You never had sweets?"

"We had baked sweets sometimes if we had the provisions, but I've never seen anything like this. Is it really to eat? The colors..." Each piece was like a little work of art.

He fought a smile and shook his head.

"What?" I asked, self-conscious suddenly.

"Your joy at something I never thought to be joyous over," he said fondly. "I love it. Let's go in."

"Really? Will you buy me some? I know you do so much for me already, but I have to know what they taste like!" I was so excited, I didn't even care I was asking for things I didn't need.

"I would buy you everything they have, Sol, but you can buy yourself some," he said, like it was nothing.

I scoffed. "With what coin?" I'd come to terms with my dependence on him for now. I would find a way to pay him back one day.

"You have your own money now." He lifted a coin purse out of the bag he was holding and handed it to me.

"What? How?"

"Trainees get paid once they are in the program."

"And you're just telling me?" I said, snatching it out of his hands. I opened it to find bronze coins, silver, and even some gold. I narrowed my eyes at him. "Explain yourself."

"We have been on the road. You haven't had any use for it. I brought it just in case you did."

"You know what I mean." I set my hands on my hips, trying to set an imposing figure.

He played dumb. "Nope, can't think what you possibly mean..."

"At the palace. Why wasn't I informed there?"

"Because you don't need coin for anything there?" He said it like a question.

I pursed my lips and stared into his eyes. "Nyx!"

He relented, looking contrite. "Okay. I was slightly concerned if you knew, you would use it to abscond. It's all safe, and it's yours. I'd never touch it, I swear."

"You may be right, but I still don't like that you lied to me about it." I wasn't mad, truly. It was just another thing between us to make me wonder where we stood.

"I never lied. I would have told you had you asked."

"It was a lie of omission." I didn't know what came over me, but I jabbed a finger into his chest.

He grabbed my finger. "It was. I'm sorry."

Heat burned my skin where we connected, spreading through my body. I broke the eye contact and muttered, "I forgive you."

He brushed the backs of his knuckles across my collarbone. "Thank you."

I leaned into his touch, closing my eyes.

"Which candy do you want to try?" he asked, breaking the moment.

"All of them."

"I'll buy you as many as you want," he said softly.

"Don't make promises you can't afford," I warned, wishing I could stay close to him like this forever. It felt so good when he was close…and then so empty when he pulled back.

"Just consider the horses before buying out the shop," he cautioned.

"As long as we bring them a piece, I don't think they'll mind."

"Come, I'll help you pick," he said, turning to the door, and the contact was gone.

I exhaled heavily. I'd grown up without much physical contact, but the tactile way my new friends were with each other was rubbing off on me. I already missed it, and I was craving it even more with each push and pull I was having with Nyx.

Maybe Kalilah wanted me to die of frustration.

FORTY-TWO

ZARIA

"I have something for you," Nyx said softly. "Close your eyes."

I closed them without question. A moment went by before something slipped over my head and settled between my breasts.

"You can open them now."

I blinked, looking down, and gasped. A large crystal hung on a long, silver chain. "It's beautiful."

"I thought you needed a new pendant–one that could heal not harm you."

"Where did you get it?"

"Back in that town, when I left you watching the candy pulling to go buy some extra supplies."

"I don't know what to say. Thank you." I lifted the stone to the light and inspected the color. I had been studying crystals to learn their many properties for power and healing. This was something I had not yet encountered. And yet...I frowned.

"Both your origin and replenishment stones happen to be varieties of quartz which can occur together. When amethyst and citrine form in the same crystal, you get the perfect stone for you. Ametrine."

I studied the point of quartz, and it was indeed half citrine and half amethyst. A clear line dividing them.

"I saw it and knew it had to be yours. I wanted to give you something to help you replenish when you need it."

"It's perfect, thank you."

Nyx slid a finger under the chain, extending it out to its full length. "And this one lifts over your head." He smiled.

I recalled the struggle to remove my old pendant and knew the consideration he'd put into making this gift a restitution for the last pendant rather than a replacement.

He tugged on the chain, pulling me against him, and leaned in, his lips almost brushing mine. Then I felt his fingers skirt the neckline of my tunic, and the fabric was pulled delicately away from my chest. I sucked in a breath.

"Keep it against your skin," he breathed, and dropped the crystal inside my clothing.

My eyes were heavy lidded from the intensity of him, but they widened at the sensation of a steady thrum from the crystal where it met my skin. A similar feeling to how I felt by the fire in the library, or under the warm rays of the afternoon sun since my powers finally became mine. A replenishment boost that filled my reserves faster than rest alone could do.

"You feel it?" he asked.

I nodded. I was feeling a lot with him so close. My breaths were shallow, and my heart hammered in my veins. I thought he was going to kiss me again.

I wanted him to.

But then he released my tunic and stepped away, leaving me breathless and wanting.

FORTY-THREE

ZARIA

ays blurred into each other. We spent long hours riding, and many, many hours training, both physically and magically. But it was the flying I missed. I never thought I would say that, but flying was my favorite thing, and those hours were when I felt closest to Nyx.

My body was changing. I felt stronger than I ever had. I slept better than I ever had, too, so exhausted by the end of the day I couldn't do anything more than eat and fall into my bed roll.

But I was beginning to realize the Goddess had other plans for us tonight. Nyx's face turned to the sky, a scowl creasing his brow. "Isn't it too early for monsoon season?"

"They have been known to come early," I replied, fear inflating like a balloon in my chest. Monsoons hit the coast of the Desert Kingdom for a brief spell each year. It was the product of a unique weather system that spilled off the volcano coast and, though brief, they could be extreme.

"I didn't consult with a weather mage before we left. I didn't want to raise suspicion. I didn't even consider…" As Nyx spoke, a few drops hit the ground—a warning from the Goddess to get under cover. The sprinkle before the downpour.

I turned in a slow circle. Not even a tree in sight. Nothing as far as the eye could see. "If the road floods…"

"Surely, the roadways are built to withstand even the worst of the flooding in the kingdom?"

I shook my head. "Maybe near the cities, but out here, the barons don't care about the fae. They hardly bring in any taxes, so they are left to fend for themselves."

"That's not right. The King provides every kingdom with military units and stipends for the fae's safety and wellbeing."

"Maybe for the larger populations that the barons care about. The ones that generate income for them. This far out, the fae are on their own."

"Maybe in your village, because they lived outside the law, but I have a hard time believing it's that way across the entire Fifth Kingdom."

"It's not just the Fifth Kingdom. We occasionally took in new followers of the Sisters of the Sands. Fae who were turned away from the kingdoms and couldn't fend for themselves any longer and were desperate. Turning to the Goddess and giving themselves in service by joining the commune. The more I think about it, the more I see that desperate fae don't ask questions and will promise whatever it takes for salvation, which is how the elders must have ensured that nothing of the outside world was ever spoken of inside their walls."

It struck me then that I understood the fae out here better than he did. He spent his whole life in the wealth and excess that was the First Kingdom, and he had no idea how other fae on the outside really lived.

"The King can't know."

I lifted my shoulders. "I can't speak to what the King knows or doesn't, but I do know we need to find cover. We can't camp out here in this."

"It's just a little water. How bad can it be?"

As if the Goddess wanted to make him eat his words, the sky opened.

The rain came down, not in drops or drips, but like stones fired from above…and it was ice cold. We were soaked before we got a mile, and with an endless stretch of desert in front of us, there was no hope for cover. We'd long passed all the giant rock formations and caves that bordered the volcanic lands.

We rode on into the driving rain, heads ducked, and faces covered, but it did little to keep the water out. It soaked even our leather boots. After sunset, the real danger would set in. The temperature dropped quickly at night, bringing the other extreme of the desert. The cold sank into my bones until my teeth chattered. It should have been impossible for water to fall from the sky in the usually arid desert to be this cold.

"We have to find somewhere to shelter!" Nyx yelled, and despite our close proximity, the wind almost drowned him out.

"Where?" I screamed.

"I don't know, but you will fall ill if we don't get out of these conditions. We have to find something with any cover at all. At least enough for me to get a fire going."

"You can't get a fire going in this even with dragon fire."

"I might be able to if we work together."

"You'll drain your power trying, and you'll never keep it alight. This rain will only get worse." I craved it, though. Anything to get warm. But I knew it wasn't worth the cost.

"Would you rather die?" Concern flickered in his gaze.

"I'm not going to die." My blue fingertips and the knowledge my lips were probably the same color were perhaps contradicting my argument, but we weren't there yet.

"Sol." His voice came with a mental bite.

"I'm not," I insisted, wiping my face in a futile war with trying to get the water out of my eyes, but it dripped from my hand and right back to pool across my lashes, making my vision blurry. "There has to be something. Anything. A village or house." But I couldn't see or even tell if we were still on the road.

"It's either find a place to shelter and warm up, or we leave the horses, and I'll fly."

"You can't fly in this. It will be more dangerous than being on the ground." Wing gusted, driving the rain even harder, making my point."

"If we can get above the worst, we might see a place to wait it out from the sky."

It might be worth the chance, but guilt held me back. "The horses will die if we leave them out here."

"If we do nothing, we all may die." He stared into the driving rain. "In another candle mark, I'm not giving you a choice."

We had to find somewhere. *Please, Goddess.* I nudged my horse on, determined to find a solution that didn't put Nyx at risk in the sky and condemn the horses to death.

We rode in silence, and as the minutes ticked by, I begged the Goddess for anything.

"We have to stop," Nyx called again. "Your lips are blue."

"I'm okay." My lips trembled as I spoke.

"I'm not giving you a choice." Nyx turned in his saddle, making a final sweep with his eyes, but there was nothing to see. Darkness had descended even before dusk. When had it set in? The rain cast a thick blanket over the land, blotting out the sun, making it seem like night had arrived.

The darkness created another world. I'd never felt this alone. So isolated.

"Sol, I'm not kidding. We have to do something." He put a

hand to his forehead, peering out into the black. "There might be shadows off the road a ways out. It may be some rocks or trees."

"What if there's lightning? Is that a good idea?"

"It's better than freezing to death. We can get in our tent." His tone carried an edge.

"Shouldn't we stay closer to the road rather than risk venturing out into a possible flood plain?"

"Whatever we are doing, we are doing it now. The horses won't last much longer. We can't hope for passersby, and you look like you are about to freeze to death. We need to make a decision."

"What about you?" I asked pointedly.

"I keep heat better than you because of my fire. It's you I'm worried about."

"Worry about yourself," I said, knowing I sounded a little like a petulant child. "If you trust me, you trust I won't let myself die."

He opened his mouth to speak but shut it and growled.

"We have to come upon a town soon. We have to. We need to keep going."

Nyx rubbed his face. "You are entirely frustrating."

"You like—" I cut myself off as something in the distance caught my attention, and I turned fully toward it, squinting.

"I like what…" Nyx trailed off, following my view.

I pointed. "Is that a light?"

Nyx frowned, leaning forward. "It is."

"It's something!" I urged my horse to hurry. I knew he was cold, too, but we had to make it.

"It could be anything, Sol. We have to proceed with caution."

"Whatever it is, it's better than dying out here. We will make it work."

"Sol, remember we need to conceal who we are."

"This is what you wanted," I reminded him, spurring my horse on. "Come on."

A single row of buildings that constituted a small town emerged through the rain once we had almost reached the source of the light, but it was life, and that was all we needed. In the middle of the row, the source of light we had seen glowed bright in the dark.

A smile broke out on my face. "It's an inn!"

"Thank the Goddess."

"I told you we'd find something." I had to get the jab in.

"You did. Good instincts, Sol."

He was being entirely too humble, and I didn't like it. It raised the hair on the back of my neck.

We dismounted and walked around to the rear to find the groom. He was asleep in a corner of the stables but quickly roused to take the horses. I moved to help get the saddle off.

"Go inside, miss. You look half drowned."

"We are, thank you," Nyx answered for us.

"I'll bring in your bags once I've seen to the horses," the groom said, waving us away. He was already working on getting the horses stripped and brushed down.

We hurried through the downpour to the inn door and entered, shaking water off. When I looked up, all eyes in the room were on us, and I drew up short. Nyx pressed in behind me.

"I didn't think anyone would be foolish enough to still be out there," the innkeeper said from the bar.

"It caught us off guard," Nyx said lightly, playing down the peril we'd been in.

"You must not be from around here if you don't know to always expect the sky to open this time of year."

"Would you have rooms we could wait it out in?" Nyx met him there while I shook water to the growing pool at my feet and tried to ignore the stares we were getting.

"I don't know if we have any. We had someone move on this morning, but I'll have to check with my wife to find out if she's promised it to anyone else. Sit down and dry yourselves by the fire, at least. If we don't have a room, you can roll out your bed rolls by the fire, so you don't have to sleep in the rain."

"Thank you," Nyx replied with a smile.

"Nothing fancy, but there's stew on. Eat something. It'll help warm you from the inside out."

"Sounds perfect. The groom said he would bring in our things..."

The innkeeper laughed. "Warm yourselves by the fire for now. That boy works slow, and to him, the horses come first. Besides, your things will be as wet as you are. Best you warm up until he's done. I'll have my wife bring your stew."

I wanted to get away from the interested gazes of the inn's guests, but he was right, and the fire was too inviting.

"We will. Thank you." Nyx turned to me, an unreadable expression on his face, and guided me to a table near the hearth.

I peeled off my outer clothes, pleased to shed the weight of the sodden fabric. We hung them on wall hooks beside the hearth and took a seat. I thought about trying to climb into the fireplace. I'd blocked out how cold I truly was until we'd stepped into the sweltering inn. Every part of me shivered, and I barely held them back. Nyx said I was fireproof-ish, which meant it was safe to sit in the flames, right?

"*Don't you think about it!*" He shot me a glare.

I smiled sweetly while peeling off my sweater. "*It was merely an idea. I don't know how I'll get warm if they don't have a room, though. I can't exactly climb into my bedroll sopping wet.*"

He blinked and then tore his gaze away. "*They'll have a washroom for you to change in, and maybe some hot water left over to wash up.*"

"*I'd take lukewarm water.*" I swiveled toward him, putting my knee on the bench. "*What?*"

"*Hmm?*"

"*Where'd you go?*" I asked, not sure what I'd done to lose his attention.

"*I'm taking in our surroundings.*"

"*Can you look at me?*"

"*Do I need to look at you?*" He was acting cagey.

"*I'd prefer it.*"

He turned, his expression schooled. "*Is this better?*"

I hated how hot and cold he was. "*Is everything okay?*"

"*You're a little...drenched, and fae are staring.*"

My brows pulled, and I looked down. The thin material of my shirt clung to my skin, but when I glanced around, I didn't see anyone staring. I looked at him again, and his eyes were on the ceiling. "*Nyx.*"

"*Yes, Sol?*"

"*Are you okay?*"

"*Perfectly fine.*"

I gathered my shirt, lifting it and twisting the fabric to ring out some of the water.

His eye twitched ever so slightly. "*Should you be dripping that on the floor?*"

"*With the amount of ale there, I don't think it will be a problem.*"

He couldn't fight it anymore, and his eyes lowered for the barest hint of a moment. A growl rumbled through him. He cut it off before anyone around us noticed, but I'd heard it.

"*Can I help you with something?*" I asked, keeping up my sweet tone.

His nostrils flared.

"The Goddess must favor your souls," a female I had to assume was the innkeeper's wife said, approaching with a tray.

"We have one room left." She set bowls and ale in front of us. "You can settle up when you collect the key."

"She must. I'll be over as soon as we finish." Nyx thanked her and poured us each a generous measure, then he lifted his glass to me in silent cheers.

FORTY-FOUR

NYX

*Z*aria's smile lit the room. Everyone around us delighted in her company. I hadn't seen her like this before. This must have been who she became on her nights out at the Flaming Pegasus. No wonder everyone fell in love with her.

Was this how she was before I took her? Had I ruined her life?

Too much had been stolen from her, and seeing her like this just made me see all that she was still missing—the freedom to make her own choices and be who she really is.

It was why I hadn't pushed her when it came to us.

She deserved to have one choice that was entirely her own, I repeated to myself.

If she made the choice not to take things further with me, I would have to live with that. I'd never be able to tell her the burden I carried, but seeing her in this light showed me what my life would be like if she didn't want me.

She was perfect, and every fae in this room could see it.

I was stuck between getting her away from their attentions as soon as possible and avoiding the fate we had waiting for us in our room for the night.

One. Room.

Goddess, spare me.

The group of males hanging on Zaria's every word laughed, and I decided.

"I should see about getting the key and settling up," I said, standing abruptly.

"Really?" Zaria looked up, confusion pulling her brows.

"It's been a long day." I knew I was being was curt, but I couldn't help it.

She studied me for a moment, then nodded in agreement.

She collected her things while I paid the innkeeper and got the key. I took the bags the stable boy had brought in, and Zaria followed me in silence. I wasn't sure if it had occurred to her that one room likely meant one bed, but I felt the weight of it with every stair I climbed.

We'd slept beside each other each night under the stars, but in our own bedrolls. This was going to be entirely more difficult.

I put the key in the lock and threw open the door to the tiniest room I'd ever seen. It was hardly more than a closet, and awkwardly shaped, like a triangle with the bed in the biggest portion, and it was barely warmer than the rain we'd escaped.

Goddess, save me.

"It's shelter to wait out the storm," I consoled us both. "I'll take the floor."

"You'll never fit." She eyed me as she edged past and into the room, where she rubbed her hands against the chill, her damp clothes still sticking to every inch of her figure. "Maybe we should have taken her up on her offer to sleep by the fire."

"We'd get no sleep. Who knows how late the patrons will stay." Not that I'd sleep here, either. Not when she was in the same room with me looking like that.

"That's true."

"It will be fine once you're under the blankets. You need to get those wet clothes off."

"You need to get yours off, too."

"Mine are fine." I put her bag on the small dressing table shoved into the cutout of a window. "I'll step out so you can change." I left the room before she could object, pressing my face into the cool wood of the door once it was closed.

"I'm finished," she called a few moments later.

I slipped back into the room, avoiding eye contact. "How many blankets are there?"

"Two. But you won't fit on the floor, Nyx. We can share."

"I'll make do with my bedroll. I wouldn't want to make you uncomfortable."

She frowned. "Why would you make me uncomfortable?"

"I…" I didn't have the energy to dance around the subject.

She slipped into the bed, and I caught sight of her bare feet and ankles.

Goddess, I'd been to shows at brothels without getting aroused. The sight of her damn ankles should not make me hard.

I dug out my bedroll to find it drenched.

Zaria lifted a brow, pulling the covers up to her chin for warmth. "Nyx?"

"I'll be fine." I blew out the candle.

"You're not even out of your clothes."

"I can see in the dark, Sol." I stripped my wet things from my skin and laid my pants out to dry, then found a clean pair of undergarments to pull on and a dry shirt. Thank the Goddess, our packs hadn't leaked like my bed roll. "Could you pass me the second blanket?"

"No."

"No?" I asked.

"You'll freeze down there. Come and get in."

"I'll be fine on the floor. Just pass me a blanket," I insisted.

"No."

"Do you want me to freeze?"

"If you're going to be stubborn about it, maybe."

I pulled out her bedroll to see if that had faired any better but they were both sodden.

Reluctantly, I accepted I'd be cold, and I tried to bed down in the nonexistent floorspace. I attempted a couple of different angles of approach, but the space was so tight, and I was so bulky, it was nearly impossible to wedge myself in. I finally grabbed hold of the bedpost and lowered myself slowly. I shuffled down until I was sitting with my back against the freezing wall and found Zaria staring in the dark.

"Are you kidding me?" she asked.

"I'm fine."

"Get up here," she demanded.

"Sol…"

"If you don't come up here, I'm coming down there to sit on the floor next to you."

"You'll freeze."

She moved to climb out of the bed, and I relented. "Okay, okay." I got to my feet. "Fine. You win."

She scooted over to make room, and I climbed in gingerly, staying as far on the edge as I could. The blankets were barely big enough, and she edged closer so they would cover us both.

I was hardly breathing; I didn't understand how she was so relaxed. Silence stretched between us, and I'd never been so aware of every part of myself. I was never going to sleep.

"What was it you liked to say to me? Your thoughts are loud," Zaria said in the darkness.

"I'm not thinking anything." I huffed. And I wasn't. In fact, I was working extremely hard on not thinking. About anything.

"Exactly. The silence is deafening." She chuckled.

"We are meant to be sleeping, Sol."

"Are you that tired?" Her tone was amused, and it was infuriating.

"Exhausted."

"Goodnight, then," she said softly.

"Goodnight," I replied.

Then I waited and prayed to the Goddess to hear her breathing even out into the soft sounds of sleep.

Instead, I heard shivering. I tried to ignore it, wait it out, but it only worsened. She huddled down under the covers more, but still, she shivered. I couldn't just listen to her freeze. It was going to kill me, but I had to warm her up.

I reached out and pulled her body to mine. She shuddered in my arms, and I realized it was more than a light chill. She was cold to her core. I wrapped myself around her and tried to rub some warmth into her skin, and she snuggled into my chest as close as she could get.

"Thank you," she whispered and lifted her face to look up. Light from the hallway crept in through the gaps around the door, illuminating her features just enough so I knew she could just barely see me, but I could see the look in her eyes perfectly well.

I held my breath.

The desire to kiss her burned through my veins despite the cold, but we were in a strange place, stuck with only one bed. She had nowhere else to go. She deserved to have one choice that was entirely her own, I reminded myself, over and over and—

And then her lips met mine.

I broke.

We fell into a tangle of exploring hands and tongues. I was desperate to be close to her in every way. Days spent watching her, scenting her, needing her had rendered me powerless to resist once she crossed that line.

I trailed my fingers over her delicate night robe, skimming across her beaded nipple. She gasped between strokes of her tongue against mine, dragging her fingers down the planes of my chest. Her leg hitched over mine, and I grasped her thigh, sliding my hand higher until it rounded the curve of her incredible arse.

I choked back my surprise to find smooth, bare skin, and nothing else beneath her robe.

"Everything else was damp," she breathed in answer to my unasked question.

I caressed her arse as she ground into me, pushing her own hands past the back of my undergarments, and kneading the muscle there. I groaned, losing all hope of making this an innocent kiss and cuddle.

I slid my fingers around to her heat and hesitated.

She deserved to have one choice that was entirely her own...

She rolled her hips. "Please," she whispered against my lips.

I couldn't deny myself anymore.

My fingers dipped into her wetness, but I wouldn't linger there. I wanted her to know pleasure before she tasted the moment of pain that would make her irrevocably mine...and that would not be today in this tiny cold room.

I circled the sensitive place at her apex, and she moaned, her hips moving to match the slide of my slick fingers. She was so responsive, and her pleasure so close to the surface, I drew it out with only the lightest of touches. She built quickly, the sounds she made something I'd never forget if I lived a thousand years.

I was rock hard, and every churn of her hips skimmed the fabric of my undergarments. Just that light brush was about to be my undoing. Power tingled at my fingertips, and as I succumbed to the sensation, coming undone, I sent the softest of pulses to the bundle of nerves at the center of her pleasure, sending her into waves of convulsing ecstasy.

FORTY-FIVE
NYX

I remembered the location of the village. The day I rescued Zaria was seared into my brain, but even though I knew what had taken place, I was still expecting a village, not a scorched patch of earth. I didn't want to go in, but I knew there'd be no convincing Zaria not to take the risk.

Reluctantly, and against my better judgment, I flew back to where I'd left Zaria with the horses and landed. She was jogging to me as I shifted back.

"Well?"

I shook my head, taking the clothes she handed me. "It's destroyed, Sol. No sign of life."

"So, we can go?" she said pointedly.

That had been the deal. I would fly over, and if there was any hint of life, we would regroup and make a plan. But if there was no life, we'd go in, and she would do what she could for her family's remains.

Now, I regretted that deal. I would do anything not to let her go in there. But I'd promised, and I wouldn't break her trust in me now, so I nodded.

We mounted the horses and made our way along a dried-up stream bed in silence. Soon, the remains of the village came into sight, and she gasped, breaking down even further as we neared.

I rode beside her and reached for her hand. Offering the only comfort I could give.

When we reached the gates, we dismounted and tied the horses, and I held her for a moment until she coughed.

My eyes watered, and I coughed, too. The essence of the burned Dragon's Bane must have been infused into every surface.

Zaria looked green, already wheezing. She felt it, too.

"We can't stay long." I pulled a shirt out of my bag, passing it to her.

She took it without complaint, covering her face.

I took one for myself and tied it, trailing behind Zaria as she walked into what was left of all she'd ever known. She walked like she was in a dream state, and I found myself at a loss for what to say or how to provide comfort. What could even be said? There was no excuse for what took place here.

I slipped my hand into hers when she stopped at the ashes of a large building. I searched my memory, trying to recall what the building had looked like when I'd picked her up, but it had all happened too fast.

"It's all gone." Her voice trembled.

"I'm so sorry."

"I didn't think..." She trailed off, bringing her hand to her mouth.

"What?"

"I didn't believe it would all be destroyed like this."

"Neither did I."

"I thought… I thought they'd get it under control and put it out." She moved forward, and we walked between burned out building foundations, taking it all in.

"There was too much destruction. There was no bringing it under control. Their only choice was to run or die fighting a futile fight."

"What I don't understand is why they were going into a cellar when all of this was happening above," she mused, half to herself.

"What do you mean?"

"My family and others. They were gathering in a storage cellar, like that would be a safe place from all of this." She waved her hand at the scene around us. "They took me there, but there were sacks of the herbs—Dragon's Bane—down there, and I panicked. They were bringing in more as I ran out, like saving that was more important than saving the village. It made no sense."

"That's when I found you?"

"Yes."

"Why would anyone trap themselves underground rather than run away from the fire?"

"It was over that way." She took off, dragging me by the hand deeper into the village. Determination made her strides faster and faster.

I coughed, the jog forcing me to breathe harder. The cloth didn't block out the fumes enough, and Zaria stopped and doubled over, her breathing ragged, too.

"We can't stay here much longer. If we both are incapacitated, we'll be in trouble." And Kol was too far away to help us if I called. We were truly alone here. We had only each other to rely on.

"I have to—" Her breathing cut her off, coming in labored gasps.

"Are you okay?" I asked, ready to force her out of here again before it made her truly sick.

She nodded, stabilizing herself. "I'm fine."

"You don't seem fine."

"I am. It's just a little farther."

"Kiera will have my arse if I land you back in the healers for this." I followed her deeper into the wreckage.

There was a building still soldering. After months?

What had they kept in there that would burn for weeks? Some kind of fuel, maybe? I had the nagging feeling all of this was even more dangerous than I'd even imagined.

"We can't go much farther. Look." I pointed at the smoke wafting from the smoldering pile.

"How is it still burning?"

"I don't know. What were they keeping here?"

She shook her head, as baffled as I was. "They never told me anything." She slowed, moving through the remains of buildings with purpose, finally stopping in front of the largest frame. "I feel so stupid."

"Why?"

"For just accepting their lies. I was so naive."

"How could you have known? This was all you knew. We are born trusting our caretakers. Why would you ever think they were lying to you?"

She slipped her hand back into mine. "The cellar was here..." She used her feet to scuff debris away and find the door. As she cleared more ash, the burned wood for the doors gave way beneath her feet, and she shrieked.

I yanked at her hand in my grasp and caught her before she fell, pulling her back and clasping her to my chest as we both breathed hard.

"Don't do that to me again," I ground out.

"Thank you." Carefully, we pulled apart and both bent to peer into the dark space. "Hello?" she called down timidly.

"You don't really think they are still alive down there, do you?" I asked her incredulously. She couldn't seriously be holding out that kind of hope.

"They can't be, I know. If they were, they'd have come out by now and either left or started to rebuild. But the hatch was covered over. No one left this cellar alive."

A nagging feeling prickled in me, and I couldn't place it, but nothing about this place was right.

Zaria set her jaw and used the stick to fling boards out of the way, kicking up more dust.

"What are you doing?" I hissed.

"Going down there."

I grabbed her wrist, pressing the cloth tighter to my face. "Maybe not the best idea while we are struggling to breathe."

She met my eyes, her teeth clamped together. "It's why we are here. I need to give them the rites so they can go to the Goddess in peace. Then we can leave."

"Sol, you said they had stores of Dragon's Bane down there. It's dangerous."

Her brows pulled. "I need to see them for myself! It's the only way I can let all of this go."

I wheezed and knew we were running out of time. Only seeing them would end this turmoil for her, and if we were going to do it, it had to be now. "I go first," I commanded. I was not taking no for an answer.

She nodded.

Carefully, I heaved the remains of the door out of the way. The ash stung my skin, a sure sign that Dragon's Bane was everywhere in this damned place. I lit a small fire in my palm—a neat trick Zaria was still trying to master.

"Wait until I say it's safe," I instructed before carefully navigating the stone steps. I used the fire to light the space and stilled at what I saw.

"Nyx?" Zaria called.

327

"It's empty," I called back.

Without waiting for my say so, Zaria descended the stairs.

I rolled my eyes. "Good waiting."

She ignored my comment, peering into the gloom. "What in the…"

The space was entirely empty. No bodies, no sacks… nothing but spiders, dust, and a few planks and boards stacked in the corner.

"How?"

"Are you sure this is the right cellar?"

"Positive."

"Then, they must have gotten out before the flames reached here. They would have choked to death on the smoke alone trapped down here."

While we both tried to think of better explanations, a breeze blew over, whipping Zaria's hair across her face. We turned to the corner where the boards were stacked, and before I could stop her, Zaria was pulling them away from the wall.

I helped her, and within a moment, we'd revealed a tunnel entrance.

"They got out! They have to be alive." She took a step, but I grabbed her back.

"Sol, there is no way I'm letting you go in there."

"We have to. We have to find them."

FORTY-SIX

NYX

"**N**YX!"

I went rigid. My brother's fear in my mind was enough to rip the breath from my lungs.

"*Kol?*" I begged. Goddess, let him answer.

Zaria had noticed the change in me. "What is it?"

"It's Kol. Something is very wrong." I reached out to him again. "*Kol? Answer me!*"

Zaria shook beside me, but the bond between Kol and me was silent. "We have to get out of here. I can't connect to him down here and with all the poison around."

Zaria took my hand, and we made for the stairs. I knew what she was giving up for me, but Kol was all that mattered.

"*Kol?*" I called as soon as we'd cleared the cellar.

Nothing.

We ran through debris and untied the horses. As soon as we were mounted, we kicked them into a flat-out gallop.

"We need some distance from the Dragon's Bane or I'll never be able to reach him," I told Zaria, mind to mind.

"I'm with you," she replied.

We ran and ran until we reached the road back to the rest of the world. I felt like I couldn't breathe, but not from the Dragon's Bane. I could feel the air was free of it here.

Breathless, we came to a stop, and I dismounted and fell to my knees. Zaria came to me, cupping my face in her hands.

"Any word?"

"No," I choked.

"Try again," she urged.

I breathed deeply, calming my body as I focused on the thread that connected us. *"Kol?"* I pleaded.

"Nyx?" he gasped. *"Tell the King...the outpost is lost. Do not send help."*

"I'm not at the capital—I can't tell him. And if I did, they would know about us."

"It doesn't matter now." The defeat in his voice crushed me.

"I'm coming." My mind was made up. I would fly to the stars for him.

"Nyx, the kingdom needs you. Zaria needs you. Go home and get the kingdom ready for war. Do. Not. Come. Here."

"Kol," I broke. *"KOL!"*

"I love you, Nyx," he whispered. And then there was nothing. Zaria held me as my world fell apart.

"We have to go!"

But we were too far away. What was I thinking? We would have been too far away if we were in the First Kingdom, even flying with no rest. Taking Zaria to her village had put me even farther away.

How could I expect to get to Kol before—

I refused to let those thoughts creep into my head. I pushed them down. I had to try to get there.

"Yes, of course," she replied without hesitation.

I dumped the contents of my pack on the ground and held it out to her. "Put what you need in here. As much food as possible." I picked through the contents, taking the things we'd need for her to survive and nothing more.

"Anything else?" She surveyed the small pile we left.

"Take the ropes."

"What for?"

"We are going to be flying straight across the kingdoms and over the Middle Sea. I won't be stopping to make camp. You'll need to strap yourself to my back so you can sleep while I fly."

"When are you going to sleep?"

"I don't need to."

"Yes, you do. Lack of sleep makes fae go mad."

"I am a Dragon of the Night. I can go without sleep a lot longer than most fae."

"Your reserves will be shot."

"I'll be fine, Zaria."

She saw I could not be reasoned with and nodded.

Without another word, I cut the horses loose and shifted to my dragon form. I lowered to the ground, barely letting Zaria get into place with the pack before launching us into the sky.

FORTY-SEVEN
ZARIA

I knelt for water in the cool steam and felt Nyx's eyes on my back, his anxiety bleeding into every connection we had. Like live wires, all the places our magic connected were fried and burned. He needed sleep but wouldn't take it. We were both short-tempered and overtired.

Something had to break.

I prayed to the Goddess for Kol to reach out to him. To say anything to him.

I splashed water on my face.

"Are you ready?" Nyx asked. He hadn't taken his fae form since we left.

"Have you had any water?" I'd given up trying to get him to eat anything. He wouldn't take the time.

"I'll take a drink from the stream." His voice was hollow even mind to mind.

I watched him, catching our reflection in the water. I couldn't get over how we looked together. A huge dragon with midnight scales, and a girl. What a pair. Except it wasn't a girl who stared back. I hadn't noticed how much I'd changed since all this

333

began. I gathered my hair to twist it on top of my head with a tie, drinking in my stance.

I didn't hold myself the same or cut the same figure. I'd been a girl when I'd left my village, and now, I was a female. A warrior. A mage. At least a little. I stood differently—I would have never stood with my feet so far apart in front of a male back home. I would never be so immodest as to wear leather ryding pants or such a tight shirt.

I smiled, lifting my chin when I finished with my hair. I liked the fae staring back much more than the one who had lived in the village.

The words Nyx had said when we left the First Kingdom came back to me. I couldn't go back to rotting in place. No matter if my family was still alive or what we faced at the outpost. Nyx and I had to find a way forward. He'd held me up through all of it, and now it was my turn to hold him.

"You must eat, or you're going to have no reserves left to help your brother." I stepped away from the stream and went to where I'd left my pack on a rock. I dug through it to find some of the bread I'd saved. *"Please,"* I said when he didn't move.

In a second, his fae form stood in front of me, naked, and as carved as a statue. He was leaner than he'd been when we left for my village. He hadn't bothered to hide his wings. They cast his form in a shadow.

I held out the bread.

"Thank you," he muttered as he took it and ate with his head bowed. He wore grief like a weighted vest. It pulled all of him forward. Rounded his shoulders. Changed him in ways that shouldn't be visible. I offered him the water skin I'd filled, too. He took it as well as a small sip while I dug out more dried food from the pack. I gave him the last of the smoked meat and bit into an apple. He ate it without a fight, which gave me some relief. I knew I couldn't do anything about the lack of sleep, but it was something.

He took another sip of the water, then I stepped around the rock to wrap my arms around him. He leaned against me, our sorrow so thick between us I didn't know how either one of us carried it.

"Thank you for eating."

He wrapped his arms around my shoulders, pressing his lips to my forehead. "Thank the Goddess I found you."

I smiled, fighting tears. "I thank the Goddess you found me, too."

FORTY-EIGHT

ZARIA

This was madness. I was strapped down to keep me on his back, but even Nyx did not know what we would face over the Wild Mountains. No one knew. According to him, they were impassable. Any who'd tried were never seen again. But we had to get to Kol, and flying around the mountains would add a day or more. Plus, Nyx felt the risk was just as high flying straight through the Storm Kingdom at the peak of its storm season, so we were crossing the uncrossable mountains, and I would pray to the Goddess to keep us safe the whole way.

Nyx was resolved, and I trusted him.

We flew in silence while he crossed the foothills, the mountains looming ominously ahead. As he began the climb to cross, the weather changed suddenly. Wind battered us in warning, and Nyx fought to stay his course. I hung on, praying to the Goddess we would make it to Kol.

But as we crested the mountain range, fairer skies were ahead. The sun broke through and seemed to welcome us into an untouched place.

"Where are the storms?" I asked.

"I have no idea." Nyx was as shocked as me. *"Maybe we got lucky?"*

We rose to cross the highest of the peaks, and as we banked to the west, I caught sight of a twinkle of light to the east. I searched for it again, and suddenly, a valley came into view. A lake sparkled from its floor.

"Nyx, look!" I gasped. *"A lake."*

"I see nothing but mountains," he replied flatly. I didn't press. His sole focus was getting to Kol, and I wouldn't distract him.

He flew on, undeterred, while I took in the view below and felt like we were in another realm of existence.

FORTY-NINE

NYX

"*It's empty.*"

I turned in place, surveying the deserted outpost.

He couldn't be dead.

I felt him.

I knew he was alive.

If he was dead, the thread would be cut.

"*Where could they be?*"

"*I don't know, but he has to be here somewhere.*" I spun a slow circle.

"*Could they have retreated?*"

I clasped my hands behind my neck. "*Octavian ordered them to hold the outpost.*"

"*Would they have retreated if the Vivi Mortui attacked?*" Zaria asked.

I knew she was trying to help, but I had to think. I had to

figure out where he'd gone. I hated myself for not telling her, not letting her in so she understood I was as close with Kol as I was with her, but this wasn't the time. There never seemed to be a good time.

"Nyx!" Zaria said out loud.

"*What? We have to be quiet. There could be anything listening.*"

"*Come here right now!*"

I turned, but she was nowhere in sight. "*Where are you?*"

"*In here.*" She sent me an image of a door she'd walked through.

I jogged over, found the cracked door, and slipped inside. "*What is this?*"

Zaria stood over sacks of something. "*Dragon's Bane.*" Terror cut off her tone.

"*What?*" My mind reeled. "*How do you know?*"

"*Because these are from my village. This are how we labeled the sacks.*" She reached to finger the stamp.

"*Don't touch it. We can't risk it affecting our magic. We need to find my brother and get out of here.*"

She hesitated, then said, "*My village is involved in this.*"

"*We don't know how that got here, so we don't know who is involved.*" I held out my hand for her. "*Come on.*"

She took my hand and closed the door on the Dragon's Bane. There was nothing we could do about it now. If I burned it, it would just put it into the air and the ground to poison anyone who came here for years. We crept back to the open courtyard.

"*Kol, please answer. Give me anything. Where are you?*'

"*Nyx!*" Zaria screamed.

I whipped around, but blackness took me.

FIFTY
ZARIA

A wall of smoke hit us like an explosion but without the sound.

Was there a fire?

I pulled my shirt up to cover my face, already coughing. My eyes burned, and I couldn't see. I reached for Nyx, but my hands came up empty.

"Nyx?" I called to him mentally.

"Zaria..." He sounded far away.

"Where are you!?" I took a half step forward, trying to reach him.

"I—" The mental link vanished.

Panic closed off my throat. *"Nyx!"*

There was no answer.

I took another step forward and almost fell face first when

my foot hit something solid. What in the Valley of the Dead.? I toed it again with my boot, and it dawned on me. It was Nyx.

I dropped to my knees next to him, franticly feeling for a pulse. I found his neck and pressed my fingers under his jaw. His vein thrummed steadily, and I squeezed my eyes shut. I didn't know what I would have done if he was gone.

My lungs burned. It had to be Dragon's Bane. It had hit us so fast—surrounded us. Not like when my village burned and the smoke spread, though. This was targeted. They'd figured out a way to turn it into a weapon. I had to get us both out of here before I was unconscious, too.

But how?

I couldn't escape by myself, and even if I could, I couldn't leave him. What could my magic do against this? Would mine even work with more poison seeping into my lungs with every second that passed?

"She didn't go down," a voice called from behind the wall of smoke.

I closed my eyes to try and listen, staying crouched to make myself a smaller target. My hearing amplified like I'd practiced, but this felt different. Footsteps on the packed dirt were like a picture in my head. I counted the number of feet and knew their positions, like I had tapped into a part of myself I'd never used before.

We were surrounded by at least forty men.

My heart stammered, and I wanted to gasp. To scream. To run. But I wouldn't leave Nyx. I had to wake him, but was that even possible with Dragon's Bane all around? It was hard to think when I was struggling to breathe. I knew the effect the herbs had, but I'd survived it before. I'd survived it my whole life. It drained dragons of their magic—that was what he said—and dragons needed metal to recharge, which I didn't have.

Goddess, what can I do?

It hit me then. We could power share, and mine wasn't

drained like his. If I could force my magic into him, maybe he would wake up.

I didn't know if it would work without him awake to accept the power, and since we weren't melded yet, it might not work at all, but I had to try. I put my hands on him and found my center like he'd taught me, then I found his. It was weak. I wasn't sure if this was the right way, but I focused on channeling my power toward his center, pushing it toward the empty vessel like I was filling him.

It was working! I could feel his center taking from mine.

The fae were closing in around us; I could pinpoint their movements.

We had to get out of here.

We had moments at most.

I pushed harder.

They sprayed another wave of the smoke.

No!

I surged my magic into him, not holding back.

"Nyx, please wake up. Goddess, please."

"Zaria?" Confusion laced his voice. *"What's going on?"*

"I don't know if you remember, but we have to get out of here now!" I urged.

He tried to move but barely had control of his body. *"I don't think I can shift."*

"Take more of my power." I forced more at him.

"Goddess, Sol. Nothing like getting water boarded with magic." He sounded drunk.

"This isn't funny. We are surrounded, and I need you to shift." I poured every ounce of what I was into him, disregarding what he'd told me about burning out my magic and making myself sick.

He wasn't doing it on his own, and I didn't know how he controlled it, but I squeezed my eyes shut and willed him to shift.

His dragon exploded out, massive and snarling. I jumped on his back, not hesitating as he leapt off the ground, and we soared into the air.

A volley of arrows followed, striking us all over.

Pain seared through my shoulder, and I bit back a cry. Arrow after arrow sliced through Nyx's wings, and I felt every one. He hissed but made no other sound. The pain drove up my nausea until I thought I couldn't bear another hit. Why was I feeling his pain?

Was it the shared magic?

I slowed the power I was giving him to a trickle...

And he fell out of the sky.

"*Zaria!*"

FIFTY-ONE
ZARIA

W e plummeted toward the ground.
"*Nyx!*"
"*What were you doing?*"
"*I was giving you my magic.*"
"*Why did it stop? Are you out?*"
"*Flying isn't magic. Why can't you fly?*"
"*I don't know!*" I'd never heard his voice so panicked.
I didn't have time to figure it out.
I forced my power into him as hard as I could.
He kept falling.
I braced for the impact.
It was too late.
I'd failed him.
Falling from this height would surely kill us both.

Why wasn't it working? What had I done on the ground that got us in the air? I willed him to fly, and his wings had spread.

I willed him again now with everything I had in me.

I reached inside my flight jacket and clasped the chain around my neck, pulling the pendant out so I could hold it in my hand. It was time to see if this would work. We were out of power and out of time. I gripped the pendant tightly and prayed to the Goddess for help. The crystal thrummed in my hand, sending energy to my reserve. It was barely a drop, but I would take anything. The ground was coming up to meet us, but I could not give up. I could amplify. With that drop of power, I could amplify the stone. Increase the replenishment. It was worth a try. I squeezed the crystal as if I could get more from it this way and pushed the last drop of my power back into it. It warmed in my palm, and power trickled into me. I heaved in a breath and pushed harder. The more power it gave me, the more I demanded. It wasn't a lot, but we'd got in the sky with less, so I stopped pushing into the stone and went back to giving it all to Nyx.

Just feet from impact, Nyx's wings spread and caught.

We soared a few feet above the ground.

"Did you do that?"

"Yes?" I couldn't figure out where I ended and he began. Our magic was too closely entangled.

Was I flying this damn thing?

"Keep doing it. I think...I'm...too...weak, and I've...been hit." There was a pause between every word, all of them strained with pain.

"Are you hurt badly?"

"It's bad, Sol."

Goddess, help us all.

I pulled back, not sure if that's how it was done, but his wings flapped and lifted us, and we rose higher and higher. I was doing it!

Another volley of arrows flew in our direction, but somehow, I knew they'd fall short. Then a frightening sound reached my ears. I knew what it was, but I didn't know how I knew. I turned in my seat to look back. They'd loaded a catapult on the garrison wall, but that wasn't the worst part. They lit it on fire, and it smoked just like the Dragon's Bane weapon they used had.

"NO!"

"You have to keep pushing, Sol. Get us as far away as you can," Nyx urged, his voice growing weaker.

"Will we be fast enough?" My inner voice trembled.

"We can only pray."

A piercing screech reached my ears. I risked another glance backwards, and my heart nearly stopped.

They had dragons.

But even at a glance I could tell they weren't right. Their color was off—the same with the ryders. They launched into the air, but even their flying wasn't normal. They were—

"They have undead flyers," I told Nyx with as much calm as I could find in me.

The sound Nyx made was guttural. Grief and sadness. *"They turned them?"*

"I think so." It had to be the Vivi Mortui. If they caught up to us, we were dead.

"We have to warn the First Kingdom. We have to warn everyone! This plague will engulf the realm if we don't stop it."

"I don't think we can make it back to the First Kingdom, Nyx. I can't fly up forever, and your wings…" At least one had a huge gash in it. I was running low on power, and I was beginning to think I was keeping us in the air with the sheer force of my will alone.

"There are pyres on the alert towers. If we can make it to one, we can send the alert."

"Where? Show me."

He gave me a mental image of a map.

"I'll try." I leaned forward, willing him to fly faster, but the strain on my reserves burned in my veins. I was running dry. *"I don't think we can make it. We need to find a place to hide."*

I scanned the ground, searching the terrain. With those dragons on our tail, how could I hope to keep Nyx safe until he was healed? It felt impossible. I knew I should turn south and head toward the First Kingdom, find any alert tower on the way, but I knew we wouldn't make it, and everything in my gut told me to keep heading east, back the way we came.

My head was fuzzy, and it was hard to think. My magic reserves were so low, and I was fighting an attack on my lungs from the Dragon's Bane smoke, too.

I needed help. I didn't know what to do. The crystal kept the reservoir from running dry, but I couldn't power a dragon for long. Desperate, I recited the properties I'd memorized, looking for anything that could help us. Amethyst calms the mind, gives courage, aids decisiveness. Citrine protects against negative energy. Nothing about piloting several tons of dragon on a drop of power, though.

Calm, courage, decisiveness. I had to make a good choice for both of us or we would die.

Then it hit me. The lake. The Wild Mountains were my only escape. No one tried to cross them; it was known that was certain death. They didn't know we already had. Dragons wouldn't follow us, undead or not. Not if they were controlled by anything real. It was our only hope.

I gathered every drop of energy I had left and banked us to the east. I prayed to the Goddess I was right about the lake. I'd find us a place to hide if we could make it there. Nyx needed healing, and if I could find some reeds… I pushed all else out of my mind. I couldn't get ahead of myself, and I couldn't waste energy worrying or overthinking. I needed every ounce I had to put into my magic.

It had to be enough.

FIFTY-TWO

ZARIA

I woke to light. Bright white light.

Was I dead?

I blinked, lifting a hand to shield my eyes. My arms hurt. I shifted my limbs, finding myself in sand. All of me hurt. Like I'd fallen off a horse.

I couldn't be in this much pain if I was dead, could I? I thought the Shores of Avalon were brimming with eternal pleasure. Pain wasn't a part of that. At least not for me.

I blinked a few times, forcing myself to sit up. A sound of lapping water reached my ears as my eyes focused.

A massive body of water lay before me. I thanked the Goddess we'd made it to the lake I'd seen. It had to be. I smiled. Trusting myself had been the right move, at least for now. The undead flyers hadn't followed us. I looked to the sky to make sure they weren't anywhere I could see.

Anyone who saw us enter the Wild Mountains would now assume us dead, I hoped.

The sun was just getting high in the sky, so it had to be the morning, and we'd been at the outpost sometime in the late afternoon. We'd been here at least overnight. If they were going to ambush us, they would have done it by now. Right?

I turned, and pain lanced through my back. I hissed, reaching behind me to find my shirt damp. The memory of being hit by an arrow came back to me. I took solace in the fact that it hadn't hit me hard enough to embed. We must have been too far away by the time it struck. I thanked the Goddess again. Then I recalled the hits Nyx had taken…

NYX!

I looked around and found him at my back. Fear took hold. He was still in his dragon form, unmoving, and blood had leeched into the sand around him. I crawled to his head, biting back my own pain to check on him. On my knees, I cradled his head and felt for breath at his nostrils. Warm, reassuring air met my hand, and I sobbed.

Alive. We were both alive. And I was going to keep us that way. I'd gotten us this far.

I pushed through the pain, getting to my feet. My stomach flipped, and bile rose in my throat. I hunched over, but that made me see red. I stumbled and fell back to my knees. A warm trickle ran down my back. I fought the tears in my eyes, breathing through the pain.

I had to think. If the lake had calm and shallow water, it would have pain reeds. I had to get to the shore.

I gave myself ten more seconds to deal with the pain.

I climbed to my feet, slower this time. I reached behind to see if I could judge how much of my skin was ripped open, but I couldn't reach the spot. My shirt was crusted to my skin and only a little damp from what I could feel. It would have to wait. I scanned the shoreline for an inlet to protect against the waves.

I thanked the Goddess when I spotted one not too far from where we'd landed. Now I prayed this was a freshwater lake, because if it was somehow connected to the inner coast of the Twelve Kingdoms, I'd be screwed. Finding drinking water would be hard, and thirst would kill us faster than our injuries. There were always roots and berries and nuts to eat, but unless it rained... I cut myself off from the fear again.

This was about doing. I knew how to source food. I knew how to make medicines. This was all females' work in my village. I could do this.

I walked into the water, not caring about my leathers. I dropped to my knees, the cool water feeling so good on my sore muscles. I cupped my hands and dipped them into the clear water before bringing it to my lips.

Fresh.

Thank the Goddess.

I dropped my hands into the water and got another palmful to splash on my face. I let myself have another minute with the sun on my face and the water soothing me, making me forget how much I wanted to collapse and sleep for a week.

Nyx might not survive a week without his injuries tended to.

I sat back in the water and took my boots off. Standing, I flexed my toes in the sand. I tossed my boots far enough up the beach to not get washed away, and started toward the inlet. I had to take it slow, but it felt good to walk with my feet in the water. My stomach hurt, but food could wait.

I needed reeds and then roots and, hopefully, white bark to mix with the reeds. I searched my memory for what my grandmother had taught me and made a mental list of plants to look for. I didn't know what would be native to this area. Would any of the plants I knew even grow here?

I hoped so.

I followed the edge of the water around and stopped in my tracks.

A village sat nestled on the inlet.

FIFTY-THREE
ZARIA

I had to be hallucinating. I must have hit my head in the crash landing. Maybe none of this was real, just the creation of my dying mind as we lay broken on the rocks of the Wild Mountains. It felt like the day I was taken all over again. Like my reality had shifted, and nothing was real.

I blinked, raising an aching arm to rub my eyes.

The village was still there.

What in the name of the Goddess is this?

Before I could fully process the shock, a blade pressed against my throat.

I froze.

"How did you find this place?" a deep, masculine voice growled next to my ear.

I jumped. I could sense the size of the fae behind me. I would be no match for him even if I could unsheathe my sword without losing my head.

My mouth went dry. I slowly swallowed. "We crashed here. We were injured, and I saw the lake from the air. It was our only hope," I said as calmly as I could.

The blade dug in, a breath away from breaking skin. "Impossible. You did not see this lake from the sky. How did you get here?" he demanded, anger thick in his growl.

I raised my hands in the air, trying to show him I wasn't a threat. "I swear, my flyer and I were chased into the Wild Mountains. We were both injured and needed to land before my magic ran out. I saw the lake and aimed us here, but we crashed. He needs my help. Please don't harm me." I didn't think about how much I was telling this stranger until it was too late. The words had already tumbled out of me, and now our fates were in his hands.

The fae sniffed deeply, his nose to my hair. I held steady. "You reek of Dragon's Bane. Explain yourself."

"We were attacked with it. My dragon was barely conscious when I got us out. We had no other choice but to land here," I pleaded. We couldn't make it this far to be killed by an entirely different foe.

"Impossible."

"What is?"

"No one from the outside can locate this sanctuary."

"Sanctuary?" I asked, not understanding what he meant.

The fae tensed. "Never mind that. Who attacked you?"

I swallowed carefully. "The Vivi Mortui."

He gasped and didn't reply right away. "Impossible."

"I swear to you. We only just escaped. If we had any other option, we wouldn't have come here."

"What proof do you have?"

"My dragon is injured from the attack." Should I have kept him hidden? Every word I said felt like the wrong one. I wasn't good at this. I needed Nyx, but no more than he needed me right then.

The blade left my throat, and I heaved a breath, nearly collapsing. But then it pressed into my back. "Show me."

I took a tentative step, and he kept the blade in contact but allowed me to lead him back to Nyx. When we rounded the inlet, he stopped, taking in the prone form on the shore.

Tears filled my eyes at the sight. I couldn't bear to see him so weakened. But he needed my help, so I had to stay strong for him.

"Goddess, save us all. How is this possible?" the fae muttered behind me, but it was clear he wasn't speaking to me. "Silas!" he barked.

A young male came over the dunes. "Yes, Jaxus?"

"Get Hadeon and have him send a healer."

"Yes, Jaxus." The young fae turned and set off for the village at a run.

I could have cried, but I held myself together. I had to show strength. "Thank you."

"Don't thank me yet. You should not have been able to find this place. It's untraceable. This is a problem for all of us."

"I don't understand. Untraceable, how?"

"Protected by magic. Hidden."

"How can you hide an entire valley?"

"The mountains can't be crossed—magic prevents it. Any who try die or turn back. Those are our protections—ones you somehow slipped by. How?"

"I don't know. We were trying to rescue my dragon's twin. We flew over the Wild Mountains to get to him faster, and I spotted the lake. When we reached his location, we were attacked and fled. This was the only place I could think of to hide. We won't tell a soul this place exists. Your secret is safe with us, I swear." I faced him.

"If only it were that simple." He met my eyes. He was larger than any fae I'd ever seen. Easily a head taller than Kol and Nyx, who were both large for fae. His skin was tanned from constant exposure, and he wore nothing but a short cloth tucked low around his waist. His sun-kissed hair fell to his shoulders with a slight wave. He was larger than every dragon we had in the palace, and looked like he'd earned every muscle he had through hard work.

Then it dawned on me what he'd said. He believed there were no dragons outside this sanctuary... Was he saying this was a sanctuary for dragons? Was he...? Now that I studied him, he couldn't be anything else.

Two more shirtless males approached with the young boy in tow, both much older than Jaxus. One was a smaller male who wore light green skirts and had ancient-looking, sun-weathered skin. The other was as large as Nyx, and though he looked younger than the first male, he had an undeniable air of authority that seemed to suggest age and wisdom.

Jaxus bowed to him.

"What do we have here?" he demanded.

"A dragon from the outside, Hadeon. Injured from battle and exposed to Dragon's Bane."

The male, Hadeon, frowned. "Pardon me?"

"I know. I don't know what to make of it either. The girl says they were flying over and saw us."

Hadeon frowned even deeper.

The older male knelt by Nyx. He must have been the healer. "Dragon's Bane, you say? Are you sure?"

"As sure as smelling it in her hair," Jaxus replied.

The healer lifted a brow and cut his gaze over to me but didn't say anything more.

After inspecting Nyx, he stood and dusted his hands together. "We need to get him back to the healer's tent. His magic reserves are completely depleted. It's a wonder he got this far."

Hadeon nodded his approval and then eyed me. "And we need answers as to how they even got here."

"I agree." Jaxus folded his arms behind his back, studying me. "I think she speaks the truth, but I don't know how she could have seen through the shroud."

I opened my mouth to speak and shut it again. Maybe it wasn't wise to give them more than I had to until I knew Nyx would be okay.

"This is his mate?" the healer asked.

"It is," Jaxus confirmed.

The healer's eyes unfocused as he peered at me. "She is a strange one. Unusual light magic."

"What should I do with her?" Jaxus asked Hadeon.

I tensed.

"She comes with me," the healer said, and his tone left no argument. When the other males looked to him in question, he shrugged. "I may need her connection to him if I can't get him replenished. Besides, she's injured too."

Hadeon grunted. "Have me kept informed, Jaxus. I'll take this to the council." He left without sparing me another glance.

"I'm sure this will cause quite a stir." The healer laughed.

"I'll report back, but it won't be good," Jaxus replied.

The healer lifted his shoulders. "They may surprise you. Magic works in mysterious ways." His eyes glinted like he knew more than the rest of us. "Bring him to me. I'll see what I can do. We need to detox him as soon as possible before the poison goes to his brain."

I gasped, and my hand went to my mouth. "Could he die?"

"Any of us could die, youngling, but I won't lie to you. He's not in good shape. We need to treat him with swiftness. Dragon's Bane is a potent toxin. Once it takes hold in the brain, it's irreversible."

They'd never told me. Not Kiera or Nyx or Kol. None of them had told me I could have died after escaping my village.

Had mine not been so bad, or had they downplayed it to not alarm me? Would I have even listened?

"Silas," Jaxus called again. "I know you're listening."

"I don't have to listen to hear you." The little boy appeared again from behind a tree.

"What have we said? Don't trust your mind over your ears until your magic is fully awoken. Now, come over here and help me lift him."

"Let me help you." I stepped forward to stand next to Nyx, not sure how we would move him, but not wanting to let him out of my sight.

Jaxus laughed and nodded at Silas. "Show her how we plan to carry him."

Silas closed his eyes and held out his hands, making Nyx elevate off the ground.

"Come with me, youngling. They wouldn't like you wandering about," the healer said.

"I'm not leaving Nyx," I told him unwaveringly. As nice as they had been, they'd shown me they were hostile and didn't want anyone in the Twelve Kingdoms to know they were here. I didn't trust them not to kill us to make the problem go away.

"Where do you think they are bringing him?"

"I don't know." I took my place next to Nyx's lifted body.

While the healer drank me in, not showing any emotion, Jaxus fought a smile, which made me feel a little better.

"Very well. We will all walk together." The healer led the party without looking back.

"And you're not a dragon?" Jaxus asked. "You have the attitude of one."

"I thought you could smell it on me?" I replied. Kol and Nyx had always made it seem like dragons always knew each other.

"I've found that anytime I think I know something to be always true, the Goddess laughs and smacks me upside the head.

The last thing I believed to be true was that no one else could find this place, and here you are."

"Nyx couldn't see it." I don't know why I said that. Maybe it would make him feel better. To prove it was only me, and maybe if I promised to not to show anyone how to get here, they would let us go.

"So, it's just you who is the problem?" he asked, dropping his voice and side-eyeing me as we fell behind the rest.

I swallowed—hard. Had I screwed up?

Jaxus nodded the group forward and spent the rest of the short journey in silence.

We passed through a small village nestled in the cove, with most of the buildings bordering the water. They were all raised off the ground on stilts, like the lake was prone to flooding. It made me wonder why they didn't build them farther back. There were raised gangplanks connecting the buildings, too, built over the sand. I had so many questions about this place, but I held my tongue. I didn't want to open myself up to give away any more information.

We reached a large tent, and as we passed through the doorway, I felt a wash of magic pass over us. Nyx suddenly shifted back to his fae form.

"Nyx!" I cried, going to him.

Jaxus put his hand on my shoulder, drawing me back. "It's okay. The magic shifted him so he can be treated more easily. Just let them settle him."

I watched as he was lowered onto a bed and a sheet was drawn over him up to his waist.

All but the healer took their leave, and I went to Nyx's side.

The tent was sweltering inside, making me instantly over-heated. I pulled at my shirt. "Why is it so hot?"

The healer bent to listen to Nyx's chest. "Heat burns out sick-ness. It aids our natural healing reserves. Energy begets energy.

We must draw it from somewhere." He took a jar from a drawer and rubbed a salve onto Nyx's chest.

"What are you doing?" I asked, remembering how dangerous it was to let a stranger treat him and snapping into motion.

"My name is Emrys. I am a healer. We take an oath. Do they not have healers in your kingdoms?" When I nodded, he pulled a rope with knots fashioned into a sort of long belt hanging with his skirts into view. "Do they still wear these with their healer robes?"

I did remember seeing something like it on Kiera and others in the healer's wing. "Yes."

"These date from before the Twelve Kingdoms were formed, back when healers trained with priests. We still wear them. Our oaths to the Goddess to do no harm are as sacred as a priest's vows. We are bound by those oaths in magic. If I tried to do harm, I would only hurt myself. The elders can do with you two what they will, but there will be no death at my hands."

My ears rang. There was too much to be concerned about, and I could only focus on Nyx. "Can I ask what you're doing so I know?" I didn't know what comfort it would give, but I couldn't feel helpless.

"Sure. This salve is winter root and spice berries to ease his breathing. His lungs are damaged from inhaling the Dragon's Bane. It's bad enough on the outside of our bodies, but inside, it can do much more damage."

I sniffed the air, and the salve was familiar. Not exactly what I remembered from my childhood, but close enough to invoke some nostalgia. "My grandmother used to make something like that."

He smiled. "Smart fae. You must have had a healer in your family at some point."

"Why do you work in a tent when the other buildings in your village are stone or wood?"

"Because different materials hold in heat and magic differently. We build our healing spaces with those things in mind. There are protections to keep the magic I'm using inside the tent as well as to prevent it from affecting someone who doesn't need it while I'm using it on someone who does."

"Healing magic can affect other fae?"

"Of course it can, youngling. What do you think blow back is?"

I'd read about blow black, but only briefly. It was when magic backfired on the caster, but I didn't know what caused it. "Are all healing spaces protected like this?"

"I don't know what the other realms do, nor how other healers operate or the types of magics they use."

"There are more types of magic?" I asked, but then I recalled the old magic Nyx had used to unblock my power. Did they use old magic here? Is that why they were hidden?

"There are many, even some long forgotten or out of popularity. Believing there is only one way to use magic is like believing there is only one way to prepare food. There are many ways to use energy. Some, I'm sure, remain undiscovered." His explanation made sense, but it hurt my brain.

I didn't need more to think about.

He continued to work, sometimes showing me what he was doing or the salves he used. Most of them I wasn't familiar with, but he did take the time to explain. I knew some ingredients because we used them in our village.

"This is the best I can do. Now time will tell if he has the strength to battle the poison." Emrys looked into my eyes. There was kindness there but also honestly. "Our bodies use magic to heal, and without any to use, it's hard to say which way a fae's body will go."

My heart sunk, but I didn't press. I couldn't bear the answer.

"Help me roll him over. I need to get to those arrows in his wings."

I frowned, looking from Nyx to the healer. "His wings aren't out; the magic in here shifted him"

"Do you think they cease to exist because you can't see them? You must see them at times. Surely, he doesn't hide them fully from his mate..." He gave me a strange look.

I returned it, not sure what he meant by that. "I've seen them. They flicker in and out of view sometimes, but only for moments."

"And you didn't think they existed outside his dragon form?" Emrys laughed, and I helped him turn Nyx.

"No..."

"Where did you think they were?" He did something I didn't catch, and wings flickered into view. They were just like his dragon wings but sized for him as a fae.

I gasped. "Are dragons born with wings like this?"

"They are. Most are taught to shield them when young because they stick out among other fae." He gave me a sly grin, and wings flickered into view around him.

My hand went over my mouth. "You're a flyer?"

"I'm a dragon. A lot of us are." He narrowed his eyes, but then nodded. "How strong is your stomach? These arrows are laced with more Dragon's Bane and maybe other poisons." He took Nyx's wing and showed me one. "See how the flesh has tried to grow over the wound but it's rotting? We have to get them out or they will continue to poison him. Can you help me, or shall I call another healer?"

"I can help."

He handed me an apron. "I like you. I hope the elders let you both stay."

I didn't reply. We couldn't stay. We couldn't leave the Vivi Mortui to ravage the Twelve Kingdoms, and we had to find Kol.

After we worked on Nyx's wings, I asked the healer to look at my back where I'd been struck. He had me sit so he could work.

"I don't really want to put you out, but this isn't going to feel good. Can you stand it, or would you prefer I drug you."

Panic cut off my throat, and it took too long to get my words to form. "I can stand it. I don't want to be put out."

"You are safe while you are in this tent, I swear to you, but I figured you would resist. Most fae born females do."

"What does that mean?" I looked over my shoulder to see what he was doing.

He ground something with a mortar and pestle. "Your pain tolerance is far superior than those born male." He laughed like it was some kind of joke. "Females are hardier and more often have stronger stomachs." He shrugged, stepping up behind me.

"Turn to face the other wall. I need your back straight so I can get at the worst parts."

I did as he asked.

"You resist Dragon's Bane better than any ryder I've seen. Especially one mated to a dragon."

I hesitated to tell him my history, but it seemed relevant.

"I was raised in a remote place by fae who grew Dragon's Bane. I was sick from it my whole life. I recently discovered they were feeding it to me daily to cut off my magic and prevent Nyx from finding me."

"Goddess forbid." Emrys gasped.

"I was wondering if I'd become somewhat resistant to it from those years?"

"Hmm. It's possible," Emrys mused.

"It's been playing on my mind. How else was I able to get us out when the exposure had taken Nyx down?"

"You make a good point, youngling."

I didn't have time to reply before he painted the mixture he'd used on Nyx over my back and pain lanced through me. It burned, and I hissed, shaking with the agony of it.

"Breathe, youngling."

I forced myself to suck a breath through clenched teeth.

"Do you want me to stop?"

363

"No. Get it done."

He worked quickly and had me wrapped up by the time my back went numb. I stumbled off the bed, putting my hands on my knees to take a few lungfuls of air.

"Maybe don't—" He cut himself off. "Too late. Don't pass out on me."

"I'm not going to," I said when I could finally manage words again.

The healer went to a drawer and brought out a heavy black chain. I had the sudden fear he was going to chain me to stop me escaping. But he placed the chain around Nyx's neck.

"What's that?" I asked urgently, fearful it could be something like the necklace I'd been forced to wear.

"Calm yourself," he soothed. "It's a tantalum chain. It will help him restore his power."

When he saw that I still didn't understand, he sighed.

"Tantalum is the rarest metal in all the realms. It's our most effective restoration metal. It won't harm him."

I relaxed.

"You should rest with him," he said. "Your presence will help him, too."

Emrys left me with Nyx, and as soon as he was gone, I climbed into the bed next to him and closed my eyes. I had to check his magic reserves to see for myself. I followed the strings of my magic to his and then to his center. I'd never seen him so low, even at the outpost. He must have been using it while we slept, trying to heal himself. I hated myself for letting it go so long before I found the village.

I held on to my crystal, hoping to restore his reserves through mine. I couldn't do nothing. My reserves were still low, and I had to heal, but I knew I couldn't live without him. I couldn't bear to lose both Nyx and Kol. We both had to survive for this to work.

I settled into Nyx's chest and drifted off to sleep.

FIFTY-FOUR
NYX

My head buzzed like light bugs swarmed inside it. There were bright spots, but the rest existed in darkness.

A body shifted against me, drawing me further into consciousness.

"Zaria?"

"Nyx!"

I winced.

"I'm sorry." Her damp face pressed against mine.

I tried to move, to hold her, but my limbs were dead weight. "Are we in the Valley of the Dead?"

"Not yet." She sobbed.

Never a good sign.

"Sol." My voice hurt to use, my throat on fire. "Tell me we aren't waiting to be made into the undead."

She shook her head.

"Kol?"

"You tell me." Her voice was as raw as mine felt.

I grasped the threads of our connection, coming to an unconscious mind. My fate might not be waiting to be turned, but Kol's was. "He's not dead."

She buried her face in my chest, and I managed to get an arm around her. "Thank the Goddess."

"Where are we, and why does it smell like a healer's wing?" There was no way we could have made it back to the First Kingdom or even another outpost.

"You're not going to believe any of this."

I did my best to pry my eyes open and listen to her fill me in. I couldn't believe there were dragons in the Wild Mountains.

"We have to leave." I tried to get up.

"You almost died. The healer didn't know if you'd wake up." Fear tinged her tone, and she pressed me back to the bed.

"I'm fine." I had to be. Kol's life depended on it.

"You're not. Your wings were in shreds. You have to heal."

I hissed, glad that whatever the healer had given me numbed them somewhat. That must have been why my limbs felt so heavy. "I don't have time to heal."

Zaria switched to mind to mind and said, "*You don't have a choice. I'm not sure they will let us leave.*"

"*It sounds like we will have to talk to these elders. They can't keep us here. The King will tear apart the kingdoms looking for my brother and me. I am his general. He has no one else to take my place.*"

Zaria sighed. "*You have to heal before we can leave. Whether they let us go or we force our way out, you need to be whole.*"

I tried to settle. She was right. I just couldn't face laying here healing while Kol's life hung in the balance.

She snuggled in beside me, and her fingers stroked my chest. "*Nyx?*"

"Mm?"

"If they've turned other dragons in the flights, why would they have kept Kol alive this long? Do you think they will use him as bait?"

The idea hadn't occurred to me. *"I can't answer that."* I didn't know what to believe. I barely understood what I'd witnessed. It was too foggy to make sense of it.

"Nyx?"

"Yes?"

"You'd go knowing it was a trap, wouldn't you?"

"Yes," I replied without hesitation. *"I have to."* I'd go knowing it would end in our death if there was even a sliver of a chance of saving Kol.

"I know. I would, too. We can't abandon Kol like that."

"We have to get me healed so we can get out of here and get back to him"

"We will. I need you, though; you know how to handle fae. I already feel like I've said too much. I keep overthinking what's important and what's not."

"You did perfect, Sol. You saved my life." I managed to lift my arm to wrap her in a weak hug. *"I don't know how to thank you."*

She lifted her face to look into my eyes. *"I would do it a hundred times over. I don't want to do this without you."*

My lips curled up at the corners, and even that was painful. *"No?"*

"Don't make me say it again," she said playfully.

"What if I need to hear it?"

"Need?" She sounded skeptical but amused.

"I need it. It could be very important to my healing."

She scoffed, but her smile gave her away. *"We need to get you fed so you can actually heal."*

I cupped her beautiful face. *"Don't go yet."* My lips found hers, but the second they did, hers glowed red hot for a second. I recoiled. *"What was that?"*

She brought her fingers to her lips. *"I don't know, but it felt a little like when I touch one of those charge stones."*

"Are we siphoning each other's magic?"

She closed her eyes. *"My reserves feel the same, but I can't exactly quantify it."*

"Mine do too. Depleted." I rubbed my thumb over her cheek. *"Kiss me again for science."*

She laughed but put her hand over mine and kissed me.

It wasn't quite a spark like the first time, but I felt better kissing her. Only fractions, but it was something.

"Maybe we didn't notice it before because you weren't depleted."

"Before?" I pushed.

"You know, when we…kissed before."

Her awkwardness was endearing. *"Maybe, but I do think we will have to test the theory."*

She pushed my chest playfully. *"You're injured and can barely lift your arm. How are you going to…"*

I loved how she couldn't say the words. *"I assure you, Sol, I will always be able to give you pleasure, no matter what state I'm in."*

She gasped softly and blushed—I loved it—then she kissed me again, her body growing warmer by the second.

"You could always sit on my face. I'm sure my tongue is working fine."

Her mouth dropped open, and she stared.

"I hear our patient is awake," a deep but not unkind male voice said, interrupting the moment.

"I am." I used the dregs of the magic I had from Zaria to try and shield us, trying to crane my neck to see who spoke.

"Zaria, why don't you come and get some food for you and

Nyx while Emrys checks Nyx over?" a second voice spoke. I instantly didn't like the familiarity of his tone and wished I could get up to challenge these males and protect Zaria. My body would not do as I commanded, though, no matter how many times I tried. My muscles were spent. My energy was sapped. Every last drop I had was gone.

The two males came into view. An elderly healer and a handsome young male who set my teeth on edge. While the older male, obviously Emrys, set about gathering items, the other smiled and… Did he scent the air?

Bastard could tell Zaria was aroused, and I couldn't get up.

Zaria climbed off the bed, and I managed to reach out my hand to stop her.

"Don't go with him," I implored through our bond.

"Jaxus? He helped bring you here. I think we can trust him."

"It's not that," I growled.

She looked between the male and me and raised a brow. *"Are you jealous?"*

"I can't move, and he can tell you're aroused. Of course I'm jealous," I snapped.

She made a frustrated sound.

Jaxus chuckled. He couldn't know what we were saying, but I had no doubt he could guess.

Zaria rolled her eyes. "Of course I'm stuck in a place filled with dragons. I thought I had no privacy back in my village, but this is so much worse." She pushed past Jaxus, and he smirked before following her out.

I tried to sit up, but I couldn't even raise my shoulders.

"Calm, youngling. You can't do anything until you heal."

It had been many years since I'd been called youngling, but to this fae, I guess I was. I sighed and relented.

"Sorry to meet you under such circumstances, but it is always a pleasure to meet another dragon."

"Likewise. Thank you for all that you did." I made sure to keep any ice from my tone. I didn't like being separated from Zaria, but we couldn't make enemies here. We had to make everyone root for us so when we spoke to their elders, we had a wave of support. I wasn't under any delusion there was another way.

"You're lucky to be alive. Your mate saved your life." I winced at his use of the term. She was not ready to hear it.

"She isn't...yet," I hedged.

"Nonsense. Your mate is destined; there is no yet."

"It's not an easy situation."

"She knows?" This healer was going right for the gut.

"I haven't found the right moment for the conversation."

He made a disgruntled sound. "No important conversations are easy."

"Fair point." I tried to move again but hissed. Giving up, I swallowed my pride and asked, "Can you help me?"

"Are you uncomfortable? I can give you another dose of the milk of poppy after you eat."

"Wing cramp. Can you move it?"

"Yes. I'm here to check how they are healing anyway." He moved behind me, collecting things. It was almost comforting because when he didn't speak, he sounded exactly like Kiera.

"How bad are they?" I kept my tone flat. He'd know what my wings meant to me.

"Hard to say until I get a better idea of how your body is processing the Dragon's Bane. You are awake, which is a good sign." He lifted the sheet over me. "Your magic stores are still quite low after nearly a full day, so your body is using that magic to heal."

"That's good."

"Can you roll to your stomach?"

I gritted my teeth and tried, but my body wouldn't do what I wanted. "Can you help me?"

370

"Persistent weakness is a normal side effect of the poisoning."

"Then, why'd you ask me to do it?" I grumbled as he moved me.

"To evaluate your progress." He moved and manipulated my wings but remained silent.

"Well?" I asked, needing to know.

"They are healing. Slowly. Your magic stores need to go up before they can progress faster. I'm going to have to ask the elders if I can give you a charge stone."

"You have to get permission to do healing work?"

"For an outsider, I do. We have our secrets, as I'm sure you've realized by now."

"Many of them, I'm sure, since the rest of the Twelve Kingdoms don't know you even exist."

"By design." His words were clipped.

"I don't know how many dragons you have here, but if we are at war—"

He cut me off, putting a salve on one of the wounds on my wing. "I know what you may think, or how it may look, but your wars are not ours. We have our reasons for being here."

"That doesn't mean our wars won't affect you if we lose. The undead will claim the continent and come here, too."

"If they have returned, I'm sure that is true. But it's more complicated than you know."

"It doesn't sound so complicated to me. We are all dragons."

"You're young, and the world has changed many times since we split off. But many here don't know you exist out there." His voice dropped low. "It's not because we don't care about our kind."

It didn't make sense to me, but no good would come from questioning the fae tending to my wings.

"Stay off your wings and eat something. I must seek permission to use power crystals," he said when Zaria returned.

"How am I supposed to eat like this?" I called after him, making a face at Zaria.

She laughed.

"I'm sure your mate can help you," Emrys threw back.

I barely held back a cringe. I guess I deserved that.

FIFTY-FIVE

ZARIA

Nyx was laying on his front with more of the salve coating his wounds. He turned his face to me, but he was still so weak.

I knelt by his bedside so I could be face to face with him. I held up the plate of food I'd been given and smiled. "Want some?" I picked a piece of fruit and teased him, then popped it in my mouth.

He gave me a flat look.

I did it again, this time brushing his lips before stealing it away.

"You are enjoying this far too much, Sol."

Suddenly, I was gripped with guilt. I shouldn't be enjoying anything while we didn't know Kol's fate. "I'm sorry."

His eyes softened. "Don't be. I didn't mean you shouldn't.

We can't do anything right now, and you're keeping me sane until we can. I should be thanking you, not making you sorry."

I couldn't respond while emotion choked my words. Instead, I fed him some fruit, and we shared a moment of understanding. We would make the best of this pause and then we would go get Kol.

We ate and talked. I told him as much as I could remember about how I somehow made him shift and fly, and he was blown away. I felt like, in a fight for our lives, I'd done the impossible. I would have done anything to get him out.

"Think the healer is returning," Nyx informed me.

"You hear them?"

"I do."

"That's a good sign." If he could train his dragon hearing outside the tent, it was a sign he was recovering.

"I've brought Jaxus to help in the replenishing," the healer said when he returned.

Nyx asked, "Why would I need help?"

"Because this is not like the magic in the Twelve Kingdoms. Old magic is forbidden there."

"How are charging stones old magic?"

"We have ways of storing more magic in stones and crystals than you do, which is why I had to get permission to use them on you. We guard our secrets closely." The healer put a crystal in each of Nyx's hands.

"Why didn't you do this while I was unconscious?" Nyx sounded accusatory, and I flinched.

"Don't bite the hand that feeds," I said to his mind.

"It's an honest question."

"Do you want to get better?"

He grumbled but returned his attention to the healer as he and Jaxus helped him turn over and then used a crank in the bed to slowly help him sit up.

"They hold a much stronger charge, but we have to guide you or they could do more damage than good."

"What do you mean?" Nyx looked skeptical, and I wanted to smack him.

"It requires you to open your mind to us. If we were to try it when your mind is not with us, we could destroy parts by trying to pry it open. You can open your mind, yes?" Jaxus asked.

"Yes, I can," he said, dropping the attitude.

Thank the Goddess.

"You can help too if your stores are replenished enough. Your meld will give us more control," Jaxus said, waving me forward to stand beside Nyx's bed.

"We can't," Nyx said before I could answer.

"Is it forbidden?" Jaxus looked genuinely confused.

"No. We haven't been able to, umm...meld," I said, embarrassment taking hold.

Emrys cocked his head and narrowed his eyes like he looked past me. "Well, that's the problem. If you could meld better, she could help you more. You have to open the flow."

"What?" Nyx asked. "We aren't melded at all."

"Yes, you are."

"What?" Nyx and I said at the same time.

Emrys and Jaxus exchanged a glance.

"Did you two not know you were melded? What are they teaching you in that kingdom of yours?" Jaxus asked.

"Impossible," Nyx said, shaking his head.

Emrys placed a hand on each of us and closed his eyes. We watched him and waited. When he opened them, he nodded and fixed Nyx with his no nonsense look. "It's there, but you're fighting it. She gives, and you block. Check for yourself. Can you not feel it?"

Nyx looked at me, but I shook my head and shrugged. "I wouldn't know what to look for."

He searched inside himself and then his eyes widened.

"It's weak, but I think I feel it." Nyx closed his eyes, and I knew Jaxus spoke the truth when he opened them again. "How? We haven't even tried to meld in more than a week, and I know it didn't work then."

"You said you helped him fly here after the poisoning?" the healer asked.

"Yes," I confirmed, not sure where he was going.

"My guess is that he was too weak to resist your control, so the flow worked."

Nyx looked utterly confused.

"Melding is an exchange. Control doesn't allow for free flow of magic," the healer said.

"Do you mean it's been him and not me?" I cried, putting my hand to my mouth when I realized I was almost shouting.

Nyx groaned, putting his palm over his eyes. "Do not answer that. I will never hear the end of it."

"She's right. You were blocking more than she was from the sound of it," Emrys confirmed.

Jaxus held back a laugh.

My smile stretched so wide my cheeks hurt.

"You have to let yourself be completely open, youngling. I thought that was a given." He shook his head.

"It can't be that simple?" Nyx asked.

"I mean..." Jaxus gave me an awkward half glance. "Depends on how easily you give up control, mate."

I bit back a giggle. "Can you give up control to me, Nyx?" I shouldn't have said it, but I couldn't help myself.

Nyx growled, sending a shiver down my spine.

"It's a fair question," Jaxus said, clearly goading where I wouldn't.

Nyx's shoulders fell.

"What is it?" I asked.

"I've ruined our meld," he explained. "I was so focused on you getting it right, but I fucked it up myself."

"What ever do you mean?" the healer questioned.

"We only partially melded because of me, and now we have to live with that for the rest of our lives. Our powers won't ever fully align."

I felt the loss as keenly as he did.

"What in the sweet Goddess' name are you yammering about?" He frowned. "If your meld isn't complete, you try again. And if necessary, again and again until it is."

"That's not how it works," Nyx snapped.

"Boy, do you think the Goddess went to all the effort of creating the two of you to fit together perfectly, only to then let you flip a coin and let fate fall where it may? You are made to meld seamlessly together. There's no reason in all the realms to stop trying until you get there."

"We are taught that once a meld happens, it's final. If it's incomplete, that is the will of the Goddess."

"What lunacy! It's a good thing you did crash here, whatever the elders say. A meld like yours can't go to waste!"

Tears filled my eyes. All the pressure surrounding our meld had nearly broken us. Nyx looked so hopeful as he took in what Emrys was saying.

We had another chance to make it perfect. Many more chances.

For the first time since fire rained down on my village, I had the hope that things might eventually be okay.

FIFTY-SIX

NYX

"Open your bond and attempt a meld, but Nyx, I want you to let Zaria take control. You be the passenger," Emrys directed.

"Respectfully, as a dragon, it's not easy to let anyone take control."

"Don't they teach you to release control as part of your magical training?" Jaxus asked.

"No, not at all. Why would they?"

"Because magic is an exchange. If you can't give over to your partner, you can never fully meld. Of course it's easier to control than to submit, so you must practice trusting your partners enough for the flow to go both ways," Jaxus explained, not unkindly. What he said made sense, but that didn't make it any more fun to have to learn on the spot. "You trust Zaria, yes?"

"I do."

"Let's try it," Emrys said.

Zaria placed her hands over the crystals in mine.

I closed my eyes, opening myself to the power burning my palms, itching to be let in. I opened the channels and power rushed in, eliciting a gasp. I choked and tried to drop the crystals searing into my skin, but they were glued to my palms. I hissed against the pain, trying to mitigate and control the power coming in, but it was too much—like trying to drink from a waterfall.

"Let go," Jaxus said as he placed his hand over ours.

"I can't. I'm drowning." I barely managed to get the words out.

"We will help you control the flow," Emrys said, placing his hand on our others. "Zaria, take control."

I instantly felt the threads of our magic light up.

"Let me in," she demanded.

I nodded, fighting the flow of the magic, trying to open up to her.

"Let go of the control. You're fighting the magic." Jaxus' tone was firm. Commanding.

"It will sweep me away," I said through my teeth. It wasn't about giving over control. I was surviving.

"You must flow with the tide to take the power. Let Zaria direct it."

I gulped air and tried to speak, but wave after wave of power hit me.

I struggled, engulfed on every side by the tidal wave of magic. Even breathing became impossible.

"We have to stop. He's going to pass out." Zaria sounded panicked.

"Not yet," Jaxus said. "Give him a chance. It's not easy if he's conditioned to maintain control. Nyx, give over to her magic. Stop fighting it. Stop directing it. Trust Zaria."

I didn't know how to let go without being swept away. I'd

lose myself to the power and burn out. I'd seen it happen before when mages pushed themselves beyond their limits.

"*Nyx.*" Zaria was no longer outside my body but inside my mind, our magic tangled, our spirits merged. Her calm enveloped me. All else around us faded. "*Let go.*"

Panic gripped my chest and flooded my veins, but I released my grip on the flow of the tide, sinking under the weight of the magic.

Zaria took hold of it, parting the flow to direct it into all the places I needed it, and I fell apart from it. A bystander in my own remaking. We had been two souls never able to connect. Now we were one. Unending. Complete.

"*Zaria!*"

"*Don't distract me.*" Joy oozed from her.

"*We did it.*"

"*We did it,*" she agreed. I'd never heard her happier.

She drained the crystals, recharging both our reserves. More than any of the crystals in the First Kingdom would have done by far.

When the crystals dropped to the floor, we were standing chest to chest, with her arms around my neck. I slipped mine around her middle and dipped my forehead to rest against hers.

"How do you feel?" Emrys asked.

"Much better than I did," I said, not letting go of Zaria.

"I told you two wouldn't be too much," Jaxus said, a smile coming through his voice.

"You were right." Emrys shifted into one of the folds of his skirts and pulled out a money purse, giving Jaxus a coin.

"You bet on this?" I asked, breaking apart from Zaria.

"Would you not have?" Jaxus had a sly press to his lips.

"Why would you make me do two? If there was an option for one, I could have controlled it myself."

"And then the lesson you would not have learned," Emrys said dryly.

"We've found that when a mage is resistant to control, this is the best way to help them," Jaxus said, no remorse in his voice.

"That was an ambush?" I asked.

"Of sorts." Emrys wasn't apologetic, and I was unable to even be mad. It sounded like something Hazel would do to a resistant student.

"Thank you," I said earnestly before turning to Zaria and taking her hands in mine. "I'm truly sorry for everything I put you through, thinking it was you resisting when it was me."

"We both had to be patient with each other." She smiled, squeezing my fingers with hers. "But we got there in the end, didn't we?"

I brought her hands to my lips and kissed her knuckles. "We did. Thank you for not giving up on me."

"Love this, but we need to get you two moved to some accommodation if you're ready," Jaxus broke in.

"Can't let us have a single moment, friend?" I scowled at Jaxus.

FIFTY-SEVEN

NYX

E ven with the meld and the advanced healing magic they used here, Dragon's Bane poisoning really kicked your arse! Days later, my body was still healing.

I was holding power now, my wings were healed over, and my blood was cleansed, but things were just slow to get back to how they were. All the power I held was still being used up at rest as my body directed it for healing. I needed to be able to maintain a full reserve overnight before I would be cleared.

I was getting frustrated.

The village we were in was a small community. There were a number of extended families who made their home here, including Emrys, the healer, whose family was overseeing our care. He was still treating me, so he had welcomed us to a hut connected to those of his family.

He seemed to be an elder of this village, but I knew we were being held on the fringes of something much bigger. Emrys would often be called away, and Jaxus came and went and didn't seem to stay here. The other male, Hadeon, who Zaria said seemed like he was in charge, had not shown his face again.

I could only assume there was more to this place that they did not want us to see, and because I wanted to be able to leave as soon as I could fly, I wasn't about to go digging around. If they wanted to keep secrets, I'd let them. We'd probably seen too much for their liking already.

We were free to come and go from our hut. Meals were taken in a larger building, where Emrys' extended family cooked and ate together. He had children older than my father, and some younger than me, and there were grandchildren of adult age, and some still running around, climbing trees. It was a village in itself just inside his family home.

I kept to our room, sleeping mostly. Waiting, planning. Trying to reach out to Kol. It was futile; nothing had changed. It was like all those years without Zaria. I knew she wasn't dead, but nothing else. The difference was that I could reach his mind, but he was just...not there. Unconscious, I hoped, and safe somehow.

Zaria's question kept playing in my mind. If they killed and turned the other dragons they took, why keep Kol alive? If I thought too much about that, I was going to drive myself mad, and I needed to keep my head. Zaria taught me a skill she'd learned while living a life with no choices, and I was trying to use it while I had none.

All the things I wondered, all the things I wanted, they were not in my reach today. That might change tomorrow, but today, I was just a fae healing. I needed to focus on that now, so that tomorrow, if the Goddess willed my fate to change, I was ready to take on whatever that brought.

Zaria was truly a wonder. She was off somewhere braiding the hair of the healer's grandchildren, and I was glad she was able to distract herself. All those years of just dealing with the present moment and not fretting about a tomorrow that was not hers to control were paying off.

I personally wanted to kill every last fae who knowingly held her to that life, and Goddess willing, I would get the chance. We hadn't talked about the fact that we found an escape tunnel in her village and there were no bodies in the cellar because Kol had needed us. But once this was over, we would face it together.

A knock at the door saved me from spiraling, and I crossed the room to open it. Jaxus stood tall and bold on the other side. I was not used to anyone standing over me, but he was truly huge, and I knew he used it to keep me in my place. I was a problem here; I wouldn't expect any other treatment.

"Can I come in?" he asked, the self-satisfied smile that never seemed to leave his face on full display.

"Zaria's not here," I told him bluntly.

"It's you I came to see."

My brows rose. He had been making a point of seeking out Zaria for things and leaving me behind as the patient who needed rest. I had bitten my tongue down to nothing over the past few days, but it was all a power game.

"Sure, come in." I held the door open, and he strolled past me into our space. He eyed our neatly made bed and smirked.

One bed was all we'd been given, but after what we'd been through, there hadn't been a question of us separating. The awkwardness of the inn was a distant memory, and we'd slept wrapped in each other each night as our magics blended seamlessly to help me heal.

Nothing else had happened between us, though. We hadn't even talked about it. We were just focused on getting me strong. And I didn't like Jaxus' curiosity. He knew we were mates, and he knew I hadn't claimed her yet—there was no hiding that fact among dragons—but I wouldn't give him the satisfaction of explaining our situation or warning him off. He could see she was mine. An alpha did not need to assert himself on every matter.

"Sit outside so we can talk?" he suggested, turning to the small veranda that looked over the water.

I followed and took the other seat.

"How are you feeling?" he asked.

"Better. I think if I can hold my reserve full overnight in the next few days, Emrys will clear me to try my wings."

"That's good news," he said.

"Is it?" I leaned forward and rested my elbows on my knees, facing him. We both knew this was why he'd sought me out rather than Zaria.

He lounged back in his chair, not showing any signs of tension, but he held my glare.

"Are they going to let us leave when I can fly?"

"I cannot speak for the elders."

"No, but you can give it to me straight. I have to assume to protect this place, they will force us to stay, and I imagine if we won't, there can only be one solution." I left our deaths unspoken since it was not a future I would entertain.

Jaxus nodded slowly. "It's never happened before, so there is no other case to reference. But I believe your assumption would be correct."

"So, what are my chances of convincing them?"

Jaxus considered my words for a long moment before speaking. "I'm going to say fifty-fifty."

I sat back. Better odds than I feared. "Tell me how I can improve that in our favor."

"Nyx, I want to help you. If I had a twin brother out there who needed me, I would bring down the Wild Mountains if it meant I could reach him. But the elders here who knew the kingdoms of old will not see the plight of one dragon as enough of a reason to risk the safety of this place."

"The safety of this place is at risk if they don't let us leave," I argued.

"Convince me," he demanded.

I huffed.

"If you can't convince me when I want to help you, you will never convince them."

He had a point. "What do you know of the kingdoms? Were you one of those kept in the dark?" I spat. I couldn't help drawing comparisons with Zaria's life, and it left me feeling bitter.

"Don't judge the elders for giving these fae a place without war and suffering."

"I judge them for giving these fae a life without choice."

Jaxus laughed. "You can't compare this place to the life your mate was kept prisoner in. She's told me all about it, and it's not the same. The fae here are free. They just don't have to concern themselves with what happens beyond these mountains."

"Can they leave?"

"None have ever desired it. We are happy here. Despite what you may think, most of us do know the history of the realms. And we choose this place."

"You can't desire something you don't know exists. Do they know dragons live outside of here?"

"No. They don't."

"Then it's not a real choice." I had to change my tune if I was going to convince him. "If the Vivi Mortui are back, they're an enemy we all face. Your sanctuary is as vulnerable as any of the kingdoms."

"The elders believe our shroud will protect us."

"But your shroud did not keep us out, and the Vivi Mortui are not bound by the same laws as the living."

"No." He inspected his nails before looking at me directly. "Nyx, I'm going to be honest with you, dragon to dragon. Emrys believes

Zaria saw through our shroud because her magic is like that of this valley. It's an older kind of magic that is unique to this place. Your kingdoms have lost the old ways. That is why they don't connect with the Goddess so well anymore. There's a misalignment."

"Old magic was abolished when the kingdoms unified. It was the only way to end darker practices and make the kingdoms safer for all," I informed him.

Jaxus shook his head. "That is why this place came to be. Magic can't be sanitized so it's safer for all. The old ways were how we thrived under the Goddess. She exists among us, her energy nurturing and providing for us, and in return, she draws power from us when we thrive. As with all magic, it's an exchange. Without old magic, you can't fully connect to her, and she can't fully provide for you. It's like your meld would have been had you not completed it. We exist here because our elders refused to lose that connection."

I took it all in, stunned. The power in the kingdoms had diminished over the centuries, and Jaxus was telling me we had done it to ourselves. Kiera had privately floated some theories in the past during our late-night discussions that were along a similar line, but now, I was seeing it. She would lose her mind if she could be here for this realization.

"It rings true, doesn't it?"

"Somewhat," I admitted.

He watched me process my new reality.

"So, how does that affect us?"

"If they let you go and you reveal this secret, our magic and our connection to the Goddess will be in jeopardy."

"And if we stay and do nothing and the Vivi Mortui find you?"

"We'll fight them. They were defeated before because magic was stronger then. We have the means to defeat them again."

"And the forces?"

Jaxus gave me a wry smile. "We have the means," he repeated, giving nothing away.

But I knew more than ever that this village was just the tip of the iceberg.

"So, where does that leave us?"

"Your battle is not with the undead. It's with your King. Unless the old ways are restored, your kingdoms will never again hold the power to fight forces like the Vivi Mortui. The elders will never allow our magic to be destroyed. Convince them you want to reverse the fate of the kingdoms, and they might be convinced to let you go."

"And my brother?"

Jaxus shrugged. "Make your case. There are those on the council who might be receptive to your plight."

"When will they see me?" I urged.

"That's why I came. They will convene tonight."

FIFTY-EIGHT

NYX

J axus collected us at sunset and escorted us across the village
to a community building filled with rows of benches facing
a raised dais where a dozen chairs stood.

Whether the community usually attended council meetings or
not, this hearing was closed. It was just us. We took seats on the
front row of benches, and Zaria squeezed my hand.

A door in the back opened, and we stood as the elders filed
into the room. Dragons could live a long time, but most didn't
see gray hairs in the First Kingdom. The sight struck a blow to
my chest. One I wasn't ready to face. I carried too many
emotions over how many of my kind had perished too young to
protect all the fae of the Twelve Kingdoms. These elders, male
and female, ranged from in their prime to old and gray.

I had to find my calm while making my case. I reached for
Zaria's hand.

She took it and looked into my eyes. *"Trust your words."*

"I will."

The elders took their seats, and as I scanned them, it was easy to tell who was in charge.

A tall fae with closely cropped gray hair sat in the middle with an air of absolute authority.

"You look to be much better than your condition when you arrived."

"I am. I cannot thank your healer enough." I nodded to Emrys, who, as I suspected, sat on the council.

She nodded. "Am I to understand your mate saw us from above?"

Again, that word rang in my ears. Zaria had not made any comment about it, but I felt the awkwardness every time it was mentioned.

"You are," I replied, then glanced at Zaria, apologizing for answering for her even though the elder had directed the question to me.

"Will you tell us how you passed through our defenses?"

"My brother was in trouble. I made the decision to fly over the Wild Mountains because going around would have taken time we did not have. We met a weather system but were able to push through it to clearer skies. I was single minded in my determination to get to my brother, but we didn't actively try to fight any defenses."

"I see." She looked to Zaria. "And you saw us from the sky?"

"I saw the lake. It caught the sunlight and drew my attention for a moment. I didn't see this village or any sign of life, though —just the lake."

"And then after you were attacked with Dragon's Bane, you were able to force a shift on your mate and power him to fly?"

"Yes."

The elder glanced at Emrys, who presented his theories on

how it had been possible. I could sense this was all just formality. They had discussed this at length already.

"So, you decided to flee back into the mountains?" the head elder asked Zaria.

"I hoped they would not follow because the Wild Mountains are supposed to be impassable. It was the only option I had."

"And you were able to locate our lake again?"

"I'm afraid my recollection of those moments is hazy. I was out of power, and we were both injured. I thought I saw it and headed toward it, but I think we crashed. I don't remember coming in to land."

"I see. Well, we thank the Goddess you survived the ordeal." Zaria nodded.

A male leaned forward, eyeing us closely.

"Hadeon," Zaria told me, mind to mind.

"Tell us how you knew your brother was in such danger from the other side of the realm?" he asked at length.

I sucked in a breath. We had known this was a possibility, and we discussed how we would handle it. I could not break my vow, but we could not allow a secret to be the reason they would not let us leave.

"I vowed to my father I would never speak it."

The council seemed to collectively hold its breath.

"Why would you vow such a thing?" Hadeon asked, confusion clearly written on his face.

"The fact that you ask the question shows that you hold a theory," Zaria said carefully, clearly not trying to out my secret. "If the council cannot make a decision on our fates without this information, then ask it of me so that Nyx will not have to break his oath to his father." She glanced at me. *"I hope this is okay?"*

"We have to get to Kol. I don't care what it takes if he's alive."

Hadeon seemed impressed by Zaria's protection of my promise. "I suspect that Nyx and his twin share a twinship bond."

"You are correct," Zaria said, and her words were like a hammer.

I held my breath, my chest aching as the truth I'd kept secret so long was revealed.

The elders exchanged glances and whispered words. We waited.

When the whispering died down, the head elder spoke. "This kind of bond is common in the kingdoms?"

"No," I corrected. "To my knowledge, they died out after the kingdoms united."

The leader of the elders nodded as if expecting my answer. "Our defenses are made to keep out all who observe the rule of the kingdoms. We've discussed this at length, and we suspect that your twinship bond may have identified you as one of us and allowed you to pass over the Wild Mountains unharmed because it's an older kind of magic. The Goddess bestowed this gift upon you for a reason, Nyx. Why would you wish to leave this place now that you've found it?"

"I have a duty to my kingdom. I cannot remain here while they are under attack. I am bound by blood to lead their dragons and protect my kingdom. I take this responsibility very seriously. Keeping me here will cause so many to perish. And my twin is still in danger. He's unconscious but not dead. I must save him, and I must return to the First Kingdom."

"You're sure he lives?"

"I am. Our threads have not broken."

"Threads continue even in death."

"I can feel him alive." I knew he was. I wouldn't let them convince me otherwise.

The fae sitting next to the leader leaned over to whisper in her ear.

"If he is with the undead, as you say, his fate is sealed. Allowing you to go to him will be allowing another dragon to die at their hands."

"If my brother is to die, then I don't know how I will live. I have to try and save him. I can't do nothing!" I yelled. Zaria took my hand to bring me down, and I drew from her calming energy. "Every hour I put off returning, my brother could be suffering. I cannot sit by and leave him in their hands. You have my word; I've sworn it. I will perform the blood oath to keep the secret of this place. Let me try to save him. I beg of you."

"And then what? Whether you can save your brother or not, the fact remains that war is coming, and the kingdoms no longer have the magic to fight off this foe. You would be safer here. We could use a dragon like you."

"I think you're wrong," Jaxus said from where he sat. "I think they need to go…and I think I need to go with them."

"Excuse me?" the elder challenged.

Jaxus stood when addressed, hands clasped behind his back. A military stance if I ever saw one. "Forgive my intrusion, but I believe you are wrong."

"Go on," she said calmer than the Regent would have been under the same disrespect, which impressed me.

"Nyx is of the Asra line."

Brows were raised. I had not known that would hold any significance in this place.

"He tells me he will take command of the dragons of all Twelve Kingdoms when he returns. I have spoken with him at length, and while he cannot change the ways of the fae overnight, with help, he could make the necessary changes within the ranks of the legions who will face the battles ahead. He is the right dragon to be in command. They cannot win this war without him, and if the Twelve Kingdoms fall, we will eventually, too. I think he is needed at their helm to win this war, and we need to know the threat against us."

"How will going with him help?" a male from the end of the row demanded.

"How else will we know what we face?" Jaxus stood firm in his conviction.

"We do not need to know the details of a war that's not ours!" The male stood, knocking over his chair.

"With respect, I believe our future could depend on his success. The undead have been gone for centuries. Who knows what armies they have amassed in that time? If the kingdoms are turned, our forces would never be a match. We are at risk, too." Jaxus believed it—I could hear it in his voice. "Any who go can swear the blood oath as well. Would you not risk a few for the sake of our entire population?"

Glances were exchanged, and then the elders stood and drew into a huddle. The head elder cast her arm over the group, and to my astonishment, their murmuring was silenced.

"Concealment magic," Jaxus told us.

They spoke at length, some more animated than others, but after a few long minutes, they retook their seats. Their faces gave nothing away, and I held my breath and Zaria's hand.

The head elder addressed Jaxus. "If you feel so strongly, will you volunteer to go with him?"

I rocked back. Was this happening?

"I will," Jaxus said without hesitation.

"Put together a team. You and two others. Choose wisely, Jaxus. As soon as Nyx's wings are healed, all will swear the blood oath, and may the Goddess grant good flight."

It was over with her words, and the elders left the small hall.

I turned to Jaxus in absolute disbelief.

FIFTY-NINE

NYX

The fire pit in the village was the center of the celebration. My wings were healed, and I could fly. Emrys' family cooked us a feast in celebration, and we ate while sitting around the fire, telling stories.

Jaxus had chosen his two with him—Augustus and Xavi, who had aided me today in testing my wings. I figured any dragon I could trust with my safety in the air, I could trust in battle.

We had all sworn a blood oath before the council that afternoon, and we would depart the hidden valley at first light, so this was our farewell.

Jaxus and Zaria were deep in conversation. Fire burned in my veins every time Jaxus leaned toward her. I kept seeing it, and I knew he was pushing me deliberately.

I glared him down to no avail; he only had eyes for my Sol.

"*What's wrong?*" Zaria asked, slipping into my mind.

"*Nothing.*"

She looked sideways, her eyes telling me she wasn't fooled.

Jaxus called her attention back to his story, and I grit my teeth.

I stretched my arm and casually draped it around her shoulders.

His eyes followed the movement, and I didn't miss the look of amusement that flickered for a moment.

I reached for my drink and used the action to slip my arm down to Zaria's waist. As I took a drink, I drew her against me.

"*Subtle,*" she said in my mind.

I flinched. "*What?*"

"*You think I don't know what you're doing?*"

Damn it. "*I don't know what you mean.*"

"*You've been inching closer and closer all evening. Now you're what? Staking a claim?*" She laughed with the group to cover our secret conversation. "*You're jealous.*"

I was well and truly caught out and had nowhere to hide. "*What if I am, Sol?*"

Her eyes shone at the admission the words were, and I was taken aback. I pulled her closer and leaned into her ear, ending our silent conversation for the sake of appearances and maybe as an excuse to claim her further under the watchful eye of the competition. I murmured my words against her skin. "You like it, don't you?"

She softened. "Maybe."

"Admit it, Sol. No maybe about it."

"Why do I have to admit it when you wouldn't?" She leaned away from me, and I felt my claim slipping.

"*Fine, I admit it. I'm jealous. I hate the way he's looking at you, and I hate the way you don't seem to mind,*" I said through the bond.

She bit her lip, keeping her amusement covered. *"I'm actually impressed you can admit it."*

Her reaction was not the rejection I'd always expected if I let my feelings be known, but if she liked that, I had plenty more, so I went for it. *"Sol, I would burn down this village if he tried to take you from me. He knows what we are to each other, and he knows what he's doing."*

"And what are we to each other?" she asked so innocently, though I was under no illusion that she knew exactly how she laid me bare with the question. It wasn't one I could skirt around and continue pretending.

"Sol, you can't ask me that here."

"Why not?"

"Because we are among friends, and I am not rational when it comes to you."

"I didn't ask you to be rational. I want you as you are."

"A possessive bastard?"

"Yes."

I blew out a breath. Aware that we were, to all outside eyes, engaged in a silent stare-off, I broke her gaze and reached for my drink. *"This is dangerous territory."*

"How so?"

"Because we are surrounded by fae who'd all have you for their own in a heartbeat if you gave them permission, and I have no claim over you. So I know I have no right to be jealous, but it doesn't change that I am."

"Then, why don't you make a claim?"

Her words landed like a bomb and blew my reality apart.

SIXTY
ZARIA

M y words had stunned him. It was clear on his face. But I was tired of the not knowing, the constant push and pull. The passionate kisses we'd stolen when emotion took over, followed by long periods of nothing. The night at the inn before everything changed.

I needed to know if it was all in my head.

I'd had enough, and if the attention of a relative stranger was what it took to push him into admitting there was more between us, I would not waste it.

"If you and your mate continue staring like that, we are all going to think you're talking about us, you know." Jaxus laughed.

Nyx shot him a hard look.

There was that word again.

"Why does everyone keep calling me that?" I asked him

mind to mind, not caring what the rest assumed we were discussing. I wanted to have this conversation privately.

"We shouldn't discuss this here," he replied curtly.

"Answer my question, Nyx," I demanded, just needing to know now.

Conflict flickered in his eyes before he pressed them closed. *"Fuck."*

"Nyx?"

When he reopened his eyes, they were filled with trepidation. What was happening?

"Sol, I wanted to tell you."

"Tell me what?" What was I missing?

He exhaled harshly. *"We are fated mates. Bonded. I don't know how else to explain it to you. Those ties that connect us, they connect us in every way. You are mine, and I am yours, and every dragon here knows it because it's a primal bond. They can sense it."*

"You mean..." There was a phrase for it in my village. *"Folie a deux."*

His face twisted in confusion. *"What does that mean?"*

"I think the direct meaning is something like 'madness shared by two.' It's a term I've heard in stories told by the field workers. But they weren't real, just fireside tales. We can't..."

But as I tried to deny it, it echoed in my head a whisper of truth. Could we be? My mind reeled.

"Why didn't you tell me?"

"When? I wanted to tell you a thousand times, but when would it have been a truth you were ready to hear?" Sadness seemed to grip him.

"You should have told me from the beginning, Nyx."

"How do you think that would have gone over? I kidnapped you from your village, and you had to learn magic in a world you don't believe is real, and guess what? You're my mate! Mine forever. Tied

to me so completely, you'll never have another. It seemed cruel, and you've never had a single choice that's genuinely yours in all your life." He looked at me pleadingly. *"I wanted to be it, Sol. The choice you made for yourself."* He sighed. *"If I told you it was fated, you'd never believe it was your decision."*

"And what if I chose another because you didn't tell me?" If we were fated, I doubted I could really choose another, but I needed to hear what he thought he would do.

"I would have lived with it. It would kill me, but all I want is your happiness."

I rolled my eyes. *"You're an idiot. Do you know that?"*

He flinched, closing one eye. *"I deserve that."*

"Yes, you do."

Neither of us said anything for a long time.

"What are they doing?" Augustus asked Jaxus in a stage whisper.

"I think they are fighting," Jaxus whispered back.

Nyx glared at Jaxus, then stood abruptly. "Walk with me?" he asked aloud, offering his hand.

I took it and rose slowly. His arm slipped around my waist, and he brought me against him as we said our goodnights.

An unmistakable claim.

Jaxus and the others exchanged knowing looks as we took our leave.

The silence was deafening between us as we made our way through the village.

Finally, Nyx broke the silence. "This doesn't have to change anything between us. You have a choice in all of this, Sol. I would never expect—"

"Do you love me?" I asked abruptly, stopping at our hut.

Nyx stopped short, and I was forced to turn back to see his face. "Sol, I've loved you since the first day I saw you."

"You can't have," I countered.

"I didn't know what it meant until I was older and understood, but I know what I felt the first time I laid eyes on you."

A part of me wanted to roll my eyes and slip into our normal dynamic, but I stopped myself. "We don't understand love that young."

"No, maybe not. But I know what I feel now." He reached out for my hand.

I slid my fingers between his and let him draw me against him.

"I love you, Sol."

And that was it. No exceptions or complications, just those three words.

I stared into his eyes in the moonlight. "I love you, too."

His eyes burned with heat. He lifted me into his arms, and I yelped.

"Ask me again, Sol."

I thought back to what I'd asked him. What we were to each other? Why didn't he make a claim? It was all the same in the end, so I asked what I really wanted to know.

"What am I to you?"

His eyes glowed for a second, his mouth lowering to meet mine. He stopped a breath from kissing me. "You're mine," he said with certainty.

And then he kissed me.

Deep. Claiming. Possessive.

I felt like I was more his with every stroke of his tongue, the slide of his fingers through my hair, the possessive hold he had on me. I was his.

When he pulled back, we were both breathless.

"Why did you stop?" I panted.

"You want to do this out here?"

I laughed, and he carried me inside.

I slid down his body until my feet found the floor, and I tugged his shirt while backing toward the bed.

"Wait!" He sounded panicked.

"For what?" I kept going.

He growled. "Sol, please, I'm trying to do the right thing."

I frowned. "And what is that, exactly?"

"I'm trying to take it slow. I don't want to rush you. It's a big step."

I was lost.

"You're a maiden. I—"

Then it all made sense, and I couldn't hold in my laugh.

Nyx's eyes flew to mine, and they narrowed.

I pressed my lips together to rein in my amusement,

"Sol?" His tone was a warning.

"I'm sorry. I just don't know where you got the idea that I'm"—I rolled my eyes at his phrase—"a maiden."

His scowl cut a deep line in his brow. "Y-you...I..." He stepped away, and I hated the space. Turning his back on me, he paced. "Everything about you, Sol!" He rounded on me, counting off his fingers with each point he made. "The religion you were raised in. The way you were scandalized when I saw you in night clothes. The way you were scandalized by me being shirtless, for that matter. You called the capital a den of sin. By the Goddess, you dressed like your body was a fortress you had to protect at all costs! And you told me you weren't permitted to socialize with the fae in your village. What else was I to think?"

I was speechless, but I could see how it had all added up in his mind. "You could have asked," I said quietly.

He tipped his head to the ceiling as if asking the stars for guidance.

This was not going well. What if he didn't want me now because I'd been with another fae?

After a long moment, he straightened and turned to me, chest heaving, hands balled into fists. "So, you've been with other fae before?" he asked with no inflection I could read.

"One," I corrected.

He crossed the space. "Did you love him?" That note of jealousy I'd enjoyed before had returned.

I shook my head.

He moved closer. "Was he good to you?"

I nodded.

"I don't know if that makes it better or worse." He closed in, towering over me.

"He didn't matter. He was just an escape from that life."

"Were you together when I…"

He didn't need to finish. I knew what he meant—when he took me away. "No."

He released a breath.

"Does it change things?" I asked, afraid of his answer. What if I'd ruined everything?

"Yes, it changes things."

My stomach dropped.

"It changes how much sleep we're going to get tonight, for one thing."

I yelped when he picked me up, wrapping my legs around his waist. He took me in a hungry kiss, walking us to the bed, and then he laid me down, moving over me without breaking our kiss. The tension of the conversation bled out of me, and my hands began to roam over his face, his hair, his collar, the buttons. I opened them one by one, and he followed, opening mine. We fought with our clothes until I was free of my tunic and his shirt was stripped off and cast on the floor.

His eyes heated, and he skated his fingers over my collarbone, down to the curve of my breast. I gasped at the sensation of his thumb stroking across my peaked nipple, arching into his touch.

He smiled, dipping his head, and kissing a slow trail down my neck. My skin came alive everywhere his lips touched, and my breaths came faster when they closed around my nipple, sucking the sensitive peak until I moaned. Then he turned his attention to the other, and I felt the sensation all the way to my core. I hadn't known that pleasure before.

I'd been with a man, but not like this. That was forbidden—rushed and basic. This was the opposite—slow and deliberate. Each move intentional. As his trail of kisses descended to my stomach and down to the buttons of my pants, I stilled. He carefully opened them, kissing the newly revealed skin there. He gripped the pants at my hips, and I lifted so he could peel them down.

He knelt over me and dropped them to the floor, leaving me bare, and just stared, unashamed, at all of me revealed to him. I cursed myself for the dozens of times I'd looked away when he was naked or insisted he'd put some clothes on.

He dipped his head again, and I froze. "What are you doing?"

He paused, looking through his dark lashes. "I'm making my claim."

I felt his words everywhere. And then everything paled into insignificance when his tongue swirled around that place where he'd stroked me to a mind-blowing peak at the inn. I didn't try to stop him even though his mouth there seemed wrong. In truth, nothing had ever felt so right.

His groan of pleasure told me all I needed to know about how he felt with his mouth there. His tongue laved the sensitive skin the same way he kissed, thorough and sure.

I began to writhe beneath him until I felt his finger brush over my entrance and slowly sink inside. I gasped as he added a second finger and slowly worked them in and out, his tongue continuing to bring me higher. His fingers curled, finding a sensitive spot, and I arched. A pleasure unlike any I'd known built, better than any I'd given myself. I ground on his tongue, free of inhibition, just seeking more pressure, more pleasure. The fingers inside me flicked over that place, and he sucked my most sensitive spot into his mouth, circling and suckling until I crashed over the edge of my pleasure and cried out in ecstasy.

"Goddess," he gasped, breathless, as he slipped his fingers out of me.

I was lost to the new feelings of pleasure which had taken over my whole body.

"Are you okay, Sol?"

"I..." I didn't have words available, but my smile said it for me.

Nyx smiled too, crawling over me again and placing a kiss on my lips. I didn't shy away, and to my surprise, a sweet, heady taste joined his own unique flavor as he kissed me deeply. I was tasting myself, and it was incredibly arousing.

I reached down and slid my hand over the bulge in his pants, caressing it through the fabric and eliciting a moan from him. I fumbled for the buttons and opened them, pushing them down over his rounded, amazing arse. He stopped me, guiding my hands away.

"We don't have to," he said carefully.

"I want to," I pressed.

"Make sure you mean it."

"I do mean it."

"You need to be sure because once I'm inside you, I'll never be able to give you up."

"I'll never want you to," I promised.

He stood to shove his pants down and pulled them off, coming back to rest over me, and I felt the length of him settle between my legs. He was large.

"Tell me to stop if you need me to." His need to reassure me warmed my heart, but I wasn't going to break.

"Please," I begged.

"Patience," he scolded.

But I didn't have any patience. I was needy to finally feel him.

"When you've come half a dozen more times and are begging me to stop, I'm going to remind you of this conversation," he teased.

And then I felt him. Thick and hard, he pressed to my entrance. I sucked in a breath as he slipped inside, and I tried not to tense when a pinch of pain accompanied the overwhelming fullness of having all of him inside me. He was much larger than my previous…experience.

He paused at my hiss. "Okay?"

I nodded.

"Words, Sol."

"You're just bigger than—"

"Good to hear." He studied me, his voice as strained as mine. "Can I move?"

I nodded again.

Slowly, he withdrew. The fullness added an entirely new dimension to the feeling. Then he pressed in again.

"You're so tight," he moaned, withdrawing carefully.

"Don't hold back for me," I urged.

"I'm holding back for me," he choked. "Otherwise, this is going to be over in seconds."

Goddess.

"Please." I didn't care how long it lasted. I needed him to move.

"Fuck." He relented, moving at last. First with slow, deep strokes that pulled sounds from him I could never have imagined. I began to move with him, building and building, our tempo increasing. He hooked an arm under my leg and hitched it up, opening me to him even further. Suddenly, the thick head of him was driving into that same perfect spot inside me over and over.

I met him thrust for thrust, riding that wave until I crashed over the edge again. I contracted around him, and he called out my name as he found his release.

SIXTY-ONE

ZARIA

A thousand fae stood surrounding the outpost, all of them tinged blue. Half of them stood in an unnatural stance or off in some way, but all of them had completely white eyes. Even without pupils, I knew their vision was trained on me. I was the center of their attention as I sat on Nyx's back on the opposite end of the field.

What hope did we have against all of the undead?

Movement flickered in the distance. I narrowed my eyes and could barely make them out, but then it clicked. More and more undead emerged from the sea by the minute. They climbed out of the water and stood to take their place at the back of the hoard.

Ice ran through my veins.

"How will we ever find Kol facing this?"

"We have to." Nyx's voice was as cold as my blood.

Dragons lifted from the middle of mass, at least a dozen of them, and right in the center was Kol. His dragon was unmistakable even tinged blue like the undead. His eyes were white, too.

My heart stopped.

I sat up in a cold sweat.

"Sol?" Nyx grabbed at me.

"Nyx." I broke down, bringing my hands to my face.

"What is it?" His arms wrapped around me, and his lips found my shoulder.

"I saw Kol...." A sob took me. I couldn't say the rest. I couldn't speak words into life. What if they came true because I'd given them a spark?

His arms stiffened around me. "What did you see?"

"An army. More than a thousand of the undead. Too many. We were facing them and..." I couldn't get the words out between my sobs.

He hugged me tighter before loosening some. "Please say it." Concern colored his tone.

"I'm worried if I say it out loud, it will it be so," I admitted when I finally caught my breath.

"Life doesn't work that way. It was probably just a dream, Sol." He whispered his words over my skin, and they calmed me some.

"Kol was one of them, but not... He was...undead like the dragons that chased us." I turned in his arms, pressing my face into his neck.

"He's breathing. I can feel him. We'll get him tomorrow. We have to." He stroked my hair.

I nodded.

"It was just a nightmare."

"How can you be sure?"

"I have to be." He kissed my temple and laid back but kept me in his arms. "Try to sleep more."

"I don't know if I can. What if I see it again?"

"I'll protect you." He soothed my mind. How, I didn't know, but I felt better as I slipped into sleep.

SIXTY-TWO

NYX

"We need to go," I whispered into her hair. "You can still stay here if you want to."

"Are you kidding me?"

"We are walking back into a death trap, Sol. I would understand if you didn't want to do that with me."

"I can't believe you're saying that. No. Vehemently no. I would never allow it. You need me. You need our magic. I am the only reason you got out last time!"

"I won't be ambushed this time."

"The entire situation is an ambush. You have no idea what they could have accomplished in the last few days." Anger creased the lines of her beautiful face. I wanted to take it all away.

"I know it's an ambush, which is what gives me the advantage. But I will never like the idea of putting you into danger."

"You have to trust me."

"I do," I promised.

"Well, leaving me out isn't doing that."

"I see your point." And I knew there was no point in arguing. I knew my mate. Her mind was made up.

Mate. It was real now. She'd accepted me, and we'd sealed it with orgasms I would remember forever.

"I can't lose you." I stroked her hair.

"I can't lose you, either, so let's make sure that doesn't happen, okay?"

"Okay."

We rose from the bed and dressed quietly. The weight of what we faced was heavy in the air.

We joined the others on the edge of the village, and Jaxus took me aside.

When we were told we could leave by the council, I'd asked him to see if the village blacksmith could make some armor and a sword for Zaria. We had left the First Kingdom with the basic swords the trainees used. Trainees weren't fitted for their own sword and armor until they graduated. But with untold battles ahead, I wanted her to be able to defend herself properly.

In the few days it took for my wings to heal, their blacksmith had not only made it happen, but he'd let me help design her sword. We'd selected titanium for a lightweight weapon, and when it caught the light, it reflected color like a prism. He'd even added Amethyst, her origin stone, to the hilt.

It was more than a weapon. It was a gift.

I took it from Jaxus, wrapped in a cloth, and turned to Zaria.

"I wanted you to have a sword of your own," I told her. "So, I had this made for you."

Her eyes lit up, and she tentatively lifted the cloth.

Her hand came to her mouth as the dawn light hit the blade and colors reflected from its angles.

THE RYDER OF THE NIGHT

"It's beautiful. Thank you," she whispered, lifting the blade from my hands. She tested the weight and looked at the details.

"We have some armor for you too," I said, turning for the armor. But Jaxus was holding another wrapped bundle out to me.

"The blacksmith thought you should have a new sword too." He pulled back the cloth and revealed a dark blade styled as a partner to Zaria's. I lifted it and recognized the thrum of the metal immediately. It was the same metal as Emrys used when my reserves were empty. Tantalum. Something I'd never heard of until we came to this place.

It was the best metal for dragon replenishment, and now I would have it with me. "Thank you."

We fitted Zaria's armor and secured both swords across her back for the fight.

"Ready, brother?" Jaxus pulled his shirt off.

"Brother?" I asked.

"If we fly into battle together, we are brothers." Jaxus held out his arm.

I grabbed his forearm, and he mine, and we pulled into a hug. "Brother."

"For here after." He pushed off his loose linen pants, and Zaria blinked before turning around. He chuckled. "Is she not used to this yet?"

I forced myself to keep my eyes on his, getting enough of an impressive glimpse to know what had Zaria turning around. "Not by far. I'm starting to think she never will be. Modesty was a big thing in her village."

"She'd be rid of it here quickly. In the summers, none of us wear clothes."

"You don't care if others look at you all the time?" Zaria said, slowly turning around. "And you wouldn't care if your mate saw others?"

Jaxus gave me a look. "Who doesn't enjoy looking at bodies? I don't have a mate, but I can say that if I did, I wouldn't mind her getting an eyeful if she got all revved up and came home to me. Plus, I like to be admired." His lips curled up at the corners.

"Let me know how that changes when you find a mate." My words were part growl—a new development since claiming Zaria as mine.

"I don't expect to find a mate, but I'll be sure to keep you updated."

Zaria smirked, pressing her lips to my jaw. "So, I shouldn't be looking?"

"Don't tease me." I hissed, finding her mouth with mine.

"You are all I see," she whispered against my lips.

"And you are my entire universe." I cupped her face. "If we don't make it, know I have loved every day with you."

She pressed her eyes closed, fighting emotion. "We will make it. We have to."

"We must go to beat the approaching storm." Jaxus cut our moment short, but he was right.

SIXTY-THREE

ZARIA

S ilence held and humbled us. There was no army of the undead awaiting our arrival.

We approached, flying in a diamond, with Nyx in the lead, anticipating an ambush. But the outpost lay bare. The only sounds were those of the waves licking at the cliffside. It felt like a graveyard.

We circled over the top of the battlement, looking for any signs of life. I leaned over the side of Nyx's back, scanning the ground. Since our meld, being on his back felt like an extension of myself. There wasn't even a fear of falling.

"Are the undead listening?"

"Why do you ask?"

"It feels like the world is holding its breath." I couldn't explain it any other way. *"They have to be laying in wait."*

"*I know, but where?*" Nyx circled back to the place we'd designated for our fallback.

The other dragons landed seconds after he did and changed to their fae form.

"It looks completely abandoned," Augustus said.

"Which makes it more dangerous," Nyx warned.

It felt hopeless. Kol wasn't dead, I reminded myself. I took solace in what I could hold on to, keeping hope alive.

Nyx paced the top of the ridge, looking over the outpost. "We need to sneak in. We'll have a better chance of finding my brother if we split up and go in groups."

"I agree," Jaxus said, and it clearly surprised Nyx.

He whipped around and looked into Jaxus' eyes. "Good. There's a cliff escape—all our outposts have them. Zaria and I should go in there. Then what do you think? Two take the front and one stays in the air?"

Jaxus nodded, considering Nyx's words. "I like that. Then one of us will draw them, and the others can get in and look around."

"We should wait until full sun. The Vivi lose power in the full sun," Augustus added. "I'll take the front with Xavi. We're lighter than you and can slip them easier."

"We need another fallback plan." Jaxus crossed his massive arms over his chest.

"And a signal," I said, finding my voice. I was part of this rescue team, too.

"Right, good point. Do you know how to send out a flair?" Jaxus asked.

"Like a streak of light? Yes." Light was becoming my best weapon. "But won't they see it?"

"Yes, but if you need help, it won't matter. Make it loud. If we're found, we're found. Best we all know," Jaxus said matter-of-factly.

"If the alarm is raised, we fall back," Nyx ordered.

"Where are we falling back to?" Jaxus asked.

"Here, in the first instance. If this spot is compromised, head straight back for the Wild Mountains. We know they can't follow, and if we can't land here to regroup or we get separated, just head back to the sanctuary," Nyx said.

"Agreed," the others said in unison.

"You're still confident they won't be able to find the sanctuary, right?" Nyx asked. "I wouldn't want to put anyone else at risk."

"I'm sure. We had dragons testing our wards and magic while you were there. We found no holes. The elders are happy that it was your unique magic that let you pass."

Nyx inhaled, holding the air in his lungs. His power darkened around him, and his wings shrouded his figure. "We need to go," he said as the shift took him.

We launched without another word. Nyx flew out over the water, coming around to approach the cliffs. I did my best to use the sun already reflecting off the North Sea to hide our approach. It wasn't something I'd explicitly been taught to do, but found I could manipulate light in ways that seem to just come naturally now. It worked fairly well.

We landed on the cliffside platform and listened. I handed Nyx a pair of pants. Once he was dressed, we both tied cloths around our mouths and noses. Emrys had spelled one for each of us to protect against Dragon's Bane. They would only buy us a few moments if we were hit with it like we had been before, but we could use it to escape. I could not get four dragons out if they were taken down.

He opened the spelled door with his command. Those still worked. He'd told me it would be a good sign.

The halls were vacant. Not a sound anywhere in the outpost.

The outpost had an extensive underground portion built down into the bedrock. We searched room by room, and they were all empty.

"*Could they have moved him?*" I asked, using our bond so we were silent to enemy ears.

"*It's possible.*" His hope slipped. "*I don't think they'd just abandon the post after taking two flights from it, though.*"

"*Is there somewhere they could fall back to?*" I asked, opening a door that led to what looked like a cellar. I pointed, and he nodded.

"*In the sea, maybe. But it wouldn't be easy for them to climb the cliff face.*"

I let him take the lead. I strained my eyes to see, but it was too dark. I put a hand on Nyx's back, feeling every step with my toes before taking it. "*I don't like this.*"

"*Neither do I.*" He stopped, and the only sound were our breaths. "*Let me make some light.*" Power gathered in his palm, and light sparked, spreading into the room.

Heavy shadows fell behind massive stores and barrels. Shelves and stacks of grain. The room was expansive, but we couldn't see past the first few shelves.

"*Let me climb one and get a better look.*"

He hesitated, then nodded, lacing his fingers to give me a boost. I got to the top of the shelf and scanned the room to find rows of shelves and enough food for an army, which made sense.

"*I don't see any obvious signs. There are other rooms, and I think a weapons store in the back.*"

"*There should be some cells down here too. Maybe another floor down? This place is like a burrow; we are never going to get through it all before nightfall.*"

"*I'll check the weapons store back there, and you find the cells. We can keep speaking mind to mind.*"

"*I don't—*"

"*Trust me. I can use my sword, and being mated to me doesn't give you an excuse to not treat me like a ryder and an equal.*"

He flexed his jaw and made a low, growling sound but said, *"You're right."*

I unsheathed his sword from my back, handing it to him. I grabbed his hand as he took it and squeezed it before taking part of the light he'd made and setting off at a jog, weaving through the stores.

He didn't follow, and I was glad. We had to trust each other.

I got to the arms store and checked the locks. I uttered the words Nyx gave me to trigger the magical lock. It clicked open, and I held my breath as I pulled open the door.

"It's empty," I told Nyx.

I even checked behind the racks of swords.

I closed my eyes, willing the Goddess to help us find Kol.

I relocked the weapons room and scanned the back corner for anywhere else to search.

"I found the cells. I'm checking them one by one, but they seem empty."

"Okay."

I made my way back to the entrance of the large room.

"Hey!" a voice called from behind me. "What are you doing?"

Ice ran through my veins, and I froze. I knew that voice.

No. Anything but that. Anything but what it would cost me to believe Luka had been against me, too. I couldn't face it. I couldn't take another loss.

Slowly, I turned around to find my old friend jogging toward me.

I slowly pulled the cloth down from my face, and he skidded to a halt.

"Zaria?" he exclaimed, moving to throw his arms around me.

"Don't." I held my hand up to stop him.

He drew back. "Don't?" Confusion tinged his voice. "Don't what? I thought you were dead. They said you'd been taken by one of those dragons."

"I was." I studied him. He looked the same. A little dirty, but not undead.

"Don't tell me you're part of all this?" he accused.

"Part of what? Trying to save innocent fae?" I said against my better judgement.

"You're not with the undead?"

"No! Are you?"

"Yes." He threw up his hands when I reacted. "But it's not what you think! I'm not dead."

"Then, what are you doing here?"

"It's a long story."

"Summarize, Luka," I demanded. "Starting with how you escaped our compound."

He exhaled heavily. "There were tunnels beneath the compound I never knew about. The elders were using them to get the herbs out before they all burned. Everyone who could carry sacks went. I looked for you, but they said you were dead."

"My parents?"

"Yes. They said you were taken by one of those dragons. Goddess, Zaria, I can't believe you're here."

"My family got out?"

"Yes."

"Where are they now?"

His shoulders fell. "I don't know. We fled to another village. They had a much smaller crop, but they took us in. I started helping with deliveries since we'd lost some workers, and we were making a delivery on the coast, like they had a hundred times, and we got ambushed. They took the lot of us hostage."

"The lot of you?"

He nodded. "The three of us who were there making the delivery. Eliezer, Callan, and me. They put us on a ship and... Goddess, I don't know how long ago that was or where we've been, but we've been with them since. They killed Eliezer because he put up too much of a fight but kept Callan and I alive to do work for them. We help with the herbs. They don't like it. It makes them sick."

Because it was poisoning them, but I didn't have time to explain that to him.

He chewed his lip, stepping forward and holding out his arms. My heart hurt, but I stepped back, not letting him get near me. I wanted to run to him and hug him. But how could I be sure he wasn't a Vivi Mortui himself? Could they fake being still alive? I hadn't asked enough questions.

"Zaria." His brows pulled, and sadness shone in his gaze. "I am not one of them."

"Prove it to me," I demanded.

He took another step toward me, and I mirrored it backward. "Feel my hands. I am not dead. The undead can't speak."

"Can't their masters make them speak?" My heart hammered so loud I could barely think straight. Could I leave him here knowing I might be wrong?

"I don't know...but they wouldn't know you. Our history. I know you, Zaria."

"Anyone might know my name. I need you to prove it to me." I drew my sword to keep him in his place.

"I'm the one who taught you to use that thing, and you'd pull it on me?" He laughed with the same humor he always had in the face of any obstacle.

I exhaled a long-held breath. "I believe you... but you have to come with me. The outpost is going to be destroyed to kill all the Vivi Mortui." If he stayed here, he'd be dead.

He glanced behind him, and I raised my sword. He held up his hands. "I have to make sure they haven't seen me down here. They trust me now to do my chores without being watched, but they sometimes check. I don't know how long I could be gone before they'd notice and come looking." His eyes trailed over me like he was taking me in for the first time. "Who are you with?"

"I can't tell you until we are out of here. Just in case."

He nodded. "A lot has changed."

"So much."

"Maybe it's better you go. If they realize I'm missing, it might ruin your plan. It's better the undead are taken out than left to claim more."

"I can't leave you." My heart was shattering into a million pieces. I couldn't lose Luka again today. Not with Kol in such danger.

"What if it alerts them you're here?"

"I will deal with it." Nyx would do the same for Kol. I knew I was making the right decision.

"I love you, but I can't risk it. Go."

I pressed my eyes closed. "Don't make those your last words to me."

"I need you to know."

"It's not okay. Not if you won't come with me." I gave him a look he was sure to understand. "Let's go. I'm not leaving without you."

"You'd stay and die by my side?" A smile edged at the corners of his lips.

"Fuck."

"Zaria! This new life has given you a filthy mouth."

I rolled my eyes. "Let's go."

"Only if you insist." He gave me that smile, the one that let me know he wanted more, and I had to stop him before he made himself dragon bait.

"You can't be that way with me anymore, Luka. Everything has changed. I've met someone."

"I see." Pain flashed in his eyes for a moment, and then it was gone. "We have to go."

Nyx did a double take when I came around the corner with Luka in tow.

"It's a long story," I said quickly.

"Is this him?" Luka asked, and I could already tell this was going to be a problem.

"Yes," I said to Luka before turning to Nyx. "Anything?"

Nyx shook his head, keeping his attention on Luka. "Who is this?"

"My childhood best friend. He's safe."

"Has he seen my brother?" Nyx asked. He should have had a hundred questions about how Luka was here, but only Kol mattered. We both turned on Luka expectantly. "He looks just like me. Have you seen him?"

Luka studied Nyx. "No, but they have a hide-out up the coast a ways where they are turning them."

Ice pumped through my heart, freezing my veins. "The fae who were holding this fort?"

"I only arrived two days ago. I don't know who they have or where they got them. I'm being held myself and just glad I'm not in the pit."

"Where?" Nyx demanded.

"North, maybe six or seven leagues. If you follow the sea, you can't miss it."

Nyx turned, storming up the stairs.

I ran after him. "Are we going there?"

"We have to."

"Do you think there is a chance he's still alive?" I asked. I didn't want to assume the worst, but how long had it been since Kol had gone silent? Too long. I felt sick.

"I don't know, Sol, but I have to see."

We found the other dragons, and Augustus agreed to let Luka ride on his back. Luka was apprehensive, though. I didn't blame him. Fear flickered in his eyes when we suggested it, but he'd rather face death on a dragon's back than be left alone to have the undead come back for him. We made him a tether to hold on to since he was not made to be a ryder.

We made a plan for Augustus and Nyx to head for the pit while Jaxus and Xavi worked on destroying the Dragon's Bane weapons and disabling as many of the undead as possible. They wouldn't die, but it would slow them down or take them out until their masters could reanimate them.

We flew north, and the sun dipped closer to the horizon. Vivi Mortui were more powerful after dark, but so was my mate.

Luka pointed out the pit he'd described a league before we were on it.

My gut dropped when I made out shapes. I didn't need a full view to know what I saw. Fae were being held in a giant pit, chained to posts. It wasn't clear if they were alive or dead, but there were too many. More than would have been at the fort.

"They have to be taking them from villages, too."

"They must." Nyx's voice, even in my mind, was void of any emotion.

"Are you sure we should go in there?" I was trying to keep my fear in check.

"Do you want me to put you on the ground here before we do?"

"No!" I wasn't scared for myself. I was scared they'd turn Kol and he'd become the dragon in my dream, but I couldn't say that to Nyx. Not when he was like this. *"Our magic works better together. Where you fly, I fly."*

"Okay."

We flew over the pit, and Nyx dove, only snapping his wings out when we were close enough to the ground to make out the faces of the fae. I scanned them one by one, trying to see every face. The worst game of eye spy. We flew too fast, and I felt like I didn't get a good enough look at half of them.

A gong sounded. My head snapped up as the undead swarmed. They crawled out of every shadow and crevice.

They'd been laying in wait. Bile rose in my throat. All the fae on the ground would be turned before we could bring an army back here.

There were so many of them. Thousands.

I screamed and threw power at the undead who stampeded over the walls of the pit. The sounds they made were monstrous. My power blasts knocked them down, but they got up and continued on their path, barely missing a beat.

I needed something more.

Nyx turned, and the sun glinted in my eyes. An idea struck me. I focused my power above them, channeling the sun's rays like a child would with a piece of focal glass. They burned, and I nearly squealed with glee. I focused, picking them off as I searched.

Nyx made a turn, coming around again, and then a magically amplified voice rang out over the chaos.

"If you want your blood, come and get him." A fae stood in the middle of an army of undead. He raised his hands, directing a hoard of them to fan out, revealing what lay beyond them.

My heart stopped in my chest.

Kol was bound to a pillar on a platform, unconscious and surrounded by dozens of sacks of Dragon's Bane, which sat among piles of hay. He was alone there, singled out, with no sign of his ryder Elvar or the rest of the flight. They were likely already turned. He was bait. Then the fae snapped his fingers, and a spark fell onto the hay.

"Nyx!" I screamed.

If Kol didn't burn alive, he would surely die from the Dragon's Bane.

Nyx nearly fell out of the sky. He'd seen what I had, and he dove for Kol.

If he could get there before the entire thing went up, he could pull Kol out.

Another snap rang out, crackling through the air, and the

entire platform went up, engulfing Kol and all the Dragon's Bane. A cloud of smoke exploded from the middle, throwing the fumes out. They'd charged it and turned my wonderful friend into their weapon.

"*Kol!*" Nyx roared. Fire spilled from his mouth and rained over the ground beneath us as he banked steeply to save us from the explosion.

He flew furiously, coming around to pass over the scene again. The smoke was so thick he couldn't get near, but even from here, I could see Kol was beyond saving.

"*Nyx,*" I warned.

"*I have to get him.*"

"*You can't save him,*" I pleaded. He wasn't seeing reason.

"*He's dying.*"

Kol was gone. Nyx just hadn't accepted it yet. I had to stop him from sending us to the Goddess with him, so I fought him the only way I knew how—with our magic.

It had to be enough.

SIXTY-FOUR
NYX

I grabbed at Kol's threads, but they slipped through my grasp. There were too many of them. Too many to keep hold of. His lifeline hung, barely thrumming in my mind. He was so close to death but too far for me to reach.

I wasn't in control of my own form. My wings wouldn't listen, and the fumes were already approaching. I fought harder to get to him, and then I realized what held me back.

Since our full meld, Zaria's power had multiplied. She pulled as I pushed, thwarting all of me.

"*Nyx...*" The word was soft, but it cut like a knife.

"*I have to get his body. I have to go get his fucking body.*"

"*You can't. You will die.*"

Grief gripped me.

I shook with it.

I lost myself to it.

SIXTY-FIVE

ZARIA

"I cannot leave him to this fate. He cannot be—" His words choked off.

"Do you want us both to die?" I didn't know how to get through to him. I tried to do the same when my village was burning down, and I understood, but I couldn't let him go to his death any more than he had let me back then.

His body shook with grief. I hugged myself to him, not letting him suffer this alone, barely keeping control of both of us.

"Nyx, we must leave. You must warn the King. You have a duty." I made up reasons as I tugged at him. Anything to get him moving. There were too many of them.

"He's still alive."

"He's not." There was no way.

"We have to fall back!" Luka screamed from atop Augustus. "Another wave is coming."

I didn't know how, but I managed to force Nyx back to where the other dragons waited on a hilltop overlooking the pit.

"We can't stay here long. If there is that many of them, they may be prowling the entire countryside." Jaxus was breathing hard after he shifted back to his fae form. "Your brother?" he asked Nyx.

Nyx couldn't even face them. He just stared out over the scene below.

"He's dead," I said somberly, tears streaming down my cheeks.

Jaxus met my eyes, and emotion flickered in his as he searched for words. "I'm deeply sorry."

"They will turn him." Nyx's voice came hollow.

I slammed into him, wrapping my arms around his body, and he sobbed into my hair.

"I can stop it." He crumpled. "I can't leave him to be one of them."

"Is it worth trading your life and mine for a body? Because I will go with you. But he is dead."

"The threads are there. Maybe he's not dead yet..." His voice cut me in ways I didn't know pain could, battering my heart to shreds.

I grabbed his face, forcing him to look at me. "Some threads stay connected in death. But he is gone." Every single word hurt, but it was true. "So, tell me if our lives are worth recovering his body, because I will follow you to the Valley of the Dead, but only if I know this is what you really want."

"Do you mean to tell me I have to feel him like that forever?"

"I don't know, my love. I don't know."

"I can't bear it."

"Then, please don't subject me to the same fate. I cannot lose both of you today. If you go, I will follow."

"We can't stay here," Jaxus urged.

Nyx looked over my shoulder.

"Please." I dug my fingertips into his skin.

"We should return to the sanctuary and warn the elders," Jaxus pressed.

Nyx's gaze flickered to him, and something in him changed. "I have to warn the King. I can't let this plague reach the First Kingdom without warning."

Jaxus wavered for a moment before determination settled over his expression. "Augustus, Xavi, return to the mountains and warn the elders. I'm going with them."

The other two dragons gasped.

"Are you sure?" Augustus asked.

"I must, and this lad needs to go with them, too." Jaxus pointed to Luka, who had remained quiet while Nyx grieved. Jaxus had made up his mind.

"May the Goddess give you speed." Augustus inclined his head in respect.

"And to you, my friend," Jaxus returned.

Augustus and Xavi shifted and took off for the Wild Mountains.

Nyx didn't say anything to Jaxus before he shifted. Jaxus followed suit, and Luka and I mounted.

Nyx shot into the air without a word.

I sobbed into his scales.

SIXTY-SIX

ZARIA

The journey home was a blur. Nyx had shut down. When we stopped briefly for water, Jaxus and Luka offered me company, but I couldn't separate myself from Nyx. I didn't know how Nyx flew. I felt barely alive. Time stopped, or maybe it flowed. It all blended together, and by the time we arrived back at the capital and landed on a platform at the palace, all of me was numb.

We must have been seen by the spotters because we had a party waiting for us, including the Regent.

Kiera sprinted to my side as I dropped off Nyx's back.

The Regent stormed to Nyx as he shifted. "Where have you been?" he said in a snarl. "You can't go running off. You're needed here. We lost another flight, and we have no idea what's going on with the outpost—" Octavian's words faltered as Jaxus landed beside us carrying Luka. "Who is this?" he demanded.

Nyx didn't seem capable of forming the words, so I stepped in, addressing the Regent for him. "There will be time for all your questions," I told him, proud of myself for my firm and steady tone. "Right now, Nyx needs a healer."

Octavian scoffed. "Not until I have some answers. I—"

Nyx cut him off. "They are all dead. They are using Dragon's Bane to incapacitate them before they kill them and turn them." His tone was flat.

A gasp rippled through the small group.

Kiera searched my face, questioning.

I nodded.

"Are you okay?" she asked quietly.

"I don't know, but check Nyx. They've created weapons with Dragon's Bane. We were close when one exploded." I closed my eyes, but the image of Kol at the center of it was burned into my soul.

Kiera whispered something to another healer, then turned to Nyx, putting a hand over his lungs to listen to him with her magic.

Octavian regained his voice. "Nyx needs to come with me to brief the King." He informed Kiera since she was now in his way.

"He's been poisoned with Dragon's Bane. He needs medical treatment."

"We don't have time for that." He lifted a lip in a sneer.

"While I understand the urgency, he's no good to anyone dead."

"He looks fine," he argued.

"Respectfully, you are not a healer, and I will pull rank if I have to."

Octavian spluttered. "I am Regent General."

"I know your position, but you know in our founding charter, the right to emergency medical care comes before even the highest matters of the crown."

He schooled his features. "Then I will come with you."

Six more healers joined us on the platform. The oldest, a tall and wiry man, stepped forward to speak to Octavian. "You may come with us, but you may not get in our way or interfere until we've assessed them."

Octavian scowled but didn't stop them as the healers led us all off the platform and into the healer's wing.

Kiera stayed by me, linking her arm through mine while Luka took my other side. She had no idea what had happened, but she knew to protect me, and I'd never be able to thank her enough for that. I had nothing left to give anyone. I was too raw. While the other healers fussed over Nyx, she got me alone in a room.

"What happened?" She searched my face.

"We went to the outpost..." My voice trembled. "To help Kol." I didn't know if I could get through the retelling. I hadn't even processed it myself.

Her brows knit, and I saw her put the pieces together. "The outpost... *Kol?*"

Tears started streaming down my face as I nodded. I tried to speak but choked back a sob. Luka sat on the edge of the bed rubbing a hand down my back like we'd never been apart.

She wrapped her arms around me, hugging me to her. "Goddess, please don't let it be real."

I sobbed harder into her shoulder. "He's dead."

We cried together like that for a long time.

She finally pulled away from me. "I really need to get myself together and check you out." She wiped her eyes with her thumbs. "I'm not doing my job. I need to check you for Dragon's Bane poisoning again. And...who is he?" She nodded at Luka, though she didn't take her eyes from me.

I let a laugh out through the tears. "Kiera, this is my childhood friend, Luka."

"It's nice to meet you, Luka," she said, using the magic to

439

listen to my chest. "And who is your dragon friend" she asked him.

"Oh, that's Jaxus. We just met, actually, but he gave me a ride," Luka told her.

Kiera frowned. "I see." Then she turned her attention back to me.

"I'm fine," I resisted. "I promise. If I thought you needed to do something, I would have spoken up."

She gave me a half glare. "Would you even know something was wrong with you?"

I lifted my shoulders. I didn't now anything in that moment. "You should go to Nyx. Who is with him?"

"My father—he's the head healer. He often travels to educate and share knowledge with other healers, which is why you didn't meet him before. Nyx is in good hands, I promise. That's why I stayed with you." She went through a full examination before she spoke again. "I do think you've built a tolerance, living around it for so long, which helped you, but I want to give you some fluids and a potion mixture to strengthen your lungs in case it brings on an attack later."

"Before you do any of that, please check on Nyx. I need to know he's okay." My anxiety over losing him, too, clouded everything else. I couldn't stand the thought of him alone. He might go mad with grief.

"Come with me. We can check together."

Luka and I followed her down the hall. Octavian paced the corridor and glared us down as we slipped inside.

"How's he doing?" Kiera asked her father once the door had closed.

I glanced at the door, concerned that Octavian was listening. I didn't trust him.

Kiera caught my concern. "It's okay. Everything we say in here is protected. Healers' work is confidential. Magic prevents prying ears."

I relaxed a little. The older healer glanced at Nyx for permission to share his diagnosis.

Nyx nodded, then stared blankly into space.

"He's fatigued and dehydrated. He's got mild Dragon's Bane poisoning symptoms. I was told by this young man"—he gestured at Jaxus—"that he was just getting over a bad case of poisoning that nearly killed him, which is probably exacerbating the symptoms. But he's awake and alert and responding, so I don't think he got much. How is his ryder?"

"She is also fatigued and dehydrated. I'm going to treat her with a preventative for breathing attacks she is prone to and more fluids. I think after a good night's rest, they will both be much better."

"I agree, and the boy?" Kiera's father asked.

Kiera side-eyed me. "He's not a dragon and shouldn't be affected…"

"I'm fine," Luka said. "It doesn't affect me."

Kiera's father looked him over before saying, "Shall we go gather those things?"

"Yes. Zaria, would you prefer to stay in here with Nyx?"

I nodded, and they left, leaving us all in silent shock. I don't know what came over me, but I climbed into bed with Nyx. He seemed to come back from his thoughts and welcomed me into his arms. I pressed my face into his chest.

"Do you want us to leave?" Jaxus asked. I'd honestly forgotten he was there.

"No," Nyx said, his voice empty and dry. He glanced at the door. "We need to get our story straight."

"Straight?" Jaxus asked, sounding alarmed.

"Do we need a story?" I raised my head to look at him, as confused as Jaxus was.

Nyx watched the door beyond which he knew Octavian waited. He couldn't hear, but Nyx still exercised caution, waving Jaxus closer. "We have a dragon with us that no one knows, who was not brought to the First Kingdom like he was meant to. I think there will be questions, and we can't risk your home being revealed, so we need to all have the same story so we don't break the blood oath."

Jaxus nodded, glancing over his shoulder at the door. "Is it normal to be under such scrutiny while you heal?"

"I am to replace him when I take my place as the general. I can only assume he is anxious about my intentions on that front."

Jaxus nodded in understanding. "Then let's decide before he barges in here."

"He could have been isolated in a remote village like Zaria and I were," Luka offered.

I nodded. "I agree. Then he'd be ignorant to the fact that all dragons are sent here to train when they are younglings."

Jaxus made a disgusted face. "As young, they are torn away from their families? Who teaches them?"

"There is a school here," Nyx replied.

"A school cannot replace family." Jaxus shook his head.

"I've never thought about it because it was my normal, and my family was here, too. For others it's—" He cut himself off. "I don't know what it is, but it's like the wool has been ripped off my eyes, and I'm seeing a lot of things I've never seen before."

I didn't know what this meant for any of us.

Jaxus clasped his hands behind his back. "Is that our story, then?"

"I think so." Nyx laid back. "I think we rescued you from your remote village, and here we are."

"Did Kiera ask?" Nyx asked me.

"I told her the basics. I will fill her in once we aren't being scrutinized."

"Okay."

We fell into silence.

"We have another small inconvenience," Jaxus said, breaking the silence.

"What?" Nyx's face pulled and creased like he was going over all our lose ends.

"If it's me, you can tell them whatever you like. You found me at his village or the outpost," Luka spoke up. "I'll go along with whatever."

I offered him a tight smile of appreciation.

"The outpost," Nyx said right away. "I'm sure Octavian and the King will want to know all you know."

"It's not much, but I'll do anything to help," Luka said.

"That's all great, but I wasn't speaking about Luka," Jaxus said cautiously.

"What is it then?" I finally asked when he didn't speak.

"I'm not sure the best way to say this...but I think that female healer is my ryder."

His words went off like a bomb.

SIXTY-SEVEN

NYX

I didn't know if it was to protect me, but Kiera kept me in the healer's wing for the rest of the night. She might have kept me longer had I asked, but I couldn't hide from our fate forever. I had to report everything to the King and tell him I was taking my place as the general. There was no maybe about it anymore. I was taking it.

I'd barely slept, making plans for how we would face this new threat. I had so many fae to speak to. I couldn't sit still any longer.

Octavian had given up his vigil outside the healer's wing sometime last night. He was first on my list to see after I showered and dressed in my uniform, the one I'd had ready for two years but never worn. I wanted there to be no doubt as to my claim when I met with them today. We didn't have time for power struggles.

We had to be a united front to win this war.

I walked into the council room, finding Octavian in the middle of a briefing. "What have I missed?" I didn't approach the table and take my usual seat. Instead, I stood staring Octavian straight in the eye and waited.

He scanned my uniform, and I saw realization flicker in his face. His nostrils flared. "How good of you to join us, Nyx. We've felt your absence."

So, that's how it would be.

"My absence was forced on me when you decided I was too close to the flight on the front to be objective." I didn't move or back down.

"I'm sure you can understand that difficult decisions were being made, and you were too personally involved. But that doesn't excuse you disappearing without a word."

"I did what I felt was best for my ryder and me."

"I see. Am I to take all this"—he gestured at my uniform—"to mean you have finally melded with your ryder?"

"I have."

He nodded and didn't answer for a long moment. "We will have to have Rakan check."

I lifted my brows, overplaying my reaction. "Strange, I don't recall any other pair ever being subject to the checking of a meld. May I ask why you think it's necessary?" I wanted him to call me a liar here with witnesses. If he was going to drag his feet in stepping aside, I needed to build my case.

"I think, after all the struggle for the meld, it's best to make sure it's secure."

"I'll see what the King thinks. We have a lot to brief him on. Are you busy here, or would you like to accompany me?"

Octavian shoved out of his seat. "It's only an update briefing. I guess it can wait while we discuss petty matters of succession with the King." He wanted it to be a barb, but he clearly wasn't getting that his time as Regent was done.

The King's private steward showed us to his dining room, where King Viktas was in the middle of his breakfast.

He took in my uniform as he finished chewing. "Can I take this as good news about you and your ryder, Nyx?"

"You can—"

The Regent cut me off. "Your Majesty, if I may interject? This is the worst possible time to hand over command to an inexperienced leader. We are on the edge of a war with an ancient enemy, and any misstep would see the Twelve Kingdoms fall."

I seethed but didn't interrupt his speech. The King would decide what he would, but none of them could keep me from my post for long. Not without a challenge. I was the rightful heir, and Octavian had sworn to keep my position open for me. This betrayal would cut deep if I hadn't seen the change in him recently.

The King considered, taking another massive bite, and chewing. He pointed his fork at me. "And what say you, Nyx?"

"I say he's wrong." I gave Octavian a half-glance, daring him to interrupt. "While I agree we are facing an ancient enemy, we are not on the brink of war. We are in the midst of a war. I think the Regent has already made an egregious error by sending another flight to the outpost after the first went missing. It cost us all those lives, and so many dragons we couldn't afford to lose...including my brother." I let my words sink in.

The King choked. "Excuse me?"

"What did you say?" Octavian spoke at the same time as the King.

I didn't look at Octavian, keeping my attention on the King. It took everything in me to deliver my next words without emotion. "Kol is dead. I watched him die myself."

"How?" the King breathed, showing a rare hint of emotion at the news my brother was gone.

I knew there would be questions, but I delivered the basic truth. "I got word from Kol they were in trouble, and Zaria and I flew directly there to offer aid. We were ambushed and barely survived, and still, we went back, trying to rescue any of the flight who survived. The only soul we got out was Luka, and we rescued Jaxus from a village along the coast when we fell back from the outpost."

"And we've heard nothing about this?" The King's gaze flicked to Octavian.

"Nothing," Octavian said, and I could tell by his tone that he was reeling. "We have a warning system. Why wasn't it utilized?"

"Because they have a new weapon. They can gas us with huge quantities of Dragon's Bane, draining our magic and incapacitating us. They have exposed a major flaw in our warning system. A watch can be ambushed and taken out before they can send out the warning. Then they are powerless to do a thing as they are killed and turned. It's mass scale slaughter."

I kept my chin up and my gaze steady, not giving Octavian a second of my attention. I was briefing the King. That was all. He didn't deserve my respect.

"I don't believe trying to hold an outpost that is vital to the Twelve Kingdom's defense was a misstep." Octavian's tone was indignant, though his panic was beginning to show. "How could we have predicted these new weapons?"

"I told you it was too big a risk to send another flight after the outpost was taken until we knew what we were dealing with," I snapped back.

The King held up a hand, silencing us both. He wiped his mouth with his napkin, then threw it on top of his plate and sat back. He assessed us both. "You are fully melded with your ryder, Nyx?"

"I am."

The King crossed his arms over his chest. "Then, I'm sorry, Octavian, and I thank you for your service, but Nyx's claim is valid. His bloodline was ordained by the Goddess to be the protectors of the realm. It's his birthright, and he has fulfilled the requirements to take it. War or not, I think we are only tempting fate by denying the Goddess' will, don't you?"

The King's way of phrasing it was genius. How could Octavian resist being ousted when it was the Goddess' will? The King had my respect for that.

"I think the timing is particularly dangerous, but you're the King, and I will abide by your decision." He dipped his head in a brief bow before taking off the heart crystal that was his badge of office. He set it down on the King's breakfast table and stared at it for a moment. "Now, if you'll excuse me, I left a council briefing for this, and as second under our new general, I still have a lot to do."

"You may go." The King dismissed him, then waved for me to take a seat as Octavian stormed out the door.

"Don't resent Octavian. He is old and thinks he knows best. He believes his experience is more valuable than your name, and most of the time I'd side with him, but this is not a case of choosing sides. Your bloodline carries the power. As first son of the Asra line, you are bound by the Goddess to lead the dragons. He doesn't fully understand the balance on which the Twelve Kingdoms were built. Your family does. You've been the protectors of it since the beginning."

"I just hope he isn't going to be a problem," I mused.

"You are the strongest dragon in many generations. Even more powerful than your father. I'm certain you can handle him."

The King stood and took the heart crystal, approaching me. I stood facing him for this important moment. He pinned the heart to my general's uniform and patted my chest. He smiled fondly.

"Nyx, first son of the Asra line, Dragon of the Night. I bestow upon you the titles of General of my legions and Head of the Dragon Council. May you be the alpha the fae deserve, and the protector the kingdoms need. And may the Goddess bless your succession."

"Thank you, Your Majesty. I swear to protect these kingdoms with all that I am."

"I know you will." He nodded, then stepped away. "Now, you'd better get to that council meeting before Octavian has the chance to start playing political games. He won't make this easy for you."

"I know." I bowed and then headed out.

Now to face Octavian.

SIXTY-EIGHT

NYX

To my surprise, Octavian handed over control of the council meeting as soon as I arrived, and after he told me he'd be out of his office by the week's end. I hated how easily he turned things over. It felt like a farce, and I spent the rest of the day waiting for the other shoe to drop.

After my meetings were done for the day, I found Zaria in her rooms with Luka. She had her feet draped over his lap when I walked in.

I growled, letting it rumble in my chest.

"That's my cue." Luka got up and leaned over to kiss her forehead. "We'll finish catching up tomorrow."

"Goodnight," she said, stepping around me to walk him out. She closed the door behind him and turned on me. "That wasn't very nice. Did you have to be so"—she waved at me—"tall, dark, and douchey?"

"Where did you get that term from?" It didn't sound like something she would say.

She laughed, and then it turned into a sob. "Kol."

I caught her as she half collapsed. "That makes a lot of sense."

She kept laughing and crying. "I'm sorry."

"What for?" I hugged her to me.

"For being a mess when I should be here for you," she said into my chest.

I pressed my face into her hair. "You loved him, too. You're allowed."

"But who will take care of you if you're taking care of me?"

"Having you here is enough." I fought tears.

"How did it go?"

"Smoother than I expected."

"That's good."

I let out a breath. "No, it was too easy. I am waiting for the other shoe to drop."

"Do you think it will?"

I kissed her forehead. "I hope not, but something just feels off."

"You can handle Octavian. I have every faith in you...General." She looked up with a smirk.

"You'll be helping me handle him. As my ryder, you'll sit on the council with me."

"I know. I've been mentally preparing."

I walked her backward toward her bed. "Now, tell me why your feet were in Luka's lap."

She laughed, going with me easily. "I was taking comfort in my friend."

"Friend?" I pressed. "Only your friend?"

"Yes, Mister Tall-Dark-And-Growly. He's nothing more."

"He's not the guy..." I didn't want to say it.

"No!"

"Good. I'd hate to have to kill him since you seem so fond of him." I rolled my eyes.

"Don't roll your eyes. He's a good friend, and he needs us."

"Us? Don't you mean you?"

"No, I mean us. He needs all the friends he can get. He's as lost as I was, and he doesn't have a big, grumpy dragon for support like I did."

"I can be grumpy if that's what he needs."

"No, you'll be nice. I just told him about being poisoned with Dragon's Bane all those years. He's in shock that my parents could do that to me. We both have a lot still to process, but at least we have each other to get through it. It helps having someone who was there, you know?"

I rolled my eyes again but buried my face in her neck, breathing in her scent.

"Oh! And Luka is still wearing his pendant. I said we'd see Kiera about finding a way to remove it without hurting him. Do you think he will have powers when it's gone?"

"Maybe." I didn't care about Luka's potential powers in that moment. I scooped her into bed, not even bothering to shed my uniform, needing to feel her. We tangled up together. "What happened with Jaxus and Kiera?"

"Nothing. He hasn't said anything, and it's not my place."

I was still reeling from that. "She isn't going to be happy."

"Do you think?" Zaria asked.

"She hates flyers." I laughed. Those are the only fae she stays away from—swore them off after a bad experience years ago.

"This isn't a mating." Zaria laughed against my throat.

"Where are Jaxus and Luka staying?"

"Kiera helped me arrange rooms for them. Jaxus will have to go into training if he stays, but I don't know what Luka will do. I don't think he'll want to go back to find our families, but what is here for him?" She sighed. "I feel five years older."

"Me, too. At least." I closed my eyes, inhaling her scent. "Are you moving to my rooms or am I moving here?"

Zaria pulled back enough to look into my eyes. "You'd move into mine? Yours have to be so much nicer."

I'd never realized she'd never been to my rooms. I'd dealt with everything so wrong, but things would be different from here on. "I don't relish the idea, but if you think I'm not going to be sleeping wherever you are, you're wrong."

A smile broke out over her face. "I will move to yours, but only because you have balconies on your wing. I've seen them."

I rolled my eyes but laughed, too. "One more thing before we can be done with this day and sleep."

"Do we have to sleep?"

I stared at her.

"I've been thinking about the offer to sit on your face since you made it..."

I groaned. "You may sit on any part of me you like as long as some part of me is inside you."

She squirmed against me, rubbing her hip against my cock. "Which part will be inside me when I sit on your face? Your tongue or fingers?"

I rolled her under me, my mouth hovering over hers. "Both."

She arched into me. "What did you have to tell me?"

"I'm not talking anymore until I've made you come a half a dozen times or so." I rocked my hips against her, already feeling the dampness pooling between her thighs.

She whimpered, grabbing me through my uniform. "Get these off."

I grabbed her wrist playfully. "Oh, no, you don't. Yours first. I was promised you sitting on my face."

She fought my hold and opened my pants with her free hand. We roughly tore each other out of our clothes, mouths and tongues clashing while our bodies ground together.

"I won't ever get enough of you."

"Promise?" she asked.

"I swear it." I broke the kiss to slide to a seat on the floor next to the bed, tipping my head back.

My movement creased her brow in confusion, but realization slowly came to her face.

"You're serious?" She slipped off the bed, standing bare in all her beauty before me.

My mouth watered. "Absolutely. I want to devour every part of you." I beckoned her forward.

She came slowly, feet on either side of my hips. I leaned forward to kiss one hip and then the other, grabbing behind her knee. I sat back again while guiding her to put one knee on the bed and the other on my shoulder, leaving her spread wide open for me.

"Fuck! I am the luckiest fae in the realm." I teased my tongue along her slit.

Her entire body reacted to me, a shiver running up her spine. I slipped two fingers into her while the tip of my tongue pushed between her lips. She moaned, clenching around my fingers, already dripping wet. I was drunk off her. I could have spent all night between her legs. I pushed my fingers farther into her pussy, curling them as I fucked in and out of her.

She gasped and half collapsed onto my face.

Breathing was overrated when her pleasure was concerned.

I sucked on her clit, finding the ball of nerves inside her.

"Nyx…"

I smiled against her, slowing to draw it out of her, taking my time to build her up.

"Please," she whimpered.

I added a third finger, and she rewarded me by grinding her hips into my face. My cock was so hard it stood straight out from my body. I ached for her to sit on me. I flicked my tongue over her, swirling it around her clit, pushing her over the edge.

She came undone, gasping and crying out, "Goddess...please...don't stop. Please don't stop, Nyx." The way she moaned my name had me leaking.

Her entire body shook with the intensity of her orgasm.

Finally, her legs gave out, and she slid down my body, landing in my lap with her arse pressed into my cock.

"That tongue..."

I kissed her with it. "You can sit on my face whenever you want."

"Now I want to sit on something else."

I growled, grabbing her arse to spread it and rock her over my length.

She smiled, rolling her arse. "Do you want inside me?"

"Please." I lifted her a little, letting my tip glide through her lips.

We both looked down to watch.

"You are so sexy."

"Nyx?" she said shyly.

It gave me pause. "Yes?"

"You know how you can have your wings out without fully shifting?"

"Yes…" Where was she going with this?

"Are there any other parts of you that can change?"

My brows lifted. "Sol!"

"What?"

"Do you think you can take it?"

She nodded eagerly.

"You won't be able to walk tomorrow." I grabbed a hold of my base, stroking myself as I focused on allowing just that part of myself to take dragon form. It was in proportion to me in this body, but it was big.

She dragged her teeth over her lower lip and lifted up on her knees, barely getting enough height to come up to the tip. "Goddess, it's huge."

I teased my tip over her clit. "It might split you in two."

She lifted one knee, planting a foot next to my hip, spreading herself open. "I want it all."

I grabbed the back of her head, dragging her mouth to mine as I pushed my tip against her opening. She moaned into my mouth, meeting the pressure.

Pleasure overwhelmed me. "Fuck, Sol."

She sat down farther, taking a couple more inches.

My head fell back. "You're so tight."

"I can barely breathe, and you're not even all the way inside me."

I sucked on my thumb and brought it to her clit, making slow circles over it. "I want to feel you come on my cock."

She convulsed around me. "If you keep doing that, I will in a moment or two."

I put my hand on her hip, forcing her down more. "Please ride me."

She grinned, knowing she held all the power. She worked me in and out of her, gradually taking more and more, stretching herself on my thickness. Watching her take me inside her over and over nearly made me come.

"Do you know what watching you is doing to me?" I cupped her breasts with both hands, rubbing my thumbs over her nipples.

She arched her back, pressing them into me. I caught one with my mouth, sucking and biting her nipple. She whimpered.

"Like that?"

"Yes!" Her voice pitched.

I moved between the two, kissing a path across her chest, biting and sucking her pink flesh. She ground into me, taking me as deeply as she could, begging with her moans.

"Can you come with just my cock?" I whispered against her.

"I don't know." Her breathing staggered, and the movement of her hips became erratic.

I bit her nipple again, and she came, exploding over me, tightening and contracting, riding me aggressively.

I couldn't hold back any longer. I came, holding her hips to keep myself buried inside her while moving her back and forth. Our lips found each other again, and we kissed through ecstasy.

She sagged, her entire body going limp, and draped over me as she came down, still lightly rocking.

"If you keep doing that, you're going to make me hard again." I picked her up, staying inside her as I moved us back to bed.

"You say that like I don't want you inside me all night."

We went again, dozing after we were spent. Wrapped in each other, we lay quietly with our thoughts.

"What did you have to talk to me about?" she asked.

"I don't want to think about it." I groaned, teasing my cock against her from behind to distract her.

She reached behind and took me in her hand, but instead of stroking me like I expected, she lined me up with her entrance. "Tell me."

I shoved forward, getting instantly hard again. "Octavian wants to meet with us in the morning."

She made the same sound I had. "Fuck me back to sleep so I don't have to think about it until tomorrow."

"I like the way you think."

SIXTY-NINE
NYX

"I don't want to do this," Zaria said as we approached Octavian's office.

"I don't either, but we have to show good will. He's still a commander in the army, and it's better not to make enemies when we have a war to fight." It wasn't my first choice, but it was the right one. "Court politics aren't fun."

"So I am learning."

"With your new position, you have to." I stopped outside Octavian's door.

"It feels so wrong."

"What does?" I asked.

"To barely get a few weeks of training and have this type of responsibility."

"Our situation isn't a normal one." I put my hand on the doorknob. "I promise it will get better."

"I know it will." She took a deep breath and nodded for me to open the door.

I knocked, not waiting for a response, and opened the door, showing Zaria in.

Octavian was sat behind his desk but stood as we entered.

Not a single thing had been moved from the shelves or taken off the walls to prepare for handing over the office. He'd said by the end of the week, but it seemed strange that he hadn't even started.

"Good morning," Octavian said, sitting back in his chair. "Please, have a seat."

It was the last thing I wanted to do, but I forced myself into one of the wingbacks while Zaria took the other.

"Thank you for taking time out of your busy day to meet with me." His tone dripped with condescension.

"Of course, and since my day is packed, why don't we get right to it?"

"I want to go over your report on the events at the outpost." Octavian picked up a piece of paper from his desk and a pen. He lightly dipped it into an open ink pot.

"Is that necessary?" My report was very detailed, but I'd known questions were coming.

"I think so. I am confused about how you even knew the First Flight needed help. No alert was sent."

"I don't see how it's relevant."

"I do if it went against direct orders from your King."

"I never went against any direct orders," I said firmly, hoping it would end the line of questioning.

"I know you're lying to me. Something about this isn't adding up. So explain again before I take my suspicions to the King."

So, that's the way it would be.

I glanced at Zaria, and she nodded. My brother was dead, my

father was dead… There was no reason to hold on to this secret any longer.

"Kol and I shared a twinship bond. A very powerful one. We could always communicate with one another."

Octavian's eyes bulged, and then he slit them as he processed all the times we'd somehow known things we shouldn't have, or covered for each other, I was sure. "You lied your entire lives?"

"No, we never lied. No one ever asked."

Octavian seethed. "This would have been invaluable information to help the Twelve Kingdoms, and you kept it from us?"

"Our father, the general, instructed us to guard our secret. And as Head of the Dragon Council and our alpha, I do believe he had the authority to make that call." I got to my feet. "I don't know why you pretended to hold his office with care, nor why you are suddenly against me assuming my rightful place, but it does not sit well with me. I need—"

Zaria cut me off, speaking quickly mind to mind. "*Nyx! Look at the letter on his desk. Look at the seal. He had it covered when we came in, but when he took that piece of paper off his desk, it uncovered the others, and you can see the corner…*"

I scanned his desk, looking for what she was talking about. "*What? Where? What are you talking about?*"

Octavian glanced between us. "What are you two discussing in private?"

"*The symbol!*" she said, strain in her mental voice.

"*I don't know what you're talking about…*"

"I demand you stop it!" Octavian hit his desk with both hands.

Zaria jumped up and snatched the paper from the desk between his palms, pointing at the symbol. The same one that was on all the bags of Dragon's Bane.

I moved in front of Zaria. "You're involved in this?"

He didn't deny it. He lifted his chin, assessing me. "Yes."

The only reason my hands weren't around his throat was

because I wanted to know why. I didn't understand his connection. "Why did you send him?"

"Because I knew you two were closing in on your meld, and good old Kol was helping you along. I had to weaken you... but I didn't foresee this turn." His tone carried so much smug satisfaction. I'd kill him.

"What is your business with the Vivi Mortui? Are you the one supplying the Dragon's Bane? Is this about money?"

Octavian laughed slowly, getting to his feet. "This isn't a fairy tale where I spill my guts, boy. You have no business in the position you are in. You have no idea how the Twelve Kingdoms function. You are too naive to hold the position you do. Your father knew how things worked."

My hand found my pommel, and I drew my sword. "My father was honorable."

"Maybe, maybe not. But he wasn't ignorant." Octavian took a half step back.

"Stay where you are. You will face the King."

He laughed, turning to dive out the window behind him.

Zaria and I sprinted around the desk in time to see Octavian shift into his dragon form.

Before I could follow, Zaria grabbed my arm.

"Don't stop me," I growled.

"Kill him for Kol," she said coldly.

I nodded before following Octavian out the window.

SEVENTY
ZARIA

I ran from the Regent's office to the healer's wing. I couldn't just stand and watch. I had to alert the guard or someone, and Kiera would know best how to help me.

By the time I skidded to a halt, I was out of breath and gasping.

"What's wrong?" Kiera asked.

I struggled with a stitch in my side. "Nyx."

"What happened?!" She grabbed her medical bag and threw it over her shoulder.

I shook my head but thought better of it, hunching over.

"Did you run all the way here?"

I nodded.

"Breathe. What is it?"

"Nyx is fighting with Octavian," I finally managed.

"*What?*"

"We were in his office." I gasped for another mouthful of air. "And I saw—it doesn't matter. He has something to do with the outpost falling." Another inhale while I tried to get my mind to slow down. "When we confronted him, he jumped out the window."

"Mister Prim-And-Proper jumped out the fucking window? I'd have paid to see that." She gestured for me to lead the way.

I nodded vigorously. "Nyx went after him. They're fighting! We need to alert —" A crash shook the palace, and I ducked, covering my head.

"I don't think we need to tell anyone," Kiera affirmed, wincing at the sound of a dragon's roar. "I think they're going to know. Come on!"

We ran toward the nearest battlement, sprinting outside where a crowd was already gathering. The two massive dragons circled each other, Nyx's oil-slick scales glinting teal and purple in the morning light, contrasted by Octavian's almost blood-red burgundy. They dove at each other in a tight circle, a blur of colors, spinning toward the ground.

I gasped, covering my mouth, but they separated at the last second, spinning, only to circle back, throwing fire at one another. Nyx's black fire blasted through the space between them, Octavian's lava pouring from his jaws.

"What if they accidentally light something on fire?" As if I predicted it, Octavian sent down a rain of lava that barely missed Nyx, hitting a building just outside the palace grounds, which burst into flames. Nyx roared, shaking the palace, and knocking me back a few steps.

Kiera grabbed my arm, steadying me. "I have to go. We have to send healers into the city."

"Go." I turned away from her, running toward the edge of the battlement closest to where Nyx was, gathering all my power as I did.

Guards tried to stop me, but I gripped the handle of my sword, and they backed off.

I ran down a flight of stairs and across to the battlement, then up more stairs into one of the guard towers. Then I doubled back to find the stairs to take me to the top of it. At the highest point, I had a much better view of Nyx and Octavian.

They were locked in each other's grasp, biting, and blowing fire at each other as they fell. I swallowed my fear. I couldn't control his flight, but I could amplify his power. I took a slow breath, then two, focusing on the threads connecting us. I let my power gather in me, amplifying it before sending it to him.

Nyx roared as our powers surged, and it shook the stones beneath my feet. I stumbled again, my eyes wide. Nyx drew back, charging, then blew a long stream of fire that drew from both our reserves. I sucked in air and watched his lethal black fire become something more...us.

It was night. Beautiful and deadly. Black fire, shot with sparks of light like the night sky. It cut through Octavian's fire like a knife. Octavian threw sprays of raining fire as he swerved, and one hit Nyx, knocking him off his flight path.

I winced, gripping the battlement as he fell from the sky. His wings spread, but black blood dripped from a gash in his side. I fought tears. I didn't have time to lose it. I had to keep our powers together so he didn't die.

SEVENTY-ONE

NYX

S treaks of lava seared through my scales, cutting down to my flesh and opening the muscle. My wings snapped closed as my body reacted to protect itself, sending me spiraling toward the ground. We weren't high enough for this. I forced my wings out against all instinct and caught air, flying back over the city. I felt the moisture at the wound, knowing I was bleeding. Very little cut through dragon scales—only dragon on dragon battle could cut this deep.

I couldn't let him get me again.

Zaria pushed even more of her energy toward me.

The charge of her power felt like light flowing through my veins. It sparkled through my black blood.

I turned sharply, sensing Octavian gaining on my tail, and cut back toward the outer wall of the city. I flew against the pain, utilizing mine and Zaria's power combined. I had to take this fight away from the innocent fae in the city.

Volcano dragons from the Eleventh Kingdom were rare and secretive. Their family lines were like spider webs, and their magic was hard to trace. It made Octavian a formidable enemy. He might not look it with his advanced age and pristine appearance, but he was a ruthless dragon with exceptionally controlled magic.

We were pretty equally matched before I found my flyer, but with Zaria, I knew I had an edge. Now I had to get him away from the city. How could he be so reckless in a city he'd sworn to protect? He had a duty to every fae below us.

I worked to push him back with every bout, trying to get him over the open land behind the palace so I could unleash the full extent of my power.

"He's charging his lava!"

"Thank you, Sol." I didn't know how she could tell, but I cut straight up, and he missed me.

He followed, beating his wings hard to try to catch me.

When he got close, I dove, shooting past him, raining fire on him as I did.

He wasn't ready for the move, and he snapped his wings in, trying to shield himself from the blast. They deflected most of the fire, but the sparks of light in my black flame, which I suspected were from Zaria's magic mixing with mine, burned tiny holes into his scales like acid.

It would leave him vulnerable.

I almost had him. I backed off, pulling him farther from the palace over the meadows.

Movement caught my attention, and I looked past him to see a horde of dragons launching from the palace. No, no, *NO!* If Octavian noticed and realized he was about to be outnumbered, he'd flee, and I could lose him. I couldn't give him that advantage.

I pulled back to hover like I was giving him an in. His red eyes met mine, and he smiled. He was enjoying this too much, and I hated him more for it.

We dove at each other, and I pulled my power and Zaria's together, amassing it to pour into my fire.

But he pulled up and turned away.

What was he doing? I shot after him.

He cut out a different direction, then dropped lower and lower to the ground, coming over a huge field, and pulled with his magic.

What the fuck was he doing?

Things burst through the ground, shooting up toward us. Tiny creatures bombarded me, hitting me from every side. They latched onto every part of me they could, biting. Their teeth broke against my hard scales, but that didn't stop them.

"What the fuck is this?"

"I can't see you. What's going on?" Zaria called.

"I don't know!" The things dug at my skin with unnatural strength.

"I'm getting a better vantage point—hold on!"

I clawed at myself, fighting them, but there were too many. I blew fire in front of me as I flew and rolled through it. That took care of some of them, but any that fell off were replaced.

I looked for Octavian, but I'd lost him as every direction was obscured by the creatures. I aimed fire up and let it fall over me, repeating the action to pick them off as more and more came. The creatures had no fear of my fire. I'd never seen anything like them. I slammed myself to the ground to regroup and ripped one off my wing to look at it.

Ice ran through my veins.

It was an undead bat.

Was Octavian a...necromancer?

Those hadn't existed since The Hundred Years War.

I pulled more of the damn creatures off me.

Fucking bastard.

I blew fire into the air, letting it rain down over me like a waterfall, burning away as many of the creatures as I could. They weren't more than a distraction to flood the sky and throw off my pursuit.

The field would burn, but it would slow his creatures as more came out of the ground.

But now I had to find him.

I listened, spinning a slow circle. Where would he be hiding?

"Zaria?"

"I'm on the north tower. I can see you. Are you okay?"

"Fine, but I need you."

She calmed and quieted to listen.

"He's gone to ground, and I need to find him."

"How can I help?"

"Can you light him up? Illuminate him, maybe? Send your power to find him in the dark?" Anything." I didn't even know if what I was asking was possible.

"I can try."

I closed my eyes as more and more of the winged creatures attacked. They chipped away at my scales, digging and biting, but I gave Zaria all my energy, letting her channel through me. We had to find him.

I owed it to Kol's memory.

I'd never forgive myself If I let him get away.

SEVENTY-TWO

NYX

"I feel something!" she told me, sending light to mark the place.

I breathed, shooting into the air to swoop to the place Zaria indicated. I couldn't give him even a second.

I accessed every last ounce of power I could gather and let it flow with Zaria's, channeling it all into my fire, blasting it at the hiding spot in the hope she was right.

It was our one shot to catch him off guard.

If she was wrong, I'd have to retreat.

The field glowed for a moment but spread out toward the mountains and trees, narrowing in on a spot part way up the rock face. All of it came to a point of focus on a massive outcropping of rocks covered in trees and huge bushes. A haven to hide a dragon.

My fire burned away rock and bushes, revealing Octavian as he ignited.

He let out a cry and tried to get into the air, but holes burned into his wings from the sparks of Zaria's light in my fire, glowing intense white as they spread. He staggered and crumpled, and I didn't let up my fire until he collapsed into a charred lump.

I stood over the singed remains of him with an empty feeling in my chest. I couldn't get my head around any of it.

Would we ever know the extent of his crimes? I had to get back to the palace and start going through his office. The letter that started all this destruction was evidence, and I hoped there would be more.

I stood with Octavian's remains until the horde of dragons caught up. Then I handed him off to them to bring back.

Right then, I didn't have the energy to do anything except get back to my mate.

I couldn't face the realization that if Octavian was a necromancer, this was about more than Dragon's Bane and money.

EPILOGUE

Nyx

The capital was quiet in the weeks after Octavian's death. Shock over the news of his betrayal was only overshadowed by the news that his crimes had cost the lives of two flights. The First Flight were a part of the city. The fae loved them, and their loss was felt deeply.

An official investigation was underway into Octavian's wrongdoings, which I used as a distraction from dealing with my grief during the long days. But at night, we closed ourselves into our rooms and quietly mourned.

Zaria saved me in those weeks. I wouldn't have survived them without her.

I delayed the ceremony that would officially swear me in as General and Head of the Dragon Council as a mark of respect to the fallen dragons. The city planned a memorial so we could collectively mourn our lost loved ones.

King Viktas arranged for a private memorial service in the palace's temple for Kol before the military service for the lost Flights. Fae turned out in droves—everyone who knew and loved him. Word of mouth spread fast, and the little temple was standing room only as the priests made offerings to the Goddess.

We filled the front row, and King Viktas stunned me by sitting by my side. I hadn't seen him attend a funeral since my father's, and it made me feel some sort of way. Too many feelings were wrapped up in this moment. I shouldn't have had to be here so soon after my father.

This was nothing like the way Kol and I swore to go out together. Living on without him felt like a betrayal to him and our promises. To our life, which was intrinsically joined.

I hated having nothing to return to the Goddess. I would do all I could to end the Vivi Mortui so that if he was turned after death, we could give him and all the other lost souls peace. I wouldn't leave them trapped and wandering the Twelve Kingdoms for the rest of eternity.

Zaria squeezed my hand and laid her head on my shoulder. I didn't deserve her, but I wouldn't have survived this without her. She brought a peace I didn't think was possible after such a loss. We'd get through it together.

I couldn't give up now. I had a duty to the Twelve Kingdoms to protect them from the coming threat.

The priests finished their prayers and bowed to King Viktas before ending the service.

After the King was led out by his stewards, Zaria and I left the little temple to head out into the city for the celebration of the two flights we'd lost—the First and the Fourth.

"Have you seen the city?" Zaria asked.

"No?" In the weeks since Octavian's betrayal, I hadn't left the palace grounds. I'd been digging through everything in his office to try and make sense of what he did. He'd either burned every scrap of evidence except the letter Zaria had pulled off his desk, or he had some hiding place I couldn't find. There wasn't a trace of money or bank accounts. No ledger or plans. His involvement in it all remained a mystery we may never figure out.

She wiped her eyes. "It's beautiful."

When we stepped out of the palace grounds, instead of drab cobblestone streets and dark-colored buildings, every surface was covered in flowers. The walls of the palace were surrounded by them piled high with notes and little trinkets for those we lost to carry into the afterlife.

I stopped in my tracks. The weight of love the city held for my brother and the Flights overwhelmed me. I fought back emotions. If I lost it now, I wouldn't have it in me to make it through the procession.

Zaria slipped her arms around my neck. I pressed into her, trying not to lose it. "You're allowed to show emotion. You're allowed to feel things. You're allowed to show you're devastated. They won't think less of you. They need to see you're grieving with them. It will help the whole city heal and come together for the war."

I cupped her face, resting my forehead against hers. "You are everything I didn't know I needed. It's hard to grieve so publicly, but as long as you're with me, I'll get through it."

"I know. I'm proud of you."

"You always know what I need to hear." I kissed her lightly. "Thank you for being by my side."

ZARIA

H and in hand, Nyx and I walked in the procession to the capital's main temple, followed by our closest friends. Our family.

Fae lined the streets, and cheers went up on each one we turned onto. I had never seen anything like it. Funerals were somber occasions in my experience, and to see the city celebrating our fallen was healing to my soul.

The Temple of Avalon sat halfway up the hill, overlooking the city, and a memorial for the lost Flights had been erected in the square outside. It was a simple monolith, engraved with the names of each flyer and ryder of the fallen flights, as well as the name of every other fae we had lost at the outpost.

I studied the names, there were too many, but Kol Asar, carved into the black marble and gilded would forever be a knife to the heart. Beneath him, Elvar, his ryder, was remembered. I didn't know him well, but he was important to Kol, and it comforted me to know they went to the Goddess together.

As fae passed the monolith, they put down flowers and other things to pay tribute before moving inside the temple.

It was packed inside, but we were ushered to a bench near the front, where all the families of those lost were seated. The priests made offerings to the Goddess. While the high priest spoke about the Flight's sacrifice and their assured places at the Goddess' side, I looked around at the fae gathered because they loved Kol.

My eyes caught on the King's where he sat on his throne in a place of honor, and I realized he was watching me. I looked away, uneasy to have been caught in his intense stare. I tried listening to the priest again, but I could feel his eyes still on me. The need to know built in me until I couldn't fight it another moment. I looked directly at him this time, and sure enough, the King's glare was fixed on me.

His eyes narrowed…in question? I couldn't understand why. After a long moment, he looked away, and I almost sagged with relief.

After the service, we were working our way out of the massive temple, and I was ready to meet our friends and say our own private goodbye to Kol, but the King stepped into our path, and Nyx stopped short.

"Your Majesty. Thank you again for doing this for Kol and the Flights."

"They deserve to be accepted by the Goddess. It was the least we could do for them." He patted Nyx's shoulder. Then he turned his attention to me, and that uneasy feeling started again. "You must be Nyx's ryder? I don't think we've been introduced."

I remembered the bow I was expected to give and awkwardly bobbed. "I am, Your Majesty."

"Do you have a name, my dear?" he asked smoothly.

"Azariah Sorelli, Majesty," I replied, smiling politely.

The King's face seemed to drain of color, and he looked taken aback. Then the look was gone, and a cool mask of indifference slipped back over his face.

"Well, I'm sorry this is the first chance we've had to meet. I'm sure we will meet again."

"Yes, Your Majesty." I bowed again. His manner had me on edge, but he was obviously done with us because he nodded to Nyx and strolled away.

"What was that about?" I asked Nyx, mind to mind.

"What?"

"He was staring at me all through the service and then he seemed...I don't know, suspicious of me."

Nyx frowned and looked for the King, but he'd been ushered away. *"I think you're imagining it, Sol. He's always suspicious about everything."*

I shrugged, but I couldn't shake the feeling I'd caught the attention of a predator.

Free from the masses at last, we returned to our section of the palace. The area that housed the flyers, and next to it, the healers, was home now, and I was happy there. So, it was there we chose to hold our own little private memorial.

Nyx had commissioned a statue of Kol to be placed in the gardens, and we were seeing it for the first time. I slipped my arm around Nyx's waist as we studied the details the sculptor had captured.

I tilted my head.

It was...off.

Not at first glance, but the more I looked, the more I had to hold in a laugh that was threatening to bubble up and ruin this somber moment.

Kiera side-eyed me, and I realized she was holding back a laugh, too.

I almost slipped and covered it with a cough.

"Are you okay?" Nyx asked, his eyes still fixed on the statue.

"Yes. I just can't believe you did this," I said trying to hold myself together.

"I can't believe you paid for it," Kiera said, making a face at it.

"It was a nice gesture," he said.

"For who?" Kiera asked.

I lost it, and Kiera and I both doubled over laughing. Nyx folded his arms over his chest and waited for us to finish.

"For Kol's memory." Nyx scowled, but a smile almost tugged the corner of his mouth.

"Do you want him remembered looking like that?" Kiera shuddered, and I bit back another laugh.

"The worst part about this is I know he'd be laughing with you and ruining this for me." Nyx muttered under his breath, "I try to do something nice."

"I think you've graduated from tall, dark, and douchey to broody." Saying it brought tears to my eyes, but I had to—for Kol.

"Or tall, dark, and moody," Kiera added.

I laughed, and my heart hurt. "Stop. You're going to make laugh-cry again."

Nyx slipped his arm around me and kissed my temple. "I miss him."

"Me, too."

"I do, too. Who am I going to gossip with?" Kiera side-eyed me again, and I had a feeling I knew what she wanted to gossip about.

"I like gossip." Luka came up and hugged me from behind. "Sorry I'm late. Did I miss anything?"

"Just the entire thing," Nyx said flatly. He was warming up to Luka but against his will.

"I had a meeting with the Board of Training to see if they would let me take some weapons lessons while I figure out what

I want to do." Luka grinned at Nyx, loving every second of the way my mate reacted to him.

Nyx had pulled some strings and secured Luka his rooms as long as he needed them, so he was definitely coming around.

"How did it go?" I leaned into Nyx.

"He said because I'm aiding the crown with my information on the Vivi Mortui, I would be welcome to take some lessons." He smiled, and he seemed happier in the capital than he ever had in our village. I loved seeing how he'd grown and how he would continue to.

"Are we going to do this? Or am I going to have to keep looking at Kol's wonky eye?" Kiera asked.

"You've ruined it!" Nyx rubbed his forehead. "It's not really that bad, is it?"

Kiera grabbed Nyx by the shoulders and set him next to the statue, looking between them to compare. "It's that bad."

Nyx sighed. "He used my image. I refuse to believe it looks that bad."

Kiera pulled a face. "I hope you don't think you look like that."

Nyx turned on me. "Tell me the statue looks exactly like me."

"I don't want to do that."

Nyx closed his eyes and sighed. "It really is bad, isn't it?"

"Kinda," I said, not wanting to hurt his feelings.

He swiped a hand over his face. "Okay, maybe it was my worst idea ever. I'm blaming it on grief, though, and we are never speaking of this again." He turned and began walking away.

I had to jog to catch up with him. "Are you just leaving?"

"Yep." Nyx kept walking.

"I thought we were having a private memorial?"

"We are. I've moved it to the Flaming Pegasus." There was no stopping Nyx now he had that in his head.

"Wait, are you just going to leave it there?" Kiera asked. "Right next to the healer's garden?"

"We are never speaking about it again."

"Where I have to look at it every day?" Kiera argued.

"Never again."

"Is he serious?" Kiera muttered to me. "Nyx, I already have to put up with that eyesore of your father outside the healer's wing; now I have to look at wonky-eyed Kol every time I need to cut fresh herbs for my work?"

"The subject is closed! I need a drink…or seven."

"So, this is just the statue that shall not be named? Kind of a mouthful," Luka said. "We need an acronym."

"No acronym!" Nyx pushed into the tavern and waved at the server. "A full round. No, make that two."

"Is the general paying? Okay." Luka sat on the other side of me.

Kiera took the bench across from us. "Did someone invite the new dragon you two brought home?"

I glanced at her, feeling awkward about him avoiding her. "Er…"

Kiera must have taken my lack of response as not understanding who she was talking about. "The massive one I could climb like a tree."

I coughed.

"This innocent thing… I can't handle it." Kiera shook her head, misunderstanding. "Not when I know how loud you two are."

"What? We are not."

Kiera gave me a sarcastic look.

"Anyway, I thought you didn't like flyers?" I turned it back on her, feeling my cheeks heat.

"I can't stand them. Wanting to climb one like a tree doesn't mean I don't know that it's an absolute no go." Kiera shuddered.

"Jaxus? He was going to come, wasn't he?" Nyx frowned. "I wonder why he didn't show."

I elbowed him lightly. *"He's avoiding her."*

"What?"

"Yes! Don't make it a big deal."

Kiera narrowed her eyes. "What are you two talking about?"

"You need to work on your poker face," Nyx said with a laugh.

"How do you know it was me?" I actually wasn't sure what I looked like when we spoke.

"It was you," Kiera said, holding out her hands when the server brought the large mugs of ale over. She took a huge drink when he handed it to her.

We all took a minute to raise them to Kol and then down some of our ale.

"I guess I'd better work on that for all these council meetings I have to go to now." I groaned. The last couple of weeks had been a blur of them, and I almost missed being a trainee.

Nyx slipped his hand into mine. "It would help a little if we are going to discuss things in front of others."

"She's always had a lousy poker face. She can't gamble to save her life," Luke threw in.

Nyx looked at me. "Gambling?"

"What else do you expect a group of kids growing up in a cult to do with all their free time? We bet on everything." Luka winked.

"Don't you start with the stories." I jabbed a finger into his arm.

"No, no, I want to hear the stories," Nyx said, leaning around me to look at Luka.

"Me, too," Kiera added, finishing her first mug of ale and moving to the second.

"We are not here to talk about me."

Nyx grabbed me, pulled me into his lap, and I yelped.

"I'd rather talk about you than anything else in the Twelve Kingdoms," he murmured over my lips, dropping a kiss and brushing his nose against mine.

"Where did this come from?" I breathed. He was lighter today. The closure was good for all of us.

"Just reminding you that you are all that matters."

"Goddess, spare me," Kiera groaned.

"And me," Luka added.

"Ignore them, Sol," he said, not taking his eyes from mine. "They just wish they had their mates in their arms right now."

"Pft! Mates indeed. I'm lucky if I see daylight some days. Where do you think I'll find a mate?" Kiera scoffed.

Nyx turned his head to look at her and grinned. "I don't know. The Goddess moves in mysterious ways."

I turned to look at what made Nyx smile so much and spotted Jaxus making his way through the tavern.

"Well, she has her work cut out for her. My life is my work, so I'd need a mate who is as passionate about magical theory and history as me, who is as happy to while away the hours in a library with me as he is to join us for an ale, and also happens to look good enough to eat. And I don't believe such a fae exists." She said it with such finality.

Behind her, Jaxus cleared his throat. "Excuse me, Kiera? I was wondering if I might have a word."

Kiera turned slowly to him, her eyes roaming his physique before reaching his face.

"Umm, sure." She stood and followed him to a table across the bar.

"Well then." I smiled.

Nyx squeezed me in his arms. "Looks like Kiera might get her wish."

"If he stays," I counter.

"He will." Nyx sounded so certain.

"How do you know?" I frowned.

"Because I offered him my former place on the council and the command of a flight."

I gasped. "And he accepted?"

"He can't yet."

"Why not?"

"Because he needs his ryder first." Nyx beamed and turned to watch Jaxus and Kiera. "But he will."

Thank you so much for reading. For more Twelve Kingdoms Preorder The Keeper Of The Kingdoms Jaxus and Kiera's story.

Turn to the next page for a look ahead at The Keeper Of The Kingdoms.

PROLOGUE

The sliver of the waxing moon was at the highest point in the night sky and the time for my task began.

The weather would soon turn, but the fire engulfing Octavian's body burned on. Cracking and illuminating several feet into the sky. The only light beyond the palace walls on this side, where the city ended and plains rolled into hills beyond.

He'd been given a traitor's funeral. No rites or prayers, only dragon fire to make sure he couldn't return to haunt the living.

My goal lay with his remains. A simple mission, but an important one. I could not fail. The Goddess counted on our success.

I kept to the shadows, covering my approach with my shadows. Cloaked in darkness the way we worked best. Our mission existed in the dark. We kept the fae safe and protected all in the Goddess' name.

The stench of charred flesh was thick in my nostrils. A nice effect.

My guardians were stationed close, looking out for any thwart to my mission. Any risk of being seen, or Flyer hanging above.

I listened for warning, but the silence kept.

I thanked the Goddess and approached the pyre. The fire around Octavian's body burned hot, but I was immune. I almost laughed at the ease of carrying out this illusion. The arrogance of the King and his new General would be their downfall.

Passing unharmed and unseen through the three rings of fire, I found what I was here for. What should long be ash, lay fully intact. Octavian's body, even devoid of the ritual cloth of funeral rites, was barely singed. I ran my fingers down his sternum, checking for the spark there.

Threads curled up out of his chest like snakes around my finger. Gripping on to anything they could hold. I pulled back sharply, shaking them off.

"Patience, my Lord."

I took the crystal from around my neck and slipped it around his.

His remains anointed by the crystal, my work was half done. I pressed it into the unmoving chest, feeding it to the hungry tendrils, willing themselves from his chest. The magic curled around the offering, probing and exploring before accepting it. It began melting into his chest. Absorbed to be used.

A smile pulled at my mouth.

Right on time, as the Goddess predicted.

I busied myself with the rest of the task, tying crystals to his wrists and ankles, then stepped back and raised my hands palms up. The body lifted, hovering above the scorched ground and I covered it, the same way I had myself with my shadow magic, keeping us from prying eyes.

I waited then, for the bells to ring at the change of hour. At last came one chime, then two. My moment had arrived. I moved Octavian forward, turning to cast a final illusion in his place. A body that would turn to ash and become nothing more than fertilizer for the land it burned upon.

With my charge in hand I moved through the fire and

vanished into the shadows beyond. I only had moments while the guards changed to reach my rendezvous point and disappear beneath the city. But the Goddess was watching over us and I passed silently beneath the guard tower and found the tunnel entrance without incident.

My guardians met me there and together we carried our ward beneath, ready to begin the Goddess' work.

Preorder The Keeper Of The Kingdom Now

ABOUT THE AUTHOR

Eden Eaves is the alter ego of two bestselling authors who have decided to dabble in magic. Based in the US and UK, Eden Eaves can't wait to share their magical world of dragons and ryders with you.

Find more about Eden Eaves on their website.

f X 🅾 ⓐ ♪

ACKNOWLEDGMENTS

Thank you so much to our wonderful publicist Sarah at Literally Yours PR. Without her encouraging us to join forces to make this project happen we never would have written Nyx and Zaria.

Thank you to our personal assistant Kalilah.

Thank you to our wonderful editor Charlie.

Thank you to our proofreader Vic.

Thank you to all the readers taking this ryde with us in the Twelve Kingdoms

Made in the USA
Las Vegas, NV
21 May 2024

90201004R00298